DEARLY DEPARTED

DEARLY DEPARTED

Mary K. Baxter

To order additional copies of this book, contact:
Xlibris Corporation
1-888-795-4274
www.Xlibris.com
Orders@Xlibris.com
19338

My grateful thanks to
Juan Dorado and Barbara Pindar for their assistance

Also by Mary K. Baxter—
ERASING MRS. LOOMIS

WHAT THEY'RE SAYING ABOUT *ERASING MRS. LOOMIS*

"— your book arrived and I foolishly started to read. And read. And read. I was hooked on page 1. I loved it! I thoroughly enjoyed your writing style, and I REALLY liked Mrs. Loomis. She kept me in suspense until the very end wondering if she really could pull it off."

__Carol Duvall, host of HGTV's Carol Duvall Show

"— just wanted to let you know how much I enjoyed *Erasing Mrs. Loomis*. I bought it because I was curious, but I was surprised at how wonderful the story was. I became completely obsessed and finished it in a day and a half! Believe me that doesn't happen very often, and I read a lot."
__Rocky Schwartz, Clinton NJ

"Mary Baxter has created a new genre – a romance for the 55+ crowd. It's a light and fun read to follow Mrs. Loomis' flight from a grumpy, carping husband, through the perils of self-sufficiency, into a new romance and a resolution with a regretful husband."
__Dorothy Vogel, Talent, OR

"*Erasing Mrs. Loomis* is an adventure/suspense story of sorts but far removed from a Schwartzenegger movie. The plot and suspense develop quickly, making it interesting to a fairly wide audience. In spite of the speed at which the action starts, character development is pretty thorough, so the book gas a sense of depth to it, and, in the end, the action and plot are really all about character."

__An anonymous reader from Bridgewater, NJ, taken from an Amazon.com Review

1

She sat crumpled in her bedroom boudoir chair, like a shaken rag doll dumped into the bright rose print. After three weeks, gunshots still fired in her brain, sharp as if firecrackers were exploding around her. Even though she had not been here when it happened, she saw the scene play over and over. Her dear Walter had been sitting at his desk, handsome, successful, and reasonably happy, surely. Certainly, he was not depressed—or she would have known, wouldn't she? Then something happened. While she was gone a few hours, Walter took his gun and shot himself through the heart. Now the ugliest word in the world flashed in and out of her head as on a neon sign. **Suicide.** A coward's way out. But Walter was in no way a coward. How could he have committed suicide?

Three weeks ago, the police had said it over and over in the library downstairs. In a matter-of-fact way, as if they were commenting on the weather. The repeated utterances of this word had made it hang in the air like a solid fact. Suzanne Wilkins sat hunched forward on the edge of her silky boudoir chair, arms folded in her lap, hugging her stomach. She was nowhere in time or space. Slowly her brain registered wetness on her wrist. She was crying again, silently, deeply from the agony in her heart. How could she cry so much after three weeks had passed? Suzanne wondered sometimes if she were ever going to stop. How could she have an endless supply of tears?

On her nightstand were several books on grieving—very popular at the moment. Actually, these were more practical gifts to the bereaved than flowers. But why were so many people losing people, she wondered. Was it kind of an epidemic of the times? Anyway, these books all gave the same advice, couched in different literary styles. Illogically her brain went off on a tangent: did they do feasibility studies to see if enough people were dying? Check out number of the dead and dying before deciding how many books to have printed? Grieve, they all advised. It was essential to give enough time to grieving. She certainly was doing well in that area.

Eventually, they promised, it would all be okay again, and she could (in their words) "get on with her life." If there could be any kind of life for her after this, she couldn't imagine what it would be like. She glanced in a detached way around the room, tears glistening like raindrops on her cheeks. Her favorite picture on the nightstand brought an unbearable yearning into the core of her, and Walter's loving glance seemed to reach out to meet hers.

Mr. and Mrs. Walter P. Wilkins—such a handsome couple. Just last year on the natural cove beach down below the Southampton Princess Hotel in Bermuda. Both looking tan, slim, and younger than a couple in their early forties. Suzanne in a knockout two-piece turquoise bathing suit, a matching headband holding her swinging blonde hair in place, laughing and leaning against Walter, his arm firmly around her shoulder. His iron-gray hair was tousled above his dark glasses, his smile warm and happy.

Close together—they had always been that way. His "second self," he called her. They talked—intimately and in depth about everything. They shared daily experiences and monumental discoveries. All the happiness and sadness of life they experienced together. They knew each other's thoughts, plans, aspirations, goals, and mutual pleasures. They knew one another's inner being. Until lately.

During the past year Walter had gradually built a wall between them, brick by brick, so slowly she had been only mildly disturbed at first. She found plausible explanations in the stress of his position as president of the Monroe Trust Company or the possible onset of the first stages of midlife crisis. Even their sexual intimacy, which Suzanne had always thought so mutually satisfying, frequently didn't work out, and she consoled Walter with admonitions not to worry: "This frequently happens with married people." She sounded like a sex therapist, but she ached inside with the knowledge that she never thought such a thing would happen to THEM. At the same time, she thought it a little strange that she worried about it more than he did. He would turn over and immediately go to sleep; leaving her with crevices in their closeness gradually widening.

Suzanne was beside herself. She fixed his favorite meals. She bought sexy black lingerie. She lightened her blonde hair. She was always cheerful and supportive. Walter didn't seem to notice. When Suzanne implied that something appeared to be wrong and perhaps they should talk about it, he gave her a strange, hard look that seemed to suggest she was out of her mind.

Now her gaze moved over the bedroom furniture, registering Walter's belongings as if they were outlined before her eyes in black magic marker. His hairbrush and comb lay on the dresser beside with the velvet-lined tray filled with gold cuff links, his gold onyx ring, and pearl studs. Colognes and after-shave lotions were reflected in the round brass oval mirror. A note pad with his scribbles was lined up precisely along the edge of the answering machine on the elegant gleaming surface of the small ebony desk. Several paperbacks were stacked in order of desired reading on his nightstand next to the alarm-radio, the dial set at his favorite classical music station. Her eyes slid over to the closed folding doors on his side of the double closet. The tears began again. She had vowed that today she would make the effort to dispose of Walter's clothing. According to the self-help books, it was time, and getting rid of his personal belongings would be a catharsis for her. A positive step she could take to expedite her own recovery.

Somehow she moved, heavy weights in her heart and feet. Slowly she folded the door back on itself, and Walter came alive again in her imagination. She could see him standing there, lean and muscular, pushing his clothes back and forth on the closet rod, considering, selecting. After that, he would turn to his three-tiered tie rack to remove the proper, expensive, conservative accessory. Of its own accord, her shaky right hand reached out and slid several sport coats of camel's hair, cashmere, and tweed along the rod, searching.

Then she stopped, her fingers lingering on a particular jacket, moving along the rough tweed, her mind and senses remembering the feel of Walter in it when she embraced him. Suzanne removed it and held it on its padded hanger at Walter's height while she stared at it and tears gathered once more in her reddened eyes. This jacket was Walter's favorite and somewhat unusual. Tailored of brown herringbone tweed flecked with rough tan yarn, the pocket flaps were outlined with a narrow dark brown suede binding. This trim was used nowhere else on the jacket.

Very distinctive, Walter had declared. She buried her head in it, sniffing the special scents of tobacco and cologne that still lingered. This personal aroma embraced her, bringing the old familiar feeling of intimacy she had felt when close to Walter. Her eyes flooded anew. Her loss stabbed at her. No Walter. Never again. She draped one jacket arm around her shoulders, and while the sobs started, she imagined Walter's arm still in it and the comforting way it used to feel. Her hand clutched it desperately as she viewed the other garments so carefully buttoned and hung. All the hangers hooked over the rod from the front with every garment facing to the right.

Suddenly she had an incongruous thought, which brought up an unexpected hysterical giggle. She could now hang anything in this house any way she pleased. Often Walter's desire for order had bordered on compulsion. And worse yet, he sometimes acted like a drill sergeant, giving her orders and the logical reasons for following them. Suzanne shook her blonde head to bring herself into the present. She was here, in Walter's closet, to begin clearing away the past. Her husband didn't live here anymore. He was never coming home again. She couldn't recover if she allowed his personal reminders to confront her each day.

She remembered her mother had a friend whose husband had died, and twenty years later clothes of the deceased were still hanging in the closet. When Suzanne had heard the story, she had shivered in distaste, thinking, "What a weird lady." Funny she would think of that story now. In a way, she could at last understand that other woman. She herself, however, had positively decided on the practical, healthy course of action. She would begin by throwing out Walter's favorite jacket and then the rest should be easier. Dabbing at her eyes, Suzanne turned to get one of the packing boxes piled in the corner by the bay window.

It was early March and still cool. Here in Edgewood, Michigan, about 30 miles east of Chicago and Lake Michigan, cool weather sometimes lasted until June. The homeless would surely appreciate Walter's clothes, she thought. And Walter had been a generous man. He would like them to be worn. But he had not been generous with her. He had deprived her of the one thing in the world she loved and wanted the most. Himself. Something had led Walter Wilkins to take his own life in a desperate and final act of separation . . .

2

A cross town, in a shabby apartment over a deli, former police sergeant Dave Monaco woke up about 2:30 in the afternoon. The formless lump of his pillow was pressing his bristly beard into his face, while his head spun around curves all by itself. He always hoped he would wake up somewhere else, or maybe in another world. He didn't know how much longer he could take this one. If he could stand himself for the next couple of minutes, he could fix it all up so he could maybe get through the next hour or two.

No matter how blotto he got the night before, he always knew enough not to drink up all the vodka. He needed a few swallows for breakfast. As it sometimes took an agonizing super-human effort to rise from the bed, he tried to keep an adequate ration handy. He moaned now as he slowly moved on his stomach to the edge of the bed so he could reach down with a twitching hand, feeling for the bottle on the floor. Panic sometimes kicked in at this point. Maybe it wouldn't be there. Or maybe it was all gone. But it was there. His fumbling fingers settled around it, and he managed to slant his head to one side and tilt the bottle to his lips.

The pain inside him began to subside and mobility crept to his limbs. He considered getting up. He wrestled with this decision each day. What difference did it make? Who cared? But long ago, his good mother had placed a tape in his brain. It played messages like 'keep trying,' 'eat the right things and exercise,' 'right will triumph,' 'evil will be punished.' Until a year ago, he had lived his life on her precepts. Then he added some of his own: 'your friends will betray you,' 'you can't trust anyone,' 'people are eager to believe the worst of you.'

His long bare legs slid off the side of the bed and his wide, flat patrolman feet finally settled on the dirty thin mat that had once been a carpet. Terrific, he thought, I'm sitting up. Some corner of his mind sickened. This was a triumph? Once there had been many real triumphs in his life: moments of incredible courage, beating the odds, tramping on evil, making powerful changes in a lousy world. Like some of his boyhood comic-strip heroes, described as 'standing up for truth and justice'. He put his life on the line every day to clean some of the rotten stink out of this world, and it felt good. Most days he felt he had made a difference.

But one night everything changed. Evil reached the arm of corruption into Dave's precinct and his partner, Barney, succumbed. The events of that evening strung themselves through Dave's brain over and over. Drinking was the only way of turning them off. He finally rose shakily from the bed and shuffled his large angular frame through the archway of the bedroom past the soiled, torn greenish tweed sofa and into the kitchen alcove. A well-worn sink with a lop-sided drain board filled one wall, a small refrigerator on the floor underneath. Opposite, a shelf straddled two slanting brackets above what seemed to be a stove, its two-burners barely visible under layers of rust and grease. A looping piece of red-checkered plastic shelf edging held by two thumbtacks testified to a minimum decorating effort by a former tenant.

Dave coaxed some water out of a reluctant faucet into a dented pan and set it on the stove over the one burner that worked. He felt weak, and for a moment, he leaned against the doorjamb, searching for his equilibrium. Forcing himself to move, he rinsed out a cup in the sink and added instant coffee from a jar on the shelf. Grasping the edge of the drain board for support, he slowly lowered himself to his knees and opened the refrigerator door. A few slices of bread confirmed that food supplies were at a minimum. He took a slice and closed the door. Cold bread was his usual breakfast, kept in the refrigerator to protect it from occasional rodents. He held the bread in his hand while he poured the steaming water into the coffee cup. Somehow his brain had enough reasoning power left to know it would not be a good idea to lay the slice down on the grimy drain board.

He returned to his bed and sat on the edge, pulling the gray blanket around him. It was cool in this room, for the April day was cloudy, and even intermittent shafts of sun had no chance against the murky glass of his two small windows. He cupped his hands around his hot cup, his thumb and first finger holding the bread. A couple of sips brought a touch of comfort to his abused stomach, and he ate some of his bread, chewing mightily on its pasty substance. He had finished and was lighting a cigarette when he heard the ill-fitting door squeaking under a sharp knock.

"What the hell!" he groaned. Who could know he was here, and who would care? Then, in his deep, husky voice, he called out, "Who is it?"

"Ralph."

Dave sighed. It was his brother-in-law. It was okay. He really didn't want to talk to him, but it was inevitable that Ralph would find him. And Ralph was a good guy—a friend. Someone who had been on his side when his other so-called friends had joined one another in a vanishing act.

"Just a minute," Dave called, and hastily picked up his pants and sweat shirt, squirming into them with some effort.

He looked under the bed, in the closet, and peered around the room but couldn't find his shoes. Had he come home last night in bare feet? In April? He had a moment of clear panic. Was his tenuous hold on ordinary life growing weaker each day? A distressing, unfamiliar feeling rolled over him. He was scared. He was damn scared. Of himself. The real enemy was living within. There was another, louder knock. This time he called out "Coming," and hurried to open it. They stared at each other for a moment, Then Dave looked away, embarrassed by the compassion he saw in Ralph's eyes.

"What in the hell are you doing in this dump?" Ralph glanced quickly around the room, absorbing the surroundings in a flash. "Sorry, pal," he then said, clamping a friendly hand on Dave's shoulder. "I didn't mean that. It's just that Lorna and I have been worried about you."

"As you can see, I'm doing great," said Dave, defiantly, waving an arm about and suddenly seeing his degradation affirmed in these neglected surroundings. "How'd you find me?"

Ralph shrugged out of his gray ski parka, looked about for a moment, and then hung it on a hook on the door. "Roberta knew where you were."

"The hell she did! I never told her. She must have had me followed. Just like darling Bobby."

Ralph crossed gingerly to the sofa, and after a slight hesitation, perched on the edge and pulled out a cigarette. "She sounded like she was worried about you, Dave. As we all are."

Dave brought up a 'humph' from deep in his throat. "Yeah. My ex-wife isn't sure she got everything I had, and now she wants to check it out." He creaked his legs into a squatting position and sat down on a splitting plastic hassock.

Ralph's eyes toured the room. "Looks to me like she left you zippo, pal." Then he fixed his glance firmly on Dave and said slowly and emphatically, "So tell me the truth. What in the hell are you doing in a run-down place like this?"

Dave's bloodshot eyes were inscrutable beneath his bushy eyebrows. His swollen lips twitched at the corners. "Hey! Be careful, you're insulting my home!"

Their eyes met in silent recognition at the poor effort at levity. Neither smiled. Ralph took a drag on his cigarette and looked about for an ashtray. Dave pointed to an overflowing one on the floor, and Ralph bent down and flicked his ash into it. He straightened and said what he had come to say.

"We want to help you, Dave. We want you to come to live with us. Now that Bob's in college, his room is available." He paused a moment. "Your sister is really worried about you."

Dave peered at his brother-in-law. "Knowing my sister, I would imagine there are conditions attached."

Ralph shuffled his feet. "Really only one. She's afraid you're drinking too much."

Dave spread his arms wide. "As you can see, she's right as usual. Look, Ralph, we've had this conversation before. I'm not ready to stop yet. When I am, I will." Dave stared at the floor for a moment, hands clasped between his knees. "It's the only way I can get through the day."

"There are other ways. There's all kinds of help available. You can lick this and start over."

"I don't think so. I just can't get what happened out of my head."

He looked at Ralph and blinked rapidly. He ran his tongue over his dry lips and wished Ralph would leave so he could have a drink. Nevertheless, he went on. He knew Ralph had heard this many times, but somehow he himself needed to hear it again. He still thought there might be a chance to convince the world he had been innocent of all charges if he could just get someone to listen.

"Damn it—I still can't believe that everyone thought I had some part in that scam. Me—with an impeccable record on the force. Why Barney would lie—God, I've been sleepless a lot over that one. Some slight or injury, I suppose. Maybe real or imaginary."

"You've got to forget all this, Dave. Hell, the investigation should be over any day now, and then you'll be reinstated. Just hang in there until then, old pal. You've got to be ready for that—be in condition, ya know? Hell, you're only what? Forty four?"

"Forty three."

"I'll be fifty next July." Ralph's eyelids dropped and his flecked eyebrows met above his thin hooked nose. He cautiously rearranged his bony buttocks along the wide arm of the couch and cleared his throat. "How's the EFOP doing with your case?"

Dave's union, the Edgewood Fraternal Order of Police, had appointed their own special investigator to look into the allegations against him. "I'm not sure. But I got a letter a few days ago that they're going to start sending me a small pittance each week."

"Well, that's good news. Maybe you can move out of here."

Dave didn't say anything.

Ralph leaned forward, his hands clasped between his legs. "Look, Dave, you know I'm your friend. Besides your brother-in-law. Can I come right out with it?"

Dave rubbed his itchy beard with a palm. "Can I stop you?"

"Look, this is only a temporary setback in your life. It doesn't change who you really are. You're still the same intelligent man who contributed a lot to bring order to our part of the world. And brave. Hell—there were many times when you were very brave. You put your ass on the line. But you believed in the value of your life and what you were doing. That hasn't changed, just because some misguided pricks choose to support the department's decision to hang a charge on you and kick you out of your job. You're still you. You can still have a damn good life. But you gotta forget yesterday, and hell, you gotta make some changes." He burned his look into Dave's eyes. "And it's for damn sure that bottle makes things even worse." He paused, as if wondering if he had gone too far. "But you don't need me to tell you that."

Dave's eyes were like stones. "You're right I don't. When I give up my friendly companion, you'll be the first to know." Suddenly he couldn't look at Ralph, and he stumbled to his feet and into the bedroom to get a cigarette. When he came back, Ralph had his parka on and was standing at the door. "I'll tell Lorna you're doing fine," he said evenly.

"You do that."

Dave stared at the floor and took a drag on his cigarette. For a moment, he felt more unstable than ever. He couldn't wait until Ralph left and his unsettling pronouncements went with him, but at the same time, he knew an unrelenting loneliness would be waiting.

Ralph hesitated, and then took a step forward, one hand in his pocket, extracting his billfold. "You know, we missed your birthday last month, and we want to make up for it." He held out a fifty-dollar bill.

A good man, trying to help, Dave decided. He hesitated only a moment before taking it. "Thanks. Of course I don't really need this with all the money I've stolen." He snickered a sharp staccato. "Give my love to Lorna."

"I will. And listen, you need anything, just call." Ralph opened the door and then swung around for one last word of advice. "Promise me—" He stopped abruptly at the warning in Dave's eyes. The rest of the sentence hung silently in the air between them: 'you won't spend it on booze'. Ralph hesitated another moment and then said, "One last thing, Dave. You used to fight for your ass every day on the street—so—ah—" He paused, looking embarrassed that his words sounded like preaching.

"Yeah, I know. Hey, don't worry about me. I'm making plans. This is strictly temporary." Ralph was good-hearted, Dave thought, and summoned up a smile as his guest departed.

He was closing the door when he heard the familiar sound. A police siren. Starting a few blocks away and growing louder as it came nearer down Division Street. He shuffled to the kitchen window and peered through the grime at the moment the red light flashed by. For a moment, Dave was in that police car with his friend and partner, Barney, flooring it on the way to the crime scene. Then the curtain rose on their last time together.

Talking to Ralph brought it all back, clearer than ever. The drug bust. Struggling with the dealers, then getting them cuffed. Confiscating the 30 kilos of cocaine and a sack with about 500 big ones. All under control, until an unexpected backup team arrives—and Steve Collier. Smart aleck—and dumb. Or, as it turned out, not so dumb. Shooting and confusion. Things getting out of control. And in the final analysis, some of the money shows up with Steve who swears on a stack of Bibles that Dave has passed it on to him for a split. And Barney supports that theory—lying, for some obscure reason. During the fracas a big share of the drug money has disappeared. The patsy—and the real idiot in the end—is Dave.

Dave's shoes had turned up under the sofa, and old habits surfaced to the extent that he wiped the mud from them with a dampened sock. He splashed water on his blotchy face and in his itchy eyes and worked his way into his navy blue parka. Unsteadily he made his way down the creaking hallway to the outside door and from there, he grasped the rotting railing and crept down the outside ladder-like steps to the alley below. An undercover cop lounged against a building at the corner of the street, blending into the environment. Casually immobile with lowered head, he fixed his eyes on the pavement, ridiculously pretending to be invisible.

Dave could always spot them. Especially as they turned up no matter where he went. He knew why they were there. He was under continual surveillance. The department still thought he had the money squirreled away and someday he would lead them to it.

Sometimes he would go up close to the guy, look him directly in the eye, and laugh. He enjoyed the strange embarrassed look he usually got in return. A distasteful, boring, duty—he knew it well. He smiled to himself at how useless this all was, and expensive. They had been trailing him now since January. How long would this go on?

Today he merely glanced at the figure to make sure it wasn't someone he knew, and then crossed Division street to walk a few blocks to the liquor store. In the 20's and 30's Colonel Lindbergh, Wendell Wilkie, and FDR himself had passed in triumphant motorcades down this street, a thriving commercial thoroughfare. Then a few years ago race riots crippled many of the small businesses with fire bombing and looting. Now the plywood-covered storefronts gave constant testimony that fear had triumphed, vanquishing livelihoods. But these commercial remnants were still useful, their cement thresholds providing a tiny piece of private shelter for the homeless, deposited there like indefinitive bags of bones and flesh. People who had reason to walk in this area made wide, hurried circles around these doorways, clutching their money.

Even Dave walked faster here and kept his glance solely on his direction. He never had enough money to worry about. It wasn't that. It was the tiny fragile gossamer web that still attached him to the real world. And in spite of it all, he wanted it there. It still told him, if vaguely, who he was. He had an identity. If he were to look into a pair of eyes in one of these doorways, he knew that thread would break. He would recognize himself as one of them, and it would be like tasting death. He drank, sure, to stop his thinking, to drift into that euphoric state of detachment. But in his more lucid moments, some kernel of his true being lay untouched, in a cocoon, submerged deep down on the edge of awareness. Waiting. He didn't know for what.

He crossed the intersection of Southern Avenue, and the sun

slid into a path across his face. Even through his tangled beard, this bit of warmth felt good. His trained ears picked up the padded sound of rubber-soled shoes matching his steps. What a jerk, he thought. Didn't this guy know that Dave had the experience to dodge him a hundred different ways if necessary?

He passed "The Second Time Around," a used-clothing store. Suddenly he stopped, and the footsteps behind him were silent. A thought struck him. If I go in here to buy something, will they still think I'm hoarding thousands of dollars? A slight smile curved his lips. Let's give them something to think about, he decided.

He turned around and paused for a moment, staring in the shop window. An effort had been made at merchandising. A headless mannequin posed in a white off-the-shoulder sequined evening gown. He smiled sardonically. If someone needed to buy an evening gown in this store, would they ever be invited to a formal affair? A half torso displayed a print blouse with coordinated slacks stretched flat before it. A man's raincoat hung over the back of a chair. Carefully folded shirts were staggered in a row on the floor below. Then close to the window on the right, there were some of those depressing-looking used household items usually found at flea markets: dingy pressed-glass bowls, florist's fake milk glass containers, an old hand mixer with the paint gone from the handle, a colander with rusty holes.

As he turned to go in, he caught a glimpse of his faithful shadow leaning against the plywood next door, lighting a cigarette. A bell tinkled several times as he opened and closed the door, and a friendly-faced plump woman in slacks and a large overblouse came forward to greet him. In the rear of the shop, three men and a teenaged girl were busy examining the merchandise.

"Are you looking for anything special?" The woman asked Dave.

He shrugged his shoulders. "As you can see, I probably could use everything."

She smiled at him consolingly. "Well, just look around. Everything is marked as to size and price."

He started at a table of underwear and socks, and located a few items for small change. Another man walked over and began pawing through the items, so Dave gathered up his selections and placed them at the end of the checkout counter for safekeeping. Then he moved over to a rack of trousers, looking ruefully down at his own. Once he had been meticulous, his police uniform always pressed, shirt collar starched, shoes he could see his reflection in. Sometimes he had shaved his tough beard twice a day. He poked through the rack, occasionally flipping out a pair for further scrutiny. He knew he needed clothes.

After their final fight over his drinking, Bobby had had the locks changed on their bungalow out in the Lowell section of Edgewood. He had been left with the clothes on his back and little else. A small bank account in his name alone. Not even a car. Bobby wouldn't listen to reason. Said that she deserved everything for putting up with his drinking every night for ten years. A statement that was greatly exaggerated.

He never drank on duty. Never then. And not really very much in those days. Not like now when it didn't really matter after all. He guessed it was a good thing they had never had children, although he often wondered how it would be to have another human in the world that shared his blood and could share his heart.

Now he shook his head as if to get free of his thoughts and idly moved to a group of jackets. Some nice stuff here, he thought, and then his hand felt a rough tweed. He had always liked tweed—so English countryside, but also rugged and manly. He lifted up the hanger and looked at the most perfect jacket he had ever seen. Not worn at all, practically new. Expertly tailored, and very unusual. No flaps over the pockets. Instead, the lower ones as well as the breast pocket were bordered with narrow strips of brown suede. A nicely tailored vent in the back. Carefully matched subdued herringbone stripes. And it had wide shoulders—made for a large man. His right hand trembled as he searched for the size. A 46. His size.

"It's smashing, isn't it?" asked the genial lady. "Here, try it on." And she waited for him to remove his navy windbreaker before helping him on with the jacket. "It's a little snug because you have that sweatshirt on," she pointed out. "But I think it's a perfect fit."

Dave had to agree. It sat on his shoulders as if custom-made. The sleeves were the right length. It felt wonderful, and he held his head higher and straightened his shoulders. He walked to the corner of the store where there was a long mirror.

At his first glance, he was shocked at his image. For quite a while now, since he had virtually avoided shaving, he had not looked at himself in a mirror. Certainly, it had been a long time since he could look himself in the eyes. He avoided it now, keeping his glance on the sport coat as much as possible. Even so, his physical appearance shot an image to his brain: a degenerate, mangy, filthy, almost inhuman thing decked out in a coat looking to belong to some kind of nobility. He was stunned.

This coat definitely did not belong in his world. So why the strange emotion? He wanted it. He had to have it. He hadn't wanted anything for many months. But now he did. What he was feeling was upsetting. He had never believed in anything that he couldn't see, understand, or explain, but somehow he now felt in his gut that this coat was to become his for a reason. Like it might have something to do with changing his life. He shook his head at such foolishness. But somehow, he already felt different just having it on.

"It's perfect," declared the lady behind him. "Would you like to see the slacks that go with it?"

"Slacks?" he asked, still in a fog from his surprising decision.

"Yes. The lady who brought in the jacket also gave us some other clothes that belonged to her husband. He died recently, she told me." She took some trousers from a nearby rack. "Here they are."

Tan gabardine. Fine quality and newly cleaned. If I take these, I'll have to be careful. Can't afford bills at the cleaners, thought Dave. Again, his size. "Any shirts?" he asked.

She took three from a shirt rack and held them up for his inspection. "I think these were his. Lucky you turned out to be the same size."

Dave smiled and nodded. The lady laid the shirts and slacks on the counter and stepped behind it. He pushed over his previous choices, adding the jacket. Slipping back into the old windbreaker, he asked, "How much?"

She pursed her lips, and scribbled on a piece of paper. "Twenty dollars?" She said it tentatively, her head cocked to one side.

Dave knew this game. "Oh, dear—" he sighed, lowering his head sadly.

"How about fifteen?" she asked, slowly. "I really can't give it to you for any less."

"Fine," he agreed, and slapped his fifty-dollar bill on the counter. Her eyes widened and she drew back a bit.

"Birthday present," he said, and then, although he didn't have to, "I didn't steal it. Honest."

She gave him his change and put his purchases into a large plastic bag, keeping the jacket on a hanger, which poked through the top and gave him a hook to carry. Then Dave walked through the jingling door with a trace of remembered jauntiness, a tiny reflex triggered by an almost forgotten and miniscule feeling of satisfaction. He checked outside for the Tail and found him looking in the window.

Dave went up close to him and yelled in his face. "I got some new clothes! Ain't that great?"

The startled look on the man's face was like a happy punctuation mark on the day's experience. He whistled a couple of notes as he ambled up the street to the liquor store, hugging his new jacket to his side. There was only one trouble with it, he thought. It was such a special garment. One would have to shape up to wear it. In appearance, certainly. Even perhaps in other areas of life.

3

The Monroe Trust Company had owned the northwest corner of Monroe and Lincoln streets since it was established in 1902. The most prestigious bank in Edgewood, it had survived several robbery attempts, some mismanaged books, a fire, and even the bank holiday of 1933. Its neoclassical facade was featured on the city's best-selling postcard. Now, however, the banking public was wondering if its business practices were judicious. Walter Wilkins, the President, had abruptly and with deadly finality resigned on March third. Under a cloud. He was the first Monroe Trust Company bank president to commit suicide. A week later, customers were still talking among themselves and asking tellers what had happened. The tellers had been instructed to play down the tragedy and reassure the investors that Mr. Wilkins' death was absolutely in no way connected with the operation of the bank. "Personal or health problems," they suggested.

In the rear of the vaulted marble lobby, a workman worked on removing a brass nameplate from one of the wide paneled doors along a row of offices. "Excuse me," said the brisk efficient voice of Dorothy Clarke, arriving at the president's former office.

In her early thirties, Dorothy was bright, arrogant, dressed-for-success. The new breed of American workingwoman. The slim black heels of her pumps beat a steady four-four time on the marble floor as the workman opened the door, and she glided smoothly around him. She stood on the old, still-beautiful oriental carpet and gazed around the office through narrowed penciled eyelids. Lustrous mahogany-paneled walls were trimmed in scroll molding; magnificent book shelves reached to the ceiling; red velvet drapes cascaded from behind cornices; a small elegant chandelier hovered over a massive antique desk.

She allowed herself some wishful thinking. Someday this office could be hers. Branch manager today—president tomorrow? A moment of inactivity was enough. That was not her style. She moved to some boxes stacked against a wall, and bent over to check the contents. Yes, apparently Walter Wilkin's personal belongings were packed and ready to go. She rifled through a few boxes at random, making sure no bank records were included. Then she went around the desk, rolling out the well worn, elegant old executive chair on its smooth casters, and sat down with a sigh of satisfaction. It fit well, and there was still, after all these years, a faint smell of good leather. She reached forward, pulling out and examining all the drawers. Finally, satisfied that only personal belongings had been removed, she moved slowly toward the door.

There was a knock, and the senior vice-president, Charles Rosenthal, poked his professor-like face around the door, thinning wisps of pale hair drifting across his bald spot. "How are you coming?" he asked, his glance flashing proprietarily around the room.

"Just fine, darling," Dorothy said, arching her neck and breasts at him. "These boxes can be picked up anytime."

Charles gave a quick look out the door, and then closed it. He strode across the carpet and grabbed Dorothy, giving her a quick, hard kiss.

"Well!" she murmured, smiling up into his eyes with pleasure while her right hand checked the back of her hair to make sure her precise haircut had not been disturbed.

"You know that old banking adage," grinned Charles. "Add up the assets and cash in on the total." He turned his attention to the filled packing boxes. "This is too much for Mrs. Wilkins to handle. I'll take these out to the house myself."

"Might as well get this office ready for you to move into," Dorothy said practically. "When the board of directors meets on Friday, you'll be the new president." She tilted her head sideways and appraised him as though inserting him into a picture frame labeled 'Bank President'. Then her expression changed to eagerness, and she asked, "Do you know anything more about Walter's death?"

"No," he said hesitatingly. "Isn't it the damndest thing?

Someone like Walter—handsome, successful, lovely home and wife? How can you figure it?"

"Maybe it wasn't really suicide."

"But it had to be. The police investigation showed that. Mrs. Wilkins and her daughter came home from the movies and found him with the gun in his hand, slumped on his desk in the library. The house had been locked up tight. They used their key to get in. No one else had one, they told the police." He paused. "What a time for Penny to be home from college. To find her father like that."

"But the note the police found. Isn't that a little strange? What was it he said? Oh, something to the effect that what he was going to do wasn't her fault, it was his. Then he started to apologize and never finished. Doesn't that strike you as strange?"

"How so?"

"Well, you know Walter, always so organized. He never left anything unfinished. Why would he shoot himself before he finished the letter to his wife?"

"I have no idea. But I suppose anyone who is about to commit suicide is hardly in his right mind. You would have to be completely out of it, I would think. Maybe he was so distraught he couldn't think of how to finish that note. Probably wanted to get the whole thing over with while he still had the nerve."

"Well", she answered, lamely. "Somehow it just doesn't seem like Walter."

Charles gave a sardonic humph. "Well, how about suicide? Does that sound like Walter?" He cleared his throat to sound more decisive. "I guess it's often like this in cases of this nature. There are a few things that don't add up and that causes speculation." He stepped closer to her and ran his fingers across a velvet cheek. "Who knows what goes on in the personal part of another's life?" His eyes bore into hers. "Do even you and I know everything about each other?" She smiled briefly and moved away. "Well, anyway, if the police have investigated and declared it suicide, we have to accept it."

Her glance swept the desk. "When are Walter's accounts going to be audited?" Their eyes met, widened, then flicked away. They were silent for a moment while something unpleasant rose between them.

Then Charles answered the silent question. "There won't be any problem there. Walter was the most honest person I've ever worked for. He's always kept perfect records on his trust and loan accounts. There was probably something in his personal life he couldn't handle. Who knows?"

*   *   *

Suzanne Wilkins was no longer crying several times a day. Now she wept only a few tears first thing in the morning and a few more at bedtime. It was a terrible way to start and end each day, but she couldn't help it. She supposed it would be better if she went to sleep in the guest bedroom, but somehow having Walter's pillow next to hers in the usual place was a strange mixture of agony and comfort. Occasionally she punched his pillow in anger that he had done such a terrible thing to her, and then cried all the harder while she moaned for his imaginary forgiveness.

When she was feeling most confused, she would sit down with one of her self-help books and search the table of contents to locate some comforting message, some direction to soothe and comfort. According to the experts, she was still in the denial stage and needed to make grieving her top priority. Although the books all promised recovery, right now she was fearful that these daily patterns of behavior would become permanent. That seemed a real possibility in her big, lonely, quiet showcase of a house that overnight had taken on a tomb-like atmosphere.

Her many friends seldom called, afraid to intrude on her grief, she imagined. Two loyal friends she had known since high school, Debbie Mahalik and Sharon Selby, came by with food and forced good cheer. They phoned every few days, but they had their own lives: families to be with and commitments in the cultural and social scene of Edgewood. In the end, it was like the books said: no one can recover for you.

When the doorbell rang at eleven o'clock on this Tuesday morning, she was dressed in tan cotton slacks and blue button-down oxford shirt, her pale blond hair caught back behind her neck with a blue ribbon. Her makeup was carefully applied and her eyes only a little clouded from the sadness within. She took a deep breath and opened the door to Charles Rosenthal, who had telephoned earlier. In spite of herself, she felt sorry for him. This was obviously a distasteful duty for Charles and an unwanted meeting for both of them.

"Suzanne—" He started and then stopped. They had known one another impersonally for many years. This moment that had brought them together was suddenly personal and awkward. He hesitated, and then leaned forward to kiss her self-consciously on the cheek. She tried to help him out and bent forward a bit. They both avoided looking at the two packing cartons on the steps beside him.

"Would you like to come in for coffee?" She didn't know why she said that. Just go away, she thought silently.

"No thanks." He finally looked at the boxes at his feet. "I have to get back. I'll just get these inside." She opened the door wider to allow him to deposit them on the slate floor in the foyer. He looked at her. "I'm so sorry," he said. I'll bet you are, she thought. I think this was just what you wanted.

"Damn," she said loudly after he had left.

She wondered how much longer she could stand it. It was as if Walter had not yet been laid to rest. Even now, the police showed up occasionally to ask the same questions again and again. Suicide was the only verdict, and yet the case stayed open. There was no plausible reason for Walter to kill himself. Neither she nor the detectives could find any explanation. The evidence refused to give up any additional information.

"Was your husband in any kind of financial trouble?"

"No. Absolutely not."

"Did he seem worried or distressed lately?"

"No." Not in the least. It didn't even bother him that he was impotent. She was the one who agonized over it in private.

"How about his health?"

"As far as I know, it was excellent. You can check with his doctor."

"Any business problems?"

"You can check with the bank." Did they think husbands told their wives every scrap of information about their activities?

"How long were you married?"

"Twenty-one years."

"That's a long time." The detective squinted his eyes at her.

"Were there any personal problems along the way that might have brought this situation about?" Damn you. You're insinuating Walter might have been involved with other women. If I knew this, would I tell you, you bastard?

"No."

"Can you think of any reason your husband would kill himself?"

"No. I didn't even know he had a gun." At this point, they usually paused and cleared a passage in the throat before going on.

"Mrs. Wilkins, is there anything you want to tell us about the note your husband left? Can you tell us how you interpret it?" When Walter had been found, the police had scrutinized the note very carefully, holding it by the edge of the paper, and then putting it carefully into a plastic bag.

They then handed the bag to her to read through the covering. She was furious. It was her note, personal, meant only for her. She felt faint and violated. Somehow, she had managed to read it, while the officer turned his head away, his idea of giving her some privacy. "Suzanne dear, none of this is your fault. It is all mine. I am so sorry to . . ." She read it several times, through a blur of tears, her brain trying desperately to find some sense in it. And it was unfinished. Why was that? She looked more intently at the handwriting as if this had to be composed by someone else. But it was Walter's handwriting without a doubt. And it was found lying on the desk next to the gun and Walter's dear head. Each time these interviews were over, the detectives would look at her impassively. No decision, no conclusion. But somehow, she felt on the defensive. Tell me what you're thinking, she screamed inside herself. Why do you make me feel as if this is somehow my fault? But after the questioning, they would only thank her and leave.

Her life stood in one place. As immovable as she felt herself to be. The insurance people wouldn't pay until the case was closed. The probate of the estate was put on hold. It was all too overwhelming. And there was the never-ending and distasteful chore of removing Walter's personal possessions from this house. She opened up a closet door and pushed the bank cartons inside. Someday. When she was stronger. Maybe not until after she figured out why all this had happened.

4

"Not too short, Mike," said Dave Monaco as he ran his fingers through his just-shampooed hair and eyed the scissors already twitching in the barber's hand.

"How'd you get such a mop, Sergeant?" The almost black curly snips of hair were already falling steadily to join other clusters of discarded tresses on the gray tiled floor.

"I've been away for awhile," Dave lied. "You know I won't have anyone but you style my hair, Mike. I'm fussy that way." He grinned sarcastically.

"And what's with the beard? Going hippy or something?"

"Hell, no. Just thought I'd try it. But you know what?" Dave leaned forward a few inches and turned his head to each side, inspecting the dark bushy addition to his face and chin. "I think I look a little like Abraham Lincoln. What do you think?"

"Was old Abe Italian?" Mike feigned surprise. He went on combing up sections and snipping across the comb. "You're better looking. Old Abe was really an ugly guy." After more clipping, he asked, "Want me to shave it off?"

Dave looked thoughtful. "No, I think I'll keep it for a while. Just neaten it up a bit."

Mike peered around Dave's head at the item of conversation. His mouth shriveled in distaste. Gingerly he poked a finger at the hairy bush. "Wash it lately?"

Dave pretended to be insulted. "Since when do we discuss my personal hygiene?"

"Humph", mused nimble-fingers. A few seconds passed. "I heard what happened to you, Dave, and I'm real sorry. Guess it's been rough on you. Come on over to the sink, and we'll wash your beard, give you a little shave here and there, and turn you into a real prince."

What's gotten into me, Dave wondered? Spending good booze money on practically a beauty treatment. He thought about the new clothes he had just bought. Strange. The poor sucker who had owned them was no more. Now Dave was going to wear his clothes, and it was kind of like picking up this guy's life and going on with it.

Just from looking at the jacket, you know the owner had been a special person, particular and well-dressed. Had good taste and probably good manners as well. Undoubtedly a well-educated, a professional type of person. Maybe even important. And not very old. An older man wouldn't buy a jacket like that. And he must have made a good buck to afford the best.

Mike snapped the towel from around Dave's neck, and Dave's thoughts flipped back to the present. He stepped to the counter to pay. "Hell, Sergeant, your money isn't any good with me. I still owe you for giving my Joey a break when you caught him slugging it out in that alley. Come back anytime."

Dave smiled his thanks and took his hand out of his pocket. He felt a little lightheaded. A couple of nice things had happened this day, and he wasn't used to that. He had a funny feeling that there might be more to come. He gathered up his packages, slipping the bottle of vodka into his jacket pocket. The Tail was waiting patiently outside. Dave went up to him and stared into his face. "Hey! Take a good look," he said. "I've been made beautiful, and I wouldn't want you to follow the wrong guy, asshole."

As he turned away, he moved past a telephone booth. He paused, thinking. Maybe he could squeeze a little more good fortune out of this day. He fished some change from his pocket and yanked the door open. He dialed his old number. After a few rings, he heard Bobby's sharp, nasal hello. "Hello yourself."

"Oh, it's you." Far from delighted, but at least she didn't hang up.

"How are you doing?"

"Terrific. I sold the house for a million dollars. Hollywood wants me to star in a movie, and there's a handsome prince who wants to marry me and won't take no for an answer. How in the hell do you think I'm doing?"

It was Bobby all right. Never relaxed, normal like rather people. Always a chip on, a beef about something or other. Taking ordinary comments and twisting them. Couching them in unrelated innuendos for no good reason. He shifted his weight and thought about hanging up. This was not a good idea.

Suddenly her voice cooled down, the anger evaporated. "So why did you call?"

He tried to sound reasonable. "I need some of my things. It's a little hard living without clothes, shoes, shaving equipment— you know, personal stuff. Plus my clock radio and papers from my desk."

"Are you sober?"

"What do you mean?"

"What do I mean?" Her voice took on an edge. "I mean just that. Don't show up here if you've had anything to drink."

Sure, he thought. Needle me some more. You love to do it. He took a deep breath. "I'm sober. What's more, I look and smell gorgeous. Just came out of the barbershop. I will walk a straight line up your walk and your neighbors will clap and cheer."

"That'll be the day," Bobby said dryly. "Okay. Come ahead and take everything that's yours. I'm sick of looking at it anyway."

Dave left the phone booth and walked back to his room, where he carefully hung his new jacket and slacks in what passed for a bedroom closet. He glanced at his watch. Almost five thirty and he was beginning to feel hungry. Maybe if his luck held out Bobby would give him something to eat. He smiled at such a preposterous idea. In the meantime, it most certainly was the cocktail hour. He took out the bottle of vodka and started to the kitchen to get a glass.

Halfway there a strange thing happened. He suddenly needed to pick up his things more than he needed a drink. Maybe just a little one, he thought. Unexpectedly a picture of himself flashed through his mind. One drink would follow another. It was always like that. He would probably never get to Bobby's. Hell. He set the bottle on the kitchen counter and left quickly, the aching desire beginning to churn within him.

The cross-town bus had just pulled up to the corner, and he hurried to swing aboard. After the bus started, he got out of his seat and walked to the back where the Tail was sitting. "I'm so glad you could make it," Dave smiled at him pleasantly. "You see, I'm going to pick up a suitcase, and you can help carry it back to my room." He started back to his seat and then turned around. "What the hell," he said. "I'm afraid you're going to be disappointed. I doubt whether you will find even so much as a nickel in it."

*   *   *

His arms ached, and he banged his clumsy burdens against the stairs as he climbed to his apartment. Dave dropped the suitcase and rope-tied packing box outside the door, opened it, and kicked his cargo into the room. Still in his windbreaker, he headed for the kitchen. There was nothing like being with Bobby to make him quiver for a drink. The bottle of vodka was like a beacon, pointing the way to his salvation for the moment. He poured a full glass and went to sit in a valley of the sofa, where he began sipping in earnest. The alcohol soothed his throat and twitchy stomach and comforting relaxation began spreading out along his limbs. A warm, mellow feeling filled his brain cells.

The day's events flickered before his eyes like skittish scenes from an early D.W. Griffith movie. Nothing much had really happened except that he seemed to have discovered a couple of things about himself. For the past several weeks, his only goal had been to eliminate his agony as much as possible, maybe even to the point of self-destruction. Doors had closed on what he had been and done. As if he had never passed that way, giving all he could. After fighting the inscrutable face of evil for most of his adult life, he had, in the end, been rendered helpless by it. He had told himself he didn't care. Now, suddenly, it looked as if it might be just the opposite. He did care. He cared too much. That was why he was drinking more than ever.

While he was married to Bobby, he never drank on the job. Only at night—to close the curtain on images like a teenager lying dead in an alley or a battered woman crying in the corner of her kitchen. Bobby couldn't tolerate even one drink—including a beer. But she had never stood in his shoes, his heart pounding in shattering moments of almost paralyzing fear. Moments when the gossamer thread joining life to the physical body could be severed at any moment. Sharing his agonies with her was impossible. She closed her ears as if to keep this degradation from soiling her own square inch of this world.

His work, his moments of excitement and fear, of triumph and despair, were what he was—the deepest part of him. She plainly said: not interested. Really not caring for HIM was the message he got. This evening, Bobby had been cool and civil to him, a stranger, someone he had known long ago. Funny. When he looked at her unsmiling face and stern eyes, he was unable to believe he had lived with her and made love to her.

He wondered how he could ever have been attracted to someone so devoid of giving warmth. The fact was, she had good legs and looked terrific in a bathing suit. They had met on the beach at Sterling Lake, and his glands had blown smoke into his judgment. Before many hours into their relationship, he discovered she was very proficient at kissing. She also loved the music of Count Basie, Italian food, and the books of Donald Westlake. Somehow, it seemed enough to go on at the time.

Tonight she offered food, and when he eagerly accepted, she looked at him disgustedly and then reluctantly put together a ham and cheese on rye. When he asked for more mayo, she angrily pulled open the refrigerator door. He saw a six-pack of beer inside, and she reached around it to get the mayonnaise jar and a coke, banging them both down on the table in front of him. Then she put both hands on her hips and said reproachfully, "That beard looks hideous on you."

Now as Dave sat quietly in his room, a small sardonic twitching played with the corner of his mouth. Thinking of Bobby always brought back some unpleasant memories. He knew he was better off alone under any conditions. All along there were signs that inevitably they would separate. How they had stayed together for ten mutually unsatisfying years was a mystery. Neither had nurtured the other in any important way. Two strangers who occasionally put out tentative feelers for some kind of communicative meshing—that was what it had been.

Dave kept turning his almost-empty glass in his hands. Slowly, subtly a thought had been building all through the day and evening. His life was not over yet. He had a ways to go. How he would travel on through the rest of it was still unclear. Hell, everyone had problems.

Dave thought again of the former owner of the jacket. Someone like that, apparently successful and probably well-educated, dying in the prime of life. Dave hadn't wondered about anything much for a long time, but now his natural curiosity started to simmer. An imperceptible thread tied the former wearer to him because of joint ownership. If only this were a magical kind of jacket and he could slip on the owner's life as well!

Dave snickered out loud. He was beginning to fantasize. He needed a drink. He got up and went to the kitchen for a refill. Carrying his glass into the bedroom, he took a good gulp and set it down on the ring-marked nightstand. Then he took off his windbreaker and went to the closet to hang it up.

The new jacket swung gently from its hanger, expensive-looking and out of place. He slid it from its perch and sat down on the bed, the garment across his lap. His hands ran along the suede binding and then flipped the jacket open to slide across the silky inside lining. There was an elegant label attached to the inside facing. 'Comstock and Harding, Clothiers', he read. This unusual jacket had come from the most exclusive men's shop in town. Then Dave saw something else. Below, on another satin label, were embroidered script initials: WPW.

He stared at them for a moment. Although still faceless, the previous owner now had a kind of identity, almost a name. He turned the garment over, ran his hand down the beautiful wool, and examined the perfect tailoring of the rear vent. All of a sudden, his hand felt a small lump in the vent placket. His sensitive fingers closed over it. Was it a coin that had somehow worked its way out of a small hole in a pocket lining to become wedged in this spot?

He kept feeling it, giving the material some slack so he could work the object back and forth in his fingers. Because of the thickness of the wool, he couldn't get an absolute make on it. He fumbled in his pocket for his Swiss army knife and opened up the smallest blade. Carefully he ripped some of the stitches that fastened the lining in place. Finally, he had enough room to stretch a finger up inside, but the vent placket was tacked in place. A few more stitches had to be eliminated so he could see where the placket was secured. He was not surprised to find that it had been ripped open and re-sewn with clumsy stitches. He smiled to himself. "Old WPW," he murmured, "what in the hell have you been up to?"

The clumsy stitches came out easily. A key tumbled out and into his open palm.

5

Suzanne Wilkins sat in a sleek chrome and leather stool at her kitchen work center, expensive polished steel European cooking pots swinging from a suspended rack over her head. The latest kitchen efficiency surrounded her in a sterile, gleaming food-preparation laboratory. Last year she and Walter had designed it and had it executed after months of research and many trips to kitchen remodeling centers. When it was finished, its simple lines, practical materials, and specialized storage units gave testimony to the world that this was to be used by a serious cook. She took a sip of the coffee at her elbow and glanced now at the built-in desk in the corner, with its radio-TV unit and ceiling high shelves of cookbooks. A special rack held several cherished notebooks of her own original recipes, many of which had been printed in the Edgewood Herald.

A bitter taste, having nothing to do with the excellent coffee she always made, began in her mouth and culminated with a queasiness in her stomach. None of this held any interest for her now. She had found joy in creating a lovely home for Walter. Planning and executing social affairs were exciting for her, her energy and creativeness accelerated by her vision of the final production. Her self-confidence was nourished in the accolades from her guests, a pay-off that affirmed her success in pleasing people. But now she glanced around her sparkling kitchen with a piteous expression, like a person who has missed the last boat from the island.

This was her frame of reference, and she was in it to stay. She had spent a good part of her life learning and polishing her skills as a hostess. Taking direction from Walter in how to create the perfect living environment for an important bank president. She choked out a weak laugh. Would they put this in her obituary someday? Was noted hostess and chef? Was famous for her dinner parties?

What a lifetime achievement! Suzanne Wilkins was born to entertain. In her big family home on the banks of the Hudson River near Athens, New York, she began her life's work at age three. Although barely able to reach the dining room table, she learned to place the family heirloom silver correctly for her mother's frequent guests. She loved being asked to do it and never lost interest. When she was only six years old she baked her first lemon pie, and the meringue only wept a little. When her mother praised it, she knew without a doubt what she wanted to do with her life. So, she went to Cornell to major in Home Economics.

Walter Wilkins, from a modest home in Edgewood, was there on a scholarship, enrolled in the business management program. Their paths did not cross significantly until their senior year, when he asked her to the corner drug store for a coke, and she supplied some brownies from the home-economics kitchens. For Walter, whose mother never baked, it was love at first bite. Of course, that was only part of the attraction. Suzanne was a fairy-tale type of girl—supple and willowy, with graceful fine bones, a tiny waist, skin like the fine porcelain she loved, hair flowing in blonde waves from a round intelligent forehead, appraising pale green eyes.

After graduating in 1968, Walter went to Vietnam with the Supply Corps, stationed well behind the jungle hell, but nevertheless torn apart by the stories of the conflict and sight of the wounded being evacuated. A year and a half later, he was home, and a week after that he married his faithful dream girl. When the lean years were over and Walter started moving up in banking circles, Suzanne honed her skills and gave him the home of his dreams.

When she entertained, her dining room table sparkled with one of many sets of French or English cut glass, sterling silver, and imported bone china. For formal dinners, she used hand embroidered ecru or snowy white linen table coverings. On informal evenings, the table coverings echoed a tint in the china. Always the color scheme was restated in a skillful mix of her favorite flowers for a bold centerpiece. She kept abreast of the fashions in table settings as some women keep a constant eye on Paris fashions to put on their backs. But she supposed at times she was like the set decorator for a movie or stage set, using the accouterments of dining in creative ways.

She made her most innovative statement when she used only black and white for a dinner honoring the officers of the bank and their wives. Gold plated tableware framed the white plates rimmed in narrow bands of black and gold. Stark black water and wine glasses were placed against a black tablecloth. Dramatically elegant, white calla lilies curved free form from a gleaming white ball-shaped bowl as the centerpiece, supported here and there with a few grape leaves, glinting in their red spray.

When the guests had uttered the appropriate oohs and aahs, Suzanne had explained the significance of her creation: gold for the bank's product; white for its record, black for the ink in the ledgers, and, hopefully, only a little red in the money supply. The guests laughed appreciatively, remembering the story to tell their friends. Even more, they appreciated and marveled at some of the best food they had ever had, framed by flower replicas carved from fresh vegetables. Often Suzanne and Walter's guests would read about their dinner party in a feature article on the front page of the living section of the Sunday Edgewood Herald. She had loved those times. Walter would hug her and tell her she had done it again. "You create such a wonderful home for me," he would tell her. "I'm lucky to have such a great wife." Funny, though. For about the last six months, there had been no comments, except for absent-minded, kind of impersonal remarks, such as, "very nice" or "great dinner."

She sat now, staring off at nothing in an imaginary space, her hands folded in her lap. Thinking about the last six months triggered some memories in her mind. Several incidents caught fleetingly at her thoughts. In very subtle ways, Walter had been different the last six months. He hugged and kissed her less often, usually as if she were a distant relative. His kisses would fleetingly brush her cheek, while he seemed intent on turning his head to put his mouth out of the way of hers. But mostly there had been the strange thing of avoiding her eyes.

Always before, in their life together, they had taken the time, no matter where, to look deep into each other's eyes, both seeming to find excitement and contentment in doing so. Dozens of times a day their glances verified their intense love for one another. But in the last few months, she often caught him apparently staring at a disturbing vision, for his brow would be furrowed and the corners of his generous mouth would be tightly drawn against his teeth.

"You're worried about something," she stated to him. She turned his head to hers and looked into the eyes of a stranger, veiled eyes that seemed anxious to turn away.

"It's nothing," he answered lightly. "Just some problems at the bank. Something I'm working on."

She suddenly remembered his next words and his tone. Forced words of assurance. He had abruptly turned toward her and stared at her as if seeing her for the first time. "You're a beautiful woman, Suzanne. I want you to know I appreciate your loyalty all these years."

What a strange thing to say! Like part of a speech at a testimonial dinner. Cold words. And almost like a goodbye. Now Suzanne, 42 and suddenly widowed, sat on a kitchen stool and looked coldly at what was probably the most extensive collection of cookbooks in the entire city. Useless, they were utterly useless. "Maybe I'll pack them away and save them for Penny. Or maybe I'll put and ad in the paper. Or maybe I'll just leave them there. Who cares?"

Thinking about Penny brought back memories of that terrible night. If only Penny hadn't come home that weekend. What a tragedy for a daughter to find her father that way. The scene began playing over again in her mind. She and Penny had had their usual close, happy time together. The movie had been so bad they laughed their way into hysterics over it. At the front door, Penny was still recalling specific scenes with gurgles of laughter. "Remember when those guys busted down the door, and he said, 'Well, hi,' and waved his hand casually as if they had dropped in for tea? God, I don't know when I've seen such terrible acting."

It had only been about ten o'clock when they entered the kitchen from the garage and walked through the dining room into the foyer to hang up their coats. They giggled into another round of laughter as they went down the center hall to the rear of the house, Penny breaking off to call, "Daddy?" as she stepped through the wide doorway of the dimly lit den. Suzanne couldn't believe it now. She had still been laughing when she saw Walter. Then, abruptly, she stopped and grew quiet, thinking he had fallen asleep at his desk.

"Honey?" she had whispered, drawing closer. Then very slowly her eyes began to assimilate details of the scene, while her mind denied each image. It was joke, a mirage, of a make-believe fantasy world. She felt unconnected to any of it. She heard her voice stumbling, grasping, and saying stupidly, "Honey, quit fooling around."

Walter was slumped over on his desk, his arms outstretched along the top, forming a semi-circle around his handsome head, which lay on its right side. The visible left side of his face was gray, the mouth slack, and the eye was closed. Next to his right hand lay a gun. As soon as she saw it, she knew the horrible truth. But where had it come from? She had never seen it before, and she knew everything about Walter. Until now. She moved to him to put her arms around him in some kind of comfort. In doing so, his chair and body swung out a few inches from the desk and then she saw it. A bullet hole through his shirt and the half-dried, still-fresh stain of blood spreading out below it. Right over his heart. Suzanne's ears began to throb from an unbearable noise. For a moment, she did not know that she and Penny were screaming.

The rest was a blurish nightmare, a series of intertwining, curious scenes. The call to the police. The questioning. The unspoken accusations. The scared, frightened feelings. And a quantity of tears. She and Penny clinging to each other in a strangely quiet house, hostile and no longer seeming like home. Death had intruded into every corner, corrupting and degrading the acquisitions and environment of the living.

The police had been business-like, although not devoid of

sympathy. While she and Penny rigidly clasped each other on the leather settee, cameras recorded the grisly scene, and everything near the desk was dusted for prints. Then the police ambulance arrived with a stretcher and a body bag. As Walter was removed, she and Penny turned their heads away and sobbed uncontrollably in a fit of denial rage.

Detective Godfrey Sohler, a weary-looking man with sad, puzzled eyebrows ascending above his nose, pulled up a chair and looked quietly at them for a moment. His glance roamed back and forth between their faces and the paper he held in his hand. And he stared down at the carpet as if finding some kind of answer there. He was obviously reluctant to start what he had to do. He questioned in a soft and apologetic tone. Was Walter in ill health? Were there money problems? Had he been depressed lately? Had she and Walter been having any problems with their marriage?

Even in her state of shock, Suzanne's mind finally grasped where this was leading. "No, no," she sobbed, tears streaming down her white face. "It's impossible. Walter would never commit suicide."

The detective's sorrowful eyes held hers. "We're still investigating. We don't know for sure. But he left a note." He held out a plastic bag with a small piece of paper inside. "It's evidence. You'll have to read it through the plastic."

Suzanne held it in a trembling hand, noting it came from Walter's note pad with his name engraved in gold ink across the top. "Suzanne dear, none of this is your fault. It is all mine. I am so sorry to—" It meant nothing. She read it again. Still nothing. She passed it to Penny, who read it and then stared at her mother.

Suzanne returned it to the detective, a huge sob twisting through her body. "I don't understand. Why wasn't it finished? Walter never left anything unfinished."

"Apparently your husband was not himself," the detective said gently. "Maybe he got that far and couldn't think of what else to say. Maybe he wanted to get on with it before he lost his nerve."

Suzanne heard him, but his words made little sense. She sat immobile, her mouth clamped shut. It was obscene, this stranger climbing into Walter's head and analyzing his final thoughts. After a moment, the detective looked up from his note pad with another intrusion. "I'm sorry to have to ask you some questions, but it's better to talk about a couple of things now while you still remember." He looked questioningly at her for her consent. She hesitated and then nodded her head. A few facts could probably show that all of this must have been some kind of accident. "When you came home from the movie this evening, through what door did you enter the house?"

"The one from the garage into the house."

"Was it unlocked?"

"No, I used my key."

"On both the door knob and the bolt above it?"

She thought for a moment. "Yes, I'm sure of it. We always locked both. We were robbed a few years ago and had special locks put on the doors, which move bolts into the doorframe casing on each side."

The detective scribbled on his pad. "First you entered the garage with your automatic door opener?"

"Yes."

"All right. Now, I know you were distraught, but when you had to open the front door to admit the police, did you have to release the bolt?"

Suzanne looked at her hands in her lap. She relived the scene: she and Penny crying in each other's arms, vainly trying so find a grain of comfort, hearing a bell far off in the night, and then finally knowing it was the police at the front door. She saw herself weaving faintly toward it and then what? She somehow had it open. Gratefully she saw them. As if their presence would somehow ease the pain of all this. But the bolt—what about the bolt? It must have been in place, only controlled by a person inside or by a key on the exterior of the door. They always kept the bolt in place, whether anyone was at home or not. People were often murdered in their homes, day or night, Walter often pointed out. He looked at her expectantly. "Yes," she said as firmly as possible through the tears in her voice, "I had to turn the bolt."

After almost a month, a videotape of that evening still played constantly in her mind, every detail still sharp and distinct. She wondered if any amount of time would ever dull it. She might be able to keep it in a little compartment in the back of her mind, but any little related bit of anything at all could start it up again. She knew it would be the same for Penny. Even worse.

Penny was back in college, hundreds of miles away from the comforting arms of her mother. Among strangers, really, dealing with the demands and pressures of the academic world while grieving for her father. Then again, the young were supposed to be more resilient, and the college environment might just be the right place for Penny to accept her loss. This was her second year at Wheaton, so she had been on her own for some time now. When Suzanne really admitted it to herself, Penny and Walter had never been really close. If Penny had been a boy, perhaps Walter would have made the time to be with his child, but as his trust accounts increased, his business success demanded a higher expenditure of banking hours.

Now in the aftermath of her tragedy, Suzanne was faced with another facet of the situation. All her life she had to have things settled. No loose ends, ever. Something had to be done to resolve every problem. Otherwise, it just sat there, looming over you day and night, irritating and spoiling otherwise contented times.

Throughout the questioning, the police remained impersonal and business-like. But when they arranged several appointments with her to go over her answers, she detected an undercurrent of dissatisfaction with the slim number of clues indicating suicide. One officer had explained it this way: "Suicide is simple. When someone wants to die, they merely leave behind their body and the means they used. Sometimes a note, sometimes not. Oftentimes their reason for doing it dies with them. Sometimes their loved ones and friends give us that. The motive." And what was your motive, Walter? And why do it so we would surely walk into the den and find you? And where did you get the gun? You were always a kind man. I can hardly believe you would inflict such pain on your family.

All of a sudden, she hurt so much she began shaking. She glanced at the clock. Five o'clock. She needed to talk to Penny. She went to her desk and sat down. Taking a deep breath, she dialed Penny's sorority house. Her roommate answered. "No, Mrs. Wilkins. She's not here. She has a dinner date tonight." After hanging up, Suzanne wished she had not called. Apparently, Penny was getting on with her life as if nothing had happened. Suddenly that seemed horrifying. Suzanne's throat began to close in the familiar numbness, and the tears began their familiar path across her pale smooth cheeks.

As if in a dream, she heard a ringing. After it stopped and began again, she realized it was the doorbell. She plucked a tissue from a desk drawer and dabbed at her face and eyes as went down the hall to the front foyer. She hoped it was not a neighbor, someone from one of the many committees she served on, or her best friend, Emilee Johnson, who seemed compelled to check on her each day. Her thoughts were churning at the moment, and she needed to think them through. These women thought they were being comforting, but their concern only served to heighten Suzanne's awareness of Walter's willful demise.

But it was Detective Sohler's narrow eyes that squinted at her through the half-opened mahogany and stained glass door. "Are you getting dinner?" he asked abruptly. She stared at him. Was it dinnertime? She had no idea. She simply wasn't hungry anymore. Food, once a big interest, suddenly seemed disgusting. He took her silence for a no. "Mrs. Wilkins, I'm sorry to bother you. Could I come in a moment?"

Oh, my God, thought Suzanne. I've had enough of this. "No, you may not." She was surprised at the coldness and vehemence in her voice. "You people are making my tragedy harder to bear by your constant haranguing which is changing nothing. It's all been said twenty times, and your department is apparently inefficient in dealing with the information you already have." She was surprised to see the detective's eyes soften and his mouth purse sympathetically.

"Mrs. Wilkins, we have concluded our investigation."

"Oh?" Her eyes widened. "Then come in."

Detective Sohler entered the foyer. "Well," said Suzanne nervously. "We might as well sit down."

He followed her to the matching floral chairs in the living room, his head down, and lowered himself carefully into a chair. She perched on the edge of a mauve and cream cushion and looked at him expectantly. He cleared his throat, obviously searching for a way to start. "We wanted you to know, of course, before you read it in the newspapers."

"Yes—go on." This man was being exasperating.

"We have been very thorough in our investigation."

"Yes, yes, I know that. Please get to the point."

"We have concluded, beyond a shadow of a doubt, that your husband committed suicide."

She stared wide-eyed for a moment. "No!" she said in a thin, high-pitched tone. "It's just not possible. You didn't know my husband. Walter would never do a thing like that. He was a strong man, used to dealing with problems—"

"Mrs. Wilkins," the detective said gently. "everyone has a breaking point. And we never know what's going on inside the deepest part of another human being."

"It had to be some kind of an accident." She blinked hard to hold back the tears.

He spoke so softly she could hardly hear him. "Dear lady, he left a note and then, with no question about it, shot himself through the heart." Their eyes met, sympathy struggling against denial.

She strained to clarify her thoughts. "What about the gun? Where did he get the gun?"

"As far as we can determine, he brought it back with him from Vietnam. It was a 38 special revolver, the kind some of the officers and medical personnel carried. He could easily have found one to bring back."

"You knew Walter was in Vietnam?" she paused. "Well, of course you people find out everything." She looked at her hands in her lap for a moment and then raised her head and then gave him a challenging kind of look "If Walter had shot himself, his fingerprints would be on that gun. Why haven't I heard anything about that? Were Walter's fingerprints on the gun?"

"Mrs. Wilkins," Detective Sohler said gently, "it is very apparent that your husband loaded and fired the gun. Not on the textured grip plate—those get smeared through handling—but when someone loads a gun, the prints are all over it, on the top of the barrel, for example. And someone who commits suicide is not concerned with eliminating fingerprints. They clearly want there to be no doubt as to their actions." He paused a moment, indecisively, then decided to press on. "The powder burns around the place of entry and the angle of the bullet tell us that your husband pulled the trigger."

"But it could have been an accident, couldn't it, somehow?" Suzanne was sounding hysterical, even to herself.

Detective Sohler answered slowly and patiently. "Mrs. Wilkins, there are two pieces of irrefutable evidence: the note and the angle of the shooting. No one shoots himself through the heart at close range without it being a deliberate action." There was no answer. Suzanne could only stare at him through her anguish.

Detective Sohler stood up. "Thank you for your time. I'll let myself out." He shuffled to the doorway where he paused for a moment. Without turning he said, "I'm sorry," and left.

When Suzanne opened her paper the next evening a black headline screamed at her: BANKER'S DEATH DECLARED SUICIDE. The story featured interviews with the detectives involved along with a recap of the evidence. She laid it down and stared at nothing. What really happened, Walter? The police couldn't come up with the answer. Maybe she could—and should.

6

A man entered the coffee shop next to the Monroe Trust Company and headed for a vacant table along one wall. He stopped beside it as if undecided. No one seemed to notice except one waitress. Theda stood still, holding a tray of food in one hand, her mouth slightly open, transfixed. Don't sit there; please don't sit there, she begged silently. As if he heard her, the customer veered away and went to sit at the counter.

Until a few weeks ago, Walter Wilkins, president of the bank, always sat at that table. It had been his custom to have midmorning break as well as lunch here, unless a business matter dictated lunching at a more elegant restaurant in the area. Now Theda breathed deeply and willed the sprinkling of tears in her eyes to go away. Other people had, of course, occupied that particular table in the past few weeks. And she had had to wait on them, choking down her feelings of loss. But she was feeling especially vulnerable today. It was March 20. A year ago today was when it had all started.

Theda blinked, shook her head, and looked at the tray she was holding. Two special omelet platters, hot coffee, and orange juice. Now who had ordered them? She ran nervous eyes over her customers. The two cashiers from the bank at the center wicker table? She started in their direction. No, it had been two men. That's right. Now she was sure. But which ones? She took a deep breath to calm her ragged breathing, but she could still feel the tingling chill along her arms that began before the new customer decided to sit at the counter.

She had served coffee to a customer with his head thrust into the middle of a morning newspaper. As she set the cup down, her eyes were only inches from the black front-page banner: BANKER'S

DEATH DECLARED SUICIDE. Oh, my God, she breathed inside, was it really true? Can I believe it's over? Maybe this is just a trick by the police. Time. That's all she needed. Just sit tight. The memory would evaporate in time like the water from a dirty mud puddle.

She tried to concentrate on her present problem. Several customers were eyeing her from their yellow-cushioned wicker chairs. This was nothing unusual because she knew she was attractive. But now she sensed something sinister in their glances, as if they could hear the guilty tapes playing in her head. Could some of these observers have a darker reason? Could any one of them be an undercover detective still dissatisfied with the verdict?

She read paperback detective stories—in fact, that's where the idea had come to her—and she knew the police used many ploys. Sometimes they fed the public false information to flush out the guilty party who thought the case was over and became careless. And about ten minutes ago, a cop had strolled in the door and taken a seat at the counter. He hadn't glanced at her at all, but she wouldn't get a real deep breath until he left.

"What's the matter with you? Got your period or something?" She jumped, and a little stream of coffee ran over the elegant "Regency House" crest on the side of a white porcelain cup. She turned and saw her boss staring at her.

She managed to smile sweetly at him, allowing a little pain to creep into her eyes. "Yes, I just had a cramp. I'll be all right now."

Two men, sitting against a far wall under a local exhibit of three atrocious watercolors, waved their hands at her, and she suddenly remembered. She hurried across the kelly-green carpet through the jungle of floor plants and smiled at them brightly, as she set down the tray and apologized. While admiring glances slid over her face and figure, she leaned down more than necessary while placing the food before them. Their glances converged on the valley exposed in the v-neck of her uniform.

Looking from one to the other, she whispered as if passing on Russian space secrets, "You know, when it gets busy in here it's sometimes hard to remember who ordered what."

One of the men managed to move his gaze to her name embroidered slightly above a lovely mounded left breast. "Theda?" he asked. "That's an unusual name."

God, she was sick of this. If only her mother had named her something else! It was so irritating, always explaining. She controlled herself and spoke evenly. "My mother was a fan of the old movie sex goddesses. I was named for Theda Bara. Most people never heard of her."

"I never heard of her," said the other man. "But, boy, your mother knew what she was doing!" They snickered like little boys sharing dirty jokes out behind the garage.

"Well, enjoy your breakfast," she said, and moved off to further duties.

Honestly, she thought, don't men ever grow up? Always thinking of sex, always yearning to be the big conqueror, and in the meantime making up stories as if they were. All except Walter. He had been so different. Polished, gentlemanly, caring, and so intelligent. A real student of everything. And so classy. Her heart began to ache. Oh, Walter, she moaned inside. Please forgive me.

Her heart broke all over again when she thought of the terrible way all their plans had turned out. She missed him. Somehow, just being with him had lifted her out of her rather drab life and made her feel different inside. Kind of important. Special. As if he saw the real person inside her curvy exterior.

No one else had ever looked at her in quite the same way. Certainly not Cam. There was always a touch of lust when Cam's eyes gazed into hers. Physical. He had insatiable desires. And no patience. Never any patience. Or tenderness. But no matter how hard she had tried to resist him, a permanent spark lay between them, too easy to ignite. Her mother had warned her persistently. It was like Mother was a mystic, looking into her crystal ball and seeing disaster ahead for Theda with Cam. Theda knew now she should have listened. But it was way too late.

A helplessness swept over her when she was with Cam. She both hated and loved the way he dominated her life. And he had been in and out of her life. When he was in it, moments were heavy and uneasy, tense with un-confronted problems and poor decisions. But at the same time, there was a sense of excitement and moments that teetered on the edge of adventure. His intense need for her rendered her helpless. When he left occasionally for another woman, she knew absolutely he would return. He would never need anyone else as he did her. His raw yearning would blaze so intently from his blue eyes that her very soul would seem to erupt in passion to meet it. At times like that, she could refuse him nothing. That very weakness had flung her into the center of her present terrible mess.

Cam was busy working out a plan. He had always been good at planning things and then carrying them out. Way back, when they had been kids together he was always cooking up far-fetched escapades that he made work to his advantage. During the three years they had been married, he hatched many schemes, some of which backfired. Because his family liked Theda, they would often supply a little capital to smooth out the bumps. But there were serious differences in the way the couple viewed life and responsibility, and two years ago, they divorced. Now, because of what had happened to Walter, Cam had found a place in her life again. She would have to trust Cam to come up with one of his plans this time as well. When it all worked out, they would be out of here and relaxing on one of those remote island beaches she had always heard about. For a moment, she felt the stab of sharp sadness. A few weeks ago, she had been planning to be on that beach with Walter.

The men she just served in the Regency House Coffee Shop stared at Theda's retreating curves while the omelets grew cold. Finally, one of them spoke. "That's the most seductive girl I've ever seen." After they left, Theda Bara Krupnick, as usual, pocketed a sizeable tip.

*   *   *

"What's the matter with you tonight?" Cameron Castore raised up on one elbow, his long dark hair falling in a tangled loop over one eye. Theda turned on her side under the twisted sheets and slowly raised her right hand to lightly flick the sparse wiry hair on his chest.

"You know," she whispered. "It's hard to concentrate when I'm really worried."

"Look, Babe," his voice was rough, impatient. "How many times do I have to tell you? It'll work out. We'll find the money, and then we'll be off."

"You make it sound so easy. Just how do we do this?"

Cam looked at her without answering. Then he rolled over, sat up on the edge of the bed, and reached for his shorts on the floor. Pulling them on, he got up, went over to the dresser, and fumbled among the cosmetics and jewelry strewn across the top. He finally turned around, a pad of paper and a pencil in hand. Pulling up a chair close to the bed, he sat down and said, "Let's go over it again."

"Shit!" Theda pulled a sheet up over her head in desperation. "This is about the millionth time!"

Cam looked at her shroud patiently. "It's important. You may think of something you missed before. C'mon. Once more."

Theda uncovered her head, and brushed her thick dark hair off her face. Her body twitched nervously under the sheet. "Let's review," said Cam in an attorney voice. "You and Walter were going to run away together and live in paradise on some far-off island— what was it called?—oh, yeah, Nevis Island. He planned it for a long time and somehow got together a lot of money to keep you two in Eden. Now we gotta find this loot. And if we don't do it soon, some other cat will. It always works that way. Now, think back to everything he ever said to you about your plans."

"Oh, my God," moaned Theda. "That's impossible."

"Okay. How about the last time you were with him?"

Theda winced and closed her eyes, trying to blot out that terrible scene. Then she began speaking, slowly. "Well, we were very happy. It was all going to happen the next day. Walter was talking about how we were going to start a new life and how good it was going to be for him to get out of the 'rat race', as he called it. He was sick of his life here. Bored. You know?"

She looked pleadingly at Cam as if she needed him to understand how Walter felt. She remembered she was skeptical that Walter would give up his important position at the bank along with the luxuries of his life just to be with her in some remote paradise. But his explanation filled her with warmth: he loved her so much he wanted a whole new untouched environment just made for the two of them. It was easy for him to give up everything in his present life. He had been tired of the routine and dullness of it all for a long time.

Theda sat up and reached for a cigarette from the pack on the end table. After she lit up, she punched up her pillow and leaned back against it. "So we went over each step of what we would do the next day. You see, Walter picked a Saturday to disappear so he wouldn't be missed at the bank immediately." She pursed her lips together and frowned. "He was upset that his daughter had come home that weekend, but he couldn't do anything about it. She just showed up on an impulse." She inhaled on her cigarette. "Anyway, he said he had the money safely tucked away and the next morning he would pick it up and meet me at O'Hare airport at noon. We were each going to rent a car under an assumed name to get to the airport. He wanted to make sure we wouldn't be seen together."

"But you need to show a driver's license to rent a car."

"Yeah, I know. We drove to Pennsylvania one day and got licenses under assumed names."

Cam shook his head. "I don't know; it's a thin plan. Walter really thought he could get away with this? Disappear forever? Where were you landing?"

"At an airport in St. Kitts, then a short flight to Newcastle," Theda explained. "Walter had a complicated way worked out to get us there. We were going to fly to Cincinnati first, then take a bus to somewhere in Tennessee, and then fly to Florida and on to the island. All under different assumed names each time we traveled. And to go to Nevis Island, you don't need a passport. Only proof of citizenship, like a birth certificate. Walter sent away and got duplicates for a guy and a girl he knew in college."

"Well," Cam said grudgingly. "I guess he spent a couple of minutes working all this shit out." His brows met over his nose and he fixed his eyes on hers. "So now all we need to do is find the money. Think hard. You need to remember everything he ever said about the money."

Theda drew back against the pillow. "You don't understand. He didn't talk about it. When I questioned him, he would always say that was his problem and I was not to worry about it."

"But didn't he ever hint at where he was keeping it?"

"Well, I'm pretty sure it wasn't anywhere in his house. Just a feeling I got when he said he would pick it up before he met me. She took a couple of puffs and flicked the ash from her cigarette into an ashtray beside her on the bed. "I asked him point blank once about it, and he said, 'Honey, don't worry about it. It's locked away safe.'" Suddenly her cigarette was frozen in mid-air, and her eyes widened in sudden memory.

"You remember something," stated Cam, leaning forward eagerly.

"It might not mean anything," Theda said almost in a whisper.

"Tell me anyway."

"Well—Walter had on his favorite jacket, kind of a brown tweed. We were standing by his desk in the study, and right after he said that I remember he slid his hand down over the pocket and patted the edge of the jacket." They stared at one another, digesting this information. "It was like when you ask someone if they have something and they pat their purse or pocket or wherever it is."

Cam scribbled on his paper, and then leaned back in his chair, crossing his arms, a big grin spread across his face. "Hey, you did good, girl. Now we go get the jacket."

7

Some threads of sunshine somehow made a path through the dirty windows and streaked across the tousled bed. Intermittent flecks of light stabbed at Dave's eyelids. He turned restlessly to his other side and was, amazingly, awake. He guessed he was pretty much alive, too, as he had an unusual and unnerving impulse to get out of bed. Instead, he lowered his hand to find the bottle. His fingers closed around it. He gave it a shake and set it back on the floor.

He glanced at his clock radio. My God—only nine o'clock? If he got up now, what would he do with a whole entire day? Not to mention the interminable night that would surely follow. He groaned and rolled back on the bed, punching his pillow and pulling a corner of the dingy blanket up over his face.

No good. Some little demon rolled a picture of the jacket around inside his mind. It needled him with an idea—maybe even a purpose. Something he had to resolve. A teeny, tiny little mystery. Nothing very much. Just a persistent question as to what the former owner had squirreled away and why. A deep secret from his past? Damaging love letters? A bank heist? A body, or maybe the parts thereof? Very possibly nothing at all. Perhaps it was just an extra key hidden away as a kind of insurance against losing the original. But all this conjecturing only increased his curiosity.

Years of probing for answers as to what lay behind the surface impressions of human behavior now seemed to demand that he see this through. Just what lock in this enormous universe would this insignificant-looking key fit into? And what lay behind the sealed opening? He groaned aloud and swore some more. What the hell, he told himself. This isn't something I HAVE to stick my thick Italian neck into. Forget the damn key. Or throw it away.

As he considered these options, he knew he could do neither. In some obscure place in his heart or brain, he didn't know which, there was an invisible cord connecting him to all of this, almost as if he were being drawn intentionally into whatever it was. "Too many years on the police force," he mumbled to himself. "Always looking for meaning, clues, motives, reasons. Always having to find the answer. Can't just let go."

Just then, he moved onto his back and a shaft of sunlight struck him in the face. It felt good. It had been a while since he had paid any notice as to what direction the weather was taking. He slowly sat up on the edge of the bed, and rubbed his arms and legs. His bones hadn't had much exercise lately. Felt kind of stiff. "Well," he said out loud, laughing softly. "As my plump Italian mother used to say, "Up and at 'em!"

When he entered the "Second Time Around" shop, the pleasant lady smiled and said, "Why, hello there" in recognition. After a pause, she smiled even wider and pronounced, "That jacket is just marvelous on you!"

After he thanked her, Dave went right to the point, bending the truth only a wee bit. "Yes," he said pleasantly. "I like it very much, and you were very helpful." They smiled at each other again. "I'm here to find out if you know the lady's name who donated this. There was a scrap of paper in the vest pocket with some kind of notes on it. I thought it might be important."

"Well—" the lady seemed to be struggling with her memory bank. "As I recall, she didn't mention her name. About all she said was that her husband had just died. She seemed awfully anxious to leave. You know, the widows who bring in their husband's clothes are like that. They feel so bad they just want to get it over with."

She considered him. "Would you want to leave the paper with me? Then I could give it to her in case she comes back with any more things."

"That's awfully nice of you," Dave said in his best-mannered voice, "but I might be able to track her down through the store that sold this jacket to her husband." He held out his hand, and she slid her little plump one willingly into it. "You've been very kind," he said in his most charismatic warm voice. She tittered a bit and watched his back regretfully as he departed under the tinkle of the bell. He glanced at the Tail, who was smoking a cigarette and leaning against the frame of the shop window. "Lovely day for the end of April, don't you think?" he called out pleasantly.

He went to the bus stop at the corner and paused. It was only eight, nine blocks downtown, he calculated. Might as well walk and save fifty cents carfare. He laughed to himself. God—hadn't he always had trouble with money? Yeah—never enough of it. He remembered when he was nineteen and lived with his folks out in the suburbs. He had gone to Junior College downtown and used to walk home, about three miles, to save fifteen cents, the bus fare in those days. Now he struck out rather vigorously with his long steps, and laughed to himself when he turned his head slightly and caught a glimpse of the Tail huffing to keep up.

When he pulled open the brass-framed stained glass doors under the cream and maroon canopy and stepped into the posh interior of Comstock and Harding, Clothiers, he almost did a three-sixty and left. But a salesperson, who resembled an impeccably attired Oxford professor, immediately approached him, complimenting Dave by assuming he was a customer. Dave reacted by stepping into his most personable self. "Good morning," he answered the clerk's greeting. "What an elegant store you have here."

He glanced about at the leather settees, the palms, and the glass enclosed areas of suits, the mannequins standing guard in their designer attire. He searched for an appropriate way to learn the information he needed. "I'm looking for a little information," he began forthrightly. "You see, a friend of mine got this jacket from someone he knew who put on a little weight and had to give it up. He passed it on to me, and I found a note in the pocket that could be very important. I'd like to return it to the original owner. My friend has moved out of town and I can't locate him. It's kind of a long story." Dave shrugged his shoulders as if agreeing that the salesperson couldn't possibly want to hear any more. "I have no idea who owned this jacket in the first place." The Oxford professor looked blank. "You will really be doing a good deed if you will help me out. This jacket has your store label in it along with the initials of the original owner, WPW."

The salesperson took two steps backward, and the air of helpfulness mostly evaporated. After a moment, he spoke. "Well, I could take it to the office and see if anyone recognizes it, sir." It was said tentatively as if he hoped Dave would just go away.

"Oh, how wonderful of you," Dave said immediately, shrugging out of the sport coat and handing it to the salesperson whose hands received it like a pair of reluctant tongs. While the clerk was gone, Dave put his hands in the pockets of the matching slacks, strolled casually to the window, and peered out. The Tail looked weary and bored as he shuffled his feet and dragged on his cigarette. The clerk-professor suddenly emerged from the office area in the rear, holding the jacket on a polished wooden hanger embossed with the store name in gold. In his other hand he held out a small piece of paper.

"I have some information for you, sir." He handed the paper to Dave. He then slipped the jacket from the hanger and held it open, albeit reluctantly, so Dave could slip it on.

"Well, thanks." Dave settled his shoulders and looked at the paper. "Walter P. Wilkins," he read. "1689 Morningside Drive." The clerk looked at Dave impassively, anxious for him to leave, but then offered a little more information.

"Mr. Comstock believes Mr. Wilkins died a few weeks ago. Otherwise our customer base is private information."

Dave feigned astonishment. "Really? What a shame. Well, I guess that's that. Thanks anyway." But he pocketed the slip of paper, and his fingers closed around it protectively as he went out the door.

*   *   *

"I'd like to see all the copies of the Edgewood Herald from about February 28 to March 7," he had told the librarian at the downtown library. He settled himself at one of the reference tables, and after a few minutes, she brought him the pile of copies from the newspaper storage area.

Starting with the oldest one, he flipped through them, checking obituaries and news stories. Suddenly, on March 4, there was the account of Walter's demise on the front page, as well as a lengthy obituary. There were several pictures: Mr. Wilkins addressing a banking convention, speaking on financial security to a group of General Motors' retirees. Finally, there was Walter in a tux, looking handsome and happy at the Governor's Ball at Christmas time, smiling a charismatic smile, his arm around his beautiful blonde wife gowned in a flowing white dress. But my God—suicide! Walter was getting more interesting every moment.

Dave took the paper to the copying machine and printed out the articles. Back in his seat, he felt some bits of excitement beginning to string together in the investigative part of his brain. His carefully honed intuitive sense picked up an undercurrent of mystery and doubt under the pat journalistic phraseology. He followed the story in each successive issue, occasionally using the copying machine to record additional information. When he was through, he turned in his papers and got the more current ones from March 7 to the present date. Finally, he was viewing the headlines from two days ago. DECLARED SUICIDE, it said and then reviewed the case in its entirety.

After making himself a copy of this, Dave leaned back in his chair and looked over the material spread out before him. A bemused expression tilted up the corners of his mouth. "Well, well," he whispered softly. "Not on your life. I think the missing key will have something to say about that." He folded up his copies and filed them in his jacket pocket. While he was returning the newspapers to the librarian, he glimpsed the Tail sitting a couple of tables away, trying to hide himself behind a coffee-table book about Frank Sinatra by his daughter Nancy.

Dave hunched over the counter and whispered conspiratorially to the lady behind. "Will you please do me a favor?" he asked, fastening serious brown eyes on her gray ones. "I'm a private investigator, and the information that I've been checking is confidential. If anyone asks you what I was looking at, I know I can trust you not to give out any information." His eyes bore into hers. She nodded, speechless, eyes widening, the possibility of a little intrigue adding excitement to her morning. Dave turned abruptly and, instead of leaving by the front door, quickly stepped into a row of stacks to carve a route back and forth between the rows of ceiling-high books. At the end of the last row, he found an exit door and slipped through it into a back alley leading to a side street.

A few blocks away he found a nice little bar where he had a beer and a sandwich. Just in time. He needed to relax and consider what he would do next. So now he had Walter Wilkins' sport coat, his key to heaven-knows-what, and papers in his pocket with all the details of Walter's death. But what of his life? He had to know Walter himself, if he were going to make sense of this scenario. He was already sure of one thing. There was only a very slim possibility that Walter Wilkins had committed suicide.

While Dave was reading the accounts, two inconsistencies kept grabbing his attention. First, Walter had shot himself through the heart. This seldom happens with suicides. For some macabre reason, suicide victims prefer to shoot themselves in the head. Then there was the note itself. It was not written in the usual suicide format. It was obscure, ambiguous, and, most importantly, unfinished. Some poor failure of a slop or a cokehead with scrambled brains might be stumped and not know how to finish a note before wiping himself out, but a bank president? Not likely. It didn't seem to fit into the picture he was forming of Mr. Wilkins.

Okay. He guessed his next move would be to look at the police records. There could be evidence that the police covered up and never released to the media. Dave frowned. This visit could be painful. He had not been in a police station since his suspension. Could be he would have to deal with animosity and the still-present atmosphere of disgrace. A few days ago, he would have been unable to handle even the thought of such a visit, consoling himself with a bottle instead. Hell, he thought. What difference does it make now? His curiosity was definitely spinning him into a strange direction, and he seemed to have no control over it. He took a gulp of his beer and snickered to himself. "What the hell, I'm on a case. One I've made up myself. God, if this isn't falling on hard times I don't know what is!"

*   *   *

Dave paused outside Precinct Station No. 5, straightened his shoulders under the tweed, and smoothed down his unruly thick hair where it tended to curl up along the back of his neck. The Tail was nowhere in sight. Great. He particularly didn't want him around this one time. It was impossible to slip unnoticed into this police station. Although he had not been based here, he knew many of the personnel, and he was sure they knew his notorious face. Dave entered the front door and merely nodded at those who recognized him as he passed as quickly as possible down the stairs to the Records Department.

Several men who had known him quite well in the past now appeared not to recognize him in his new beard and expensive jacket. In fact, it took a minute or two before Vince Polari, the officer in charge of records, realized who he was. Then Vince's manner became cool and impersonal. That's okay, thought Dave. As long as I don't face any open hostility. Then I might decide to throw this completely insane idea right out the window and the key along with it.

They shook hands, and Vince asked abruptly, "Is there something you want?"

Dave smiled pleasantly. "Yes. I'm working as a PI now, and I need to go over a case for my client."

Vince looked at him, deadpan. "Well—you know these records are confidential. Police only."

"Sure, Vince. I certainly don't want to put you on the spot." Dave made a pretense of fumbling in his pockets. "I have a note here from Detective Sohler who handled the case." He fumbled some more, taking out some of the printed copies he had made at the library and ruffling them. Then he looked apologetically at Vince. "Hey, I'm sorry to hold you up. I've got it here somewhere."

"Just whom are you working for?"

"Penny Wilkins. The daughter. She and her mother are not satisfied with the suicide ruling. I've been hired to see what else I can sniff out."

"You're working on the Wilkins suicide?"

"That's right." Vince leaned on the counter before him and doodled some chicken scratches on a pad. Dave decided to use the clincher. "I need this job, Vince," he said softly.

"Okay," the officer said finally, pushing a register pad toward Dave. "Fill this out with the case name, time, date, and your name. Then you can go to a table in the back and I'll bring you the file." He stared at Dave. "Don't tell this to anyone, or I'll have your neck."

Dave smiled back easily. "The police department already has it in a noose, and maybe a bit more."

*   *   *

He looked at all the evidence. He read the interrogations. He studied pictures of the body slumped over the desk, sections of the room, a close-up of the gun, the body on the autopsy table. Constantly he asked himself questions. He juggled possible scenarios in his head.

Could it have been an accident? People seldom shoot themselves in the heart at close range by accident. He kept thinking about the gun and the note. If Walter was not about to commit suicide, why was his gun on the desk? And why was he in such an all-fired hurry to eliminate himself before he finished the note? If it were an accident, there wouldn't have been a note.

Dave's thoughts began to whirl. Maybe Walter's last message wasn't intended as a suicide note. He could have just written a little note to his wife for some other reason. Could they have had a fight, and he wanted to apologize? Dave began tacking a few endings onto the note. If Walter had finished it, he might have said: "Suzanne Dear, None of this is your fault. It is all mine. I'm sorry to cause you so much pain. I'll be a good boy from now on." Or, "I'm sorry I forgot our anniversary and you thought I didn't love you." Perhaps even, "I'm sorry we had that fight over the grocery bill."

These conjectures sounded pretty weak, he had to admit. But they proved one important fact. No one could know what was in Walter's mind and what his intentions were. Anything was possible. Another phrase from the reports nagged its way into the list of questionable suicide evidence Dave was forming in his mind: 'no forced entry'. The police seemed to emphasize this piece of evidence to substantiate the suicide decision. "Flimsy," he labeled this to himself.

What about the possible existence of another door key? Who else had one? Pretty shoddy investigation in that area, he decided. For one wild moment he diddled with the idea of turning the key he had found over to the police. This would certainly reopen the case. The idea died quickly. Very possibly they would do nothing with it. Under the burden of a heavy caseload they loved to get an open-and-shut case they could wrap up quickly. Deciding that this case was a suicide almost immediately, the detectives probably failed to look for any evidence to the contrary. Dave patted the breast pocket of his jacket and felt the key securely fastened inside with a safety pin. He knew he was the only one in the world who realized there was a whole other side to this case. Except perhaps for one other person.

*   *   *

After his session in the records section, Dave's dry thirsty mouth led him into a beer and burger place around the corner. He emptied a couple of frosty mugs of tap beer while smoking three cigarettes. Twirling his last, almost empty mug in his hands, he contemplated giving up the investigation for the day. He hadn't walked this much since his patrol days, and his brain had had an unusual workout besides. Adrenalin was flowing again.

Finding the key had stirred interest into his life, giving him a purpose. Still, he thought, it would be nice to go home and take a late afternoon nap. He flipped a couple of dollars on the counter and stood up, automatically patting his breast pocket to make sure the key was still with him. What the hell. A few blocks away was his old friend, Frank Nelson, who had a locksmith shop. Might as well stop in on his way home. Dave paused outside the restaurant and checked the street. Apparently, the friendly Tail had not caught up with him. That was good. He didn't need anyone else knowing he was messing around with this case.

Frank Nelson seemed glad to see him. Dave had worked with him at several times in the past, and Frank had given valuable testimony in court on a few occasions. "Hey, Dave!" Frank came around the counter of the shop and shook his old friend's hand briskly. "How've you been? What have you been up to since your business associates cut up your ass?"

"Not a hell of a lot. Until now. I'm doing some PI work and I need some information."

"Sure. You know you look pretty good. Distinguished with that beard. Well, maybe a tad, anyway." They laughed, eyes flicking together over the ridiculous assumption that brawny Dave could ever be so described.

Dave reached into his pocket and unpinned the key. "Take a look at this, will you? What kind of a lock would this fit into?"

Frank turned the small flat piece of silver back and forth in his palm. "Off hand, I would say it belongs to a locker or a padlock. Maybe even a trunk. There's no way of knowing."

Dave stared at the key. "Any special kind of locker? You know, like in a school gym or an air terminal?"

"Well," Frank paused, his brow furrowed. "My best guess is a type of school locker. This key works with a very simple mechanism. You understand, this is only a guess."

"Sure. But I thought kids in school used padlocks."

"Perhaps." Frank turned it around in his hand. "This is not like any padlock key I've ever seen. Did you notice the number on it?"

"Yeah. Forty-three. Mean anything?"

"Well, could be a model number, but I suspect it's the number of the locker." He smiled at Dave, his eyes twinkling. "Now all you have to do is check every locker in the city that has this number. That should keep you busy and out of trouble."

"I doubt it. I may be stepping into a heap of shit."

*   *   *

The shadows were lengthening and, without looking at his watch, Dave knew it was fast becoming cocktail time. It had been an unusually active day for both his long legs and the cortex of his brain. Gratefully he swung aboard the first bus leaving from the downtown Mall heading up Division Street. He was let off a block from his room and right in front of the Methodist Church, whose outdoor bulletin board advised "Let God Run Your Life" in rather wobbly letters. Dave thought that was probably a good idea, but surely the Lord would demand that he give up the booze for this to happen. As if reaffirming this condition, smaller letters beneath simply stated: AA MEETING THURSDAYS 7:30 PM. That let him out. What a relief! He was only a heavy drinker and already he had cut down a lot.

Slowly Dave creaked his way up the outdoor steps to his second floor apartment. When he pushed open the door, an envelope lay on the floor just beyond. His infrequent mail was delivered to the sandwich shop below him, and eventually a kind-hearted person pushed it under his door. He saw right away what it was. Hurrah! His unemployment check had come just in time. He would go down to the sandwich shop in a little while, they would cash it for him, and then he would get something to eat. But right now, other urges took priority.

Dave moved quickly into the kitchen and poured a glass of vodka. A large gulp settled him down, and he sighed with relief.

He had been so good all day. Only a few beers. He could now have a few vodkas and still be okay. He shrugged out of the sport coat, held it up for a moment of admiration, and then went to hang it carefully in the closet. With glass in hand, he spread himself in the most comfortable depressions of the old sofa and began studying the pictures of Walter Wilkins.

Aha. He was amused to find he had pegged Walter Wilkins correctly just based on his wardrobe. A large man—but that was no surprise, because Dave knew they were the same size. A good, clean American look. Kind of sandy hair, as far as Dave could tell, with a fair complexion. Not swarthy like himself. Good-looking and apparently amiable and friendly. Just like me also, Dave laughed to himself. But there the similarities ended. Even a slightly fuzzy newspaper picture of Walter Wilkins seemed to give off vibrations of power and influence. The confident, easy set of his shoulders, the alert, perceptive gaze through conservative dark-rimmed glasses, the charismatic smile curing around perfect teeth all drew an unmistakable portrait of a winner.

Dave concentrated next on the adoring wife. Quite a beauty, he decided, but prim and uptight. Not a hair out of place. Wearing the perfect simple dress with a single strand of pearls. Probably jumped when he husband called. No mind of her own. A perfectionist who is unable to take chances. Doing what is expected of her, but probably never having a good time. Providing the correct background support for her high-powered executive husband. Just the kind of boring woman Dave couldn't stand.

"So, old WPW," he mused softly, taking another drink from his glass. "Did she bore you to death? Is that why you took a path to the great unknown?" Another drink, another thought. "Maybe you survived with a little extramarital activity?"

8

Before Theda could insert her key into the lock on her apartment door, it opened suddenly, and Cam's glowering eyes met hers. "Where in the hell have you been?" She could tell immediately that he had been drinking. Or shooting up—or both.

She walked past him as confidently as possible, and tried to keep the trembling out of her voice. "I had to stay late. I had some customers who wouldn't leave, and I didn't want to lose my tip."

He followed her into the bedroom, glaring while she hung up her coat. "C'm here."

He grabbed her around the waist and slammed his lips down on hers. She responded as well as she could. She knew this mood. Anything she said or did could send him into a towering rage. Oh, please, God, she pleaded in her head. I just can't take anymore. I've just about reached my limit.

In a weak moment, reeling and distraught over Walter's death, she had foolishly told everything to Cam, hoping for some strength and comfort from him. Now Cam was in charge, somehow taking over Walter's part in the scenario. When he was sweet, it aroused passion in her, and she ached to be close to him. But when his eyes got that dark look, fear made her hastily agree with him while her body ached to escape. But actual escape was impossible. Cam knew it all, down to the smallest detail. Even everything that had happened those last terrifying moments.

"Sit down," he now ordered, pulling her over to the edge of the bed. She settled herself close beside him, smiling at him with what she hoped was a loving look. He seemed to mellow a little. Gazing at her, he murmured, "I'm worried about you. I know you're upset, and that means you might blab to somebody else."

She made a negative noise in her throat and shook her head.

"Don't think for a moment about getting rid of me. Don't forget I know what really happened, and I could turn you in any time."

His eyes were menacing as they bore into hers. "You're in a spot and you can't get out of it without my help."

"I'm okay," she whispered, pleading. "The case is closed. Suicide. I can forget about it in time. I don't need to be worried. I can just walk away. No one is ever going to know." Her voice wavered on the last word.

His sinister grin sent a tremor through her body. "Except for me, baby—except for me." His meaning was clear. And then he made it clearer. "You will do exactly as I say on this, or I go to the police and tell them what really happened to Walter." Tears of fright formed under Theda's exotic lashes. Cam suddenly looked pleased by her reaction. "What do you know about Mrs. Wilkins activities?"

"What?"

"Well, you must have known her schedule pretty well to be making out with her husband for a couple of years."

"I don't know what you mean."

"Oh, for God's sakes, Miss Innocent!" Cam exploded. "When was the lady usually out of the house?"

"Oh, Cam, no. You can't do that!"

"Do what?" He gave a cat grin, playing with a mouse. "You can't be thinking of breaking in!" He shook his head in disgust. "How in hell do you think we're going to get the jacket?"

"But it might not even be there! Maybe she got rid of Walter's clothes." Theda swallowed at the idea.

"Oh, my God. You are a piece of work. But we aren't going to know that until we check it out, are we?"

Although Theda reluctantly saw the logic in this, her dismay increased. A new tangled web was about to ensnare her, and there seemed to be no way to escape. The corner of her mouth twitched nervously as she answered, "Once a month on a Tuesday she played bridge—I don't remember which one. Then on Wednesday afternoon, I think it was, she went to a meeting of her garden club. It was—let's see—the first Wednesday of the month. She always did her grocery shopping on Thursday mornings. And on Thursday nights she went to some kind of a class at the county college—it had something to do with books, I think."

Her cooperation was rewarded with a toothy grin from Cam. He suddenly rose, stretched, and held out a hand. "C'mon, Babe. We're goin' for a ride."

"What?"

"Isn't this Thursday evening?"

*   *   *

"Come on," said Emilee Johnson. "It'll do you good."

"I know," Suzanne agreed into the phone mouthpiece. "But I'm just too weary tonight. I've been going over Walter's assets for the probate of his estate. Then I spent a couple of hours with our lawyer discussing all the things that have to be taken care of. It's really drained me."

"I guess I understand." Emilee said. "I'll take some notes and you can go over them later, if you wish."

"Thanks. I just want to vegetate in front of TV tonight and try to forget all the stressful thoughts floating around in my brain."

*   *   *

Cam and Theda sat in Cam's '84 red Firebird, parked on Morningside Drive, the nose pointed toward the Wilkins house in the middle of the next block. They were hardly inconspicuous. It was seven o'clock and dusk was only beginning to fall. They slouched down in their seats as far as possible while still keeping their attention on the Wilkins driveway in the distance.

"It's risky," Cam acknowledged, "but it will soon be dark. We'll just have to take the chance." Theda wriggled nervously every few minutes, which got her looks of irritation from Cam. She had protested going along with this scheme. She never wanted to see Walter's house again, let alone actually set foot in it. But Cam had explained it, looking at her with disbelief at her stupidity. "If you don't go, how in the hell am I going to find the right jacket? We gotta be in and out in a hurry. I can't search every damn piece of clothing in his closet."

So, here she was with flutters in her stomach, about to risk her very life. If they got caught, she could be accused of a great deal more than breaking and entering. It grew darker and harder to see the driveway down the street. Cam started the car and moved it up to just past the corner in the next block. They sat. Theda looked at her watch. Seven forty five and nothing had happened.

"She should be leaving any minute now," Cam announced with conviction. He had called the college and was told that the class on great literature was held at eight o'clock. The college campus was only a mile or two from here. The minutes ticked away. Nothing. At fifteen after eight, Cal released a few expressive swear words. Then he started the car. "Might as well go home. Jees—I hate to wait, but I guess we'll have to try again next week." Theda didn't know if she were relieved or not. Now she had the whole week ahead to worry about it. But with any luck, Cam might forget the whole thing. Who was she kidding? Cam would never forget a plan that might net him some money.

*   *   *

The second day of his investigation, the tweed sport coat stayed in Dave's closet. He put on his windbreaker and was ready to leave around ten o'clock in the morning when he suddenly thought of the key in the breast pocket of Walter's jacket. Call it instinct, whatever you will; he got a sixth sense about it. He unfastened it and looked around for an unlikely place to leave it. But leaving it at all was making him uneasy. Small objects could almost make themselves disappear sometimes. Funny. He knew without any reservations that this little key was all-important. With some luck and a lot of determination, he would discover why. Before someone else did. He ended up fastening it under the pocket flap of his windbreaker.

When Dave entered the Monroe Trust Company, no one

seemed to notice. He walked quietly on his rubber-soled shoes to one of the rear desks. A nameplate said she was Dorothy Clarke—Branch Manager. "May I help you?" She smiled impersonally, a trained, dutiful smirk.

He fired what he hoped was his most irresistible grin. "Aren't you too young to be Branch Manager?" It didn't help much. She stayed cool and remote, the fake smile gone. He decided to get down to business. "May I sit down?" he pointed at the leather chair studded with brass nail heads.

She nodded and gestured with one hand. "What can I do for you?" A cucumber kind of voice, he decided.

"My name is John Darby," he told her. "I'm a free-lance writer, and I need some help for a story I'm writing. Do you have a minute?"

"Just about, Mr. Darby. I'm really very busy." She waved an index finger at a stack of papers on her desk.

"Well, I'm doing a profile on your former bank president, Walter Wilkins. I thought you might be able to give me some human interest information about him—you know, the personal kinds of things that didn't appear in the papers."

That seemed to stir her, and Dorothy Clarke straightened up in her chair. "What kinds of things?"

"Oh, you know. Who his real friends were, what he was interested in, what his hobbies were. What kind of a man he was."

She glanced at the imposing clock mounted on a marble pillar. "I can give you five minutes." She folded her hands over a pile of papers and leaned toward him. Dave opened his notebook and took a pencil from his breast pocket. "You don't have a tape recorder?" she asked, surprised.

"It's in the shop. Now, what kind of a man was Mr. Wilkins?"

"He was very nice. Business-like always, but fair and kind to work for. Rather a private person, however. A little hard to get to know."

"How long did you work for him?"

"A little over two years."

"I guess you got to know him pretty well. What was he like?"

"Very pleasant, but almost totally concentrating on the business. We shared a few laughs once in a while."

"Did he ever talk about his family?"

"He mentioned his daughter occasionally. He was very proud of her," she said.

"What about his hobbies, recreation, that kind of thing?"

"I really have no idea." Annoyed now.

Dave fastened his warm brown eyes on hers. "There's nothing you can think of?" he prodded.

"The only interest we shared, other than the banking business, was tennis. We used to talk about that."

"Really. He was an avid tennis player?"

She nodded. "Played every Saturday morning at the Centerline Tennis Club out on the South Beltline."

"Do you know who his partner was?"

Dorothy decided to loosen up a bit. "I think he usually played doubles. I would think Centerline could help you there."

Dave was thinking the same thing. He suddenly veered off in another direction. "I guess Mr. Wilkins had an impressive career here at the bank."

"Yes. He had been here about twenty years, and worked his way up, starting as teller and moving up through the management level. His financial expertise was formidable, and he was very successful as a loan officer and investment counselor."

"He handled trust accounts, both living and testamentary?"

"Oh, yes. He was trustee for several inter vivos trusts, you know, reinvesting the principal, buying and selling stocks and other commercial paper. Some of his clients had been with him over ten years. In fact, he had a couple of famous people as clients." She smiled briefly. Dave looked at her inquiringly. She quickly shook her head. "Oh, no. That's privileged information."

"Of course." Dave nodded pleasantly at her while closing his notebook. He stuck his pencil in his shirt pocket, and stood up. "I suspect my five minutes are up." He allowed his eyes to crinkle in appreciation at her. "My thanks, Miss Clarke. You will be getting proper credit for helping me with my story."

Dorothy's eyes followed his muscular frame as he ambled across the bank lobby. Not bad. Rather an interesting man. Looked rough and oafish, but actually intelligent and not unattractive. Friendly brown eyes and marvelous thick curly hair. She had a strange yen to run her hands through it. And she liked his walk. Light on his feet and swinging from his wide shoulders like a puppet held by taut strings. But a writer? That was straining her credulity. More likely an undercover cop. If so, why was he interested in a case that was closed? Or did the police want the public, or more specifically real human beings, to believe in a closed file so certain information could drift unrestricted to the surface? Dorothy tapped her pencil absently on her desk blotter. Walter's connection to the bank nibbled at the back of her mind. Had there been something going on? Walter had been a mite irritated last month, an abruptness occasionally cracking his impeccable manners. Under the cool exterior Walter was probably as susceptible to the effects of stress as anyone else. The bank auditor wasn't due until May 1. But Walter's files had already been transferred to Charles, who had, with a positive sense of accepting them as his responsibility, scrutinized each loan authorization and investment decision with a critical eye. No apparent conflict of interest. Substantial assets behind every loan decision. Nothing was wrong there. She folded her hands on her desk and stared into space for a moment, considering the possibility of any other irregularities. There were none. Walter Wilkins was the most honest man she had ever known.

*　　*　　*

Leaving the hushed vault of the bank lobby, Dave stepped out into the swirling wind and stinging raindrops of an incipient April squall. A stab of thunder rolled away overhead. He paused for a moment in the shelter of the entrance and glanced at his watch. It was only a little after eleven o'clock but already certain cravings were demanding satisfaction. He licked his dry lips and mentally gave himself a small lecture. Now where? He noticed a coffee shop next door and decided a cup of hot coffee might help him get through a few more hours. Buffeted by an increasing wind and pelting raindrops, he was already shivering in his light nylon jacket when he opened the door. It seemed to be a popular place, with the stools at the counter already holding the full number of backsides, mostly men. Dave scanned the tables through the potted plants, and found an available one against a far wall which seemed to double as a gallery area for amateur watercolor artists of varying talents. He settled himself, and craned his head backwards and to the side, observing a large painting of sand dunes and ocean waves with what he thought might be a sailboat riding on the tip of a whitecap. There was no way to know for sure. A movement beside him caused him to turn, and he saw that a waitress had dropped a menu on the table.

"Hey," he called to a retreating back. "All I want is coffee."

She wheeled around, and came back, getting out her pad and writing it down. "Anything else, sir?" she asked very politely, smiling a commercial smile.

She looked directly at him and something constricted in his throat. Here was one of the loveliest creatures he had ever seen. Lustrous olive skin and smoldering eyes. Yes, that adjective definitely fit here. He couldn't remember if he had every known anyone with eyes like these. Slim waist and ample, earthy breasts. Curved, sensuous lips with corners like dimples. Early twenties, he guessed. She must stay here for the tips, he decided. It was worth plenty just to have her show up at a table and take an order. He had already noticed the grid of glances converging on his table. He watched her fluid convolutions as she moved off, as did almost every other man in the place. She walked in slow ripples, apparently comfortable with her sexuality. When she returned with the coffee, Dave gave her his best smile and saw her eyes grow wary. Of course, he realized, this girl is being hit on every day.

He made his voice business-like and asked, "Do people from the bank next door come in here a lot?" He noticed she seemed to flinch and wondered why. But her voice was cool and collected when she answered.

"Of course. We're right next door." She started to leave, but stopped dead still at his next question, her shoulders stiff and her chin high and immoveable.

"Did Mr. Wilkins, the former president, come in here?" Bingo, thought Dave. For some reason I've struck a nerve. Did old Walter make a pass at her? This case was growing more intriguing by the minute.

She avoided his eyes. "Yes, occasionally. Now if you'll excuse me, I have other customers."

Dave sipped at his coffee while he ruminated on her reaction. He had noticed her name embroidered on her uniform. "Theda," he said to himself. "Could it be you're the real key to this mystery?"

*　　*　　*

At seven o'clock that night, Theda left by the back door for the alley parking lot and got into her blue mustang with the rusted, dented fenders. She sat for a few moments, taking deep breaths and shivering. It was still raining and the temperature was in the 50's, but she knew it was more than the weather that caused her trembling. If only she knew what to do. Cam always sounded so reasonable and convincing, so sure of his scheme. She, on the other hand, was scared to death. All kinds of things could go wrong, and then she would be guilty of fleeing the country with stolen money as well as her other serious crime. She wished she had a good close friend she could talk with about all this. Well, not all of it, of course. She considered her mother, but only briefly. Mrs. Krupnick was now Mrs. Baker, living in California with a new husband. This physical separation had had little effect on the mother-daughter relationship.

Theda's brief marriage to Cam over her mother's protests had driven a wedge between them years ago that left mother and daughter estranged. Hate welled up at the thought of Cam. Not hate for him, but a loathing for herself that she could have been so stupid. After that horrible night, when her life was shattered, she desperately needed a friend, someone to turn to. When Cam had turned up a few days later, professing his love and swearing he had changed, his unexpected tenderness drew it all out of her, It was a relief to gush it forth, a babble of words, tumbling over one another.

She expected sympathy, soothing and balm-like, a mutual understanding that whatever happened was not her fault. She expected to feel better, sharing her agony with one who loved her. But almost immediately, Cam had seen an opportunity to step into Walter's plans and take his place in escaping with the money and Theda. Now things were worse than ever.

She had trusted Walter as a respected, successful man to carry off the scheme in his usual cool and confident way. On the other hand, it was not possible to trust Cam with anything. His moods changed hourly, and he could blow up in anger over the least little thing. Now she gripped the steering wheel and tears trickled down her face. Two years ago, her life had been happy and exciting. She and Walter had fallen genuinely in love—really in love. Never had she known such caring and attention. He respected me, she now thought. He really did. He loved the real me. With such a splendid man at her side, she felt lifted into another world. A shining, polished world with good fortune anxious to burst through the door. She couldn't believe how much Walter loved her and with such devotion. Being together only occasionally was agonizing for both of them—they longed to share all of each other, every second. Their disappearance together would never be believed. Someone like Walter who had it all would never chuck everything to be with a simple waitress. But no one knew Walter like she did.

He talked often about how his dad had pushed him into a banking career and how he always found it boring. His life revolved about making money. He was sick of the whole scene, and especially the mountains of regulations and paper work. "I want to be free— really free," he would say. "I want to be out in the sun every day. I want to find peace and quiet and some meaning." When he explained what they would do to make their wonderful private world a permanent thing, it had all seemed possible and even practical. Never preposterous. Wasn't this man a bank president, used to controlling situations and making things happen? When she was with him, she always felt safe. For the first time in her life. To be with Walter forever would be to live in paradise.

They carried on their love affair in complete secrecy, and she never worried that anyone would find out because Walter was in charge. His self-confidence was awesome to her. The world he created for the two of them was special and safe, separate from ordinary activities all other humans were involved in. She only thought of Suzanne fleetingly, usually when Walter was at home. Then she agonized over whether Walter was making love to his wife. He swore repeatedly to Theda that there was no closeness between them, but Theda knew a bit about men's sexual drives and the difficulty of controlling them. She would argue with herself on this point and fasten on the comforting thought that before long Walter would belong to her completely.

Then that terrible night happened. Without warning. When she had been her happiest. She sat now, the rain sprinkling steadily against the windshield, the scenes of Walter's last few moments moving slowly before her eyes. If only—if only. If only she hadn't gone to his house that night. If only she hadn't gotten so playful, because she was so happy to be going away with him the next day. If only she hadn't made such a fuss about his note. Then the gun. That had been a shock—the very fact that Walter had it lying on the desk. He had showed it to her proudly, a souvenir from Vietnam, explaining how it worked. They needed to take it with them, he said, in case they ran into trouble.

They were going to Nevis Island, a little-known paradise in the Caribbean. No one would find them there. They would have a beautiful pink stucco bungalow on the white sand beach, or maybe one of those glass and wood-beamed houses on a cliff with a deck soaring out over the gorgeous blue water. Although Walter reassured her over and over that he had planned it all very carefully and nothing could go wrong, there was the matter of the gun. "Then why the gun?" she asked.

"We'll be carrying quite a bit of money," he explained. "There may be some rough characters on that island. I'll just feel better if I have it with me." He had laughed a little and stroked her cheek. "Just because I have it doesn't mean I intend to use it, honey."

He never entirely convinced her. Having a gun around could attract trouble, not prevent it. She wanted nothing to do with it.

Which was ironic considering what eventually happened. The scenes separated out into the sequence of events that she relived over and over as if that in itself could change what happened. After his wife and daughter left for the movies that night, Walter telephoned. "Sweetheart," he said softly. "I'm home alone, and I want you with me. We need to go over our plans for tomorrow. Suzanne and Penny went to the movies, so come as soon as you can."

Theda had left almost immediately, taking time only to pull on a blouse with a plunging neckline, a favorite of Walter's. She parked her car up the street in the next block and entered Walter's lot by the side yard, keeping close to the large sweeping evergreens that defined the lot line. She crossed the rear terrace and rang the back doorbell. She smiled as she heard the chimes playing the first few notes of "Lara's Theme". So romantic and appropriate, Theda thought. Her heart pounded with the excitement of being with Walter again, and in a moment he had eagerly opened the door and swept her into his arms. They stood in the back hall, fastened together in long, passionate kisses, rubbing their inflamed centers of sexual desire together. After a few moments, Walter gently pulled away and looked at her in the tender and loving way she loved. His hand slowly caressed a breast. "I could easily forget why I asked you here," he said hoarsely. "After tomorrow we can spend all our time making love." Such an idea definitely brought a sparkle to his eyes. "But right now we need to go over our plan, and make sure we know exactly what we're going to do."

So, hand in hand, they had gone to Walter's library. Walter sat down in his desk chair, while Theda leaned over him from behind, her arms around his neck clasped together on his chest. She rubbed her cheek contentedly against his. He laughed. "You're very distracting, but don't stop." She noticed some notepaper and pen lying in front of him.

"What's that?" she asked.

"I'm writing a farewell note to Suzanne." He was still, his eyes scanning the words he had written.

"I don't think that's a good idea," Theda had said. "You never know. She might figure out something from it."

"No, not the way I'm going to word it. And I'm mailing it to her. She won't get it until Monday. We'll have started our new life by then." He turned his head around, puckered his lips, and made a chirping, kissing noise. Then Walter opened a desk drawer and took out the gun, looking at it for a moment and then laying it beside the note.

Theda's eyebrows lifted in surprise. "I was hoping you'd forget about that," she said, disapproving.

"We need it for protection, honey. Remember, I explained that to you?"

Theda recoiled in disgust. "I hate guns. I'm scared of them."

"Hey, honey," Walter had smiled at her, amused. "You ought to learn how to use this. It's easy. I'll give you a quick lesson."

She remembered now how repelled she had felt. If she had only gone with her instincts at that point and refused his instruction, Walter would be alive today. Why didn't she? Because Walter had become her hero, her prince with an intelligence she respected and eagerly agreed with. Since that night, she had relived this moment a hundred times. If only—if only.

He picked up the weapon, and turned his hand over to show the gun lying comfortably in his palm. Her arms loosened around his neck as she pulled away, and he laughed, tilting his head back against her neck. "Come on now. It could be important for you to know how to use this. You should know how to protect yourself." She saw his point, and her arms came down around his chest. "Okay," he said. "Now this is a revolver. Don't worry, it's not loaded." He flicked the cylinder out and checked, then spun it around. "When it's loaded, it can't be fired unless it's cocked."

"And how do you do that?"

"Like this." Walter pulled back the hammer. "But you have to be very careful. Some guns are hard to fire. This one is very easy. Touchy, you might say. But that means it's faster to fire, too."

Theda had been squirming. "For God's sake, Walter, will you put this damn thing away?"

He had seemed amused by her fright. "Hey, relax, honey." Then in an unusual teasing way, he swung it towards his chest.

"Bang bang, I'm dead." he said, laughing. "Would you miss me, sweetheart?"

In retrospect, the next few moments blurred into a shattering nightmare. She didn't want to play any games, even with an unloaded gun. As clearly as she could recall, she had reached forward and placed her hand on top of Walter's right one to force him to lay the gun back on the top of the desk. He was right about it being easy to shoot. His finger seemed barely to touch the trigger when there was an explosion. A spasm jolted his body against the back of the chair, hitting her in the chest and knocking the breath from her. It wasn't possible. But it had happened. Somehow, one of the chambers still held a lethal shell.

What followed was even more agonizing to remember. As she sat in her car this evening, tears ran down her face, matching the rivulets on the windshield. Shock had made her an automaton, the horror pressed down inside, the screams only in her head. At first, she denied it. That noise couldn't have been the gun. Walter was play-acting again. But his body was definitely out of control, slipping and sliding from the chair and then, lying on the floor.

She had gone to him, trying to help him up, pleading with him to speak to her. Then she saw the powder burns on his shirt, and the red stain spreading above his heart. Her own heart dissolved in overwhelming grief. She had desperately wanted to flee immediately, to escape the horror of this scene, to pretend it had never happened. But from deep inside, she knew what Walter would want her to do. He loved her and would have done anything to protect her. This she knew without any question. Walter would not want her to be involved in this. And he would expect her to protect his reputation. Could she lift him? She had good strength in her arms from lifting heavy trays, but still Walter was six feet of dead weight. She sat down on the floor beside him, placed her back against the desk, and turned him to move his head into her lap. Tears splashed down into the beloved face. Then she pulled and tugged, bracing herself against the desk as she got to her knees and then her feet. With the strength born of desperation, she managed finally to get Walter back into his chair.

She lowered his head to the desk, placing his arms on either side. The gun had fallen onto the desktop, and she left it there. Mustn't touch anything, she reminded herself. But blood—what about blood on the floor? Weeping, she got down on her hands and knees and looked about. There seemed to be only a few drops. Taking a tissue from a box on the desk, she blotted it up as best she could and stuffed the telltale evidence in her pocket. If there was more, it seemed to blend into the rust-color carpeting. It was time to leave. But not quite. My God—what about finger prints?

Her head was spinning. Had she left any? She really hadn't touched anything but Walter. No, there was the doorknob. She would wipe that off when she left. She leaned down, her eyes blurring in tears, and kissed Walter's cool, graying cheek. Rising, she picked up her purse and jacket from a nearby chair, and then turned for one more look. Something was wrong. My God, where were Walter's glasses? Theda got down on her hands and knees and scanned the carpet again. She found them a few feet away, blown off Walter's nose by the bullet's impact. Reaching for them, she stopped suddenly. Could they get prints from eyeglasses? She stood up to get some tissues with which to hold the stems. Leaning over the back of the chair, she managed awkwardly to settle Walter's glasses where they belonged. Even looking down at him, she was grateful his eyes were closed. Somehow, Walter had lowered his own lids while fleeing into death.

She took a few deep breaths on the edge of sobs and forced herself to look at the scene objectively, as the police would undoubtedly view it. Walter slumped on his desk, the gun only a few inches from his right hand, and then the note. Thank God for the note. The scene had all the impact of a suicide. Captive sobs were aching to escape from her throat, and she clamped her hand over her mouth as she looked at him for the last time. Only, this shell of fading flesh in Walter's clothes didn't seem like Walter anymore. She had never been so intimate with a dead person before, and she was suddenly revolted, her stomach reacting in kind. As she looked back now at the tragic accident of that evening, she was amazed that she had remembered to lock the house and wipe her prints from the doorknob. Once when Suzanne was visiting her mother for a week, Walter had a duplicate house key made so Theda could get in if she arrived before he did. It was kept in one of those fake stones made for the purpose, hidden away among the pachysandra plants near the back door.

When she left that tragic night, she dropped to her knees and searched among the plants until she felt the hard plastic exterior. Extracting the key, she locked the back door bolt and returned the key to its hiding place. Now she had to be sure no one would see her leaving the house. It was already dark, and she kept to the row of tall evergreens until she reached the sidewalk. When Theda reached the last one, a dog began to bark, close by. She froze, trying to stand still with liquid kneecaps while she heard a voice murmur and the sound of steps receding down the street. A man walking his dog, she thought. She felt a bead of moisture skid down her breastbone. Close call. After a moment, she covered the few yards to the sidewalk and casually walked the eternity to her car a block away, her pace so uneven she was afraid she would trip over her own feet any moment.

Once inside the car, she began shaking and crying, trying to get control of herself in case someone looked out of a window and saw her. Eventually she was able to drive away. Walter would have been proud of her, she decided. She had taken care of everything. Brief thoughts of reporting his death to the police came and went. But she knew it was already way too late. Walter's relationship to her would come out, and, when that was known, who would believe it was an accident? She would certainly be suspected of murder. Dearest Walter's reputation would be ruined.

Now she wiped away her tears and blew her nose. She started her car, turned on the lights and the windshield wipers, backed out of her parking space, and headed for the apartment. And Cam. Maybe the worst of this nightmare was still waiting for her.

9

Detective Sohler transferred the receiver to his other ear and listened to the telephone ring for the ninth time. He was about to hang up when he heard a click and she answered. "Hello?" Suzanne said, slowly, in her low, cultured voice. He visualized her head tilted, the classic blond haircut swinging, the perfectly manicured nails coiled around her receiver.

"Mrs. Wilkins? Detective Sohler here. How are things going?"

She took her time replying. Her voice was cool. "What do you want, Detective?"

"Well, I'm sorry to bother you, but I thought I'd better check something out."

"What is it?" She certainly was direct, he thought, and not very gracious. Not that he blamed her after all she had been through.

"A man came to our records bureau to check the file on your husband. Said he was a private investigator hired by you to investigate your husband's death." No answer. "Mrs. Wilkins? The department wanted me to call to see if you've hired a special investigator."

"Certainly not! Whatever for? Is something funny going on here? Why would someone do such a thing?"

"We don't know, Mrs. Wilkins, but we're going to look into it."

"Thanks, Detective Sohler, I wish you would." The voice was decidedly warmer. There was a pause, and then Suzanne made a strange request. "Could you give me the man's name, please? I suppose it's possible my daughter may have contacted him, although I'm sure she would have told me about it."

"Well—I guess that would be all right. His name is Dave Monaco, and he's a former police sergeant."

"A police sergeant?" Surprise. "Why no longer?"

Sohler hedged. "There was some kind of trouble, and he was suspended."

"I see. Well, thank you for calling and giving me this information, although I must say it is pretty baffling."

"Yes, well, I agree. If we find out anything more we'll let you know."

Suzanne hung up and looked at the name she had written so neatly on the pad by the phone. Dave Monaco. Why would a stranger to her be interested in the police file? And an ex-policeman who was no longer involved in criminal investigations? What had happened to get this man involved? Not for a moment did she really believe Penny would hire anyone and certainly not without checking first with her mother. She sat quietly, staring at the name on the pad.

Since the night Walter was found, a strange uneasiness mingled with the sorrow of her grief, making it impossible for the grieving process to repair her life. Something certainly unexplained, or maybe even evil, simmered just below the level of reality. No matter what evidence the police believed to be conclusive, Walter had not committed suicide. In the deepest part of her, she knew this was the truth. And it was not just because the suicide of her husband raised ugly questions about their life together, directing the guilt of responsibility for the act right at her. No, it had to do with the basic character of Walter himself.

Walter had never been a coward in anything. He had always faced up directly to every problem. But the clinching argument against suicide was that Walter was a cool, unemotional person. Never distraught or out of control. If he had been unhappy with her, he would have analyzed every aspect of the situation, considered every angle, and then, if there were no other solution, would have asked for a divorce. She and Walter had always talked freely about everything. If any aspect of his life caused him to be desperate enough to consider suicide, he would have shared it with her, and they would have worked on the problem together. But Walter was contented with his life. There was no evidence to the contrary.

She tried to remember the last few days they had spent together. Walter had been as sweet and thoughtful as ever. They had held hands as always while watching TV. They had played tennis the previous weekend with some good friends and then gone out to dinner. She pictured Walter relaxed and laughing, telling some of his favorite jokes. He had brought her flowers, for no reason at all. He had been so attentive she had anticipated making love, but Walter seemed to relax into sleep almost immediately after kissing her goodnight. Her mouth now curled ruefully, and tears gathered on her lashes. If she had known how soon her marriage would be over, she would have taken more sexual initiative. She would now have the memory of that final act of love to cling to for reassurance.

She gave a little shudder and once again looked at the name before her. Maybe now was the time to look for more answers. And here was a good place to start. She pulled the phone book towards her and began looking through the M's. She found Monaco, D and dialed the number.

"Yes?" An abrupt, sharp woman's voice.

"Is Mr. Monaco there?"

"Who wants to know?" Definitely a rude, uncooperative person. If this is Mrs. Monaco, thought Suzanne, her husband must be a real prize as well.

She thought fast. "I need his help on a private matter," she said coolly and authoritatively.

"Hmmm. Well, he doesn't live here anymore, so I guess I can't help you." The woman sounded ready to hang up.

"Wait a minute. This is really urgent. Don't you have a telephone number for him?"

"No, the bum can't afford one." Silence. "I guess I could give you his address, if that would help."

"Yes, please."

"Okay. It's 1401 Division Street, upstairs over the deli."

"Thank you. Mrs. Monaco, is it?"

"The former, thank God."

Suzanne had just hung up when the door chimes tinkled. She opened the front door to a muscular young man with stringy dark hair tied back in a ponytail. She noted a red Firebird parked at the curb and had the disturbing thought that he might have stolen it. Instinctively, she drew back and wished she had checked through the peephole first.

The visitor spoke rapidly, almost as if he had rehearsed what he had come to say. "Mrs. Wilkins, I'm Bob Davidson. I played tennis sometimes with your husband. I wanted to come by and tell you how sorry I was to hear of his death." All said in a singsong voice.

An alarm went off in Suzanne's head. Walter would never associate with a hood like this. Funny. First the information about Dave Monaco and now this strange encounter. Whatever this game was, she would have to become a player to learn what was going on. Suzanne gripped the half-open door, determined that this person would never gain access to her house. She attempted a smile. "That's nice of you. Thanks for coming by." She waited. She knew there would be more.

"Uh, well—" said Cam Castore, "there's something else." He cocked his head questioningly, as if waiting to be invited in.

"Yes? What is it? Please, I'm very busy right now."

Cam shifted his feet around on the step. "Well, your husband had a great tweed jacket I always admired. I know I've got balls— I mean, it's nervy of me to ask this, but Walter always said if anything happened to him, I could have his jacket."

In spite of herself, this caught Suzanne off guard, and her eyes widened in surprise. She almost laughed at such preposterousness. But there was an undercurrent of intrigue here. This young hippy apparently knew Walter. How else would he know about the tennis club and Walter's favorite jacket? But Walter would never have allowed this type of person to own his favorite piece of apparel, even after he was gone. So—part of this story was fabricated. This person wanted the jacket for some unfathomable reason. It seemed to Suzanne there was a gleam of desperation in the visitor's eyes. Suddenly, she feared that he would push her aside and ransack her house, looking for the desired garment.

She spoke quickly. "I'm sorry. But I got rid of all of my husband's clothes." She felt a spark of anger flare at her. Out of fear, she spoke the truth. "I took everything to the 'Second Time Around Shop' on South Division Street. Maybe you can find it there."

The ponytail bobbed as he backed down a step. A brief thanks, and he was bounding down the walk to his chariot.

*   *   *

The Firebird circled the block, while Cam looked for a place to park. "Damnation," swore Cam, pounding the steering wheel in frustration. Every minute counted. What if someone else was in the store buying the jacket at this very moment? Calm down, he told himself, or you'll forget what you're going to say. He slowed to 10 miles an hour, while the traffic bunched up behind him and horns began singing a nasty little chant.

Suddenly a man walked around a car at the curb and got in. Behind him, Cam pulled in tight alongside the parked car and switched on his right turn signal. The traffic began swerving around him. The would-be driver took his time, fiddling with his side view mirror and fastening his seat belt. My God, thought Cam, can't he see I'm waiting? Finally, the car moved slowly from the place, and Cam zipped expertly into it, front forward. The car was barely parked when he was out and running into the "Second Time Around" shop.

Once inside, he looked desperately around before finding the rack of sport and suit jackets in the rear. Gees—there was no prospective buyer checking them out—that was good. Rapidly he began to fumble through them, pushing the wrong ones rapidly out of the way.

"Can I help you find something?" A sweet-faced little lady was looking at him with puzzled eyes, her arms crossed and feet planted firmly on the tile floor. Cam turned his best smile on her.

"I hope so. I'm looking for a certain sport coat. It belonged to a tennis buddy of mine who passed. He always said I could have it, but his wife told me she brought all his clothes here."

"How long ago was this?"

"Maybe a week ago?" His eyes pleaded for her to give him hope.

"What did it look like?"

"Well, it was very different. Custom-made, I think. A brown tweed, with the pockets bound in suede." Where is it? God damn it; find it for me, lady, his eyes demanded, narrowing his gaze at her. She backed away, and her voice became cold and dispassionate.

"That was sold several days ago."

"Are you sure? How can you be sure? You must have a lot of clothes going in and out of here."

The lady took a few steps back, as Cam thrust a clenched jaw in her direction. "I'm sure. We've only had one such garment as you described in this shop—ever."

What the fuck! What shitty luck, thought Cam. The lady turned around and Cam called out to her. "Well, can you tell me who bought it?" Then he allowed a little wistfulness to creep into his voice. "I did so have my heart set on finding it." The little-boy approach always worked well with older women. Sometimes with young ones, too, he thought with an inner grin.

The lady turned toward him. "I don't know his name, but I think he lives in the neighborhood. I've seen him several times on the street."

"Can you tell me what he looks like?"

"About six feet one, muscular build, dark hair, beard. Of Italian descent I would think. Forty-ish."

"Well, thanks," said Cam, trying to hide his disappointment. Not very much to go on, but then again he just might get lucky.

*   *   *

Cam couldn't sleep. He got out of bed and went to the dresser to fumble around among the papers, keys, and pocket change for his crumpled pack of cigarettes. Hell, only a couple left. He lit up and went to sit on the side of the bed, slanting the sagging mattress, and sliding the other body toward the middle.

The body turned over and Theda said sleepily, "What's wrong?"

Cam dragged on his cigarette, scowling in the dark. He had described his search for the sport coat to Theda, and they had agreed there wouldn't be much chance of finding it. It seemed their future plans didn't stand much of a chance. Not without the key to all that money.

"I can't give it up," he said now. "God, we were so close."

Theda pushed herself up on one elbow and looked at the outline of Cam's back in the dark. "What are you thinking?"

"That I'm going to find this guy somehow, whatever it takes."

"How are you going to do that?"

"I'm going to park myself outside that store and watch for him. I think I'll know him. He might even be wearing the thing. That would be a break. The lady thought he lived in the neighborhood. Across the street, there are apartments above the stores, but none in the block where the second-hand store is. "

"So—if you find him, are you going to go up to him and say, 'Pardon me, sir, but you have a jacket I want'?"

"Don't be a fucking asshole," he said. "I'll follow him and find out where he lives. Then when I see him vacate the premises, my sweet, I'll check out the apartment."

Theda sat up straighter. "Cam, you can't do that. You get caught breaking and entering, and back you go to prison. It's too much of a risk."

Cam gave a heavy chuckle. "And what do you think we're involved in now? Covering up a murder and stealing a bundle of money? Get real, my love."

*   *   *

It was an unusually warm day for the middle of April in the mid West. Even through Dave's windows, the day was shaping up to be bright and cheerful. Something like energy stirred inside him, and he put down his coffee cup suddenly and did some deep knee bends, stretching his arms out before him. When he was a cop, he had exercised every morning, a routine as established as brushing his teeth. When had he stopped? He couldn't remember.

But somehow now, this moment, he felt more alive than in a long time.

Last night he had only had two drinks. Then, at about 7:30, when he was ready to pour another, a strange thing happened. He remembered the AA meeting at the church next door. He had stood motionless, the bottle in his hand. Should he or not? Some inner voice passed judgment on his way of life, and reasonably suggested he could attend. He didn't have to join. Just go and see what it's like, it said. If it's not for you, get up and leave. The booze will still be here. So he had cleaned up a bit and shrugged into the new sport coat.

When he turned out of the alley into the street, it was dark, the old streetlights flickering unsteady strings of light through the weathered glass. He automatically checked for the Tail, but the street was fairly deserted, except for the permanent homeless and a couple leaving the deli. Several people were entering the church door at the same time, and they smiled at him and said hello. At the entrance to the church all-purpose room, a nicely dressed young man squeezed his hand firmly.

"Hello," he said. "My name's Tom. Welcome to our meeting. I don't remember seeing you before. Is this your first time?" Dave acknowledged that it was. "Well, there are others besides you. But we're all after the same thing. Sobriety. We're here to help you get sober, if you decide that's what you really want." Dave wasn't sure, but he grinned, nodded his head, and glanced awkwardly around the room, ill at ease. But Tom wasn't through yet. "There's coffee over there," he said, waving at the kitchen pass-through counter, where people were clustering about. Dave got in line, got a Styrofoam cup of brew, and went to sit in an unobtrusive spot in the back row. Near the exit in case he decided to leave suddenly.

There were two speakers, a middle-aged man and an attractive dressed-for-success woman. In spite of himself, he was caught up in the accounts of their lives. Here were the real stories of horror. Stories of alcohol and drug abuse that caused the loss of family and jobs, serious car accidents, blackouts and completely unmanageable lives. But out of the chaos of hitting bottom, these people had turned their lives around. Because of AA. He found himself realizing these people had courage and guts. He felt a glow of admiration for them. While Dave was listening, he congratulated himself that he had never known such degradation. After all, he was only a social drinker.

Then he heard some words that cut into his introspection. "Some of you out there are probably thinking, well, I don't need this program because I've never suffered such experiences. Well, if I had had the courage to enter the program sooner, my life would not have been the hell it was. Remember, all it takes to turn your life around is to stay off the booze and come to meetings every week." There was more about "working the program" and admitting to being powerless over alcohol and needing the help of a "higher power." At the end of the meeting everyone joined hands and said "The Lord's Prayer." He mumbled the words, feeling uncomfortable holding hands with two strange men. This was a little heavy. Maybe he wouldn't come back.

When he got back to his room, he had read the newspaper and gone to bed. No vodka. Now Dave stood in his kitchen and remembered some of the things that had been said last night. He smiled. He was feeling good. His brain was awake and ticking away, making plans. He was more than ever determined to find what lock the key would fit. It was crazy, but this morning he was sure he could solve this thing. All he needed were the right breaks. His glance fell on the half empty bottle of vodka, and he picked it up, gazing at it for a moment, and then putting it out of sight below the sink. Symbolic, he thought. Out of sight, out of mind. But he wasn't sure it was going to work that way.

It was time to visit the tennis club. He looked through his meager wardrobe hanging in the doorless closet, his fingers lingering for a moment on the sport coat. He would love to be able to wear it this morning; he was in a good mood and the coat would make him feel even better. The corner of his mouth creased plaintively. But someone at the Tennis Club might recognize it, and he had to be as inconspicuous as possible. He put on his old navy windbreaker, patting the breast pocket to make sure the key was pinned inside. A quick check in the stained mirror above the dresser, a pat to the top of his unruly head of hair, and he left the apartment, clattering down the outside stairs and whistling "Bye-Bye, Blackbird" under his breath. He headed for the telephone booth in front of the Deli. A young man with a ponytail was leaning up against the side, and jumped in a startled way when Dave opened the door.

"Perkins and Lombardo," announced a crisp voice.

"I'd like to speak to Ralph Skalnick," said Dave.

"Just a moment, please." In a moment, Ralph answered.

"It's Dave. I need a favor."

"Sure, Dave. How are you doing? What do you need?"

Ralph was some kind of brother-in-law. Always there. Willing to go all out to help a guy, and not even asking what for. Sometime he should remember to tell Ralph what his friendship meant to him, thought Dave. "Well—now that you ask." They both laughed. "I was wondering about Bob's car. Did he take that to college with him?"

"Uh, no, as a matter of fact. It's a small campus, and cars are discouraged. Would you like to borrow it?"

"I sure would, if it's okay."

"Of course! It's in the garage, and I think Lorna's home today. You can get the key from her. I'll call and tell her you're coming. Do you need a ride out there?"

Dave was sure Ralph would leave work to come pick him up if need be. "No, I'll catch a bus."

"Okay, and listen, Dave, we don't need the car. Why don't you keep it for a week or so?"

What a guy! Dave mumbled some emotionally gruff thanks and hung up. He swung the door back on itself, and stepped out on the sidewalk, hunching up his shoulders and taking a few gulps of warming spring air. Immediately he felt someone staring at him and knew with his cop training that this was not just a flicker of superficial interest from a passerby. Without turning his head, the corner of his eye registered an intense scrutiny coming from the young pony-tailed man, who was now leaning against the front ledge of the Deli window, casually staring at his Reeboks and flicking ashes from his cigarette. Dave allowed himself to turn his head for a second, during which his brain recorded the features of this person: a once-broken nose, pale, sallow complexion, thin eyebrows, and a long face. He was about 5 feet 10 with muscular arms, (probably from working out), and he had a pretty good start on a beer-belly. His feet looked humongous in white Reeboks. His long stringy black hair was gathered back with a rubber band. Without looking back, Dave strode to the corner for the bus. While waiting, he felt the eyes still on him. When the bus came, he half expected to see this person suddenly appear in the small group of boarders. However, when he took his seat and the bus began moving past the Deli, he glanced from the window and the young man had disappeared.

*   *   *

There were three apartments over the delicatessen, one facing the street, one on the alley side, and a third off a small hall in the rear. There were no names posted on any doors. Cam hesitated. He couldn't risk knocking on any doors to ask for the right apartment. Someone might identify him later. He had only to find out which apartments were vacant. Any pretense would do. God, how stupid of him. He should have thought of bringing along some disguise. Well, if it became necessary, he could cut off his precious long hair later on. That would really make him look different.

He moved quietly to the side apartment and put his ear to the door. A radio was playing, but that didn't mean anything. Many people left music playing to discourage break-ins while they were out. As if anyone would want to rob these dingy places. Of course, you never knew. Some people hid diamonds in their mattresses while they scrimped on their food. Suddenly he heard a flurry of movement behind the door and barely had time to pull away and continue down the hall before the door opened and someone left. He glanced back over his shoulder in time to see an attractive young girl smoothing back her tangled curls as she started down the stairs. He began to breathe heavily. This was more complicated than he had visualized. What if this guy was not living alone? He hadn't considered this before. However, he was now fairly sure the just vacated apartment was safe to enter, if he found that was the right one.

He rounded the corner of the back hall and listened at the door of the rear apartment. Hearing nothing, he knocked. There was a shuffling noise inside, and an old withering cracked voice called, "Who is it?" This could be the guy's mother. He couldn't be sure it wasn't.

He decided to blow his cover—maybe her eyesight was bad. "I'm looking for someone. Could you help me?" he called out.

After a minute or two of some sliding noise, the door opened slowly and an old lady with spiky gray hair, her hunched shoulders rounded in a shawl, peered up at him past the wire-rimmed glasses sliding from her nose. "Who in hell are you looking for?"

Cam blinked at her language. Old people had no business using such words. "I'm looking for Mr. Monaco's apartment."

"It's the apartment in the front, sonny." She peered up at him, her thin wrinkled lips pulled back in a sparse-tooth smile. "Hey, would you like to come in for a cup of coffee?"

This invitation started Cam's knees knocking. God, this old lady was really scary. "No, thanks" tumbled quickly from his lips as he turned back down the hall to the front of the building.

Finally, at the right door, he listened again, heard nothing, but knocked hard for good measure. Nothing happened, so after a minute or two, he bent down and examined the door lock. He was in luck. The hardware was ancient, and the whole assembly was loose. A few deft twists of his handy pick and the lock retracted. As the dead bolt above it was a single cylinder and could only be thrown by someone inside, he creaked open the door and slipped into the living room.

Cal stood for a moment and glanced about. "Christ," he said. Even he, who had been in some pretty bad places, was surprised by the overall grunginess and dingy atmosphere of the place. A kind of blue smoky film lay in the air, whose scent threatened the act of breathing. Cal's gaze took in the overflowing ashtray on the floor, the spotted threadbare sofa, several unwashed glasses, and then traveled to the bedroom area beyond, with dingy sheets spilling off the bed and a mound of dirty clothes covering the floor of the closet. He gave a low whistle and moved around the sofa and into the bedroom area.

Next to the closet was an old bureau with a sprawl of papers on the top. He glanced at the top one and the name 'Walter Wilkins' sprung to life, stopping him in his tracks. He picked up a few and leafed through them. They were copies of all of the publicity about Walter's death. Cam was stunned. What was this guy's interest in all of this? How did he get involved, if indeed he was? Maybe he had been a friend of Walter's and that's why he had these clippings. No, scratch that. This character definitely had never moved in the same circles as Walter Wilkins. He was just a down-and-outer who had bought Walter's sport coat at a second-hand shop. That must be it. This guy got curious about the former owner. But some instinct told Cam that was not all of it. A chilled feeling ran through his body. This was not going to be the easy pickin's he had planned. Something else was going on here. Something kinda weird and unpredictable. He had to find what he came for and get the hell out of here.

As soon as he stepped to the open closet area, he spotted the jacket. A sleeve of quality tweed protruded from a cluster of non-descript garments. He expelled a large breath, grabbed it from the hanger, and looked around for some way to carry it from the building. Under the sink, he found a brown grocery bag and stuffed the jacket into it. Next to it was a half-full bottle of vodka. "Thanks for the hospitality," he mumbled, grabbing the bottle and adding it to his prize.

Hardly anyone was on the street, and he was sure no one saw him leave. He went directly into the telephone booth and called Theda at the restaurant. It was ten-thirty, and the breakfast crowd had tapered off. He had only to wait a few minutes when she answered.

"I've got it," he said, a little pride creeping into his voice. He heard a big sigh of relief.

"I don't believe it. How did you ever find the guy?"

"I asked around the neighborhood. Then I found the barber who cuts this guy's hair, and he gave he the name and address. I staked out the apartment, and I got in when this character left on the bus this morning."

"Oh, I can't believe it. Listen, I can't talk now. I'll see you later tonight."

Cam crossed the street and got into the Firebird, tossing the bag into the seat beside him. He smiled widely. Wait until that jerk gets home and finds the jacket gone. He'll go nuts wondering why someone else wanted it.

10

It was good to be driving again, even though Dave's big frame was constricted in the bucket seat of the Nissan Sentra hatchback, and the top of his head brushed against the roof. The air from his open window gusted across his face, and the rock beat from the radio caused his fingers to tap in time on the rim of the steering wheel. A faint feeling of well-being began to trickle through him. Ridiculous, when he still had no job, no reputation, no friends, and very little money. The only thing he had going for him was this imaginary "case" he was involved with. And that was even more ridiculous. He was an outsider, poking into things that were not his business. If he found anything of substance, what then? Who would listen to him? The case was closed. Certainly, the family of the deceased would be the last to thank him for stirring up more unpleasantness. So why was he involved in all of this? Because the deceased and he shared the same sport coat? Come on, Monaco. That's too spooky. You're getting vibes from the dead that you should check all this out for him? This kind of thinking was getting him nowhere except to the loony bin. He had to get on with it. No matter what, he was just too interested and too curious to let go of it all now. What would he find—drugs, money, counterfeit plates, some kind of damaging evidence—what? When—and if—he got some of the answers, hell, then he could decide what to do with the information.

The Centerline Tennis Club was housed in a low sprawling building centered behind a large parking lot, circled by abundant green shrubbery and a gleaming green lawn. Dave walked into the lounge area, where groups of people, mostly women who could play during the day, were milling about in their cute little brief shorts, apparently waiting for partners or vacant courts. He slipped

around the edge of the room as quickly as possible, and headed for
a door marked "men," noticing a separate area on the other side of
the business counter marked "women." As he walked down a narrow
carpeted hallway, he heard the smacking of tennis balls from the
courts curtained off on the left.

Dave ducked into the men's dressing room, and was relieved
that no one was there. A brief check showed a bank of showers,
urinals, several hot tubs, and then finally a row of lockers set against
a far wall. As he walked toward them, his heart sank. He saw
immediately that they were the kind in which you inserted a quarter
and took out a thin little key. No resemblance to the one he was
hiding. Obviously, the answer was not here. So the key fit some
locker in never-never land. There was no way he could find it by
himself.

He needed more information, more clues. It was beginning to
look as if he should go to Mrs. Wilkins and spill the beans. Her
husband might have left another trail of some kind. His feeling of
optimism about this day faded away. He started down the hall
back to the lounge, when a side door suddenly opened and he
almost collided with a young man carrying two racquets and several
cans of balls. They both apologized, and the young man walked
quickly down the hall to enter his court. Dave stood for a moment,
smiling broadly. This might be a good day—no, make that a great
day—after all.

When the door opened, he had seen a bank of lockers. Off in
this special room. He would bet anything that these lockers were
rented by the month by members who wanted to keep their
equipment at the club. Dave opened the door and entered quickly.
No one was there. He began checking locker numbers. Fifty, sixty—
no, not in this row. He swung to the row behind him; twenty,
thirty—where the hell was it? He rounded the last locker in the
row and saw number forty against a separate wall. The third locker
from that was number forty-three. He hadn't realized he had been
holding his breath, and he now let it out in a swoosh. With
trembling fingers, he extracted the key from his breast pocket and
inserted it in the handle. He heard a wonderful click, twisted the

handle, and the door opened. There was a tennis sweater hanging on a padded hanger, two racquets in cases upright on the floor along with several cans of tennis balls and, behind these items, something else. Dave stared at a dark blue duffel bag. His heart pounding, he pulled it out. He paused a moment, listening. Satisfied that no one else was in the area, he opened it.

He should have realized all along it would be money. Walter had been a banker, hadn't he? Still, he was shocked at what he saw. Stacks and stacks of hundred-dollar bills. The bag was full of them. He stared, while his head spun. What now? He couldn't take this out of here. If he were caught with it, it would confirm to the police that he was indeed guilty of the narcotics heist. Maybe it was safest right where it was. After all, he was the only one with the key. Or was he? Walter could have had the key duplicated. Knowing of Wilkins' death, no doubt the tennis club had called the widow to pick up her husband's possessions. He had to make a quick decision. Someone might come in at any moment. He removed the bag and relocked the locker. Then in the remote possibility that someone might recognize Mr. Wilkins' property, he took off his windbreaker, tossed it over the bag, and carried both items from the premises as casually as possible, his head down to avoid any eye contact.

He had picked the most remote parking spot around the side of the building. Even so, he inspected the area carefully for any sign of the Tail before he got into his car. Dave had spotted his shadow a few yards from the apartment this morning, but managed to lose him at the bus stop. As the bus started up, Dave had walked past it as if he had no intention of boarding. In the last critical moments, he had spun around and run to knock at the door, and the driver had stopped to admit him. Dave swung aboard, smiling at the glowering driver and ducking into a front seat in time to catch the despairing look on the Tail's face. Even so, he couldn't be absolutely sure the Tail had not caught up with him. Or someone else. The flatfoot could have called a backup patrol car to follow the bus, but Dave guessed this whole operation of following him was on the low priority list. At the moment, there was no one outside the tennis club, not even sitting in the cars he could glimpse in front of the building. He opened the car's hatch, stuffed the bag down beside the spare tire under the hatch's floor covering, and quickly shrugged back into his jacket.

He was perspiring when he was settled behind the wheel. What should he do now? He had no doubt he was the possessor of stolen property. He couldn't go to the police; they would never believe his story. He smiled grimly. Isn't that why they were having him tailed? They expected him to lead them to the money they thought he had confiscated. He had no idea how many thousands of dollars were in the bag, but it seemed very probable at the moment that the police would somehow equate it to the missing narcotics money he himself was supposed to have tucked away. He had to separate himself from this incriminating bag of suspicious money as soon as possible. He thought hard. He needed a safe place to keep it until he decided what his next step would be. Well—what about another locker? He started up the car and was soon on the beltway, back to the center of town. On the way to the train station.

*　　*　　*

On his way back up Division Street, he began to feel good again. What the hell! He had certainly accomplished something today, and he had these great wheels besides. Freedom to move around. He hadn't realized how he had missed it. Up ahead was a little hamburger joint with a most conspicuous sign dangling below the name above the entrance. Beer, the sign declared joyously. Dave looked at the dashboard clock. Well, it was almost noon. A little celebration for a good morning's work was really required. He pulled in. The memory of last night's AA meeting flitted briefly through his brain, but what the heck, surely a beer with lunch was okay. Or maybe two at the most.

At about two o'clock, he shuffled up the weathered steps to his apartment. A sleepy feeling was beginning to engulf him and his next move would surely be to stretch out on his bed. But when he went to insert the key in his door, he found the door was slightly open. Immediately his body and brain clicked together into a familiar alertness, honed by all the self-protecting measures learned in police work. Someone had broken into his apartment. But why? A second later he knew the answer to that one. He had only one thing anyone would want. But who would know about it? The widow, maybe. Maybe she killed her husband for this money, and had somehow figured out that the key was in the pocket of the jacket she had given away.

He surveyed the living area. Hell, he couldn't tell if anything had been disturbed or not. It was still the same mess, as far as he could see. He took another look. He really should do something about living like such a slob. He ambled slowly around the sofa and into the bedroom, his eye on the closet, knowing already that he would fail to see the tweed sleeve hanging among his familiar shirts and trousers. Nevertheless, he pushed hanger after hanger aside, hoping he was wrong. Then he sat heavily down on his bed, the desire for a nap completely gone. The sport coat—his handsome sport coat—had been stolen. He felt bereft. It had become dear to him, a symbol of something better ahead. Wearing it, he had felt handsome, confident, assured that his fortunes would change. It was as if he had been robbed of his one chance to get out of this kind of life.

He recognized that these thoughts were pretty dramatic over the loss of an item of clothing, but this was the strange way he was feeling. The jacket had come to symbolize a kind of hope of rebirth— perhaps a new understanding of himself. He sighed and then another thought struck him. He threw back his head and gave a giant laugh! Wait until the burglar discovered the key was gone, because obviously that was what he was after. Dave smiled to himself for a few seconds, visualizing this person ranting and raving when he—or she—discovered that the key was no longer in the jacket. Then abruptly he stopped smiling. This whole thing was becoming very serious. Obviously, someone else now knew about the money and was after it. That meant that this person would probably be back, to search again for the key. Only now, Dave had the advantage. Only he knew where the money was.

He took out his well-worn billfold, and felt for the new key he had tucked behind his driver's license. He needed to find a safe place for number 166 immediately. The best thing would be to keep it on his own person at all times. After a moment, he untied his well-worn right tennis shoe, removed it, and placed the key under the innersole at the very end of the shoe. He put it back on and stepped on it. Not too uncomfortable. It was something he could get used to. Dave was lacing it up when he heard a noise. He froze, immobile, concentrating on the sound. At first, it seemed his door was creaking, and then he heard a faint tapping. "So! You're back already, you bastard!" he yelled, bounding up and rounding the corner of the bedroom doorway. He stopped almost in a skid.

An attractive forty-ish blonde lady in a navy blue designer suit, a vivid scarf of blue and turquoise artfully entwined about the neck, stood primly in the doorway, In a moment, he knew who she was, although they had never met before. She was shorter and thinner than her pictures had indicated, and, surprisingly, she was obviously ill at ease and quite a bit dismayed. No wonder, he thought. She left the social whirl to come to this wretched part of town. To think he had yelled at her besides! He hastened to correct her impression of him. Although he feared he was already too late.

"I'm sorry," he said. "I've just been robbed, and I thought the perpetrators had come back to do more damage." What in the hell was SHE doing here and how did she find him?

"Oh." She didn't seem to know what else to say. Her glance swept around the dismal apartment, and suddenly he felt like a teen-ager standing in a messy room under the eyes of an unforgiving parent. It WAS disgusting, he had to admit. It made his story completely unbelievable. Who would rob him—and of what? "Excuse me," she said, suddenly remembering her manners. "I'm Suzanne Wilkins—Mrs. Walter Wilkins—and I need to talk to you about something." Cold gray-green eyes bore into his brown ones like flints of steel. "I'm sure you know who I am."

Yes, indeed, he thought, trying to smooth down his cowlick,

but why was she so angry? She enlightened him. "You have been prying into my husband's death. I want to know why."

"I, uh—how do you know that?"

"Detective Sohler, who investigated my husband's death, felt obligated to tell me you had been to police headquarters to check out the files." She stood stiff and straight, primed to do battle if necessary. Dave shuffled his feet back and forth.

"Well," he said as casually as possible, "I think we better talk about this. Why don't you sit down?" He swept some newspapers off the stained sofa. Her answer was direct.

"Sit there? You can't be serious."

Even Dave had to admit she had a point. "Look," he said, "I know this is a miserable place. I'm moving out tomorrow." The minute he said it, he knew it was the right thing to do. That guy would surely be back again to search for the key.

"Just answer me," she said with a nasty nasal twang. "What is your involvement in my husband's death?"

What an unpleasant broad, Dave thought. Just like I thought when I looked at her picture. "It's complicated," he said evenly, trying to control his temper. "We need to talk at length about this. How about a cup of coffee in the deli downstairs?" She was silent. "I guarantee the seating is clean, although not aesthetically gorgeous."

She rewarded him with a faint smile and a brief dip of her wedge-cut blonde tresses. She then turned and moved like a couturier's model out the door. Slowly enough for Dave to glimpse a beautiful pair of legs and to detect a faint delicate perfume. She was silent, only clicking her high heels down the wooden stairs and onto the street. He moved ahead of her to open the door of the deli, allowing an enticing medley of freshly cooked food odors to escape. A few people, casually dressed in jeans or slacks, sweat shirts or parkas, were standing at the food counter placing orders.

When Suzanne entered, heads turned like the "wave" at a baseball game, as if a celebrity had just walked in. She gave no sign that she felt out of place, but walked to the one empty booth and slid onto a shiny red vinyl bench. Dave stood by the table. "Cream?" he asked. She nodded. "Sugar?" She shook her head. God, this dame is spooky. How uptight can you be? He went to the counter and came back with two thick white ceramic cups. She looked at hers like some kind of poison was deposited in front of her. Dave fought with himself to maintain some kind of civility. He took a sip from his cup to reassure her. "It won't kill you," he said, trying to put a little kindness into his voice.

"It's not the coffee," she said finally. "It's these cups. These thick rims make me wonder about all the other mouths that have drunk from them. They never look very clean."

Dave looked at his cup, and it suddenly seemed like a valid point. "That's no problem." He picked up her coffee and headed for the counter. In a moment, he was back with a Styrofoam cup.

Her eyes met his, and she smiled slightly. "Thanks."

The immediate climate became a degree warmer. Dave fortified himself with a few swallows and then decided to plunge in. But he certainly wasn't going to divulge all he knew until he had some more answers to this caper.

She was looking at him expectantly. "Mr. Monaco? Please tell me what is going on here."

"Call me Dave. I have a feeling this won't be our only meeting." She was silent, as if this was such a repulsive idea she didn't want to think about it. He went on. "It all started when I bought your husband's sport coat at the secondhand shop down the street."

Her head snapped up and her eyes widened. "You bought Walter's jacket?"

"Yes. And because of that, I got interested in your husband. It was funny, but when I put it on I got vibes as if your husband needed me to check out his death." As he said this, he was astonished to find it was true.

Her eyes were far away and looking strange. "Walter's jacket," she murmured, almost to herself.

Dave pressed on. "I used to be a police sergeant, Mrs. Wilkins," he said as if to a child. "My curiosity was aroused. The lady in the shop said your husband had died a few days before, and she described you. I checked at the clothing store and found out your husband's name."

She was now looking at him skeptically. "But then you went to police headquarters and went through the files. What gave you the right to look at the evidence? Walter's death was declared a suicide. The case is closed." Her voice rose angrily. "You had no right to involve yourself in my personal tragedy." A tear escaped the corner of one eye.

Damn, thought Dave. I don't know if I can deal with this right now. This lady was angry, resentful, and grieving—all at the same time. He leaned forward and placed both arms on the table. His gaze held hers. "Mrs. Wilkins, I have something very important to ask you."

Suzanne pulled back against the booth and folded her arms. "You have no business asking me anything. You're the one who has overstepped the boundaries of good taste and invaded my privacy."

"Yes, that's true. And I'm really sorry. But I need to find out how you really view your husband's death. Do you yourself believe he committed suicide?"

"That's no business of yours. I'm only here to find out why you have gotten involved—a stranger with no credentials except a weird story about how my husband's jacket has affected you. You are no longer a policeman, and you are in no position of authority. I should think you would have better things to do with your time. You're not even a private investigator." So—she had checked him out. He reluctantly admired her for that. This was an intelligent lady, not to be taken in by anyone. But then she twisted the knife. "You were suspended from the force for stealing money."

That statement hung in the air between them. Their glances clashed like blades of steel, and he lowered his eyes to escape the disgust in hers. Was there any use in explaining? Would she buy into any of it? He suddenly became very weary. She was right; he had no business meddling in any of this. No matter what he discovered about her husband's death, she would never believe it. He could have no credibility with her. He had stolen money that might belong to her. But what if she were guilty in some way?

He took a drink of lukewarm coffee and thought about leaving. To hell with her. He had been spending his own time probing into all of this, and she didn't give a shit. Wouldn't you think she would want to get at the truth if there was the least doubt that her husband had not committed suicide? He risked another look at her. She sat rigidly, arms folded, like a tiger waiting to spring. A small, beautiful tiger full of grief and anger. He had a strange feeling of wanting to protect her—now where in the hell did that come from?

"Mrs. Wilkins, I really don't care what you think of me. But the truth is that I was framed by a fellow officer. Now you probably think all policemen are the good guys, so I would have a hard time convincing you of that. It would be foolish of me to try. Anyway, it has nothing to do with the issue at hand."

She said nothing for a moment. Then, "I'd like to have my husband's sport coat back. I'll pay you twice what it cost you."

He was surprised. "Why?"

She spoke in a whisper. "It was all right when I didn't know who had it. It was then only a memory—like it had disappeared. But now I can't bear to think of you wearing it. And that's how I would see it in my mind."

What a fairy tale. Obviously, she only wants the key. Whatever, Dave could no longer avoid revealing the rest of the story. He had realized a little while ago that he would have to tell her about the key. He hadn't yet decided about the money, but definitely, she had to know about the key. She herself could be in danger when the present owner discovered the key missing from the jacket. Dave could see she was already visibly perturbed by what she had learned so far. This additional information about the key could really string her out. He decided to come right out with it and judge her reaction. "Mrs. Wilkins, I no longer have the jacket. I'm sorry."

Her reaction was unexpected. She sighed with relief. "Well, then that's okay." A faint attempt at a smile. "It's anonymous again."

So. It seemed she no knowledge of the key. Dave felt a strange sense of relief. He could have left it there. But she still might be in danger, and there were still a lot of questions. "Mrs. Wilkins, there's more. I didn't just give it away."

"What do you mean?"

He plunged in. "It was stolen. The jacket was stolen. Today. From my apartment just before you came." She stared, wordless. "You wondered why anyone would break into my place. It was to steal your husband's jacket."

"But why?"

"Apparently there was something of value in it."

"Nonsense! I went through all the pockets."

Dave said nothing. They stared at each other for a moment.

Then Suzanne spoke slowly. "I think I know who it was. A young man came to the door a few days ago pretending to be a friend of Walter's—a tennis buddy, I think he said. His name was Bob Davidson, and he claimed Walter had promised him the jacket someday. I knew right away he was a phony. Walter would never associate with someone like that. He struck me as being a hood."

"Did he have dark hair worn in a ponytail?"

"Why, yes," she said surprised. "How did you know?"

"I've noticed him hanging around out there on the street. He seemed to have an unusual amount of interest in me."

"Did he see you—uh, wearing the coat?" Apparently, the mental picture of Dave in her husband's jacket was hard to take.

"I don't think so."

"Then how do you think he found you?"

"Did you tell him what you did with the jacket?"

Her hand went to her mouth. "Oh, my. Yes, I gave him the name of the second-hand shop."

Too much was being made of this. Dave tried to ease her conscience. "So the lady gave him a description, and he made a few inquiries. Happens all the time. Hey—it certainly wasn't your fault."

"Well—good Lord, what do you suppose this all means?"

"I have a few ideas," he said, leaning forward. "Mrs. Wilkins, you are going to have to be very careful. This young man did not find what he was looking for. It is very possible he will return to your house to search for it."

"How do you know all this?"

"Because I have what he wants."

She understood immediately. This lady is sharp, he thought. Nasty disposition, but sharp in the head. "You found something in Walter's jacket." Dave looked down at his cold coffee. "What?"

"I don't know if this is the right time to tell you."

"Well, for God's sakes! You have something that belongs to me! I could have you brought up on charges."

"True," he admitted. Then he turned on his most persuasive voice. "Mrs. Wilkins, I found a key. I'm not sure what it means yet, but it could be important." This was not the right time to bring up the money. She obviously distrusted him, and definitely, at this stage he could be charged with stolen property.

"A key? In Walter's jacket? How odd." A gray fog moved into her eyes. Dave read the meaning. Her husband had kept something from her. A secret perhaps. "I'd like it, please." She stretched an open palm across the table.

He spread his legs and leaned back against the red padding. He couldn't believe what he said next—or why. "I don't have it with me." Actually, it was partially true. The original key was gone.

"So get it for me." Her eyes blazed. "It belongs to me."

"What do you plan to do with it?"

"I don't know. Find out where it fits, I suppose."

"And why do you want to do that?"

"Good Lord! This is a regular inquisition. I don't have to account to you for anything. You're the one who is meddling in my affairs without my permission!"

They were two antagonists, poised and standing firm. Then Dave shot his ammunition into the battle scene. "Mrs. Wilkins, maybe now you have some idea of how important it is that you answer a question I asked you awhile ago. Regardless of the police report on your husband, do you believe he committed suicide?"

She sat ramrod straight on her bench. The eyes fastened on him were blazing with animosity. "Mr. Monaco, I have had enough of this. I'll tell you once more, and maybe you'll get it through your head this time. I want you to butt out." She's certainly mad, he thought, to use language like this. And she wasn't through yet.

"I'll give you until tomorrow to deliver that key to me. If I don't get it by the end of the day, I'm going to the police and report you. I'll also get a restraining order if necessary. Do I make myself clear?" He nodded his head, while some little section of his brain noted admiringly that this was one tough broad. So tough she had somehow drawn the truth out of him and then trampled all over him for his honesty. But very attractive, especially when she came to life and got excited. Mrs. Wilkins was quite excited now. About burying him.

*　　*　　*

When Dave got back to his apartment, he headed for the kitchen. If he ever needed a drink, it was now. But there was nothing but paper bags under the sink. He was puzzled for a minute, but then he laughed. Pretty smart burglar. He had managed to find and steal the only two things that mattered to Dave. He pulled out his billfold and checked its meager contents. Not enough to buy a bottle and have anything to eat tonight. He opened the chipped refrigerator door and found a wrinkled apple in its remote depths. He took a bite and sat down to think. Once again, he went over the conversation with Mrs. Wilkins. He pulled the card she had given him out of his pocket and studied it. Her name flowed in script across the top with her address and phone number in tiny gothic type below. He tossed it on the coffee table and crunched on a bite of apple. He would have to give it up. There was no alternative.

Somehow, his instincts had misled him. His feeling about the jacket and an almost certainty that the owner was not a suicide—surely that was just an illusion. None of this was any of his concern, nor should it be. I'm losing it, he thought. A day or so ago, he had viewed this case as if preordained; as if this problem had landed in his lap to save him from his fast slide to degradation. He smiled grimly. Did he really think some higher power had smiled down on him and led him to the sport coat just to give him a purpose in life and pull him up out of his despair? And yet that is what happened. For a brief time his confidence returned, and he began again to acknowledge some abilities still deep inside himself. It had been a good feeling.

The key had provided an urgent call to find a locked door. There were still locked doors within himself. As the popular saying of the day went, he should "get on with his life." Find the keys to those other locked doors. God, that Mrs. Wilkins was one hell of a tough broad. Shows you couldn't tell anything by looking at a picture. So delicate and refined, but the heart of a tigress underneath. It had been a surprising afternoon. She had been strong enough to win. He would deliver the key tomorrow and explain about the money. The rest was up to her. Anyway, he was out of it.

He glanced about the room and remembered his resolve earlier in the day. By Jove, he WOULD move out. Definitely. He was no bum, and he certainly deserved better than this. He still had a few hundred in the bank, and perhaps he could get a job as a security guard somewhere. He suddenly noticed a white envelope lying on the floor near the door, apparently shoved under the door by the deli. Dave had been so immersed in depression when he entered that he had failed to see it. He got up now and picked it up. It was from the Edgewood Fraternal Order of Police. There was a letter and a check for two hundred and fifty dollars. They had assigned a special investigator to his case, and until it was resolved, they would be sending him a similar check each week. It was certainly a bright spot in an otherwise rotten day. It's always good to know where the next drink is coming from, and he certainly could use one now. Whether to drown his sorrows or to celebrate his good fortune, he wasn't sure.

He clumped down the stairs to the street and the newspaper-dispensing machine in front of the deli. No matter what twisted turns his life decided to take, it would be best if he found another place to live. And fairly soon. Not only was he sure his surreptitious visitor would be back, but scrutinizing his living quarters through the eyes of his blonde visitor had been a shock. He had two good reasons to move. There was a wobbly third. He had, after all, located the money. There was comfort in that fact, as if somehow such an achievement meant he should take more positive action in his life.

He was losing his desire to fade out of the picture. Extracting the local paper from the display case, he tucked it under his arm and walked to the bank on the next corner. He had enough sense to deposit most of the check, keeping out only enough to keep him going for a few days. Kind of a self-imposed restriction against allowing all of it to evaporate in alcohol. Later, he sat at a table in the pub two blocks down, gratefully sipping his second beer, the want ads spread out before him.

He was on his fourth one when he read about an apartment he thought he could manage. Or rather, it was a furnished room and bath, and it was right around the corner. A good location because it was still near the bus line. He found a quarter and went to the phone. Yes, it was still available. He could move in anytime. A woman's friendly voice on the phone asked if he wanted to, he could come over now.

Mr. and Mrs. Romano—Milo and Sophie—met him at the front door of their brick 1930's home and eagerly took him upstairs to the room they had recently painted and decorated. It was one of those spacious front rooms of a bygone era with three large windows looking out on the flat tin roof of the porch below. A tree-lined side yard came into view through a window on the other outside wall. Next to that was an outside door.

"It's a private entrance," pointed out Mr. Romano, and Dave glanced out the window to see a covered outside stairway. The double bedspread was in a small floral pattern that matched swags hanging over starchy white curtains. Even Dave noticed the sparkling clean windows, the rays of the setting sun making them glimmer. The faint smell of furniture polish hung in the air. There was a huge old-fashioned walk-in closet, a big chiffonier, two well-worn but comfortable lounge chairs, two nightstands with plain white ceramic lamps, and a TV in one corner. A door in the south corner stood open, revealing an old-fashioned bath with white ceramic bowl and base, a tub with claw feet, and a circular curtain for a portable shower. It was roomy and sparkling clean. Big enough for a large man like himself to move about in comfort, Dave thought. While he made his inspection, the Romanos stood with arms crossed, beaming at him.

"It's wonderful," he said, and he meant it, standing in the middle of the pale gray carpeting and looking around. It was an oasis. He felt the comfort of home. "You've done a lot of work," he declared to their smiling faces.

"So—you want it?" asked Milo Romano. When Dave nodded his head, Milo asked for two references. Dave gave him Ralph's name and number and then, searching his memory, he came up with Mike Polarski, his barber. What the hell—Mike had known him a long time and was sympathetic to his present distressful situation. Besides, he was in the neighborhood. Dave could do worse.

When he divulged to the Romanos that he was a former policeman, the deal was cut. An older couple, probably in their seventies, they seemed delighted to be having live-in security. The rent was most reasonable—two-fifty a month—and Dave was sure they lowered it because of his previous profession. Move in anytime, they told him. He decided it would be tomorrow. On the way out, they showed him the kitchen.

"You can cook anytime you want," said Mrs. Romano, an ample Italian woman of ruddy complexion with a huge smile. "We got a toaster oven and a microwave. And you can put anything you want in our refrigerator." A huge pot of spaghetti sauce was bubbling away on the stove and Dave's nostrils and stomach twitched to the familiar stimulus. He somehow knew that after he moved in here, he would be eating dinner often with the Romanos.

Dave left smiling. He was starting something, even if he didn't know what. But tomorrow he had to deliver the key to "the dragon lady." His smile vanished and his teeth meshed. He wished he never had to see her again.

11

Suzanne's heels clicked like typewriter keys as she hurried down the street to her parked dark blue Thunderbird. Not only was she anxious to put this unpleasant afternoon out of her mind, but also she couldn't wait to distance herself from this miserable and depressing section of town and from the feeling that several pairs of derelict eyes were fastened on her every move. She would not have been surprised to find her car stolen, or the tires slashed, or the tape deck ripped from the dashboard. But it still glimmered at the curb in unblemished condition.

Once on her way up Division Street to take the beltline to her own exclusive neighborhood, she groaned aloud. What a situation! This big burly man—definitely a low-life, living in wretched circumstances—had insidiously wormed his way into her affairs. No, correct that. It was worse. He was prying into Walter's life and death. What a ridiculous story about how wearing Walter's jacket affected him! Well—she raised her chin—there could be a grain of truth in that. It was certainly obvious that this man had never before had any garment as expensive and elegant as that one.

Then there was the matter of the key. Her lips drew a straight line. This was really disturbing. Mr. Monaco had stolen something that belonged to Walter, and therefore to herself as well. When he found out that Walter had owned the jacket, he should have gotten in touch with her at once and returned the key. She would then have turned it over to the police. Apparently, this Monaco person had been suspended from the police force for pulling some shady deal, and here he was again, stealing someone else's property. Walter's property! The thought made her livid. If she hadn't found out about this guy, he would never have contacted her. She was sure of it. Whatever was locked up under that key Mr. Monaco intended to appropriate for himself. Maybe he already had it.

She exited from the beltway and accelerated to move into the line of cars in the right lane. Adjusting back to the speed limit, she settled against the seat and thought again about the key. It was certainly mysterious. Why would Walter have such a thing hidden in his jacket? Walter, always so organized and so business-like about the minutest detail, kept keys on key rings, or in safety deposit boxes, or in desk drawers. Unless it was in a pocket. She smiled in satisfaction at resolving the problem. Well, that must be the answer. There was nothing odd about this key situation. It had been in Walter's jacket pocket all along, and it had somehow escaped her scrutiny when she was folding the clothes to take to the secondhand shop. It didn't really matter what the key opened. Walter had been an important man with many responsibilities. She never pried into his activities. This key probably opened something at the bank. Suzanne turned on the radio and found some cheerful Dixieland jazz. She tried to hum along to "Sunday," but Dave Monaco's face kept intruding. A strange man, but not wholly unattractive. She remembered she had had a strange impulse to push down his cowlick. Also, sitting across from him she had been uncomfortably aware that he and Walter fit into the same size sport coat. She drove off the highway at exit 51 and then right onto Madison Boulevard, a wide, spacious tree-lined street whose large estates were hardly visible through the carefully nurtured colonnades of privacy. A few blocks south, she turned the corner and drove down Morningside Drive and into her own driveway.

She sat for a moment, looking at her house with mixed feelings combining the pleasure of possession with the sadness of now being the sole occupant. It was true that Penny occasionally came home on a weekend. But at those times, her daughter was an impermanent presence, almost like a guest. Now the campus was more Penny's home than where she grew up. She was immersed in stretching her brain with academic stimulus and her emotions with personal involvements. Perhaps home meant distant memories that surfaced during the rough times when a little comfort was needed.

As usual when she thought of Walter the old question, "Why?" persisted in running around in her brain. She thought of Dave Monaco. Was she wrong, or hadn't he hinted that he didn't believe Walter had committed suicide? And she had been so angry that he had involved himself in her business, she had cut him off. But deeply within herself, didn't she want someone to think as she did? Ever since the police had made their decision, she had been uneasy. To be honest, her intuition and emotions were telling her the verdict was wrong. Now she had found someone who believed as she did. Although this man was offensive to her, maybe she should find out what he had been hinting at. But what if this Monaco thought it was murder and she herself was involved? She shivered for a moment, then lifted the garage door with her opener and put the car away. Before Suzanne entered through the side door, she had reached a decision. No matter how obnoxious Dave Monaco was, she would force herself to be pleasant to him until she learned what he knew. She could hardly wait for tomorrow, when he returned the key.

*   *   *

"Damn, damn, damn," Cam hunched over in the gold boucle' club chair, his shaking head in his hands. How many times had he examined the sport coat, running his hands over every seam, feeling every inch of the lining, prying deep into each pocket, even laying it flat on the breakfast table and moving his big palms in pressing motions back and forth? He had felt nothing, found nothing. He tried not to panic, but went over Theda's story again, her description of Walter patting the jacket. Perhaps he had moved the key elsewhere. Or if not, Mrs. Wilkins may have discovered it when she gathered up his clothes to dispose of them. Then again—that big Italian ex-cop could have removed it and hidden it somewhere else. Cam's head was splitting over the possibilities. He'd have to wait until Theda came home to discuss it further. In the meantime, he'd have some beers and think about it. He got a cold one from the fridge and tuned the TV to Oprah Winfrey.

He was asleep on the sofa when Theda came home around seven thirty from the early shift. She pounced on him, and his body stiffened in shock. "What the hell!" he screamed at her. She was smiling happily at the sport coat dangling from the closet doorknob.

"Hey—it's wonderful! You got it!"

"Sure—wonderful. Absolutely wonderful." She didn't seem to notice his sarcasm, but got up and went to run her finger wistfully down one sleeve.

Without turning, she asked, "So where's the key?"

"You tell me." A low growl.

"What?" She whirled and stared at him.

"There was no key in it."

Her eyes widened in dismay. "But there has to be. When Walter said he had it in a safe place, he patted his pocket, and I knew what he meant."

"Well, it's not there now." Theda turned and ran a hand into the lower right pocket. "Check it out. Be my guest." Cam's voice was tight.

"But it has to be here. I know it is." She slid onto the floor, the sport coat in her lap, frantic fingers slipping and sliding into and over every part. At last she looked up, eyes full of despairing tears. "I've lost my ticket out of this mess."

Cam pulled himself up to a sitting position and hunched forward, hands clasped between the spread of his legs. "Not necessarily." Her puzzled look met his. "It's got to be in one of three places," he said. "Either Mrs. Wilkins or our friend Monaco has it, or Walter shifted it to another hiding place."

"Walter wouldn't do that," she said slowly. "The way he patted his pocket and looked at me, well, I just knew he meant to keep it there because that was what he was going to wear when we took off. Shit—that was his favorite jacket. He would never leave it behind."

Cam got up and clumped back and forth for a moment, his head lowered in thought. Finally he stopped. "Okay, I think we should go with your gut feeling on this. And there's something else I thought of. If Walter wanted to hide the key in that jacket, he wouldn't just leave it in a pocket. He'd rip a seam, probably, and hide it in some other part. And if he did that, Mrs. Wilkins would never find it." His eyes blazed at Theda, and he grinned. "That leaves our good friend, Mr. Monaco. An ex-policeman who's used to butting in. Let's just say he checked it over and found the little devil."

"But even if that's true," wailed Theda, "it's gone now and we have no clues."

"True, my pet, but have some faith in old Cam. If Monaco found that hidden key, he's gotta figure out it's important. So— no way would he leave it lying around his apartment, especially after a break-in." He paused. "He could've turned it in to the police."

"Oh, my God!" Theda's hand flew to her face.

"But we don't know that. First we can find out if he still has it."

"How do we do that?"

"Well—it's been my limited experience that the safest place to hide anything is on your person. And anything small like a key— well, there are several possibilities." Theda began to cry. "Dry your tears, my love. I have a plan."

*   *   *

After three or four vodka martinis, Dave was beginning to feel better. He had been battered by Suzanne's accusations and hostility, but then comforted somewhat by the Romanos' acceptance of him into their home. After this day of emotional contrasts, he was hanging over the edge of uncertainty. Being involved with all that money could seal his doom. What if he hadn't lost the Tail and somehow the police knew? And to think a few days ago he thought fate had taken charge of his affairs, showing him a faint glow at the end of the tunnel. He sat twisting the stem in his hand. A comforting mellowness began creeping over him and turning his limbs to spaghetti. He guessed it was long past dinnertime and that he should order some food, but he didn't want to interrupt the glow he was getting.

When a small rock group began to play in the back of the bar, he was astonished to realize it must be nine o'clock. He flicked a wavering finger at the waitress and ordered straight vodka, ice on the side. Sometime during the evening—he had no idea what time it was—a person pulled up a chair and leaned close to him. Blonde frizzy hair, plucked eyebrows, thick pouty carmine lips. Something about her seemed familiar. Did he know her?

She flashed a red-rimmed toothy smile two inches from his face and then enlightened him. "I hardly knew you, Sergeant, with that beard. You in disguise or something?"

He shook his head. "Who the hell are you?"

"Why, Sergeant Monaco. What language!" She pouted for a moment. "I'm Curfew Harris. You picked me up a few times for hustling." She threw him a disappointed look. He pulled back and looked her over. Curfew Harris—he certainly remembered that name. When he had first heard it, he knew here was a hooker with a sense of humor about her profession. The beat of the band was getting in the way of the conversation. She stood up and grabbed his hands. "Hey—c'mon, sweetie, let's dance."

After that, the evening became a blur of dancing, drinking, and a little hands-on activity. How long that went on, he didn't know, but, my God, he had fun. He twisted and turned on the dance floor as if he were a teen-ager again, and everything he said was amazing and wonderful. Curfew hung on every word and around his neck. They understood one another perfectly.

Once back at their table for a little refueling, he had mumbled, "I don't have any money, you know."

She knew he wasn't referring to paying the bill. She snuggled up close to him, her big boobs resting on his left arm. "That's okay. Sometimes I do it for fun."

What happened after that he didn't know. His last memory was taking an elevator to Curfew's apartment, laughing all the way. He didn't even know if they had fun or not. When he woke up around nine o'clock the next morning, alone in Curfew's bed, there was no laughter left in him. Out of the events of the day just past came a nagging concern. He filtered it through the mush that used to be his brains and remembered this was the day he was to deliver the key.

He struggled to sit up although he knew a truck had surely run over him last night. He was alone, but it was not Curfew's apartment. It had the dingy transient aura and aroma of a cheap hotel room. His clothes were strewn on the floor, along with his sneakers and socks. He regarded them idly, without much interest, rubbing his aching forehead. Suddenly, his head exploded. Sneakers! He reached for them, but even before he stretched his finger down inside the right one under the innersole, he knew what he would find. Nothing. The key was missing. It had been a setup. Again.

*   *   *

"Bring me a whole pot of black coffee," he told the waitress in the hotel coffee shop. "Oh, and a couple of aspirins."

"Tough night, eh?"

He didn't answer. His spirits had found a new low. Whoever had the key was probably on the trail of checking out lockers. He had to take a few minutes to clear his head with some strong coffee. Dave tried to examine his problem in an objective, impersonal way. It was impossible. His very life was at stake here. The fact was, he had promised to deliver the key. Why in hell hadn't he given it to Mrs. Wilkins yesterday? He knew why. He was overly intrigued by the mystery of her husband stockpiling money in a locker. A lot of money. He was so interested in these strange clues he wanted to solve the mystery. And yet how could he? Even if he still had the key and was somehow able to find the answers to Walter Wilkins' strange activities, what would he do with the money? Forget the idea of going to the police with his theories and the bag of loot. So, you found a key and it led you to a pot of gold? He could already see the scorn and disbelief in their eyes. With the legal staff of the police union preparing his defense on the

drug bust case, which would not be a good idea. His activities of
the last few days would blow that right out of the water.

It all came down to one pitiful thought. He had promised to
return a non-existent key to the "Dragon Lady" today. If he were
only able to do that, he could get rid of this whole strange case. It
would be better anyway to spend his time organizing his life and
keeping his nose clean until his case came up for a hearing. But he
didn't have the key, and he could still be involved if she reported
him. She definitely had grounds to charge him with larceny. Even
though he could argue that when he bought the sport coat he also
purchased what was in it, a judge could find fault with that
reasoning. Especially when it appeared the lost item was so valuable
that the former owner had sought to conceal it.

Dave propped his elbow on the table and held his aching head.
His indiscretions of last night were causing him more pain than the
booze. He shook his head to get rid of a brief unwelcome thought.
No booze would have equaled no lost key. He lit a cigarette. On very
flimsy evidence, he had found the right locker. Surely if he could clear
his head he could think of a way to get back the key. He began laying
out a sketchy plan. It was crazy—preposterous—but it might work.
If not, if he got caught, he would be in deep shit.

He had very little time. If he figured it right, the pony-tailed
creep had the key and was probably now on his way to the tennis
club. After that, Dave would bet it would be the nearby airport
before the creep showed up downtown at the bus depot and the
train station. There would be a special reception at the last stop.
But first, he had to cancel his appointment with Mrs. Wilkins.
God—maybe she'd had second thoughts and filed a report on him
by now. He pulled out his wallet, extracted her card and enough
money to cover the bill. Nice of Curfew to leave his other belongings
intact. Especially his small amount of money. There was a pay
phone in the lobby. Might as well get this over with.

Her voice was cool and wary. When she heard his, hers began
to drip icicles. "I'm sorry," Dave said pleasantly. "I can't make it
today. You'll be happy to know I found a new place to live, and I

promised to move in today. It's around the corner in a much nicer neighborhood. Isn't that great? I'm really excited."

The feeling of excitement was not mutual. "I don't like this— I don't like this at all, Mr. Monaco. You have gone back on your word. You promised me faithfully you would bring it to me today."

"Oh, I know, I know. And believe me, I feel terrible about this. But what difference can one day make? I'll get it to you for sure tomorrow." Suzanne didn't answer. "Mrs. Wilkins? You're not going to report me, are you? Believe me, that would be a bad move. If the newspapers got wind of this key thing, the facts of your husband's death would hit the headlines again."

"I don't know," she said slowly. Then, "Is there somewhere I can reach you?"

He was making progress. He gave her the Romano's telephone number and volunteered his new address: 615 Hawthorne Street. He needed all the credibility he could get. He waited. Finally, she said, "You have until five o'clock tomorrow afternoon. Not a minute longer." He hoped she didn't hear the whoosh when he let out his breath.

The hotel was downtown, and his car was parked around the corner from the deli, so Dave rode the bus back up Division Street and thought about his next move. That was difficult because he had no idea what the enemy was scheming. But he held the trump card. Only he knew where the right locker was. But when had this kid started on the search? Dave scratched his chin. This punk looked like kind of an acidhead to him. It could take him a little while to add two and two and get four. Nevertheless, Dave didn't have a lot of time. He swung off the bus in front of the deli and went inside to tell the manager he was leaving the apartment upstairs.

As he wrote a check for this week's rent, he made a request. "Listen. If a thin young man, dark straight hair pulled into a ponytail, should come around asking about me, you don't know where I went."

The manager and the two waitresses agreed. As he walked around the corner to get his car, he was so absorbed in thought he hardly noticed the blustery weather. April seemed to have found a few scattered snowflakes left over from March. Goosebumps were just beginning to form beneath the windbreaker when he reached the car and got in. He drove it completely around the block until he could park it out in front of the deli. Then he went upstairs and threw his belongings into his suitcases and his dirty clothes into a pillowcase. Another trip up to get the things he had removed from Bobby's house, and then he was climbing back into his car in a matter of minutes.

As he was about to pull out, he spotted the Tail, a distinct look of surprise on his face. Dave rolled down the car window. "I'm moving around the corner—see you there," he called out and spun away from the curb.

"Is this all you got?" Mrs. Romano asked when he arrived. Dave shrugged his shoulders. "You poor boy!" she gurgled. "We'll take care of you!"

Dave was sure she would. He deposited his meager belongings in his new bedroom. The bag of dirty clothes somehow disappeared with Mrs. Romano in the direction of some wonderful laundry room. He caught the Romanos sneaking furtive glances at his disheveled appearance and spiny whiskers, and he thought longingly of staying long enough for a shower and clean clothes. But every moment counted. The pony-tailed genius might already be on the real trail. In about ten minutes, he was back in his car, the key to his new home swinging on his key ring.

*   *   *

Rock music thumped relentlessly from the Firebird's super, fore and aft speakers, while strange guttural voice gymnastics came from Cam's throat. He grinned happily, imagining over and over Dave's awakening this morning and discovering the key gone. He— Cam—was a genius, no doubt about it. Imagine putting together the scenario that had just happened. He whooped louder. That was certainly one of his finest efforts. He and Curfew had been friendly over the years, and not long ago she had called him to rough up some guy that was giving her a hard time. Cam was delighted. He was good with his fists, but he didn't get much of a chance to prove it anymore. So, when he called Curfew and explained what he needed, it was easy. Easier because she knew this Dave Monaco. It was a long shot, thinking Monaco would have the key on his person, but at the same time, it was worth a crack.

His instincts had paid off. Curfew called him this morning. He met her at a coffee shop to take delivery of the key while they had a good laugh together over a cup of coffee. He had the time. He knew the money was at the tennis club and that didn't open until ten o'clock. Besides, there was no hurry now. He—and he alone—had the magic access to the pot of gold. Christ! It hadn't been too bad for Monaco either. After all, he'd had a very good time last night.

So here Cam was on the south beltline on his way to the Centerline Tennis Club. Before Theda left for work this morning, they reviewed what she remembered about Walter's plans. When Walter mapped out their escape route, he had been adamant about making one stop—at the tennis club. The key certainly looked to fit a locker, so there it was. One and one added up to two with no problem. A piece of cake.

Two hours later, Cam pulled into one of the parking lots at the Edgewood Airport, five miles east of the tennis club. The smile was gone, and the radio dead. He sat for a moment and pounded on the steering wheel. He simply couldn't understand it. It figured so neatly. It had to be the tennis club. He had crept in quietly, unobtrusively, sneaking into the men's locker room, searching corners, finally discovering the locker section back of the reception area. He even asked a feminine member to check the women's locker room. The trouble was, there was no number 166. Not anywhere in that building. So that was why he was now at the airport. With one stop on the way.

His nerves were so shot he stopped for a couple of beers. Now fortified, his anger slightly abated, he was certain this was it. After all, the airport was only a few miles from the tennis club. Walter probably figured the money would be safer here. It was more convenient for renting a car and throwing the police off the trail of his disappearance. He locked his beautiful red car and went in to begin his search. There were three different terminals stretched out in spokes from the main terminal, and they all had lockers. In fact, there were lockers in the corridors, lockers in the men's rooms, lockers in the luggage claim areas. His stomach began to hurt. Also, the numbers were crazy, with the sequences out of order. After an hour, he knocked off and sat down in a restaurant area for a cup of coffee and a burger. Think, he told himself. You can find it. It has to be here. He felt better after jacking himself up and went off to continue his search.

It was another hour before he found it in the Delta terminal building. Number one hundred sixty-six. He glanced quickly around to make sure no one watched him and inserted his key in the handle. Nothing. It didn't seem to want to turn. He kept insisting, swearing under his breath, turning, forcing. Nothing happened. He paused for a moment, sweat glistening on his forehead. His gaze fell on the locker next to him. An unused locker, the key was in the lock. He found two quarters, inserted them, and removed the key. He looked at it. Then looked at his. His was smaller and flatter. The other had a small scallop design at the top on each side.

Anger flushed up inside. He would have kicked the locker, but too many people were scurrying back and forth. What now? He thought of the bus station. He'd try that next and then the train depot. He cursed under his breath all the way to the parking lot to get his car. Then he found out this was really a bad day. It wasn't there. His beautiful Firebird was stolen. He wanted to drive a fist into Dave Monaco's face.

*   *   *

It was about four-thirty before Theda could get off work long enough to go pick up Cam at the airport. By that time he had spent more than two hours circling the airport parking lots with the security people, filling out a report, waiting for the Edgewood police to show up, and then answering more questions and filling out more forms. He went outside the terminal building to wait for Theda to swing by. He lit a cigarette and bent his head, staring at the walkway. Anger ripped a seam in his gut. When Theda drove up, he got in the car without a word.

"I'm so sorry about your car," she offered, trying to find a break in the solid line of cars on her left. Cam sat with arms crossed, staring trance-like straight ahead. Theda finally moved the car away from the curb and crept along toward the tollgate. She glanced at him, and then concentrated on maneuvering into the right lane for the exit to the beltway. "Aren't you going to say anything?" she finally asked.

After a moment, he turned his head and iced her with his look. "Yeah. You're one stupid broad, and I wish I'd never come back to you and got into your mess. Once the verdict was suicide, you were in the clear. You should have kept your damn mouth shut."

"You can't blame me because your car got stolen," she said in a low, tight voice. He leaned toward her and his left hand grasped the back of her neck. As his finger tips dug into the cervical nerves, her eyes bulged and then filled with tears. The car swerved onto the middle line for a moment. "Please—don't," she said.

His arm moved away, and he clenched his hands between his legs. They were silent for a few moments. "You're not going back to work," said Cam between clamped teeth.

"What?"

"We've wasted enough time. Turn down Robinson Road. We're going to the train station."

"What?" she asked again.

"Stupid!" he said. "You're one stupid broad. It wasn't at the tennis club or the airport, so now we try the train station. Get it, Madame Einstein?"

*   *   *

They had met a few times over the years—Dave and Rupe

Feeney. Occasionally Rupe conquered homelessness and alcoholism to use his superior intellect to earn a living, but primarily he tapped his unusual wits to wheel and deal with the more challenging elements of street life. Basically, Rupe was a good guy, true to his word, operating on the fringes, but not into any heavy crime. Also, he steered clear of drug pushers. Any con game was more to his liking. If people were willing to be taken in, he couldn't see that it was his problem to enlighten them in any way. His connections brought him a variety of stolen items that had no problem slipping along a network to eager buyers. Dave drove over a few blocks to Garfield Avenue and down to the boarded storefronts of Garfield Square. He parked at the curb and walked the block in both directions, always keeping the car in sight while he questioned the homeless huddling in doorways.

The snowflakes had given out, but April had found some blustery March wind in the bottom of its weather bag. He knocked at the door of the now-defunct Garfield Theatre, and the piece of plywood that boarded up the entrance creaked open enough to allow entrance. A scholarly face looked back at him: bright blue eyes behind horn-rimmed glasses, sparse pale hair above a high forehead, straight nose, small mustache, and goatee. The man stepped back, revealing a nice looking quilted parka, pressed dark wool slacks, and shined wing-tipped black shoes. Dave acknowledged his own shabbiness for a moment.

"Well!" said Rupe, obviously glad to see him. "Sergeant Monaco. Welcome to my office."

"I can see business is good," said Dave, shaking his hand. "Such elegant surroundings."

"Well, they'll do until I get my first million. Then I figure I'll move over to your territory on Division Street." They laughed. "So what is it you want from me?"

"It's just a small favor."

"Oh, my God! That's what you always say! The last time the small favor almost got me killed!"

"Quit complaining! You know you love excitement, or you wouldn't live like this."

"Okay. Shoot."

"First of all, do you still have your 38?"

"Sure, but I don't know if I'm up to wasting someone, even if it's for ex-fuzz like you."

"That's not what I had in mind."

"Enlighten me."

"Someone has something I want. I need you to help me get it back."

"Where?"

"At the railway station."

"Lots of people around?"

"We hope."

"Hmmm. Tricky." Rupe's eyes narrowed. "Where does the trusty 38 come in?"

"Only as a little persuasion. It's got shock value. Especially when held against a guy's back."

"Not exactly my line of work. How big is this guy?"

"He's a punk."

"He could also be a giant."

"Well, he's not," said Dave. "Slender, skinny, small-boned, a leech." He thought for a moment. "Got a source for some M?"

"Hey—this is serious," said Rupe. "Sure—that's no problem."

"Make it about 16 milligrams. And we need a spike."

"Of course. I figured that was coming." They stared at each other, speculating on might happen in the next few hours. "What if he's got a gun too?" asked Rupe.

"More the knife type, I think. Anyway, we'll work out the details later."

"How much later?"

"In a few minutes. Get your equipment together. I'll be waiting in my car." He pointed out the red Nissan three parking spaces from the theater. "We got to beat this guy to the depot."

*   *   *

Dave drove slowly around the station block and finally spotted a car leaving a spot four spaces from the front loading area, but with a good view of the entrance. He pulled in and got out quickly to hurry into the station to check on the locker. He was smiling as he came back down the steps.

"He hasn't been here yet," he told Rupe as he got back in the car. "We might have a long wait."

It was about five o'clock in the afternoon and commuters were already spilling down the steps and across the street to their special parking lot. The aroma of McDonald hamburgers began to smell better and better, and Dave finally reached behind him and got the bag of burgers they had picked up on the way. They split up the food and coffee and settled back in their seats.

"You take the entrance, and I'll watch the street," said Dave.

They settled back to eat, drink, and converse about people they knew and didn't know, sports, fighting in the middle east, TV programs. After the calisthenics of the previous evening on the town and the pressures of today, Dave began to relax and his eyelids insisted on closing. He forced himself to drink some more coffee and introduce another topic of conversation. But after only a half an hour passed, Rupe poked him in the arm. "That him?"

A blue Mustang with a large dent in the right rear fender was moving slowly past their car, looking for a parking space. Dave spotted a dark ponytail on the driver's side. He was not alone. Dark curly hair tumbled about the head of his female passenger. Abruptly that head turned, scanning for parking possibilities. Something about the profile under the faint glow of the streetlights disturbed Dave. I've seen that girl somewhere before, he thought, but where?

Three spaces ahead of Dave's car, a parked car abruptly pulled out, and the Mustang drew up close, ready to move in. Before it pulled to the curb, Dave and Rupe were out of their car and on their way into the station.

"It's number 166," said Dave as they turned down a corridor featuring lockers and the restrooms. He had picked out the last locker along one wall where traffic would be light. They moved across the corridor and stood at the end of the opposite row of lockers. "All set?" asked Dave.

Rupe patted his jacket pocket where he had placed the needle full of morphine in a ready position. "Piece of cake."

An unintelligible voice crackled over intercom system, apparently announcing important train schedules. A moment later, a young man came around the corner, jerking past the lockers as he stooped to read the numbers, his ponytail flicking nervously. Then he stopped in front of number 166.

Dave looked at Rupe. "Now," he said.

Cam had a big smile on his face as he inserted the key easily in the lock. Then it faded fast. Something pushed up under his jacket, and a ring of cold hard steel pressed against his back. Two rock-like arms held his own immobile. While he froze, some other fingers removed the key from the lock.

"So how have you been, old pal?" asked a voice conversationally. Then it turned ominous. "Keep looking straight ahead, and you won't get hurt."

Cam found some squeaky parts of his own vocal chords. "You can't get away with this. You wouldn't shoot me in a public place."

"Don't count on it, buddy. There's two of us and only one of you. We could easily push you into a utility closet and take care of you there. But we've got other plans. You've been a bit annoying, so how would you like to go on a little vacation?"

Before Cam could answer, a side of his t-shirt was lifted, and the sharp prick of a hypodermic needle punctured his skin. His eyes widened and he tried to turn around, but his arms were pinned against the locker, his body shielded by Dave and Rupe, their free arms around his shoulders.

"Hey, our buddy here is in pretty bad shape," said Dave smiling across Cam's back at Rupe and at questioning looks from the few people walking in the area. "Do you think he'll make his train?"

"Sure," said Rupe in a loud voice. "He's only had a little too much to drink. We'll help him on, and then he'll be okay."

Euphoria and listlessness were starting to make jelly out of Cam's extremities, and he sagged against his captors. Dave managed to glance at his watch. There was a commuter train to Chicago every half hour. "Hey, old pal," he said loudly to Cam. "You're in luck. You can just make the next train out of here." Cam mumbled a goulash of syllables. "He says that's great," Dave reported heartily to Rupe. "Let's go." They turned as if glued together, Cam's head lolling from side to side, his dragging Reeboks making squiggly tracks along the dirty tile floor.

They entered the main lobby area and were sucked into the pushing crowd of commuters maneuvering into a line for the gate. The sleek Amtrak cars were posed momentarily at the platform like racehorses ready to spring down the track to Chicago. A few passengers hung back to make room for the strange trio, as Dave made frequent pronouncements, such as, "He's not feeling well, M'am, so we're just helping him on."

Finally, Dave and Rupe deposited their cargo in an aisle seat. "Goodbye, old pal," said Rupe, pulling on Cam's ponytail. "Be sure to give them your ticket when they come around to collect." He looked at Dave and laughed.

"And don't forget to write," said Dave. Cam struggled to rise but his legs flailed aimlessly. He opened his mouth but there were no real words in it. "That's okay, old buddy," said Dave. "There's no need to thank us. After all, what are friends for?" Dave and Rupe were still laughing when they started down the entrance steps. "Hold on," said Dave, suddenly, putting out his hand.

"What?"

"Keep going, but check out that babe over there on the sidewalk who looks like she's waiting for someone."

"Yeah! You can pick 'em, Monaco."

"You don't understand," said Dave softly. "I've seen her somewhere before."

"And you can't remember where? Monaco, you're in bad shape."

"Keep moving and don't look at her," said Dave. "Could be she has a long wait. I think her boy friend just left on a little vacation."

12

When Dave awoke the next morning, his first thought was of the Dragon Lady. He might be in for a very sticky, unpleasant encounter, if the first meeting was any indication. Then again, he would be mighty relieved to get rid of the damn key and separate himself from these strange incidents, no matter how intriguing they seemed at times. He stretched himself out on Mrs. Romano's delightful innerspring mattress for a moment, and then swung his legs over the side to sit up.

His gaze drifted around the room. Surroundings certainly affected your outlook on life, he decided. A comfortable feeling of being home and well cared for surprised him. He hadn't remembered feeling like that since he left his mother's old house and his boyhood room. Another pleasant feeling surfaced this morning. He liked himself—that surprised him even more. Although he had taken a shower last night, he couldn't resist another this morning—plenty of pressure sending unlimited hot water down his back. After shaving and trimming his mustache and beard, he located clean underwear in the bureau drawer, courtesy of Mrs. Romano, and then contemplated how he would form the rest of his wardrobe for the important appointment of the day. He spent the next half hour pulling rumpled clothes from suitcases and hanging them in the closet. A corduroy sport coat didn't look too bad.

He went to the window to check on the weather and was pleased to find a thermometer attached to the outside frame. Sixty degrees with the sun struggling to find a path through a few wispy clouds. The sport coat would be just right with a tan v-neck sweater under it. Walter Wilkins' tan slacks would look great with the rust corduroy. Did he dare? Yes. Lots of men had slacks like these. Mrs. Wilkins would never notice.

After Dave was dressed, he looked at himself critically in the long mirror on the back of the closet door. His reflection startled him. He turned his body from side to side, rubbing his beard, peering into the whites of his eyes, and combing some stubborn strands of hair down with his fingers. He pulled in his gut, and swung the jacket out of the way to get a full profile view of his figure. Not bad, he decided. All this running around with little food has pared a bit off the love handles which rounded above the belt. My God, he thought, I must have looked like a bum before. Now he was almost handsome, he decided. He turned his head, and his cowlick popped up. When he lived with Bobby he used to give it a squirt of her hair spray each morning. Now he searched through his Dopp kit and came up with an old tube of hairdressing. A little dab did the trick—for the moment.

He heard a knock, and then Mrs. Romano called out, "We have coffee and rolls in the kitchen. Come down when you're ready."

What a setup! Lady Luck had begun to smile on him. He was sure of it now. Once in the kitchen, Mrs. Romano couldn't help doing what she did best, spoiling people. The continental breakfast expanded into a diner special, with scrambled eggs, bacon, and hash browns. Dave told her he had never had such good food, and he meant it. She beamed.

"A little celebration for your first morning in our home," she said. Afterwards, Dave went out into the hall to call Suzanne.

"I've been wondering when I would hear from you, Mr. Monaco, or if I ever would." Dave decided the "Ice Lady" would be a better nickname. He worked on controlling the anger bubbling inside him.

"Mrs. Wilkins, I never break a promise. I have the key and can get it to you immediately. When would be a convenient time?" He glanced at his watch. It was nine thirty.

"How about around eleven o'clock? I'd like to get this over with. I'll feel much better when this key is in my possession—

where it belongs." Her voice was hard. "I didn't sleep much last night." Accusingly, as if it were Dave's fault.

"I'm sorry." He was unable to keep the chill out of his own voice. "I'll be glad to get rid of it too. It's been a nuisance." You don't know the half of it, lady, he thought. And once you have that key, your troubles may really be starting. Not that I give a shit. "Okay, Mrs. Wilkins. I'll be there about eleven."

After she gave him directions, he hung up and climbed the stairs to his room. Thank God, he would be free this afternoon to enjoy other pursuits, maybe check around and see how his own case was coming along.

The picture of a young man slumped in a train seat flashed through his mind. That could still be future trouble. Definitely. But he was only slightly worried. He had been trained in the most sophisticated protection maneuvers, and his instinct for self-preservation had always been high. No matter what might hit the fan, he was able to handle it. He had the experience of protecting himself from all kinds of street violence. But there was one slight problem now. Maybe even a serious one. He had no gun and no badge. Well—he pushed this uncomfortable thought from his mind and got down to priorities of the moment.

Whistling softly, he unpacked his books, papers, cassettes and tape player, knick-knacks and mementos. When he was finished getting organized by filling bookshelves and drawers, he went down the street to the cleaners with the rest of his rumpled but wearable wardrobe.

*   *   *

Dave stood on the wide front brick steps at the front door of the imposing Colonial home and heard faint chimes announcing his arrival. His hands went in and out of his pockets, and his weight shifted between his polished tan shoes while he waited for the Dragon Lady to open the door. Even standing outside he felt ill at ease. He turned 180 degrees and peered up and down the street through the trees and shrubbery. No suspicious cars seemed to be

parked on the street, and no people moving about. On the way
over here, he kept checking his rearview mirror, but no one was
trailing him. Not even the Tail. Matter of fact, his shadow had
been nowhere about today. Was the police investigation over with?
Did that mean they had reached a decision, good or bad?

At last, the thick mahogany door opened with a faint creak,
and Suzanne stood there, her tiny frame smaller than ever in snug-
fitting jeans and a waist-hugging blue sweater. Her blonde hair
was pulled back into a barrette, and she wore no makeup except
the faint blush of lipstick. She bore little resemblance to the dressed-
for-success, antagonistic, assertive lady he had sipped coffee with
in the deli. Dave looked at her skeptically, while the vision of the
Dragon Lady skittered off somewhere. But it could return. Dave
prided himself on pegging people correctly at first meeting. This
was still a tough broad, no doubt dressed today for a little
manipulation.

She invited him in, not really looking at him, her head bent
and her blue eyes clouded in evasiveness. He got the idea
immediately that now he was here, she regretted her invitation.
Probably would have preferred to meet him again at the deli. But
she was all business, and something else. As she ushered him in,
she backed away from him as far as possible. Then he got it.

The aggressiveness she had shown over the coffee they shared
at the deli had dissolved into fear. Now that he was here, she was
suddenly aware of being alone in her house with a strange man.
He saw it from her perspective. Here he was, a graceless dark-
complexioned muscular man, in disgrace with the police force,
who was living in rented rooms and buying second-hand clothes.
No one in their right mind would trust such a person, especially
this delicate, pampered, and now unprotected little lady.

He summoned up his kindest smile to put her at ease. As they
stood for a moment in the hall, he plunged in. "Mrs. Wilkins, let
me say something. I've had considerable experience dealing with
all kinds of people. The one emotion I'm easily able to identify is
fear. I know that right this minute you're scared to death of me."
He paused, reading agreement in her face. "You have no reason to

be. I promise you that I will not harm you in any way. For years my job was to protect people. If you can come to trust me, I think I can be of help to you."

Now why in hell did I say that, he wondered. I don't want to be involved in this. I just want to shake it loose and forget it. She was silent for a moment, looking at the floor. Then she raised her head and gave him a wan smile. "How amazing that you understand what I'm feeling. I'm sure you also understand that it's nothing personal. I've had to deal with a lot of unfamiliar business since Walter's death. It hasn't been easy."

A little rapport fluttered between them. He followed her across the gleaming marble hall tiles to the den, where she motioned him toward matching chairs on either side of a stone fireplace. He settled himself into a leather club chair. "This is a very nice house," he offered lamely. What an understatement, idiot, he said to himself.

She stood behind the other chair and looked at him. "Would you like some coffee?"

"Yes, thanks." He managed a twitch of a smile.

"I'll be right back," and she left, presumably for the kitchen. He turned his neck enough to catch a good view of her trim little behind going through the hall door. He settled back, discovered his chair swiveled, and turned himself so he could examine the room: rich paneled walls, bookshelves to the ceiling, polished tables, and shiny brass lamps. A bay window almost filled one wall, its window seat cushioned in a hunting print with matching drapes caught back on either side. It was a fitting backdrop for the massive mahogany desk and several chairs. On the far wall, built-in TV and stereo cabinets shared the space with a full bar and sink. He had never been in such an elegant room in all his life. Suddenly he felt like an actor in a stage setting. Any moment a servant would come through the door and address him as Lord Monaco.

"Wow," he said out loud.

Suddenly Suzanne was standing next to him, carrying a tray with a coffee carafe, cream and sugar, and a plate of some tiny filled croissants. She set it down on the coffee table and turned to glance at him. "Did you say something?"

Remembering his manners, he rose out of his chair as soon as he became aware of her. "Sorry," somehow feeling he should apologize. "I was—well, this room is very attractive."

"Well, thank you." She seemed pleased. Then her voice clouded over. "This was Walter's favorite room."

"Really." He sat back down, feeling like a schoolboy. She perched on the edge of the other chair and leaned over the coffee table, filling two cups. "This smells wonderful," he said as he accepted a cup. She gave him a napkin and passed the flaky pastry. He smiled inanely.

"My husband was killed in this room," she said suddenly.

Dave almost choked on the morsel he was swallowing. He remembered now. Deliberately he kept his eyes from the direction of the desk. He glanced at Suzanne. Small and forlorn, her face bleak, she perched on the edge of her chair like a survivor adrift in a lifeboat. He put his cup down on the table and swiveled his chair toward her.

"Suzanne," he said, catching her green eyes in his, "I'm really sorry about your husband. I know it's been tough, dealing with such an accident."

Her eyes caught on fire. "Accident?"

"Certainly. All unnatural deaths are accidents. Even self-inflicted, they're accidents of the twisted thinking of the mind." She seemed not to notice the use of her given name.

Her words came out measured, staccato. Like she was reading from a prepared speech. "Nothing was ever twisted in Walter's mind. He had the clearest, sharpest way of thinking and reasoning of anyone I ever knew. Walter never allowed anything to defeat him. He welcomed problems, challenges."

Dave nodded at her. He certainly had no grounds for argument. "You don't believe he committed suicide." It was a statement, not a question.

"No, I don't." Suzanne answered. "But I can't prove it. And no matter what really happened, Walter isn't coming back." She turned in her chair and gestured with a slight wave of her hand toward the desk. No theatrics, no drama. "That's where I found Walter."

Right on. Not, 'that's where Walter was found.' This lady faces up to things, thought Dave. Maybe she can take it after all. He decided to plunge in. He reached under his open shirt collar and lifted out the chain, the key dangling from it. He spun the clasp around until he could work it free and then, reaching forward, he opened her right palm and laid the key in it.

She stared at it, as if she expected this piece of metal to give her the secrets of the universe. Dave leaned forward, his brown eyes warm and sympathetic. She met his look and said, "Why do I have the feeling I'm not going to like what you have to tell me?"

"That may be true, Suzanne. I don't know you very well, but I think you're a tough lady. I think you can handle what you have to." He read some uncertainty in her eyes, but went ahead anyway. God, let's get this over with and get out of here. He held up his palm toward her. "Now, just let me tell you all about the key, and then we can discuss the entire matter. First of all, the key you now have is not the one I found in your husband's coat pocket."

Anger flared in her eyes, and she started to rise from her chair. Dave motioned her back down. "Please just let me tell my story. And try not to judge me until you have heard me through." So he described his investigation which had identified Walter as the original owner of his sport coat, how he found out Walter was an avid tennis player and reasoned the key might fit a locker at the tennis club, and how he had been right. He had found a duffel bag. There he paused a moment, not knowing how to go on. Suzanne's eyes were blazing.

"All of this nonsense is about a bag in a locker at Walter's tennis club? It's probably full of tennis equipment."

He held up his hand again. "Wait a minute. Don't you think it's strange your husband hid the key in his jacket?"

"Maybe there was a hole in the pocket, and it simply fell through and into the lining."

"Suzanne," said Dave softly. "The key had been deliberately sewn into the lining along a seam."

"What? Who would do a thing like that? You're implying Walter would? That's ridiculous. Walter couldn't thread a needle, let alone use one. And why would he? If he wanted to hide a key, there are many places he could do that."

"That's true," said Dave, "but you yourself said the jacket was Walter's favorite. Apparently he wanted it with him." He leaned forward, retrieved his coffee cup from the coffee table, and took a sip of slightly warm coffee. There was no way he could mollify the information he had to give her. "The bag was full of money."

She sat back abruptly, stunned. "Oh, my God. How weird. Why would Walter keep money at the tennis club?"

Dave said nothing while she digested this information and maybe added two and two. She seemed numbed by this evidence of her husband's strange and uncharacteristic behavior. In a moment, tears formed and wiggled down her pale cheeks. But after a few moments, anger replaced grief, and she stabbed Dave with a furious look.

"You had the key and you knew there was money in that locker. If I hadn't traced you, you would have kept it for yourself. Obviously you need it." Her look was scornful. "You stole the money and put it someplace else. You—you who were a cop! You knew where that money belonged. It belonged to me, as Walter's heir. It was up to me to decide what to do with it."

"It looks like that, I admit," said Dave. "But it's not true. I had no plans to keep the money. I don't know if I can convince you of that, but, what the hell, if I'd wanted it, I could be in Mexico right now." He leaned forward and caught her angry eyes in his.

He kept his voice low, emotionless, convincing. "But I'm definitely guilty of meddling. When I read about your husband's death, I felt the police did an inadequate investigation. It was none of my business, but somehow, after I got your husband's coat, it became my business. Very strange. It was almost as if he became my client. Like he wanted me to clear up some loose ends."

Her eyes widened, but she said nothing. Dave went on. "I told you before that I'm on suspension because money disappeared during a police drug bust. I'm innocent. Anyway, I couldn't be caught with a bag of money, so I moved it to what I considered a safer place—the train station. I wanted time to think what to do.

I thought perhaps your husband had been in some kind of trouble, and there might be some way to straighten it out. Then when that young man stole the jacket, I knew there must be a lot at stake here."

Her eyes were blazing again. "You expect me to believe you would care about my husband's reputation, a man you didn't even know?"

"I know it sounds crazy, but it was turning into an interesting case." He stared at the floor for a moment. "Somehow, owning that jacket got me involved. And when I read about your husband in the newspapers, a lot of things didn't add up."

"Well, un-involve yourself, Mr. Monaco. This is as far as you go. I can handle it from here."

"I'm not so sure of that, Mrs. Wilkins. You've forgotten the other interested party in all of this. The guy with the ponytail."

"Is he still a problem? I know he stole my husband's jacket, but we have the key now."

How could he tell her that he—Dave—had almost lost everything one drunken night? Better just let the information lay as it was.

"He strikes me as being very persistent. He's been here once before. Somehow, he found out where your husband lived. That disturbs me. He obviously knows that the bag contains money. Maybe he was in some scam with your husband, otherwise, how would he have all this information?"

He looked at Suzanne intently. "I'm worried about you. He could come back."

She thought of something. "Couldn't he get access to the locker—maybe say he lost his key and get the station security to open it?"

"It's not in the same locker."

She flashed him a look of admiration and opened her hand, glancing at the key. "So now it's in locker 100?"

He nodded, and then went on. "Mister Ponytail took an unexpected trip to Chicago. But he could be coming back anytime today."

She seemed to read additional information in his eyes and she laughed. A brief, bright tinkle. "You're really something."

He grinned. Then he grew serious again. "Do you have a really safe place for that key?"

She didn't answer right away. Instead, she said, "How do I know this is the right key now? How do I know this will unlock a locker that contains Walter's tennis bag full of money?" She leaned forward and placed the key on the coffee table.

"You don't know. You have only my word. If you like, we can go down to the station and unlock number 100 right now."

She scrutinized him for a moment. "I don't know what to think." She looked away and shook her head from side to side. Then she glanced back at him. "And I don't know what to do. This is too much, coming so soon after Walter's death and the investigation." She twisted her hands in her lap. "I don't even know you, but I guess I have no choice except to believe you. I have to trust someone. And I can't tell anyone else about this strange business until we have resolved the mystery of all this money."

Dave took notice of the 'we'. He sighed with relief that apparently Suzanne was accepting the description of his unorthodox activities. "Even though the money is now in a different locker, I don't feel comfortable leaving it there very long," he said. "Then there's still a problem in getting it. This pony-tailed punk could be making his home in the train station until we show up. I say we, because I can't take the chance of being caught with the money, and you could be in real danger if this guy fingered you with it."

"And I see now that I can't go to the police with any of this," said Suzanne slowly. "If Walter did anything he shouldn't have, I want to keep it from the media if possible."

Dave thought of something. "Did you and your husband have joint bank accounts?"

"Always."

"Then you would have noticed any large or unusual withdrawals, perhaps over a period of time."

"Yes. There was never anything like that." Suzanne sat for a moment, head down, staring at her hands in her lap.

Then she leaned forward and picked up a silver cigarette box from the coffee table between them. The box shook as she offered him a cigarette and then took one herself. He brought out his lighter and lit the tips, avoiding her eyes, which appeared to be suddenly wet. They smoked for a few moments in silence. Then he reached forward and snubbed out his cigarette in a shiny ebony ashtray. Now was a good time for him to get the hell out of here. He rose from his chair.

"Well," he said. "You have the key and you know the whole story. So I guess I'll be going. You can always call me if you have any questions."

Suzanne swiveled her chair to look at him. "Dave, wait a minute. I've made a decision. I need some help, and I can't go to anyone else on all of this—not yet, anyway. Could I hire you, as a private investigator, perhaps?" Her blue eyes pleaded, and her tiny person seemed swallowed up by the chair and by life itself. Dave groaned to himself and made a quick decision. He sat down again.

"Look, Suzanne. While I'm on suspension, I can't get a PI license. But I'll be glad to help in any way I can. No charge, of course."

"Good. To start, I want to know why you think my husband didn't commit suicide." Suzanne leaned forward, her hands clasped between her knees. A white light sparkled and flashed. She was twisting a large diamond ring on her left hand.

"Are you sure you're strong enough to go into all of this now?" Dave asked. Her face turned toward his, brows straight over serious eyes.

"Dave," she said. He was glad to hear they were back to first names. "I have been upset myself over the police investigation. I am positive that Walter could never have been in the deranged state of mind to commit suicide. Now this money thing has turned up. Maybe he was involved in something shady, but that wouldn't have been Walter either. I'm terribly confused. But I want to find out all I can, no matter how bad it might be. I need to know the truth. I can't go on living with all this uncertainty."

"Well," said Dave, caught by the intense look in her blue eyes.

"Let's start with where your husband was found." He got up, walked over to the desk, and leaned over the side, his palms on the top. "The newspaper accounts said your husband was here in his chair, his head lying between his arms on top of the desk."

"Yes, that's right," said Suzanne, who had come to stand on the other side of the desk.

"The gun was lying near his right hand, a 38 special I believe the police report said?"

"Yes. Walter had apparently picked it up in Vietnam."

"Was he in the action over there?"

"I don't believe so," said Suzanne. "He mostly worked in supply depots. But he didn't talk about it much. I didn't even know he had a gun."

"Hmmm."

"We didn't tell each other everything," Suzanne said a bit defensively. "But we loved each other."

Dave's eyes met hers. "Of course," he said gently. His eyes swung back to the desk. "I'm puzzled," he said. He went around the desk and looked at the oak chair behind it. Then he bent down and examined the four arms and casters that comprised the base. Next, he looked at the spring mechanism under the seat. He took hold of the back of the chair and moved it easily toward and away from the desk.

Suzanne moved over to stand next to him, and he was distracted for a moment by the tantalizing scent she was wearing. He recovered and explained his comment. "Walter was a large man, about my size." They both knew that, and Dave knew he was even wearing Walter's trousers. He hoped Suzanne wouldn't notice. "Being shot at close range packs a wallop. Someone like Walter sitting in a chair like this would probably have been thrown up and out of it by the force of the bullet."

Dave sat down in the chair and demonstrated, suddenly throwing his body against the back of the chair. The force lifted the front casters off the carpet and spilled him off the side of the chair into a sprawl on the floor.

"Are you okay?" asked Suzanne.

"Sure, I do this all the time for a living." Dave got up, rubbing his right hip. He stood for a moment looking at the carpeting around the chair. "Have you done anything to this carpet since that—uh—night?"

"No." Suzanne looked puzzled.

Dave got down on his hands and knees. "Got a magnifying glass?"

She got one out of a desk drawer and handed it to him. He moved around, spreading the pile of the thick rust carpet apart with his fingers and peering at it intently. Then he sat up. "How about some small scissors?"

"Did you find something?"

"I think so. But I need to take a sample. Would you mind if I cut just a few strands of your carpet? You won't even notice it's gone."

"Of course. If it will help." She left the room for a few minutes and then came back with some manicure scissors. Dave got his sample and put it in an envelope. He creaked himself upright and leaned against the desk.

"Please tell me what you think," Suzanne asked breathlessly.

"I think it's strange your husband was found in his chair. The force of the bullet entering his body at such close range would have blown him right out of it. Especially this particular kind of posture chair." Her eyes widened as she began to understand. Dave went on. "In the pictures I saw of your husband, he wore glasses. Did he always?"

"Oh, yes, he had several pairs. Special ones for tennis and skiing, and bifocals the rest of the time."

"Where were they when he was found?"

"He was wearing them. His bifocals, of course."

"With his head on the desk."

"Yes."

Dave stared at the desk and chair, his thumb and forefinger stroking his chin.

Suzanne's brow wrinkled. "What are you thinking?"

"If the force of the bullet spilled him out of the chair, I doubt that his glasses would have stayed on."

"So," she said slowly, working it out in her mind. "Someone else was here. Someone who got him back in his chair and put on his glasses. Oh, my God." She suddenly turned very white and leaned against the desk.

Dave went to her quickly and put an arm around her. "Are you all right?"

She smiled weakly, her face inches from his own. His heart skipped a beat. "Yes, I guess I'm all right. All this is so unexpected, plus I haven't been sleeping very well."

Dave's arm fell away, and he moved back to the coffee table to light a cigarette with slightly trembling fingers. By the time she too had picked up a cigarette, he was able to light hers with a steady hand. They sat down again. "Do you still want to go on with this?" he asked.

"Definitely." She inhaled deeply. "So now we think there was someone else here with Walter on that Friday night. But how could that be? Only Walter's prints were on the gun, and there was no evidence of forced entry."

"Your husband obviously admitted someone."

"But how did that person leave the house? The bolts were on both doors when my daughter and I got home from the movies."

"I don't know the answers yet to those questions. Maybe he gave someone else a key."

"Walter? Give someone a key to our house? No, I don't believe that's possible."

Dave uncurled his long legs and stood up. "While we're on this subject, do you mind if I examine the doors?"

"Of course not," said Suzanne, getting up also. They went down the hall and opened the front door. Suzanne showed him how the bolts entered each side of the doorframe when the lock was engaged. Then Dave stepped outside onto the wide cement stoop. He ran his hand behind the coach lamps over the door and checked up under the eaves. He looked under the doormat. Then he bent down and fumbled around with the wood chips under the low evergreen shrubs on either side of the house.

He looked up at Suzanne and shook his head. "Nothing here. Let's try in the back." The back door opened onto a bricked terrace, outlined in low, green, spreading pachysandra. Dave crouched down and felt among the plants nearest the door. After a moment, he stood up. "Would you have a Kleenex?" he asked. "I've found something that might have prints on it."

Suzanne stepped inside and in a moment was back with the tissue. Dave took it and crouched down, reaching into the green plants. In a moment, he extended his palm to Suzanne, a round brown stone lying on the tissue.

"Eureka," he said, and smiled at Suzanne before he thought what this might mean to her.

"What's that?" she asked.

"It's one of those fake rocks with a hiding place for a key." He rolled it over in his hand and, holding the sides carefully, slid out a flat plate along the bottom. A key lay on its side in a special compartment. Dave tipped it out and into the tissue. Then he moved his thumb and first finger to grasp the edges of the key from underneath, protecting it with the tissue. He went to the door and inserted it in the lock. The bolt slid out of its resting place on the edge of the door. He tried not to look at Suzanne. My God, what was she thinking by now? She stood by the door, her arms still hugging her body, keeping out more than the cold.

"So now we know how someone got in." Her voice was a whisper. Another shiver.

He followed her lithe little figure back into the study, resisting a very strong impulse to give this embattled lady a big hug. He quickly stepped on any ideas along this line. Effusive Italian urges had gotten him into trouble more than once. He said nothing for a while, giving Suzanne time to absorb the astonishing information he had presented.

"I always knew Walter didn't commit suicide," she said finally, "but what about the note he left?"

"Didn't the police think it was strange that it was unfinished?"

"Perhaps somewhat. But then I think they thought he suddenly decided to—ah—do it before he lost his nerve." She looked at him. "But you don't think so."

"No. Suicides finish notes, if they decide to write them. This one could have been a note about anything. If I remember correctly from the newspaper reports, Walter never mentioned taking his own life. Then again, very rarely would a suicide shoot himself in the heart. It's usually the head." Suzanne drew back and shuddered. "Sorry. I know it's hard for you to hear about all this."

"So what do you think really happened?" Suzanne asked in a voice came out in a whisper. "Are you saying you think he was murdered?"

"Perhaps. But the note bothers me. Why did your husband start to write it? Was he trying to tell you something when someone surprised him? Also, how could someone get that close to shoot him with his own gun?" Dave slowly shook his head from side to side. "Then there's the bag of money. We can be pretty sure that ties into this in some way."

"So what do we do now?"

"Well, there's a couple of things. Our ponytail friend is involved somehow. I can check him out. Then I have this carpet sample and the key from the fake rock." He felt the envelope in his jacket pocket. "If you agree, I can look into this. With more concrete evidence we can get a case to take to the police, should we decide to."

"Well, of course. Whoever did this has to be brought to justice!" Her eyes burned into his.

"Yes—we're agreed on that," he said firmly, spacing his words, trying to convince her of his intentions. "But I don't think you'll want to do that until we know more about the money." He paused, thinking how to phrase this. "It might be best to find the source of the money first, just in case it might reflect on your husband in some way."

"You think he stole it!" She was furious again.

"I didn't say that. But if we uncover something—uh—unusual,

maybe it can still be fixed." His voice trailed away awkwardly. Suzanne slowly nodded her head while looking at him hopefully. He went on. "Did the police find any other finger prints that you know of?"

"No. Detective Sohler told me the only fingerprints he found were Walter's. That's one of the things they based the suicide verdict on. Is that why they missed this evidence you just found?"

"Possibly. With the suicide note, they had no suspicions of anything else. Then again, maybe they were too involved with other more difficult cases." Dave went on. "Hmmm. Well, then there's the problem of tracing the money. If we can find out why your husband had that cash, we can learn more about his death, I'm sure."

"My God, this is awful." Suzanne's eyes filled with sad tears. "Where would Walter get money except from the bank? And yet Charles Rosenthal found all the accounts in order." She leaned toward Dave, her cloudy blue eyes beseeching. "Whatever you find out, you must tell me, not the authorities. I can't have Walter's reputation ruined. It's bad enough now with him a declared suicide. It certainly raises questions when a bank president commits suicide."

"Of course. I'll be very discreet," he said.

"I know I wasn't very nice to you in the beginning, but there's no one else to turn to." Her green eyes fastened on his brown ones. "Besides, you know all about police business and investigations. I'd be so grateful if you could help me with this."

"Sure," said Dave, trying to keep it light. "It's not as though I had a lot of other business to occupy my time lately." He smiled at her and glanced at his watch. "I guess I'd better be going," he said, although he had nothing to do for the rest of the afternoon. All this must have drained Suzanne, he thought. Better give her some rest and time to sort through everything he had told her. She was seeing him to the front door when suddenly she stopped.

"I've been so devastated by what you told me," she said quietly, "that I forgot something. Charles brought me a box of Walter's personal papers from the bank. They're here in the hall closet. I never got around to look at them. Maybe you could find some clue there that would help you unravel this mess."

"Maybe so. Why don't you call me when you feel like going through them?"

She surprised him. "How about tomorrow afternoon? I have a hair appointment at one o'clock, but I should be home by three."

"Okay. I'll call to make sure you're home." He paused. "By the way, the money is safe where it is. I think it would be a good idea to leave it there while we untangle this thing."

She nodded her head and suddenly held out her hand. "Partner," she said, half statement, half question. She managed a hint of a smile.

"Partner," he agreed, accepting her small graceful hand into the warm shelter of his own. The warmth began to spread elsewhere in his body. He said an abrupt goodbye and thanks for the coffee and started down the front walk to his car. Halfway there he stopped abruptly and turned.

She was still standing in the open doorway, like an uncertain wistful child. "Are you going to be all right?" he called.

He strained to hear her scared child-like voice. "I don't know," she said.

Dave kicked at an imaginary stone on the path. Damn. Why did he feel responsible for her hurt? It was her husband that was responsible for this mess, not himself.

"Call me if you need me," he said in an impersonal tone that contradicted his real feelings.

*　　*　　*

He turned abruptly and walked briskly to his car. On his way home, he drove slowly in the right lane while keeping one eye on the rear view mirror. Everyone else whizzed by him. After a few minutes, a familiar craving began in his dry mouth and spread to his stomach. Hell, it was early afternoon and already he needed a drink. Or several. After all, so far this day had been very stressful. A drink was certainly indicated to give a little support to someone like himself who had somehow agreed to unravel some very questionable circumstances. With not much to go on.

He had to trust his own brain and gut to give him the right signals along the way. That was the way it worked. One tiny bit of information leading to something else. Then the gut reactions as to what to discard and what to check out. You counted on breaks along the way, too. You had to believe you would get those breaks. Because without that hope you could never get started with any of this.

When he reached Division Street, he parked in front of the cleaners and retrieved his clean clothes. After putting them in his car, he locked it and started for the liquor store. What he needed was to relax this afternoon on his new bed with a few drinks and mindless TV. He went into the store and back to the counter that held the various brands of vodka. He picked up a half-gallon jug and started for the checkout. Halfway there he stopped, the handle of the jug swinging from the crook of his third finger. A strange thing happened. Abruptly his mind filled with images of Suzanne, small and trusting, counting on him for the answers. He swore a few choice words, and the clerk looked up, startled. Dave turned around and put the bottle back on the shelf.

"Shit," he said. He walked slowly to the rear refrigerated compartment and removed a six-pack of coke. "Shit," he said again.

When he parked the Stanza at the Romano's, there was no one about. Apparently, the ponytail was either still in Chicago or hadn't located Dave's new residence. And the Tail must have been withdrawn from Dave's official investigation. He went to the kitchen and spoke with Mrs. Romano who was putting a pan of brownies in the oven. He took a moment to absorb the cheerful scene of the bustling motherly figure wiping her hands on a flowery apron, speckled gray hair framed by the bright yellow curtains behind her. She smiled at him happily—this inventor of a heady mixture of delightful smells.

He suddenly realized that he hadn't had any lunch. She seemed to read his mind and offered him some bran muffins. He was soon eating several while she reheated coffee to go with them. He began to feel better. The hunger was satisfied and the craving for alcohol lessened. He went out to the hall with his coffee cup and placed a call to the Chicago police department.

"Hagerman here," said a weary voice.

Dave lowered his voice and measured his words. "This is a survey. Do dogs still love you?"

"WHAT? Who is this?"

"We understand dogs are crazy about you, and we want to know your secret."

"For God's sake—Dave?"

"Yeah. Guilty". They laughed, remembering past incidents in their Police Academy days when all canines ran from Paul Hagerman as if he had rabies.

"How the hell are you, Dave? I sure was sorry to hear about your trouble. Straightened out yet?"

"I'm not sure. Maybe. Anyway, I'm helping out a friend, and I need a little information."

"Sure. Anything."

"Last night a guy left Edgewood on the eight o'clock Amtrak to Chicago. He had no ticket, and he was stoned out of his mind. Can you check and see if he was booked? I need full ID and any record." Dave described the ponytail. Paul agreed to check and call back later in the afternoon.

Dave put a couple of dollars on the hall table for the call, picked up his cleaning from the hall tree, and went up to his room. About four-thirty Mrs. Romano's cheery voice floated up the stairs, calling him to the phone.

"His name is Cameron Castore—known as Cam," said Paul. "A punk. Some breaking and entering, simple assault, on parole since February. Twenty-two years old, high school dropout. From a good family—his father's a vice-president of the Edgewood Chair Company. Kicked him out when he was seventeen. Let's see—was married briefly to a Theda Krupnick."

Dave was busy making notes. "Current address?"

"He only gave his parent's address. Concord Drive Northwest. Twenty-eight sixty," said Paul. "I have the name of his parole officer. Matter of fact, he's the guy who got him released this morning."

"He came to Chicago?"

"No, he did it through our parole department. He seemed to think this guy was framed."

"What's this guy's name and address?"

"John Garrison, 26 Carlton Street in Edgewood." There was pause, and then Paul asked, "Well, Dave?"

"Well what?"

"Nothing. Anything more you want?"

"No," said Dave. "Thanks. So this punk is back in Edgewood by now?"

"I would think so. And I guess by the tone of your voice that you wish we had shipped him overseas."

"Exactly," said Dave.

*   *   *

At seven o'clock Dave left his room and headed for the deli. While he ate a Reuben and smoked a few cigarettes, he twirled some pieces of information around in his mind, hoping they would jell into a plan. Obviously, he had to locate Cam Castore before this jerk came after him again. In that case, Dave had a gut feeling there could be a really bad scene. Deadly, even. Frustration had probably lit a fuse in this guy that could blow up into hell-bent revenge. Right at this moment, the vengeful ponytail-person could be lurking about. At a quarter to eight, he paid his bill and left by the back door, which exited into an alley.

He crossed the side street and ended up behind the church. He circled it and entered with a group of people from the street, following them down the stairs to the meeting room. Tom, whom he remembered from the first AA meeting, came up to him with a smile.

"Dave," he said, and pumped Dave's hand. "It's good to have you back."

"It's—uh—good to be here," said Dave automatically, and wondered briefly if it really was.

But after the meeting started and some of the personal experiences connected with his own, he began to feel responsive and also amazed. The speakers, male and female, were gut-wrenchingly honest. Traditionally used to hiding emotions, the men hung their heads, stammered, and but finally told their stories to the audience. My God, Dave thought, he could never get up in front of a group and expose the dirt of his life to a bunch of strangers.

They recounted their chilling stories to "keep the memory ever green." It was important to remember the terrible times to protect the precious sobriety born of painful self honesty. And out of these ashes, they were rebuilding lives in brave new ways while mending the relationships that alcohol had destroyed. As he listened, Dave admired their courage, the tough faith they had found.

At the end of the meeting, he sought out Tom. It was time to make a start. He didn't know if he could make it, but after all he had heard tonight, he knew he was no different from those who had succeeded. He asked Tom if he would be his sponsor. Tom agreed and shook his hand. They got more coffee and Tom picked up literature for Dave from a table in the rear. After they talked a while about the program, Dave left to walk the side streets back to the Romano's house.

13

By midnight on Thursday, Theda was distraught, worried, confused, and generally out of her mind. For almost two hours she sat immobile in a chair in her apartment living room, still in the clothes she had worn to the railway station. She had waited there for Cam until ten o'clock, unable to believe that he would not reappear. She couldn't believe it even now. Even after all this time had passed.

Cam never showed up again. There could be only one explanation. He had scammed her again and taken off with the money. Tears ran down her face, and sobs stuck in her throat. Just when she thought things would work out and she would be free of this mess, everything was worse than ever. Cam had the money, and she was left here with her guilt and the constant piercing fear that she would someday be found out.

She had waited in the car for about an hour, eagerly scanning every person leaving the station entrance. The scary feeling in her gut kept growing until finally she knew that Cam had somehow vanished. Even after she felt this was true, she got out of her car and paced up and down on the sidewalk, feeling that activity on her part might make Cam materialize.

Finally, she went into the station and walked the corridors, pushing by people and walking next to where the lockers were. Maybe Cam was sick in the men's room. She waited for about ten minutes, leaning against the opposite wall, staring at the word 'Men'. Not a sign of Cam.

When she went out to her car, she had a parking ticket. She got into the driver's seat, put her head down on the steering wheel and sobbed in frustration. Then she lifted her head, peered once more at the station through wet eyes, and drove home.

Now exhaustion began creeping through her body while her mind reluctantly gave up its exercise in futility. She managed to push herself out of her chair and go into her bedroom to get ready for bed. The telephone rang. It was Cam. Her heart jumped in relief. It was going to be all right.

"Oh, my God," she said. "Where are you? I've been worried sick."

His voice sounded strange. His words were slurred and strung out. "I'm in Chicago. In the slammer." Oh, my God. It wasn't all right after all. It was worse. She tried to stay calm. At least he hadn't skipped with the money. But then again, he must have been picked up by the police WITH the money. That could be much worse. "What happened?"

"I was jacked-up by Monaco and some other dude. They gave me a shot of something and put me on the train to Chicago."

"But why are you in jail?"

"I had no damn ticket. Besides, I was fried. So the fucking conductor turned me in. The fuzz grabbed me when I got off."

"Now what?"

"Looks like I'll be here a couple of days. They found out I'm on parole. Now I'm in violation because I left Edgewood."

This was terrible, but suddenly Theda thought of something else. "You lost the money, didn't you?" She asked sadly.

"Hell, it's not my fault! Quit sniveling. How would you like to be in jail? Besides, I feel lousy. I'm sick." There was a pause. Then Cam said, "Listen, I've got to hang up. This is my one phone call. Do me a favor. Call John Garrison, my parole officer. Tell him what happened. Not about the bread, but about these guys jumping me and shooting me up. Have him call the city jail here. Maybe he can get me out." He gave Theda the number and hung up.

*   *   *

Suzanne took another aspirin with another sip of coffee. She propped her elbows on the kitchen table and massaged her forehead with the tips of her fingers as if this would control the thoughts that wanted to fly off in all directions. She moaned his name over and over—Walter, Walter—as if this would sharpen her understanding. Her husband for over twenty years was now a stranger, the kind of person who was apparently involved in strange activities with strange people. How could she not have known?

She got up suddenly and went to the living room to pick up a recent photo album from the long library table behind the sofa. She sat down with it in her lap and began to look intently at every picture Walter was in. And even more so at the pictures of Walter and her together. Viewing these had always given her the pleasure of reliving some special moments. Now, as she turned the pages, she saw strangers, impersonal people posing as if for a magazine.

There was Walter, smiling, his arm around her—was he really more of an actor playing a part than her husband? Was the loving way he seemed to look at her maybe just a trick of sun and shadow? As she turned the pages, she saw that Walter's expression was the same in each picture. Always his head turned slightly toward her, his welcome-you-at-the-bank smile in place. Well rehearsed. Playing a part. Stiff. His body stood at attention, she realized. The self-contained bearing of an officer on important maneuvers. Secretive ones.

So, she hadn't known him at all. At least not during the last few months. But if he was unhappy, perhaps longing for something else, why didn't he come to her about it? She looked around her elegant living room and got a glimmer of an answer. She was the one completely hooked on the proper, elegant, materialistic life-style. Always the perfect surroundings, the proper wines and food, the appropriate dress, accepted manners.

She suddenly remembered an old movie from TV a year or two ago: "Craig's Wife." In it, Rosalind Russell was a housewife who had a greater attachment to her home than to her husband. Was there a parallel here? In the early years of their marriage, the Wilkins' common goal was to establish a beautiful home. Somehow in the passage of time, maintaining and improving the beautiful stage setting became more important to her than what was happening—or not happening—between the actors.

But she had always loved Walter; surely, he knew that. After all, she was the image of the perfect wife as he himself had ordained it. If—and it now seemed more than likely—Walter was unhappy in some way, it may have been impossible for him to ask her to sacrifice her way of life for some substitute. To the debilitating emotions of grief, confusion, and fear she had been carrying around with her since his death, she now added a new one. Guilt.

She had felt a particular closeness to Walter that she assumed was also the way he felt about her. Now it seemed that this was probably not true. She had given him all her love unconditionally, but Walter's passion for her had dwindled the past few years. She had not been too concerned, knowing that being in love does not last forever, but real loving does. However, before she hardly realized it, Walter seemed content to forget all about making love. She made efforts to rekindle his passion, risking rejection and subjecting herself to embarrassing moments. Memories of these times now spread the hurt deep within her.

The telephone rang. "It's Dave. Monaco." As if she wouldn't remember.

"Yes. Well—hello."

"Just wanted to make sure you're okay. It guess it's been a tough day for you."

She sighed, almost a sob. "It's definitely not been one of my best."

"I'm afraid there may be some tougher ones to come. Are you sure you want to go on with this? We could go to the police right now, and you would be out of it. There might be some way we could get them to hush up the money part of it—you know, get them to replace it. Wherever it belongs."

"No, I'm more scared of that than anything. If Walter did something wrong, I want to try to make it right. I feel I owe him that much." Even as she said this last part, she wasn't completely sure it was true.

"Sure. Well, I'll see you this afternoon," said Dave.

"Come around three," she said and hung up.

Suzanne picked up the album again and studied a close-up of

Walter, his trademark smile aimed at the camera. She leaned down and tried to peer into his eyes behind the rimmed glasses, as if she could learn somehow what went on in his mind. During their last few months together she had convinced herself that Walter still loved her, but it was the male menopause syndrome that had diminished their relationship. So, she tried hard to love him an extra amount and be patient.

Now she laughed aloud at her stupidity. She had been duped, conned, completely fooled by her conservative, straight, trustworthy, prudent, community-leader husband. In fact, it now appeared that Walter Wilkins could be an embezzler. My God, Suzanne thought, how can you live with someone for such a long time and not know him at all? This was dangerous thinking.

There were strange things going on here, the truth of what really happened still shrouded in an unpleasant aura. Maybe there was a good explanation for the money. She shouldn't jump to conclusions. But her brain refused to stop there, and raced ahead to grab at some other repulsive possibilities. Maybe Walter was writing her a note to say he was leaving. If that were true, would it be with another woman? But in that case, who would shoot him? Maybe a jealous boyfriend?

That's it, she thought, and sat quietly for a moment. It had to be the pony-tailed young man. Otherwise, how would he know about the money? Walter was probably set up by some girl and the ponytail. Somehow, that made her feel better. Walter was not completely at fault. Some young thing threw herself at him because of his position at the bank and worked out a plan with her boyfriend.

She remembered the key and felt a sudden chill. The boyfriend would be after it again, maybe attacking Dave and maybe putting two and two together and coming here to search her house. She got up and went into the den to slide out the copy of Shakespeare's plays from the bookshelf and feel the key lying in place behind it. The existence of the bag of money was a problem needing to be dealt with immediately.

Mr. Monaco would be back this afternoon, and they would

make that decision. It was good to have him in her corner. She sighed in relief. All this was too much to handle alone. And he was a man with expertise in matters like this. A good man. I can trust him, she thought. And strangely, I like him. He's not like anyone I've every known before—he's what my mother called common— a blue-collar type, a little clumsy, ill-at-ease, not many social graces. But I'm glad he's on my side.

Before she went out into her garden to cut some daffodils, she had one last thought on the subject. "He has lovely soft brown eyes." Another thought tried to intrude, but she dismissed it. The brief touch of his arm around her shoulder had made her feel warm and safe—for a moment or two.

Dave was on her doorstep promptly at three. Just back from the beauty shop, Suzanne opened the door dressed in a silky kelly-green shirt tucked into off-white slacks, her hair shiny and swinging. The blush on her cheeks looked natural. She glanced up at him in an appealing shy way with eyes that were greener with the same color on her eyelids.

He couldn't help staring. But it was hardest to keep his eyes off her mouth. Outlined in coral, it was just the right size. And provocatively curled up at the ends. "Wow," Dave said to himself. To her he said lamely, "Your hair looks nice."

"Thank you." Her eyes widened, and she gave him a little smile.

Maybe old Walter didn't notice things like that, Dave thought. She led the way into her gleaming laboratory kitchen. Dave stopped just inside the door. "Wow." he said again. This time aloud.

"I'm a serious cook," she said. Then her voice clouded over. "Or I used to be."

"That's a real accomplishment. As someone who appreciates food," Dave put his hand on his rounded stomach, "I can swear to that."

She brightened. "You really think so? I've been thinking lately how I've wasted my life."

"Of course you haven't. Good wives and homemakers support the structure of our society." His eyes were puzzled as if he couldn't believe he said that.

She waved a hand at the box of Walter's papers from the bank, which was on the marble and chrome kitchen table. "Would you like a drink before we start? Wine, beer, scotch?"

"Do you have a coke?"

"Of course. I guess I just took you for a beer or scotch man. Actually, most of our friends drank scotch so I did too. I wonder why now. I really can't stand the taste." She made a face and they both laughed.

"Drinking is very overrated," Dave said lightly. But his eyes were serious.

She opened the largest stainless steel refrigerator-freezer he had ever seen outside a restaurant kitchen and took out two cans of coke and a container of ice. She fixed two glasses and then sat down across the table from him.

"Before we get started, I have some information," said Dave. "I have a name for the pony-tailed character—Cameron Castore. An old friend in Chicago helped me out. This Castore is a punk, has done time, and is now on parole. I know who his parents are, but I don't have a current address for this guy as yet. Shouldn't be too hard to get."

"And then what?"

"Hopefully then we'll find out more about him. Information that will help us find out if he had some connection to your husband."

"What about this Cameron's parole officer? Couldn't he help us?"

"I'm not sure. If they believed any of this guy's story in Chicago, he might have fingered me as the one who loaded him. That busts my credibility."

"So what do we do when we find out where he lives?"

He smiled at her. "I'll probably tail him. His habits could tell me a lot. And I have the name of his ex-wife."

"Oh, good. That should help. But what about the money, Dave? I'm really worried about it being safe."

"I think it's in about as safe a place as it can be right now. Our best plan may be to find out where it belongs as quickly as possible and then arrange to get it there."

"How do we accomplish that?"

"We can hire armored motor delivery to transport it. It'll be perfectly safe. We'll never have to go near it."

"Oh, that's a great idea! Thank goodness you know about things like that."

"Well, we'll see. First let's go through all these papers and see what we can find out."

There were fewer things in the box from Walter's office than Suzanne had expected. She and Dave emptied the items onto the kitchen table and spread them out. There were two pictures: one of Walter and her on their last vacation to Bermuda and the other a happy studio portrait of Walter and Penny taken for Father's Day last year. Suzanne scooped them up with only a cursory glance and took them to a counter to lay them face down.

There was a Rolodex which Dave took an instant to flip through. Business numbers, professional numbers, a few names to check later. Then Walter's personal appointment book. Business expense receipts. Employee evaluation forms. Interoffice memos. Lists of clients and account numbers. A box of index cards separated by tabs—apparently, notes for speeches Walter gave on financial planning. A file folder labeled "Maude Hills."

"Is that THE Maude Hills?" asked Dave.

"Yes, the old actress. She was a good friend of Walter's family. A few years ago she went into a nursing home, and she gave Walter her power of attorney."

Dave moved the other items out of the way and spread the contents of the file out on the table. It appeared to be mostly receipts, for things like taxes, insurance payments, housekeeping services, plumbing and heating repairs, new storm windows, landscaping. He went through them again. Except for the tax and insurance payments, which appeared to be quarterly, all the other receipts were for payments beginning the previous November. Why such a sudden flurry of attention to the upkeep of Maude Hills' estate?

"Look here," he said to Suzanne and laid the receipts out in date order. "It's as if Miss Hills suddenly decided to upgrade her estate. Did Walter mention any of this to you?"

"Not that I can recall." She frowned. "As a matter of fact, every time I asked about her condition, Walter would say it was deteriorating. She spoke to him sometimes about going home, but he seemed to feel she would never make it."

"Maybe she was getting ready to sell the property and had to make some repairs."

"Well, perhaps, although he never mentioned that."

"Wait a minute." Dave picked up three other receipts from the table. "What about these? Here's a bill from the Dover Furniture Company: one sectional, $2500; a breakfront, $3000; two tables, $1500; and arm chairs, $1500. Total $8500." He stared at Suzanne.

"What are you thinking?" she asked.

"I don't know yet." He held a receipt in each hand and his eyes swung back and forth between them.

"What else?" She leaned forward.

"Why would an old lady order $5000 worth of stereo components? And a whole roomful of exercise equipment? Totaling around $10,000, I might add."

"Oh, my Lord. I don't believe this."

"Is this Miss Hills senile?"

"Oh, no, not as far as I know. At least Walter never mentioned it. You know, she's still a celebrity. None of the tabloids has ever hinted that there was anything wrong with her mind. I went out to the home with Walter about six months ago, and she was bright—even witty, as I remember."

"Well, there's a lot of craziness going on here. I think your husband as her attorney-in-fact had an obligation to talk her out of this spending."

Suzanne's voice was defensive. "I'm sure he tried to, but she's a strong-willed person."

Dave picked up some other papers and held them out to her. "There's more, Suzanne. A bill for a new roof. New siding, brickwork, landscaping, interior painting. Expensive vases from an antique shop." He paused. "One is totally unreal. Repairs on a car." This last had the recent date of February 26 this year. Walter had died on March 1. Dave looked at Suzanne's face, white with strain, her eyes showing the hurt of struggling with the acceptance of Walter's deceit. He turned aside and took a drink of his coke, silent while he gave her time to compose herself.

She was shuffling the bills back and forth in her hands, her smooth forehead now laced with lines above the disbelief in her eyes. "Walter could never do anything like this. It just wasn't in his makeup."

"Do you have a telephone book handy?"

Suzanne went to a shiny hi-tech desk in the corner of the kitchen and pulled a telephone book from a drawer. She passed it to Dave without a word and sat down again across from him.

He flipped it opened and began checking. "Nothing for a Dover Furniture Company," he said.

"What's the telephone number?" asked Suzanne. Dave recited it from the business letterhead. Suzanne went back to her desk and dialed. Someone answered, and she asked for the furniture company. After a moment she asked, "How long have you had this number?" and then, "I see. Thank you." Her voice trembled. Dave looked at her expectantly as she moved slowly back to her chair. "Someone else has had that number for 20 years," she said.

"Well," Dave said lamely, "that still doesn't prove something's wrong. Could be a printing error on the bill." It was a ridiculous, impossible supposition, but he had a very strong desire to hold back the proof of Walter's stealing as long as possible so Suzanne could grasp it gradually.

She sat with her hands in her lap, her head down as if she would lose control if she lifted it to look at him. "Look up another one," she said finally.

"Okay. Let's try Maxwell's Roofing and Siding Company." Dave found the page and ran his finger up and down uselessly. Then he flipped to the yellow pages and looked there. Finally, he glanced up, shrugging his shoulders.

"What's the number?" she asked. He read it from the receipt, and she went to the phone once more and dialed. Again, she talked to a residential telephone subscriber.

She sat down and they looked at each other for a moment, comingling conclusions in their glances. Dave ruffled through some papers. "There are quite a few more here."

After a while, she asked, "But where did those letterheads come from? They look so real."

"My guess is they were computer-generated. You know, with desktop publishing there are all kinds of software programs that will produce practically anything you want. And certainly the bank has work stations."

She nodded and then spoke slowly, working it out in her mind. "So—you think Walter wrote checks from Maude's account to these fake companies and then cashed them himself?"

"It looks that way. In his position at the bank, who would question a double endorsement? Probably signed as an officer of the bogus company and then with his own name. I have no idea how he got away with this. But then again, there were no personnel from these companies to investigate anything. And as Walter was handling all of Miss Hill's accounts, all the cancelled checks came back to him."

She sat crumpled in her chair. "I guess I was foolishly thinking that somehow Walter's records would vindicate him, and there would be some other explanation for the bag with the money." A sad piece of a laugh escaped. "Like maybe he had collected it for a good cause."

Dave reached out and covered Suzanne's pale cold little hand with his warm substantial one. "Go ahead and cry, if you feel like it," he said gently. "I'll understand."

Her hand stayed in his until she caught her breath. "I'm okay." Her words jerked. "It just takes some time to get used to this."

"I know. It's hard when people you trust screw you." He hadn't meant to use such language, but somehow his own situation got into the act.

"I think I'll have a cup of tea," she said, getting up and keeping her face averted. She filled a pint-measuring cup with water and set it in the microwave to heat.

"I think I'd like one too," he said without looking at her. My God, had he said that? It had been a thousand years since he had tasted tea.

"Sure." She put tea bags into two mugs and stood until the buzzer sounded and she could add the boiling water.

She set the mugs down. "Sugar?"

"No. This is fine." He tried to find a smile that would say everything is going to be all right. But there was no way he could promise that. To his surprise, the hot tea was fragrant and good. A sip of comfort for the wounded inner core.

"Maude Hills is out a lot of money," Suzanne said suddenly. "My God, this is so awful." She lowered her head over her teacup and a tear splashed onto the tabletop.

Dave couldn't think of anything comforting to say. Finally, he reached over and patted her arm. "Look, we can't be absolutely sure until we verify the absence of these purchases. We should get out to the Hills house and check it out. The roof and landscaping for instance." He tapped a finger against his mug. "I think first of all we should pay Maude Hills a visit and get some answers. And it would be good if you can get her to appoint you her new attorney-in-fact."

"Why? I don't know anything about such things."

"No matter. I don't know how we're going to replace the money yet, but we may need that authority to do so when the time comes."

"Well—"

Suzanne seemed ready to collapse, tear-stained lines on an ashen face, streaked eyeliner over heavy lids. Enough for today. He stood up. "I'd better go," he said. "Tomorrow being Sunday, would that be a good day to visit Miss Hills?"

"Yes, it might be." She rose slowly as if it took her last bit of energy. Dave stood aside at the doorway to the hall, and she passed in front of him as if sleepwalking. As he looked down on her, an ache crept into his heart.

At the door, she raised her head and looked into his eyes and his heart broke. He—big tough Dave Monaco—who had seen every kind of degradation, human tragedy, hate, wickedness, the casual wasting of life, was now touched by this little lady as deeply as by anything else in his turbulent life. Their glances built an invisible thread between them, which hung silently in the air and blotted out all ugliness of this day. Without thinking, he opened his big arms wide and she came into them to rest her head against his chest. He placed his own face against her lovely shimmering hair and lost his senses in the fragrant smell of her. Then he felt himself getting aroused and held her gently from him. What on earth was he thinking of? He tried to find an impersonal smile to cover up the surprising way she affected him.

"I guess you needed a hug," he said lightly. "I'll call you tomorrow morning." Before he did something he might regret, he opened the door and stepped into the patter of an April-rain.

*   *   *

Theda got a call from Cam early Saturday afternoon and left work to pick him up at the railway station. He was waiting on the sidewalk, and she hardly recognized him. The bloodshot eyes of a madman blazed from their sunken niches. A half-inch growth of bristly wheat-like whiskers covered a white taut face. He teetered back and forth and seemed likely to lose his balance any moment.

"You're sick," she said, after he finally made it into the car. She reached over to give him a sympathetic pat. It was like patting a snarling cat. He slammed her arm against the steering wheel and hissed at her through drooling clenched teeth.

"You bitch—you goddamn bitch. Why I ever took up with you again I'll never know. You and your stupid goddamn schemes. Look what you've done to me. I almost got thrown back in the slammer for good."

Theda slumped down in the seat, biting her trembling lower lip and whimpering. Then she started the car and drove off. Neither said a word on the way back to the coffee shop.

She parked the car and heard a click. A quick flash of silver and Cam's thin fingers suddenly held the long thin blade against her throat. She gulped air laced with fear and thought she might never breathe again. Then his wild laugh broke the spell. "Surprise! A little something I bought in Chicago. No, I'm not going to use it on you, my love, though I'm mighty tempted. I still need you because you owe me a lot of money. If I can't get it from that fucking Monaco, you may have to pull a few tricks on him." His laugh screamed at her. "That shouldn't be too hard for you—he's not bad looking."

She said the wrong thing. "You shouldn't have that knife."

He began screaming again. "What's this kind of crap! You don't tell me what to do—ever. You got that straight! Now get the fuck out of this car 'cause I'm going after Monaco. I'm going to make him a hell of a lot sicker than he made me."

Cam tried to leave a little rubber on the pavement, but the old blue mustang grumbled and strained. He thought of his beautiful red Firebird and nausea rose in his throat. My God, how could things be so bad? If he felt like crap, he still had to show up at his job at the container company on Monday. His pal Joe who worked in personnel couldn't cover for him any longer. Then there was his parole officer. He'd be on top of Cam more than ever after Friday night's fiasco.

He drove up Division Street and stopped by the Deli. There was a sign in the upstairs apartment: "To Rent." Damn. He went into the deli to inquire, but it was no dice. They were evasive. He sat down with a cup of coffee and thought of possible moves. No use getting mad all over again. He needed a clear head. Possible scenarios flashed through his head.

Maybe Monaco returned the money to the Wilkins widow. Then maybe again he was keeping it for himself. You never knew about a former policeman. What the hell happened to make him a 'former'?

His Reeboks squished through a few puddles on his way to the Mustang when he remembered about his Firebird. He splashed through a few more puddles to the corner pay phone while water began to drip off the ends of his ponytail. He called the security people at the airport and then the police. He waited endlessly for people to check elusive files while streaks of water raced down the window in front of him. Sorry, fella, no news yet. We're working on it. Do we have your right telephone number? We'll call you. Cam's rotten mood intensified. He slammed the doors of the booth into an accordion pleat and went back to his car.

So now what? He had no idea where Monaco might be. Maybe miles from here. But he used to live here above the deli, and he probably had friends in the area. And habits were strong. If he used to eat here all the time, he might still do so. He decided he might as well hang out here for a while.

He went back into the deli and ordered a corned beef sandwich to go and a big cup of coffee. They sold magazines, so he picked up a copy of Playboy magazine. Then he went back to the car, drove it around the corner, and finally parked it in the first space in the preceding block. In front of the church. He had a good view of the deli area from here.

He mused about Theda for a second. She could find her way home from work as best she could. He had something more important to do. He was going to settle the score with Monaco. Now. Tonight. It was all a nasty business. What the hell was he doing in the middle of it?

*   *   *

All the way home from Suzanne's, Dave asked himself that question. Hey, he could have suggested she hire a regular PI. Turn over the evidence—the fake rock and key, the blood sample, the suspicious invoices—and let someone else worry about finding the solutions. So why didn't he? He skirted that question in his mind with the answer already lying there, his subconscious scurrying around finding ways to cover it up. Honesty finally forced it to the surface. He was attracted to Suzanne. It might even be more than that. Being with her released familiar feelings of long ago, both wanted and unwanted.

She had definitely touched something inside him. And that fact got him in over his head. "You damn fool," he groaned as he chugged along on the beltway. "Now you've promised to do the impossible. Put the money back—if you can figure out where it belongs. Keep Miss Hills from learning the truth—if it is the truth. Find out what really happened to Walter Wilkins—if he didn't actually commit suicide. So why is Castore involved in all of this?"

All these thoughts ran back and forth in his mind. Then the chilling, most important one of all crept to the surface. His biggest responsibility was to keep Suzanne from danger.

Dave climbed the outside stairs to his room about five thirty. His head ached, and his insides craved their usual sedation. The cocktail hour was always the worst time of the day. He hung his corduroy sport coat in the closet, then reached in the pocket and removed the plastic bags containing the key from the fake rock and the darkened carpet fibers. He put them in a sock in his underwear drawer, took an aspirin, and flung himself on his bed.

He twitched inside and out—thought of going around to the deli and getting some coffee, but he needed more than that. The way he felt now, if he went out the front door, the liquor store would pull him across the street like a magnet. Reason and need battled inside him, and temptation had only to crook a little finger. He tried to fight it off by facing the truth. One drink always led to another and then another. He owed it to Suzanne to think clearly tomorrow when they continued their investigation at the nursing home.

With an effort, he sat up, fished a card from his wallet, and went downstairs to the phone. The phone rang on and on. "Please," he mumbled. It was almost a prayer. Finally, Tom answered.

"It's Dave," he said, and didn't know how to go on. How do you ask for help when you've never done it before?

"Cocktail time is the pits," said Tom, as if reading Dave's mind. "Hold on and I'll be right there. It's around the corner, next block down from the church?"

"Yeah", said Dave and gave the address. He had sent for the cavalry, and they were on their way. He went to his room for his windbreaker and then returned to the chair by the phone to wait. He was afraid to move. If he stood up, his feet might carry him out the front door and down the street. He heard the Romanos talking in the kitchen and hoped they would stay there. This was not a good time for idle conversation.

The minute the doorbell rang, he was out of his chair, calling out, "It's for me. I'll get it," while opening the door.

"Hey, take it easy," Tom said, looking into Dave's face through his wire-rimmed glasses. "It's going to be okay. I'm going to help you."

It was an openhearted statement. They got into Tom's car and drove to a quiet little restaurant in one of the beltline malls. "You need good food," said Tom. "It helps during a time like this. You see, alcohol destroys a lot of vitamins." So, Dave had a steak, baked potato, crunchy broccoli, and a salad.

While they ate, he began to feel better. When Tom asked questions about his life, Dave surprised himself by responding openly.

"Don't hide anything," said Tom. "It's best to get all the shit out. Also all those feelings that go with it." He brought up some violent memories of his own past life and told of the devastation his addiction had caused his loved ones. Factually, unemotionally. He was a man rebuilding a life in present moments.

During dessert, Dave got a shock. Tom had been a physician, an M.D. A professional man who had a successful career. But gradually his addiction to alcohol took over his life, leading to a malpractice suit and the loss of his license. Now he had a job as a counselor in a rehab program. Dave could hardly believe that the bright, intelligent, together person across from him had ever suffered through such a nightmare. Tom's journey out of despair was reassuring and inspiring. As he talked, Dave began to sense the possibility of a similar path for himself. Tom kept emphasizing, "One day at a time," and "trust your higher power." Dave hadn't done much thinking about God in the last few years. It was comforting to know that He was active in other people's lives and apparently just waiting for a sign from Dave to give a little help to him also.

Maybe another time Dave could talk about his suspension and the false accusations. For now, the words rolled around in his head, but refused to form sentences. When they left the restaurant, it was seven-thirty and already semi-dark. A brisk wind twirled bits of trash along the curb. They pulled up the collars of their jackets and hurried to the car.

"And now to the meeting," stated Tom, giving Dave no chance to refuse. There was no danger of that. At this point, he would have followed Tom anywhere.

*   *   *

There was an empty parking place in front of the deli, and Cam idly watched a strange foreign two-seater pull into it. Two men got out and started walking toward him. The streetlights were on, and when they passed under the one at the corner of the side street, Cam said, "Holy shit," and sat up straight to get a better look. One of the guys was Monaco. Jesus, what luck. He slid back down in his seat as the two men ambled by his car and turned up the walk to the church entrance. The sign on the church billboard read, "AA Meeting, 8 pm."

Cam grinned. His blood ran fast and warm. "Yeah, get sober, Monaco," he said to himself as he watched Dave enter the sanctuary. "You're gonna need all your smarts later on when I jump you." He ran his fingers over the switchblade in his pocket. Then he huddled down in his sweatshirt to rest and wait.

After the meeting, Dave and Tom stood for a few minutes in front of the church. "It was a good evening," Dave said simply. "And thanks for dinner." They shook hands.

"Give you a ride home?"

"No thanks. I'll just slip down the alley by the deli, around the corner, and I'm there."

Later on, Dave cussed himself out for not being more alert. Pretty stupid of an ex-cop to let his guard down. Especially when he knew he was in danger. But his thoughts were on the evening, his new friend, and the great group of people he had just left. Suzanne's face wafted in and out of his musings. It was still a blustery evening and the wind whistled down the alley, dancing empty drink cans about and rattling the covers of trash containers. Dave pulled the parka collar up around the back of his neck. He wrapped his arms about himself, not bothering to zip up the front of the windbreaker. He would be home soon.

He never heard Cam come up behind him. Suddenly a body bumped against him with knees slamming into the backs of his own. Dave slumped, and his body sagged forward. His flailing arms were pinned to his side by two long ones that wound like wire around his upper body. Immediately Dave knew who this was although he couldn't see Cam's face. While he considered his predicament, some crazy thoughts popped into his head. Cam was not the gangling weakling he had thought. He's been working out, Dave decided. Then he heard the snap of a switchblade next to his right ear. The next instant a ribbon of cold steel pressed against his throat.

"Don't move," Cam advised. Dave had no such intention.

"You try to break away, and I'll get you in the back. I can throw this knife like a javelin." There was no reason to doubt this statement. "Now where the hell is it?"

"Is what?"

"Damn you, Monaco. Don't give me that crap, or I'm going to cut you in little pieces. Maybe I will anyway." His voice stabbed Dave's eardrum. "One way or another I'm gonna get that fucking key. Understand? I don't care what I have to do to get it, understand?" He tightened his grip and Dave could only gurgle in reply, paralyzed by the feel of the knife blade against his skin. "That property belongs to me, and if you don't deliver, maybe I'll have a little fun with that cute little blonde, Mrs. Wilkins. I have a funny feeling she might know something about this." Cam's voice lowered to a snarl. "You think you're so fuckin' smart, loading me and planting me on that fuckin' train. I'm gonna take care of you for that. A few cuts on your gorgeous face, and your little bitch will kiss you off."

Dave's mind was a roller coaster, racing toward a solution. He mumbled, trying not to move his lips or throat more than necessary. "I'd like to help you out, but the truth is, I've turned this business over to the police. Haven't they called on you yet?"

Cam's hot breath hissed in his ear. "Damn you to hell. What do you think I am, some goddamn amateur? I want that key and I want it now." Cam was desperate and determined. He slid the razor-sharp blade an inch across Dave's neck, and Dave felt warm blood begin to drip slowly down his throat.

"Damn," thought Dave. This punk is making me really mad. "I don't have it," he said. "Feel free to search me."

"No, you don't," said Cal. "I don't fall for that old trick." In a flash, he transferred the knife to the back of Dave's neck. "Now, ya either throw the key on the ground, or tell me how I can get it. If you don't level with me, you can be damn sure I'll be back to cut you into little pieces and feed your body parts to the lions at the zoo. I'll cut Mrs. Wilkins, too. On her face."

Dave was wondering how to respond when he heard the faint sound of crunching footsteps mixed with the swishes of gusty wind. Cam's body stiffened against him, and his arms loosened as his head whirled to check the alley. But before Dave could move, the narrow thin blade slid like a buttered knife up under the windbreaker and into Dave's right side. The moment froze as Cam's voice hammered in his ear and then trailed away. "This is a sample. You've got until Wednesday to get me the key. I'll find you."

Dave stood for a moment, confused, denying what seemed to have happened. Then the pain and blood seemed to break loose at the same time, to co-mingle in a whirling pit of dark confusion.

A strange, but welcome, weakness began covering him like a blanket. He sank to his knees, his eyes lifeless and unseeing. Then he pitched forward on his face and lay still on the cold damp alleyway.

*   *   *

By noon on Sunday, Suzanne hadn't heard from Dave. She decided to call the Romano's number. Mrs. Romano's voice fluttered with emotion. "Mr. Monaco is in the hospital. He was hurt last night."

"WHAT?"

"Yes, apparently some mugger knifed him in an alley. Fortunately, some undercover cop found him right after and got him to the hospital. He's at John Ball Memorial." She sounded on the verge of tears. "Such a nice man. What is this world coming to?"

Suzanne's head spun. Some mugger indeed. It could only have been that Castore person. But why would he try to kill Dave, who was his only lead to the key?

"How is he? It's not serious, is it?"

"It doesn't seem to be. He was lucky. He's going to be all right."

All the way to the hospital, Suzanne said little prayers for Dave's recovery. The crazy case they were working on faded in significance. It was only important for Dave the person to get well.

When Dave struggled into consciousness on Sunday morning, he was lying on his stomach and very much aware that his right side was bandaged. He raised his head as much as possible to look around and glimpsed a white coat standing at the foot of the bed writing something on a clipboard. He lowered his face to the pillow and felt the adhesive pull where his neck was bandaged. "How do you feel this morning?" asked the doctor.

"How do you think? Aren't you the doctor?"

He was, and he was blunt. "You drink a lot, don't you?"

What the hell! "Nice greeting, doc," said Dave.

"Well, I thought you'd like to know what happened. You see, your liver was distended to the degree that it pushed your kidney aside. You were lucky. The knife slipped under the margin of the rib cage and missed your organs. If your liver had been normal and in the correct position, the knife would have sliced your kidney like a ripe tomato."

After the doctor left, Dave lay quietly, reflecting on the strangeness of life. His affection for alcohol had saved his life. Now there's a strange one for you. He went back to sleep.

When he woke again, there was a man sitting in a chair beside him. It took him a minute to recognize the shadowy figure who had dodged his footsteps. It was the Tail. Here now as a real person, the long face relaxed and amiable, laugh lines around eyes and mouth. He was all in tan: trousers, bomber jacket, sallow face.

As his image became clearer, Dave saw that the eyes were serious and the mouth firm. Dave could only see his visitor out of his right eye. His other one stayed buried in his pillow while he lay on his left side. He tried to move but the bandage seemed to go completely around him and made it difficult. The upper part of his body felt like one big bruise.

The Tail seemed to sense Dave's questions. He sat forward. "You got knifed. Then you fell on your face and got dirt and gravel in it."

Dave lay quietly, his brain darting around in the remembered pieces of last night's incident. "You were following me," he stated, peering at the Tail with his one good eye. The visitor nodded. "I think you saved my life."

"Possibly."

"I'm very grateful." Dave paused. "I think." They smiled wanly at one another. "I thought you'd given up on me," Dave said.

"That's what we wanted you to think."

"Hmm. I also think you're good at your job. I had no idea. Anyway, it was lucky for me you didn't stop tailing me."

"You didn't make it easy. You were pretty good at giving me the slip."

After a moment, Dave asked, "What's your name?"

"Elmer Botsworth."

"ELMER?"

The Tail looked him straight in the eye. No smile. "They call me Peep."

"I would say that suits you better."

"I didn't get it on this job. I got it in school. Got teased so much because of my name, I used to sneak around getting the dirt on the other kids." A corner of his mouth twisted. "Kinda prepared me for my life's work."

Dave was surprised by the sudden confidence. But when someone saves your life, isn't it true that a kind of special bond develops? "So how long have you been an undercover cop?"

"I'm not. I'm a P. I."

Dave struggled to move his head for a better look. "What? I thought you were working for the Prosecutor's office. Trying to get the goods on me."

Peep shook his head. "I'm working for a private party. You know I can't divulge my client."

Dave tried to nod. What the hell. Was someone else mixed up in all of this?

He smiled weakly. "At least I know your client didn't hire you to waste me."

Peep leaned back in the visitor chair. "I've got a hunch you're working on some kind of a case of your own. That's okay; I'm not interested in that. But this guy who knifed you. I saw enough to know he's the same punk who's been hanging around the deli. I get the impression you know him." He waited. Dave said nothing.

"I've given a description to the police. They'll probably pick him up in a few hours."

Dave struggled to roll more of his body onto his back. He was getting a crick in his neck. He winced.

"You were lucky," said Peep. "The knife missed your vital organs."

"Yeah," said Dave, feeling luck had nothing to do with any of this. The whole damn thing should never have happened. He had been careless. Had allowed himself to forget that Castore would be coming for him at his first opportunity.

After Peep left, a police detective showed up to ask the usual questions. Dave thought fast and made his decision. The right word from him and Cam would be picked up and charged. He might get out on bail, but his parole officer would be keeping him under wraps. Dave would have a better chance at solving this case without that punk's interference. Would Cam talk about the bag of money? No way. Not if he still wanted to collect it later on. Neither Cam nor Dave could spill the beans to the police or anyone else. Or a crowd of people would come out of the woodwork, like in the movie, "It's a Mad Mad, Mad, Mad World," to join the chase. He gave the officer Cam's name. Then he decided to take a little nap.

At noon, a nurse showed up with some pills and a tray, which she put on a table on the left side of the bed. Dave managed to raise his head off the pillow enough to eat some tasteless pasta and chicken mixture and to take his medication with some coffee through a furrowed straw.

He had just finished when a sweet, worried voice spoke from the doorway. "Dave?"

Suzanne took a few steps into the room and stood, a vision in a long white coat with a scarf triangle of purple hues draped around the neck.

After a moment, Dave realized he was staring. "Hi. Come in." She came in slowly, tentatively, like people do when they enter a sick room. As she came closer, he saw the worry lines between her brows and questions in her eyes. He made an effort to sound hearty, although his voice cracked in spite of it. "I guess you called Mrs. Romano."

She stood beside the bed and looked down at him. His neck hurt from trying to see her face.

"Why don't you sit down?"

She stood unmoving for a minute. Then she said, "I can't believe this awful thing happened to you. You got knifed and it's all because you decided to help me." Her voice was low, backed with anger. She backed away and found the chair.

"Hey," Dave said. "That's not the way it goes. Don't forget I blundered into this all by myself. Besides, lots of punks hate me. I can get jumped anytime. Kind of an occupational hazard." He strained to give a little laugh.

Dave twisted his neck to look at her and found she had her head cocked on the side so they could regard one another on the same plane. It was ludicrous. They both laughed at the same time. Then she straightened her head and leaned forward from the edge of the chair. "He meant to kill you."

"No, I gather this time was a warning. He said I had a few days to come up with the money and then he would be back. Only he may have some difficulty keeping the appointment. The police will put out an APB on him. Because of his past record, his bail could be very high or none at all."

Suzanne continued to look worried.

Dave went on. "This guy is so angry he's out of control. That could work to our advantage or disadvantage. He could become careless, reckless, and get himself put away for a good stretch. But if he gets to us, his desire for revenge may be more important to him than locating the money." He saw that his statements were hardly reassuring Suzanne. That was okay. He had to really scare her to make her careful. He went on.

"This guy is not very smart. He demands I come up with the key, and yet he's so mad he cuts me up so there's no way I can get it for him right away. But if the Police don't pick him up very soon, he's got time to cool off and think of his next move. Stabbing me probably got rid of some of his anger. He's happy he's paid me back for his trip to Chicago."

It appeared that Suzanne was gazing at him admiringly. He caught her gaze in his, loving it.

"I think you must have been a wonderful policeman. You seem to be good at analyzing people."

"Well—" Dave turned the left side of his face into the pillow and let his right eye wander to the floor.

"What do your doctors say?"

He looked up at her again. "I should be out of here in a couple of days. Then I come back to get the stitches out after I'm healed."

Suzanne regarded him for a moment. Then she said, "I'm still going out to see Maude Hills this afternoon." Dave opened his mouth, and she held up her palm.

"I can do it. It's time I took an active part in this. I think I can ask questions that are unobtrusive enough so she won't suspect anything. Anyway, I've made up my mind." She straightened in the chair and stuck out her chin. Dave suddenly noticed it had a dimple in it.

"What can I say? But listen, be careful. This Castore guy probably isn't in custody yet. Maybe holed up somewhere." Then Dave thought of something else. He pulled his head up from his pillow as far as it would go and spoke urgently. "Listen, Suzanne. You can't go home tonight. Castore mentioned your name just before he cut me. He might be trying to get to you, too." He watched her widened eyes understand this possible new danger,

and a part of him grew afraid for her. He went on. "I just thought
of something. Why don't you use my room tonight? I'll have the
nurse call Mrs. Romano and arrange it. She'd love to take care of
you. So, after you go to see Maude Hills, don't go home at all. This
guy is wild, and we can't be sure what he'll do until the police
grab him."

Suzanne gave a stiff little laugh. "Oh, for goodness sakes. I can
take care of myself. I'll call my local police, and then lock all the
doors."

"No, you won't," Dave said firmly. His eyes held hers. "You'll
do as I say. I can't have anything happening to you." This last
statement came out in a throaty whisper. As Dave looked at her,
those green eyes grew soft and a nameless something crackled the
air between them.

Right." Suzanne stood up and fixed the strap of her brown
leather handbag across her shoulder. "Off I go now, to play
detective."

"Take care—"

"You, too. Get well fast." She came over to his bed and looked
down on him. She started to laugh.

"Hey—I'm here flat on my stomach, and you're laughing?"

"Sorry, I can't help it." Another giggle. "It's your cowlick."

"MY COWLICK?"

"Yes—you look like Alfalfa in the "Our Gang Comedies."

"Even with a beard?"

"There's still a resemblance." She reached down and fluffed it
up some more. Then, still giggling, she left.

*   *   *

Plainsong Acres was a nursing home complex masquerading as
condominiums in a country—club setting. In the hills beyond
suburban Edgewood, it accommodated the wealthy elderly and ill
with carefully researched environments to provide the best care in
all circumstances. Patients requiring constant nursing care were
housed in suites in the main building, while those partially

ambulatory and in wheel chairs lived in individual cottages monitored by scheduled visits from the nurses. Some cottages had two bedrooms so that spouses could be together. In Maude Hills' case, a companion shared the cottage with her. Beverly Cramer was only about 68, but still goggle-eyed over the fact that she was actually allowed to take care of what was still an American treasure, a pioneer from the old serial movies filmed on the cliffs at Englewood, New Jersey. Later in her career, Maude Hills demonstrated more acting ability than hanging by her hair from a prickly bush while waves dashed on the rocks below. She also made the transition to talking pictures with grace and appeal, putting charm into the slow seductive way she had of speaking.

This Sunday afternoon Suzanne found Maude in a wheelchair and her companion in a lounge chair in the comfortable sitting room of their cottage. They were watching, of all things, a Chicago Cubs game on TV.

"I love the Cubbies," said Maude in a different kind of voice now—slower still, hills and valleys in the syllables as if reciting a script printed with a worn out typewriter ribbon. She focused bright, round child-like eyes on Suzanne. Under a curly white wig, her crinkled face was a ghostly image of the gamin beauty that once captivated America. "My dear," she said, extending a shaking hand slowly with concentration. "It's so good to see you again."

"I didn't know if you would remember me," said Suzanne, saddened by the feel of a skeleton hand covered by thin, cold, wrinkled flesh. Would her own lovely hands come to this some day?

"Of course I do. I have thought of you often since dear Walter's death." Maude's eyes watered and her lids almost closed. She drifted away for a moment, and then rallied. "Shut that damn thing off," she said, waving at Beverly, who promptly picked up the wand from her lap and darkened the screen. "Beverly will take your coat," said Maude. Suzanne shrugged out of it, and Beverly got up to take it into the bedroom. "Now," said Maude to Beverly when she returned, "get us each a glass of white wine and then go for a walk." She was imperious, dramatic, her frail hands gesturing and then falling limply onto her lap. Beverly gave her a hurt and reproachful look, but said nothing, only getting up to go out to a small kitchen to do as she was told.

"Sit down, my dear." Maude pointed a long red fingernail at the vacated chair. A Mexican shawl, knit in a vibrant red, green, and blue totem pole patterns, sat loosely on her shoulders over a long green dress. She smiled as she noticed Suzanne looking at her shoes. Red toeless, heelless pumps with the chunky high heels of the forties rested on the footrest of the wheelchair.

"I wore these in the movie, 'Red Heels', that Russian comedy I did in 1947. They've always been my favorite pair." Maude's voice was tremulous and a bit hesitant. It appeared her mind supplied the words promptly, but it took a while for the vocal chords to get the message. She gazed down at her feet and was silent. Suzanne wondered if she was remembering the famous scene that had been on all the movie posters. The definitive moment when woman gleefully ensnares her man. A waist-down picture of a man embracing a girl who was kicking up one red shoe on a shapely leg behind her.

Maude spoke. "You know, when I was a girl, we only had two pairs of shoes—our everyday shoes and our Sunday best shoes. I could hardly wait for Sunday to put on those shiny patent leather shoes my mother usually bought me." She looked at Suzanne with memories deep in her eyes. "So, these have been my Sunday best shoes for many, many years now. If I can't walk in them, I love to wear them anyway. They make me feel young again." She gestured at a pair of black orthopedic shoes on the floor nearby. "I'm not giving up altogether," she said. "While I'm sitting immobile in this damn chair I can at least look down at these sexy pumps and believe I haven't really changed."

In a moment, Beverly was back with two Waterford stemmed glasses. Although her hand shook, Maude managed to resolutely hold up her glass. "Here's to Walter. Stupid man though he was."

Suzanne was startled. Could she drink to such a toast? Maude noticed her hesitation. "Don't mind an old lady, my dear. I don't think there's any excuse for suicide. Life has problems for everyone. Challenge is what we need. That's what creates the soul in each of us."

Suzanne had the opening she needed. She took a sip of her wine and plunged in.

"Miss Hills, I don't believe Walter committed suicide. Some things don't seem to add up. Well, you knew Walter. Was he the kind of person who would ever do such a thing?" Maude's head gave a wobbly shake. "Well, I'm glad you agree with me."

"But what about the police? They've already closed the case, I understand." Suzanne leaned forward to hear her. "Call me Maude, my dear. After all, we're practically related. You know, Walter was my sister's nephew."

"Yes, I know. Walter was very fond of you. Anyway, I've decided to check out a few things myself. If I find anything unusual, anything that maybe would show it was an accident, for example, I could get the case reopened." Dave flashed into Suzanne's thoughts and out again. Better not to mention she had a partner in all of this. It would be hard to explain how that had come about.

Maude's eyes were getting brighter. "Accident? Or maybe murder?"

Suzanne was startled. This remarkable lady was one step ahead of her. "Possibly. I don't know. I'm just trying to find out everything I can about Walter's business affairs. I keep thinking there must be a link between some business he was involved in and his death."

"You poor child," Maude said. "It's a lot to handle, isn't it?"

Suzanne blinked unexpected tears from her eyes. She took a deep breath to compose herself.

"How can I help?" Maude asked gently.

Another deep breath. Suzanne leaned forward and took a frail hand in hers. She needed to be straightforward and honest. No pretense. "Maude, Walter had your power of attorney and took care of your financial affairs. Was there ever any problem with this arrangement?"

"Oh, no. Walter did a good job. Paid all my bills and took care of my house."

Oh, my God, if she only knew. But Maude would never know, Suzanne pledged to herself. She suddenly felt crushed by her inherited responsibility.

The old actress turned her wheel chair slightly to look more directly at Suzanne, pleating her trembling lips into a straight line. "I sense there's more to this than solving Walter's death. You've come to see me for other reasons." Suzanne opened her mouth, but the red fingernail flicked up from Maude's lap. "I'm not going to pry, my dear. I trust you. I always told Walter he married a real lady, with intelligence and guts." Suzanne looked startled. "Yes, I believe you have guts. I think Walter kept your light under a bushel so you wouldn't outshine him. But I've been proven right, because here you are, tackling some big problems, I'm sure."

"Well—" Suzanne paused and then said stiffly, "Thanks for the vote of confidence. I'm not sure it's justified."

Maude suddenly leaned back in her chair apparently overcome with weariness and closed her eyes. Suzanne sat quietly thinking about this strange conversation. After a few minutes, Maude opened her eyes, and once again, they were bright beads. "How can I help you, my dear?" she said as if there had been no break in the dialog.

"Well, now that Walter's gone, you don't have anyone tending to your personal affairs. Walter and I talked often about your situation since you came here to Plainsong Acres. I have Walter's records, and I'd be willing to continue in his capacity as your attorney-in-fact." Mustn't sound so eager that Maude might suspect something.

She wondered if Maude heard her. The actress once again had dropped her head to her chest and seemed to have left the room for a moment. Then she got back into the conversation. "Yes, that might be a good idea. There have been some problems lately that I mentioned to Walter. He said he would check them out, probably some bookkeeping snafu."

Oh, my Lord, thought Suzanne. It's too late. Maude already knows something is wrong.

She tried to look innocent and unknowing. "What kind of problems?"

"Well, it seems my stay here at the Waldorf has not been taken care of for the last two months. Walter was checking it out, looking for cancelled checks, that kind of thing. Then I haven't received any bank statements from him for sometime. He said it was a computer problem at the bank." All of this was recited in a stagey whisper, an old actress stepping into a role. She knew. Maude already knew what Walter had done. Suzanne was sure of it. Now the hopeful plans to keep Maude from finding out the truth about Walter had no chance of succeeding. Her depression must have showed in her eyes, for Maude patted her again with a bony hand. Yes, I know, the still bright eyes seemed to say. But you can straighten everything out. Suzanne couldn't think of a thing to say.

"I think you're just the person to take over where Walter left off," said Maude. Or further back than that, thought Suzanne. "I'll call my lawyer and have a power-of-attorney drawn up. He'll send you a copy."

"Thank you, Maude. I'll check out all your bills and see that your charges here are taken care of." It was a pledge, perhaps to do the impossible. The women stared at one another for an instant. Then Suzanne tore her gaze away and looked about the room. After living in sumptuous homes in Paris, Greece, Rome, Hollywood, and Edgewood, how could Maude accept living in this small, neat, and rather hygienic room?

But she said, "This is really a nice place. Do you plan to stay on or are you going back to your own house?"

Maude suddenly looked exhausted. Suzanne had to lean forward to catch her words. "I wish I could go home, oh, how I wish it. A few years ago, I really thought it might be possible. My beautiful home." She sighed and her eyes closed as if she were seeing it again. "But Beverly has arranged for someone to drive us out there next weekend. I don't know if I'll be able to get inside, but I know I'll feel better just looking at the house."

An alarm rang in Suzanne's head. Rather too quickly, she asked, "You still have your car?"

"No, I sold it when I moved here. We'll take a taxi." After a pause in which Maude seemed to be looking at a picture in her mind, she went on. "But right now it's better for me to live here. You see, there's more wrong with me than just a broken hip. And life is simple here. It's all I can cope with these days." She gave a snort, and her head slumped forward on her chest. In a second, she was asleep. Suzanne picked up her purse and stood up, undecided what to do. She went into the bedroom for her coat and then walked slowly to the door and opened it. Beverly was coming down the path. Suzanne said goodbye and left.

An hour later Maude opened her eyes and turned to look at Beverly in her accustomed chair. "What we supposed is true," she said. "Walter Wilkins has embezzled my funds." Beverly stared and said nothing.

"I have no idea how he did this, but that's not important. The thing is, Mrs. Wilkins is going to going to put the money back."

"How can you possibly know that?"

"Call it instinct. But it's more than that. Mrs. Wilkins is a real lady, a person of integrity. She was devoted to her husband, although he didn't deserve it. Anyway, honor is important to her. She's the kind of person who always does the right thing. I may be old, but I still know people, but that doesn't always apply to distant relatives." She fussed for a moment with the edges of her shawl. "When she asked for a power of attorney, her face gave her away. She's an innocent involved in something nasty. But she'll do what's right. So, I want you to call John Talbot first thing tomorrow morning and get the papers drawn up. Then we'll see what kind of courage this little gal has."

*　　*　　*

Before she left the nursing home grounds, Suzanne knew she had a distasteful task she could not avoid. She needed to check out Maude's estate. And she couldn't delay. She had to do it now. She prayed she wouldn't find what she feared. Surely, Walter would have arranged for the perpetual care of the lovely old place.

But how much checking could she do? Walter must have had

a key to the place, but where was it? Anyway, she couldn't go back
to her own house to look for it, it might be too dangerous.

Years ago she and Walter had been invited to one of Maude's
rare parties and she could still remember how beautiful the house
was. Almost like a palace, she had thought at the time. Large rooms
with Persian rugs on polished wood floors, long casement windows,
antique furniture, priceless paintings and sculpture. The terraces
that wound around the brick and stone exterior of the house were
circled by exquisite gardens. The views from three sides of the
house swept over hills of perfect grass down to a river's edge where
the water formed a loop, setting the grounds on its own private
peninsula.

Pulling off a country road into an overgrown lane, Suzanne
thought she was lost. Nothing was familiar. Then she glimpsed
bronze roof tiles glinting in the sprinkles of sunshine that wove
through distant trees. She turned into what was once a shorter
replica of the Apian Way with dozens of poplar trees bordering the
edges of the road. Gone were the expansive green lawns on either
side. The road was a dusty trail cut through what seemed to be a
farmer's field, ankle-deep in brown grass and weeds. The end of
March and first of April had been rainy, and Suzanne's own yard
was thick with bright green grass. Her yard boy had been mowing
for several weeks now.

There was no resemblance to the estate she remembered. She
drove her car up the circle driveway and stopped at the still gracious
portico. Azaleas struggled to bloom through the weeds. The once
perfectly shaped evergreens were shaggy and untamed. Old brown
rose blossoms hung from spindly stalks that needed pruning.

She sat for a moment, peering out of the car windows at the
neglect. A sob hung low in her throat. At that moment, Walter's
crime was worse than stealing money. What had Maude called
him—stupid? No, it was more evil than that. What he had done
to the trust and respect Maude Hills had given him was damnable.
For what reason had he sinned to this degree? Would she ever find
out? And if she did, could she stand knowing the truth? She knew

one thing: something—or someone—had been very powerful to cause Walter to do such a terrible thing.

Suzanne got out of the car and walked slowly along a brick path that ran beside the library on the west side of the house. She wrapped the white coat snugly around her—not exactly the right wearing apparel for this kind of effort. There were French doors for access to the terrace from the library, and she peered in. The grimy glass overlaid the interior scene like a mist, but Suzanne could still make out the elegant furniture, the enormous wall of books, the gold-framed oils on the walls.

There was the Oscar for 'Red Heels'. It sat on a fringed scarf on its own little table next to a Chippendale settee. Suzanne stared at it for several moments while her eyes filled with tears. My God, Walter, how could you have taken advantage of such a great lady?

She wandered around the house and peered into other windows that she could reach. At least the furnishings of the house seemed to be intact. Before she got back in her car, she knew what she had to do. This place had to look shipshape when Maude made her visit next Sunday.

She herself was the only one who could make that happen.

14

The key wouldn't turn in the lock. Cam worked it back and forth, but the tumbler refused to move. Damn. He tried a couple of more times until it hit him. His father had had the locks changed. Goddamn, his own father had cut him off. His legs grew rigid and his muscles tensed. He stood on the entrance steps of the imposing Georgian house while his rage grew into a white heat.

It was two o'clock in the morning, and he had driven around for hours, not knowing where to go. Back to Theda's was out of the question. Her address was on his police records. He finally decided to go back home, sneak in for a couple of hours of sleep, and then leave early in the morning before his parents were up.

He stuck his finger in the doorbell and left it there. After several moments, the door opened slowly, and Cam looked into the furious eyes of his father.

"Get off my property," said Mr. Castore. Even in a flannel bathrobe, he was an imposing man with bushy eyebrows over grim eyes that said he meant business.

"Dad—please. I need help. Just let me get something to eat and have a few hours sleep. That's all I want. Then I won't bother you anymore."

"You won't bother me now. You've wrecked your life, and I won't have you messing with mine. So beat it." He started to close the door.

"But I'm your son!" Cam's tough exterior crumpled.

"You gave up that privilege a long time ago."

The door was almost shut when Cam heard his mother's anxious voice in the distance. "Who is it, Bill? Is it Cameron?"

"No, it's a mistake. This person has the wrong house," Mr. Castore called out behind him.

Cam made one last effort. "All you care about is being a big shot at the chair company!" He felt like a little boy again, begging, pleading for his father's attention and approval.

"That's correct. And don't forget it." The door shut with finality.

Cam couldn't help it. Tears leaked into his eyes. This had been his last chance. Monday's newspapers would most likely carry an account of the attack in the alley. It could even identify him by name and artist's drawing. Just his dumb luck to have that other guy come up behind him.

The only way he could get out of this mess was to get hold of the money. That was the ticket out of here. Then he and Theda could blow this town for good.

So, what was he going to do now? He went back to Theda's car and tried to plan something. But his brain wouldn't work—he needed some sleep. He drove up the street to little lane that wound dead end into a wooded lot, parked the car, and fell asleep.

*   *   *

Theda had a restless night, checking the bedside clock frequently, wondering where Cam was and when he would come home. On Sunday morning, she still hadn't heard anything. Worse yet, there was no one she could call. She had kept her distance from Cam's hoodlum friends. Certainly, she couldn't call Cam's parents. Good thing this wasn't a working day. Her car was missing, too.

Finally, the phone rang about ten o'clock. She sighed in relief as she answered it. But it wasn't Cam. Of all things, it was the police asking for him. Seems they had located his Firebird, and it was being held for him at one of their impounding locations. How wonderful. She said she'd be glad to give Cam their message.

A moment later, there was a knock at the door. Not Cam, who

never knocked but inserted his key and blew in the door like the king of a palace. But maybe this was news of Cam. She flew to the door to open it. Anticipation faded from those sultry eyes as she confronted two policemen with hands on their hips, ready to pull their weapons.

"What—what do you want?" she managed to stammer. After looking at Theda it seemed to take the two officers some time to find their tongues. Finally, they told her. "We're here for a Cameron Castore. We understand he lives here." One of them was looking at Theda in her tight jeans and snug black t-shirt as if he'd like to take Cam's place.

She backed away and gave him an icy look. "He's not here."

Please God; don't have him call me now, she prayed. "And when do you expect him, Miss?"

"Mrs. Castore." Maybe her old title would put this fresh guy in his place. The way both of them were looking at her now stabbed her heart with fear. Everyone knew you couldn't trust the police these days. The papers were full of their brutality. She would have no chance against two of them.

She tried being business-like. "What do you want with him?"

They gave each other a look. "I guess he didn't come home last night?"

"I don't see where that's any of your business. I'll tell him you were here. Now, if you don't mind, I have an appointment." She saw amusement in their eyes.

As they started to leave, one of them said, "Give him a message from us. Tell him he has been identified in that stabbing last night, and it's just a question of time before he's picked up for questioning. Might as well give himself up." He reached in his pocket and extended a card—Sgt. Ron Ambrose, 4th Precinct. "It'll be better for him if he calls as soon as possible," he said.

Theda stood behind the closed door staring at the card. No wonder she hadn't heard from Cam. It was much worse than she could have imagined. A stabbing. What could he be thinking of, risking their whole plan like this? Her despondency grew. There was no way they could start a new life now. The police were going to catch up with Cam, and then he would go to prison again. Maybe for a long time.

The telephone buzzer made her jump. It was an operator with a collect call from a Mr. Jones in Hamilton, a city forty miles away. Yes, she would take it, she breathed in relief. She knew it was Cam.

His voice was low and dispirited. He was brief. "You've heard?"

"Yes. Two policemen were here looking for you. How could you knife someone?"

"Hey—it was Monaco. It was only a scratch, and he had it coming. I told him he has only a couple of days to get me the key or I'll really get him."

"Oh, my God," she moaned. Then, "Are you all right?"

"Are you kidding? You're a damn idiot. I'm on the lam. I've got nowhere to go. I've got a couple of bucks to my name."

She wanted to cheer him up. "They've found your car. It's at one of the impounding lots."

"Well—" For a moment a bit of good news, then, "What the fuck! There's no way I can get it. Can't ride around in it anyway. What a shitty world."

She sounded him out gingerly. "Cam, I need my car so I can get to work. Can't you leave it somewhere for me?"

A wild laugh hurt her eardrum. "You bitch! All you think about is yourself. We're talking about my life here, and you're worried about getting to your stinking job. You work it out. Meanwhile, send me a hundred clams care of general delivery in Hamilton. Right away."

"Where am I going to get that? I don't even have the rent money this month."

"How the hell do I know? Just do it. I'm holing up in an alley with the homeless until I can get one of my pals to take me in. So hustle, babe."

I hate you, she thought. I really hate you. My mother was right. But how can I get rid of him now?

He wasn't through. "It's up to you to get the money now. And pronto. You started this caper, and now you're going to end it."

"And just how do I do that?" she asked in a tremulous voice.

"You make up to Monaco. And you've got just the machinery to do it."

"You mean, have sex with him?"

"Hah! Such an innocent! What the hell do you think I mean? Look, doll, just think of it as a job you have to do. I'll still love ya!"

Theda bit her lip. Then she ventured, "But how'm I going to meet him?"

"Up to you, baby. Use your stupid head. He's in the hospital now, no doubt. Maybe you could play nursey-nursey." He laughed. "Don't forget to send money, mom. And next time I call I want to hear about you and Monaco."

She hung up and then took the receiver off the hook. She stared at the living room wall for a moment, thinking. Her mother really had been right about Cam from the beginning. But teen-age rebellion was strong, and the sex between her and Cam was stronger than all else. It still was, and it had made her so weak she had babbled to Cam about that tragic evening. So wake up now, she told herself. Like Cam said, you are stupid—but only about him. She spoke out loud, defiantly, making a promise to herself to tell Cam how she felt. "I'm sick and tired of the way you talk to me, Cam Castore, and the way you put me down. And the way you order me about. You do you think you are? You're the stupid asshole."

How could she have gone back to Cam after Walter? My darling, she thought. Such a loving, gentle, thoughtful man. So tender when making love. Tears seeped through her thick black lashes. She had known what it was like to love and be loved by an intelligent, successful gentleman.

The howler beeped at her, signaling the receiver off the hook, and she came back to the present. She looked at the card Sgt. Ambrose had given her and dialed the number. The call was transferred to his mobile phone.

"I'll tell you where Cam Castore is if you'll do me a favor," she said.

"Such as?"

"He has my car, and I need it."

"Make, year, and license number?"

She told him. "And the rear fenders are a little banged up."

"We'll get it back for you. Where does he have it?"

"He's in Hamilton. Hiding out with the homeless in some alley. Expects to pick up some money from me at the post office tomorrow."

"He'll be gone before then," the sergeant said. Then, "Listen, Mrs. Castore, you did the right thing, calling us. Someone could have been killed last night. He'll never know you turned him in, I promise."

Theda wasn't so sure about that last statement. If Cam ever found out what she did there could be a killing after all.

*   *   *

Suzanne saw the florist's sign up ahead on the beltline and made a quick decision. Didn't men enjoy flowers as much as women? But someone like Dave Monaco? She wasn't at all sure about that. She flicked on her right turn signal and turned in. There were a few Sunday buyers milling about, looking at the shrubs and spring flowering plants outside. She decided on an azalea plant, bright red with opened blossoms. Suitable for a man, she decided.

After that, she was on her way to the hospital, eager to share with Dave the results of her detective work. She caught herself smiling and was stunned. It had only been about six weeks since Walter's death, and here she was, her interest and adrenalin at a high pitch. It was good to feel so alive after weeks of depression. She searched for some remnants of guilt, but found none. She could hardly go on mourning a man who was not her intimate husband but a person she hardly knew. A deceiver. And worse, a criminal.

When she parked her car at the hospital, she remembered the fugitive and glanced carefully about. Surely, Castore wouldn't chance a visit to Dave in the hospital, or even surveillance on her.

She shivered as she remembering Dave telling of the threats on her own life and hurried into the visitor's entry.

*   *   *

"Press the flesh gently," Dave told the nurse who was turning him over to check his face.

"God, you're a piece of blubber," she said. "Don't you ever exercise?"

She was large-boned and strong, with a wide, humorous mouth. "That bad, huh?" asked Dave between clenched teeth. "Ouch! Hey, it was my love handles that saved me. If I'd been some lean, mean machine I'd be dead by now. Exercise can kill ya." It was much better being on his back rolling toward his left hip. The nurse cranked up the bed to raise his head slightly, and he began feeling like part of society again. Actually, being in the hospital had some plus sides. Three meals a day. A buzzer to ring for instant gratification to his requests. Security police outside the door for protection. Goodies from Mrs. Romano. Nurses and doctors acting as if he were important. Visitors too: the police, the press, friends, and relatives. He felt as if he were being celebrated, like it was his birthday or something. No cocktail hour here, either. Then in the middle of Sunday afternoon, Dave had a visitor from Internal Affairs. Friend or foe?

"I hear you got knifed, Dave," said Speed Carlson, slouching into a chair in his rumpled raincoat. Everyone told him he looked like Lt. Columbo on TV, so it seemed he felt obligated to dress like him also. Speed got his name not from his efficiency in the department, but from his former passion: driving in demolition derbies.

Dave flicked him a look and said, "I didn't know you cared."

"Hey, don't get feisty. We're just doing our job, you know." He leaned forward and twisted a battered cap in his hands. "You say you're innocent, well, then help us prove it. Don't hold anything back."

"You guys have it all. The problem is you don't know how to run with the fucking ball."

"Maybe. But we're confused. Straighten us out. You get knifed in an alley. Do you get robbed—wallet, credit cards, crap like that? No. So why? Just for fun? I doubt it. This guy's on parole— he's not going to take chances, the stakes are too high. So what's going on here? Are you making out with his wife? Did you cut in line in front of him at the supermarket? Did you put him away the first time? No, we checked. Something big is at stake here, something like ah—" he paused for emphasis. "Money," he said.

"Money?" Dave repeated inanely. Then, "What money?"

Speed shook his head sadly from side to side. "Dave, Dave," he said slowly. "When are you going to level with us?"

"I can repeat it for you a thousand times if you want," said Dave. "I have no money. There is no money. I never took any money. I live in a rented room. I have no car. I own nothing, not even a decent suit. Don't you think I'd be easing my situation a little bit by now if I'd heisted any of that drug money?"

Speed slouched further down in the chair and regarded Dave with a depressed look on his face. "So why do you think you were attacked?"

"Because this punk read the news and thought like you guys. He figured I had some of the green on me or would tell him where it was." So far not a lie, thought Dave. But we're not talking about the same lettuce here.

"Your wallet was still in your pocket."

"Because some guy surprised the work in progress," said Dave. "And thereby saved my life. A sweet story, really."

"You're a fresh bastard," said Speed. He pulled a notebook from a raincoat pocket and flipped some pages. "An Elmer Botsworth. A private eye, no less. Who just happened to wander along. What a coincidence!" His tone was getting angry. "What the hell is really going on here, Monaco?"

Dave didn't answer for a moment. Then he spoke seriously and quietly. "I don't have all the answers. I can only swear to you that I am not guilty of taking that money. Hell, I was in on many drug busts where the take was bigger than on that night. Look at my past record. Look at my life. I'm a simple guy. I'm not materialistic. I've never lived beyond my means. All I've ever wanted was to be a good cop. You know damn well that doesn't spell yuppie success.

"You're after the truth? Go after my ex-partner and pretty-boy Steve Collier. Find out what Barney had on Steve to make him lie about who gave him his cut. Have you checked the trashcans in Barney's garage? Probably full of cash."

"Know what I think?" asked Speed. "You're full of crap." He stood up and blinked. "Have a nice day."

Dave closed his eyes. Had anyone won that debate? Someday that problem would all be over, decided one way or another. Anyway, there was nothing more he could do. Besides, there was a more pressing crime to engage his talents.

An hour later, his sister Lorna and brother-in-law Ralph showed up with a basket of fruit and cheerful talk. Dave began to feel better again. After they left, another visitor came hesitatingly to his bedside.

"Ralph read about you in the papers and called me," said Bobby. She looked down on him for a moment and then bent awkwardly to lightly kiss his bearded cheek. "It tickles," she said, with a coy smile.

"That's what all my girl friends tell me," he smiled. This is hard for her, he thought.

Bobby slipped off a brown vinyl jacket and sat down, her tan mini skirt up to her eyeballs. Her ear lobes rattled large orange and silver loops, and several chains swung around the neck of an orange T-shirt. Tight brown boots made her still shapely legs go on forever. Her eyes were well defined in what Dave used to call 'glop' as in, "Why do you cover up your eyes in all that glop?" Dark hair frizzed around her round face in the fashionable squiggles of the day. The scent of "Passion" perfume wafted toward Dave and he sneezed. There was a sharp pain in his right side. He began to hope she wouldn't stay long.

"I'm so sorry you were hurt, Dave," Bobby said sweetly.

"Really? I thought you hated my guts," he said. "I figured you'd be rooting for the attacker."

"You never did get anything right." Her eyes flashed. Aha. The old Bobby was back. "You always read me wrong. You never took the time to find out how I felt about things."

"I didn't have to. You were always telling me, and in a loud voice."

Their eyes met, and after a moment, they both laughed. "Just like old times," said Bobby softly. A bit wistfully. Their eyes wandered together again and softened.

"All of the memories aren't bad," said Dave gently. "You know, the good times we had together will always be ours alone." My God, he thought. What am I saying? I sound as if I expected to croak in this hospital bed. But then he looked at Bobby's face. It was young and sweet again. He had, after all, said exactly the right thing.

So there they were, Dave and Bobby, gazing at one another in rather a tender way when another visitor arrived. Suzanne. Looking like a movie queen about to be interviewed. A fashion cover from Vogue with her arms full of red blossoms. Cheeks flushed and eyes bright. Then her lights went off and the green eyes changed to gray. Looks went back and forth, criss-crossing among the three of them, and tension mounted.

Bobby stared at Dave, her eyes now cold. He made the introductions and waved Suzanne to a vacant chair on the opposite side of the bed. She placed the plant on his bedside table.

"I thought some flowers might be in order," she said and sat down. The two women sized up each other across his legs. He couldn't keep his feet from twitching. "Have you known Dave long?" asked Bobby in clipped tones.

"A while." Suzanne smiled graciously while Dave groaned inside.

Bobby brought out her claws. She leaned forward and put a hand on Dave's arm. "You know, honey, you don't seem at all like Dave's type. Where in hell did you two meet?"

Dave's arm flew up as if he wanted to smack her. "For God's sakes, Bobby, Mrs. Wilkins is a client of mine. We're working on a case together." It had slipped out. Damn. The less Bobby knew about his present life, the better for him.

"Oh, really," Bobby was flippant. "You're still a fast thinker, Dave. Always good with the fucking explanations. How dumb do you think I am? Don't forget I know you, creep. I saw the look on your face when this dame came in. But forget it. She's a real lady. You've got nothin' she could want." Bobby stood up, picked up her jacket and purse, and went to stand close to Dave. Then she leaned over and kissed him on the mouth so long that her perfume made him nauseous, and he thought he would stop breathing.

After she left, Dave and Suzanne glanced aimlessly about in embarrassment. Then Suzanne spoke.

"She seems very nice," She said primly, inanely.

"Is that so," Dave said seriously, looking in her eyes. Then they burst out laughing.

"She still loves you," said Suzanne matter-of-factly.

"Not really," said Dave. "It's an illusion. We were rotten together. She has a bad memory. She can't seem to remember those times."

"I would guess most of us want to blot out the bad things that happen to us." Dave understood she was talking about herself.

He reached up his right arm and held out his hand. She put hers into it. It was cold. He wanted to warm it forever. "It's going to be all right," he said. "Just remember the bad times pass away."

"I'm working on it." She smiled weakly. Then she stood up and shrugged out of her coat, revealing gentle curves under a powder blue knit dress. She folded her coat neatly and sat down with it on her lap. "I have a lot to tell you," she said and described her visit to the nursing home, everything Maude had said, and her visit to the estate.

"Hmm—" Dave digested it all.

"And listen to this. Maude knows that Walter emb—misplaced her funds. I'm sure of it."

"What?"

"Well, she didn't come right out with it, but it was in the tone of her voice and the way she looked at me. I'm sure of it."

"Then why didn't she blow the whistle on him?"

"Well, he was kind of a relative for one thing. And I think she's a lady who moves slowly on things. Doesn't rush to conclusions. I think she was just getting ready to confront Walter when he died." Dave was as fascinated by Suzanne's graceful hand gestures as with her words

"I've got to get outa here."

"No, you don't. I can handle it." Her eyes were green again and determined.

Dave almost got lost in them. "I can see you're busy planning."

"Yes. Tell me what you think. Tomorrow morning I'm calling my landscaper. I'm sending him around to the estate with as many men as he needs to get it in shape. I want to get all the windows washed, too. I don't have the money for all of this, but I've figured out how to get some." She twisted the large diamond solitaire on her left hand. Dave noticed but said nothing.

She reached forward and put her hand on his arm below the hospital gown. "There was something about the way Miss Hills treated me. It's hard to explain. Like she trusted me to put things in order. As if she knew I could do it." She smiled. "I didn't even know that myself."

"I'm with Miss Hills," said Dave.

"Well—" Suzanne went on. "I'm positive I'll get the power of attorney in a couple of days. Then when we get the money we can put it back in the bank in her account. I want to go over some more of Walter's papers, I need the cancelled checks from Maude's checking account, savings records, things like that."

"But you are not going home until we know that creep is behind bars."

"What if they pick him up and he gets out on bail?"

"Possible, but bail may be too high. Don't forget he has a prior, and he's violated his parole. Anyway, go to Mrs. Romano's tonight. We'll see what happens tomorrow."

"All right."

The nurse entered with the evening meal. She looked at Suzanne. "What's a nice lady like you doing, visiting an old grouch-head like this?"

"Living dangerously, I guess," Suzanne smiled at Dave who

was appreciating the graceful way she was moving her attractive body parts into her coat.

The nurse cranked the bed up a little higher and then tucked a large napkin under Dave's chin. "Be a good boy and don't spill now," she said.

"Gee," said Dave in a little boy voice. "I'll try." When she turned around to get his tray, Dave made a face at her broad backside while Suzanne giggled.

"That smells good," Suzanne said after the nurse left. "I just realized I didn't have any lunch."

"There's a cafeteria downstairs," said Dave. "I don't think it's a good idea for you to go anywhere else. And then go immediately to the Romanos."

"All right."

"Listen, I almost forgot." He moved his head to look at the glowing plant. "It was great you brought me flowers. A first." He turned back to her. "No one ever gave me flowers before."

"Well—" she made a fluttery movement with her hands. "It seemed appropriate for an invalid." She moved closer. Their eyes clung. "I want to find out something."

"What?" Ah, those green eyes.

"If beards really tickle." She leaned down, kissed his cheek, and then was out the door.

He lay still, his pot roast dinner growing cold on the tray before him. By God, she was flirting with him. This elegant, charming, beautiful lady—a real lady—who shouldn't be giving him the time of day—was flirting with him. Him—a battered, street-worn, disgraced ex-cop. Overweight and scroungy-looking, no coins to jingle in his pocket. This wasn't an act. She didn't have to put out for him to help her straighten out her life. He committed himself to that long ago, or was it only last week? How strange. They were from different planets, and yet he felt so at ease and comfortable with her. She was far above him and still he felt no pressure to impress her. What they had in common was a spirit, an essence of their beings that moved between them when their eyes met. An indefinable something. Dave suddenly felt hungry and attacked his dinner. It was a little hard to chew when he was smiling so often.

$$* \quad * \quad *$$

After dinner, Tom came to see him. "I called to see if you wanted to go to a meeting tonight and Mrs. Romano told me what happened," he said.

"She's been very busy today," said Dave. "I should pay her a secretarial fee."

"So how are you doing?"

Dave knew this wasn't just about the injuries in the alley. "I'm okay. Very okay." He grinned at Tom.

"I'm mystified," said Tom, "after all you've been through. But I'm mighty glad to hear it. Let me know when you're released."

"So we can celebrate?" Dave grinned, the meaning clear.

"Yeah—we'll go to a meeting, smoke, and drink coffee."

$$* \quad * \quad *$$

About eight o'clock, when Dave had just started watching the Sunday Night Movie on TV, he felt someone staring at him. His neck bandage only allowed him peripheral vision, but he got a general impression that it was a young woman. She stood there for a moment, hesitating, and then took a couple of slow steps into the room.

"I'm sorry," she said in a low husky voice. "I'm afraid I have the wrong room. I'm looking for my girl friend."

She was close enough now for Dave to see she was gorgeous. Probably the most beautiful sensual creature he had ever laid eyes on. "Well," he said. "You can obviously see you have the wrong person. What number did you want?"

She looked at the plastic-coated tag in her hand. "Room 436?"

"I think that's in the other wing. This is 416."

"How stupid of me. I always get lost in hospitals." But instead of leaving to find the right room, she took a few steps nearer.

Dave got the shock of his life. He knew this girl. For a moment, he couldn't think where. Then he remembered. He had seen her twice. Once in an old blue Mustang parked outside the train station. And once in the coffee shop next to the Monroe Trust Company. Where Walter Wilkins was president. His brain was adding two and two and coming up with a bagful of information. Walter went next door for coffee breaks. Walter went next door for lunch. Walter obviously went to this girl's apartment for something else.

Her name came back to him now. Theda. He remembered her reaction that day in the coffee shop when he had asked her about Walter. Aha! So now she was here. In his hospital room. On purpose, using a flimsy excuse. This could be a real break. He gave her what he hoped was his most charming smile.

"I remember you," he said. All of a sudden, she looked scared and took a step backward. "From the coffee shop. Isn't your name Theda? That's a name that's not easy to forget."

He saw her sigh in relief. "Yes, I know. People kid me about it." She was now standing at the side of the bed. "I've never forgiven my mother for being such a fan of that old movie star."

"I think it's a lovely name. Very fitting for such a lovely young woman." He gazed softly into her smoldering eyes and let her know he was available. Pleasant work, this. He wasn't surprised when she batted her fabulous lashes and came onto him. He knew why she was here. He played out the rope of romantic intrigue and hoped she would trip on it. In the meantime, it was a pleasant game and even sexually arousing.

"Look," he said. "Do you have to visit your girl friend? I'm all alone here, and I'd sure like some company. After all, don't you think it's your civic duty to cheer up someone who almost got killed?"

He noticed she didn't ask him why he was bandaged and in a hospital bed. Another fact was added to his bagful of interesting items. She knew what had happened to him, and that was precisely why she was here. Castore and she were a pair. First Walter and then Castore. A busy lady, thought Dave, admiring her wonderful curves below a waist-tight jacket.

She came around the bed and settled into a chair. "What movie are we watching?" she asked.

At ten o'clock, all visitors were gone, lights were dimmed, and the nurses had dispensed their sleeping pills. Dave had been cranked back down, and he lay on his left side ready for sleep. But not quite. He couldn't stop smiling. His mind jogged back and forth over the events of the day, his injuries and discomfort forgotten. Dear Suzanne. Where were they headed? He didn't care. However long the trip together, it would be worth it. His mother used to tell him, "Let go and let God." Exactly it, he thought.

Then there was Theda. They had gotten cozy during the movie, playing their little game of pretend attraction, exchanging telephone numbers, cooing and aahing at one another like a pair of teenagers. Talking of future dates. Deception was not his bag, but in this case, he had to play along for Suzanne's sake. Theda was after something, and Dave knew exactly what that was. Theda and Walter—an interesting pair. Easy to see how a man could get tangled up with a broad like this one and firebomb his entire life.

So how far was Theda planning to go with him to get the money? Dave suspected it was enough for a few romps in the hay. Now that was an enticing idea. Why did the thought of Suzanne suddenly get in the way? Friendly visitors, romance, intrigue—these had been the elements of this day. Here I am, thought Dave, flat on my back in a hospital bed, and this has been one of the best days of my life. Oh, he thought, and flowers too.

15

"I put clean sheets on the bed," said Sophie Romano as she led the way up the stairs to Dave's room.

"Well, thank you," said Suzanne. "I didn't want you to go to any trouble."

"My goodness," Sophie turned in the doorway to look at her overnight guest. "You're no trouble. We're glad you're here. Me and Milo don't have many guests. And Lord knows we think a lot of that Dave. Such a nice man and going through such a trying time."

Suzanne stood uncertainly in the middle of the bedroom and looked around. "You mean because of the knifing?"

"Well, yes, that was bad. But there's all that trouble with the police department. His being on suspension and all. Imagine a good cop like him, risking his life every day, and then accused of something he didn't do. You just can't figure it." Sophie's voice sharpened with indignation.

Suzanne laid her purse and her coat on the bed. "You know he's innocent?" she asked.

"Well, of course," Sophie's hands were on her ample hips. "You can just tell by being with him. I have a good sense about people— good instincts. Dave Monaco is okay."

Suzanne patted her on the arm. "I absolutely agree with you."

"I thought you would," Sophie said with a sly smile. "Now, is there anything else you need? Cookie? Glass of milk?" For a moment, Suzanne was back in her childhood bedroom being tucked in by her mother. She shook her head and smiled. "When you get up tomorrow, come down to the kitchen. We'll have breakfast waiting."

After Sophie left, Suzanne sat down on the bed and looked around. This large, old bedroom with its long windows and wide old dark woodwork had a faint scent of its own. A bit of Boxwood, pressed rose petals, cloves perhaps. Mixed together. She sniffed and a memory jarred loose in her mind. Her grandmother's bedroom had smelled like this. When she was little, it had been a favorite place to be. Her grandmother allowed her to search through the treasure-troves that were her dresser drawers. Little Suzanne had reverently looked through the trinkets and jewelry, holding necklaces to her throat and earrings to her ears. She lifted out hand-embroidered handkerchiefs and smelled them. Jeweled hair combs went into her hair, and fancy pearl shoe ornaments onto her loafers. She took big enthusiastic sniffs from each fragrance bottle on the dresser top, sometimes dabbing a bit here and there. She was a princess making herself beautiful for her waiting knight. At this moment, she was there again. Strangely, the familiar scent in this room had gently wafted her back in time.

But it was Dave's room. A big, bearded, outspoken man who lacked the social graces that defined her world and who hardly filled the image of Prince Charming. Walter had stepped into that role perfectly. His handsome, commanding presence turned the head of any woman within fifty feet of him. A glossy exterior apparently hiding a darker side.

But what of that other fairy tale, where the ugly frog turns into a prince when he is finally loved for himself? How interesting. She felt her face flushing. This kind of thinking was dangerous. She remembered how she had kissed Dave on the cheek, and she shook her head in despair. Whatever had come over her? What must he think of her, being so forward? It was so unlike the Suzanne who was always so cool and in control. Reserved. As Walter distanced himself from her, she saw now that she herself had kept people at arm's length. Much of the time she had been in the audience at the drama of life. But now there was this bearded, rumpled alien from another world who looked at her with a strange kind of promise in his eyes.

She shook her head in dismay and moved about the room, looking out the window at the average middle-American street, checking out the old-fashioned bathroom, and eventually inspecting

Dave's few belongings. If he read at all, she would have expected some paperback detective stories, but lined up on the bookshelves were some hard covers that surprised her. Thoreau, Fitzgerald, Michener, Emerson, and Emily Dickinson. *The Bible, Clan of the Cave Bear, Look Homeward Angel, The conquest of Everest.* Several books about the Titanic, and, of all things, a jazz encyclopedia. She took down the Bible and fanned the pages. Corners had been turned under and phrases underlined. She put it back quickly. She had intruded into the spiritual side of Dave Monaco and that was too intimate.

There was a picture on the dresser of a Navy lieutenant in dress whites with his arm around a laughing brunette, her hair in a 40's roll around her head, A little boy about five years old stood between them. He wore a navy blue sailor suit, and the wistful eyes in the small serious face were familiar. Next to the picture was a brush and comb and a dopp kit with some shaving essentials.

Suzanne looked at the drawers for a moment and then gave in to temptation. She was shocked at herself for opening them. A well-bred person would never do such a thing. They contained only a few socks and a meager supply of underwear. The usual traveler staying a couple of nights at a hotel would have filled all the drawers with no problem.

She hung up her coat and noticed a couple of jackets and slacks. A raincoat of sorts. Three pairs of shoes on the floor and some rather old sneakers. Walter had had dozens of everything. And apparently it wasn't enough.

Suzanne herself had never known anyone who had as little of the world's material goods as Dave. She had stepped into a world she only knew about from books. How could someone in these conditions get along and be happy? What about ambition?

As far as she could tell, all Dave wanted was to get his old job back. Was this the way to live a life? To be satisfied with so little? She was totally confused. And yet, Dave was not a worrier, as far as she could tell. She finally realized something else. Dave had a certain grace under pressure. A laissez faire attitude. The ability to live in the moment and make the logical surefooted leap into the next one. Like pulling back to make a void so the good Lord could fill it with something you really need.

She shook her head and went into the bathroom to get a drink of water. How strange all this was. While she had been sunk in depression for the weeks following Walter's death, she wondered if she could continue living. Now she had met this funny man who had the ability to remove the plugs that bottled up her feelings and emotions and who seemed to be dangling before her some new ideas about life.

Later when she lay in Dave's bed, she was surprised to feel the beginning flutterings of sexual arousal. An aura of his presence hovered over her. There was something erotic about lying where he had lain, her head in his pillow. It seemed as if he rightfully belonged beside her. Heat flushed up inside her, and a very faint voice in the back of her mind whispered an astounding truth. It would have been comfortable and natural to have him there.

*   *   *

The night passed as in an instant. It was her first solid sleep since Walter died.

She woke about nine o'clock to the sound of rain lashing against the creaking old windows, and lay for moment feeling cozy and safe. Then she realized. "Oh, my God." She sat up in bed with a sinking heart. She needed good weather all this week if she were going to get Maude's grounds in shape. Well, she would do what she could. "Damn you, Walter," she said out loud and felt better.

She took a shower in the old-fashioned bathtub and put on the silky beige brassiere and panties she had rinsed out the night before. After she was dressed, she brushed her hair slowly with Dave's hairbrush, searching her eyes in the mirror. Then a little pale lipstick and blusher went on, and she was ready to go down to the kitchen.

She caught the Romanos at the sink in a fond embrace. Seventy plus years old and obviously still crazy about each other. "Excuse me," she said.

They turned to her, laughing, but still hugging each other. "This is why I like to cook and wash dishes with Sophie," said Milo. "I get some squeezing time in."

"I'm envious," said Suzanne, meaning it with all her heart. Why do so few people find exactly the right mate? Her own parents were divorced, she had aunts and uncles who were always fighting, and her close friends complained constantly about their spouses. Dreary thoughts on a dreary morning.

Sophie seemed to notice the look on her face. "Sit down," she said, pulling a chair out from the kitchen table. A plate decorated with red cherries was laid on a yellow checked placemat. "Is orange juice okay?"

Suzanne got settled and nodded. "I'm afraid you're going to too much trouble."

The Romanos grinned at her. "You remember the La Paloma restaurant down on West Cutler Street across the river?" Milo asked. She didn't really, but they looked at her so expectantly she nodded her head. "That was ours," he said, looking proudly at Sophie who was pouring Suzanne's coffee. "We were in business there for over forty years. Finally decided to sell and take it easy."

Suzanne was remembering something. "Weren't you reviewed on the food page of the Herald as the best Italian restaurant in the area?"

"Several times." Milo's back was to her as he flipped over a mushroom and tomato omelet.

"I was interviewed for that page," said Suzanne. "As a hostess."

"No kidding," said Milo, turning the perfect omelet onto her plate. The three of them passed smiles around and laughed. "We have a lot in common," said Suzanne, and meant it. She was suddenly ravenous and took a bite. "I love to cook, also," she said between mouthfuls. "But this is the best omelet I have ever had in my entire life."

After breakfast, Suzanne made some telephone calls. First, the Edgewood Groundskeeper Company, who maintained her own lawn. She described the work to be done on Maude's estate. "We won't be able to do anything today in all this rain," they told her, as she expected. "Maybe later in the week."

"I don't care what it costs," she said. "It absolutely has to look cared for by the end of the week." They promised to do their best.

Next, she called a window-washing firm and got the same answer. Later, Mrs. Wilkins. They would do their best. Suzanne sat for a moment and considered the situation. She could really do nothing until the weather cleared up. Later in the week she go out and do some trimming and pruning herself even if it was too wet to mow. As a member of the Garden Club for many years, she could do a good job.

She dialed her code numbers and got her answering machine. There were several messages from Emilee Johnson, the last one this morning. Emilee sounded ready to call the Missing Persons Bureau. "I'm worried about you. You missed my little dinner party Sunday night. Where are you?" asked Emilee Johnson. Oh, my. Emilee had talked her into joining two other couples along with her husband and herself to have dinner and go to a concert. Suzanne had completely forgotten. And now Emilee apparently knew that Suzanne had not been home on Sunday night.

Suzanne bit her lip and dialed Emilee's number. Well, thank goodness you're all right," said Emilee and waited. Where the hell were you, the silence asked.

"Look," said Suzanne. "You're my best friend. So, stay my best friend and don't ask questions. Let me just say that some business came up about Walter's estate, and I had to go out of town overnight."

"You couldn't even call." Accusing, hurt.

"I'm sorry. I got absorbed in what was happening and completely forgot." She was ashamed of what she said next. "You know, I haven't been myself lately."

Emilee calmed down. "I know."

"Listen, Emilee. I'm not going to be able to go to the Great Books class or the Garden Club or play bridge for several weeks. There's a great deal of work to do to settle Walter's estate, and there are some things I want to clear up."

"I thought your lawyer was handling all of that."

"Well, of course. But there are records, papers, insurance, things like that that I need to research. There's a lot to get settled."

"Hmmm. I don't know what's going on, but whatever it is, I approve. You sound more like your old self today. Well, I'm here if you need me."

"Thanks for being my friend."

Suzanne hung up and Sophie Romano came into the hall, the morning newspaper in one hand and a smile extending her cheeks. She flipped the paper open to the front page and held it out to Suzanne. "Look."

It could rain as hard as it wanted today. This was a good day after all. SUSPECT NABBED IN ALLEY ATTACK, the banner screamed. There was a picture of a haggard Cameron Castore staring blankly from beneath the headline. Seems the police got a tip and picked him up in Hamilton. Bail was set at $50,000. "That didn't take long," said Sophie.

"I wonder who tipped them off?"

"A punk like that—in trouble before—well, I guess maybe he has some enemies. Came from a good family, too. Honestly, I don't know what's wrong with kids these days."

"I suppose some of them have too many pressures in today's society," said Suzanne, thinking of Penny who was coping with the loss of her father. She must call her daughter soon.

"That's no excuse," said Sophie indignantly. "My word, me and Milo—well, we didn't have it easy. You know, like the kids today have everything—cars, TV, clothes—well, shoot, we both worked through high school. There weren't no college money, so we both worked in restaurants. That's how we got our own business—by working hard. Kids today don't wanna work hard."

"That may be true," smiled Suzanne. "Well, I guess I can go home now. But I think I'll stop off at the hospital first and share this good news with Dave."

"I'll loan you an umbrella." Sophie turned toward the kitchen. "Stop in the kitchen before you leave. I made him a coffee cake this morning."

Dave was lying on his left side, his eyes riveted on the open doorway when she walked in.

"You're a bright vision on such a day," he said.

"Even wet?" she laughed, self-consciously, shaking out the huge flowered umbrella. "Well, anyway, I come bearing the usual comforting food from Mrs. Romano." She went to the side of the bed and stood, holding the coffee cake. The dark pools of his eyes were disconcerting this morning.

"Did you hear the news?" she asked.

"Yes, indeed." He flicked a finger at the newspaper folded on the bed stand. "This is a real break for—us, Suzanne." He gave her a wide smile. "With this character out of the way, we should be able to safely transfer the money to Miss Hills' bank account, once you get the power of attorney."

She placed the coffee cake on the nightstand and sat down, shrugging her arms out of her coat. "But you can't be involved, Dave. Because of your own problems, you can't go anywhere near that money."

"Well, we'll work that out later."

"Anyway, this Cameron is behind bars. Will he stay there, do you think? What about bail?"

"I doubt very much if he can raise that kind of money. Unless his parents come through for him. That's always a possibility."

"So he still could be a threat?"

"Maybe. Depends on how scared or desperate he is. I would guess it could go either way."

"I wonder who turned him in. The newspaper account mentioned a telephone call from a woman."

"Probably a girl friend. Or an ex-girl friend. Maybe a woman scorned kind of thing."

She grimaced and shook her shoulders. "I can't imagine any girl caring for that kind of a person." Dave's glance wavered from her face.

"You know something," she said suddenly.

"Not really. Just a hunch."

"You're not going to tell me now."

"No." His voice was firm.

"All right. Then tell me how you feel this morning and if you had a good night."

"I'm feeling better, thanks. The doctor thinks I'll be out of here by Wednesday."

"Wonderful."

"And did you have a good sleep?" She read the rest of the sentence 'in my bed' in his eyes.

"Yes, thank you." Then, "I used your hair brush. I hope you don't mind."

"No." Dave's eyes circled her face, lingering on her shining hair, as if he himself were brushing it. She felt the heat rising in her face. She turned her head and stood up. "Going so soon?" he asked wistfully.

"I think I'd better get home and check on some things," she said. There really was no reason to go except that being with this man made her restless and jumpy this morning. She stood away from the bed and said goodbye. If she stood nearer, she might lose control and touch him in some way—again.

She passed by the nurses' station on the way out and went to wait for the elevator around the corner. Before it came, she got a real surprise. The nurses were laughing and their voices drifted down the hall to her. "Wow! That guy in 416 sure has the beautiful women visitors. First that gorgeous brunette last night. Did you see them holding hands and watching the movie? Then this blonde shows up this morning. She brought him flowers yesterday. Wonder which one he's married to!" Laughter. Then, "Probably neither one. His wife is home with the screaming kids." Ha ha. Ha ha.

With each descending floor, Suzanne's heart grew heavier and heavier. When she stepped out into the rain again, she was perfectly in tune with the weather. Depressed.

*   *   *

Someone else sighed in relief over the morning's headlines. For the time being Cam was off her back. Theda had bought herself some time and she had a plan. After last night, she knew that Dave Monaco was half in love with her already. All she had to do was seduce him and then convince him to run away with her. With the money, of course. She knew she could do it. Ever since she was twelve years old, boys and men had practically driveled at her feet with lust and desire. She knew she had a special appeal few other women had. Now was certainly the time to use it. Once she got him to turn over the money she would figure out a way to get rid of him. Not that he wasn't attractive. There was something kinda boyish and appealing about that big ex-cop. But she wanted a new start for herself somewhere. Maybe Hollywood. She could change her name, dye her hair, and who knows? She knew how those starlets worked their way to the top. She could do the same.

Theda was feeling better than she had in days. Cam's absence was spreading a balm over life's rough edges of the past few days. She expected he would call her anytime now, but she was ready for that, too. He would never find out she was the one who blew the whistle on him.

She could hardly wait until her working day was over so she could get to the hospital. While Dave was flat on his back in a weakened condition, she had the perfect target for her trap. Theda stood in Dave's doorway about seven o'clock.

"Well," he said, running an appreciative eye over her from tip to toe. She slipped off a yellow slicker and stood for a moment in a bright red jersey blouse criss-crossed tightly over full rounded breasts. Snug black knit leggings hugged the lower curves nicely above up-to-the knee black boots.

"Well," he said again. It looked like another interesting evening was about to get under way.

"I hope you don't mind," she said. "I thought you might be alone here tonight and want some company." She came over to the side of the bed and intertwined his fingers with hers. A lock of her thick dark hair tumbled seductively over one smoldering eye as she looked at him. His nostrils filled with the provocative scent of her perfume. Oh, oh, he thought, tonight is serious business. He hoped he was up to it. Disturbing thoughts of Suzanne had flitted back and forth through his head all day. Something interesting had been building up between them, but then this morning she had definitely backed off. He knew what had probably happened.

When she stayed in his room among his meager belongings and got a sample of how he lived, she must have recognized the economic and cultural gulf between them. Things like that mattered to women—most women. Why had he thought she was different? Just because she was nice to him? Get real, Monaco. She's a lady of breeding, taught to have nice manners in any situation. The only reason for your association with her is to help straighten out her present problems. After that is done, you have no further reason to see her—ever. But now Theda was here, gazing at him with faked adoration. He became aware that she was suggestively caressing the palm of his hand with her finger, and he came back to the present in a hurry.

He decided to do his part. He gave her a limpid look with his brown eyes. "Come here," he said softly, and gripped her arms to lower her face to his. Their lips met tentatively, then again more firmly. She was delicious. A real pro. Her lips were like waves, pressing and retreating. Then her mouth parted and her little pink tongue darted ever so tentatively between his lips. He took his cue, and covered her perfect lips firmly with his own, unleashing his own tongue to mate with hers. She leaned against him apparently in passion, and he winced with pain. "Ouch," he said, turning his head aside.

"Oh, I'm sorry, I forgot," she said, straightening up. "I was just so glad to see you again."

"I understand," he said with a smile. Oh, baby, do I ever understand!

"I'll try to be good." She gave him a coy look. "But it's going to be hard, Dave. You're such an attractive man."

Okay. Sure. Don't overdo it, kiddo. You're a temptation, all right. She settled down beside him, holding his hand, and gazing adoringly at him. He stifled an urge to laugh and tried to look at her with equal yearning. Now was his chance to twist the hook, to couple the two of them seriously. He was sure he knew how to do that.

"Do you realize I know very little about you?" he asked. "Of course, I see that you are very beautiful, but what about the real you? The part that is deep inside, you as a person? I want to know everything about you. What were you like as a little girl? What were your parents like? Have you been married—or are you now? What do you like to do in your spare time? Just anything about you—whatever you want to tell me."

He saw the surprise behind the long dusky lashes. But he had guessed right. He was probably the first man who wanted to get behind the sexy exterior and understand the private Theda. This was the way to really reach her.

Theda stared at him, and then the seductive look peeled away, leaving the sad eyes of a little girl whose puppy had just died. She began slowly, tentatively, and spoke of her father leaving when she was young and of her mother's remarriage.

"I suppose that's why I got married young," she said. "I wanted some kind of home. Trouble is, I picked the wrong jerk."

"You're still married?"

"Oh, no. Uh, that—uh, we broke up a while ago." Dave noticed the hesitation.

"So you're free now?" He squeezed her fingers.

"Yes."

"Good." He summoned up what he thought would be a suggestive grin. "I imagine there were some others since you and your husband split."

"A few." She smiled, then lowered her face. "There was one—a special one," she said softly.

"What happened? Was he married?" Theda's head shot up and she looked at him in surprised shock. After a moment, she lowered her head again and whispered, "He died."

"I'm sorry," Dave said sincerely. It was obvious she had really loved this person.

"What was he like?" he asked.

"He was wonderful." A little glow crept back into her eyes." A real gentleman, you know, educated and stuff. Nice manners, and. he was fun, too. And so good to me. He was a big executive." She said the last proudly.

"So he got sick?"

"Not exactly. It was more like an accident." She moved restlessly in the chair. "Hey, that's enough about me. Let's watch the tube."

Dave picked up the remote and turned on the overhead TV. While he pretended to watch, his brain spread out the information he had just heard and made some assessments. How could he have been so stupid? All this time he thought Cam was connected to Walter in this scam. Why had he forgotten cherchez la femme? There was Theda in the coffee shop next to Walter's bank—and apparently, the temptation was too great. Turn this around, he said to himself. Then there was the money. Suppose Walter stole the money for Theda and Cam found out about it. Then which one of them is probably the murderer? Maybe both of them? But something wasn't quite right here. Something didn't fly. Theda had loved Walter too much to kill him. He would make book on that. Then Cam. But if Cam did it, then Theda would have nothing to do with him or the money. Dave didn't know much about her, but somehow he felt she would be loyal to the memory of her lover. Well, he had found out a few things, but he was still far from solving the case. If this were a mystery novel, the killer would probably turn out to be the least likely player in the drama: in this case, Suzanne. Only in real police work it rarely worked that way. A lot of hard police work uncovered minutiae connected to minutiae, building a reverse pyramid of indisputable evidence.

Theda continued in her role as vamp, leaning over occasionally to kiss him on the face and twice more hotly on the lips. She seemed to enjoy her part in this fictional romance, as did Dave. He felt desire for her increase as the evening went on. My God— what would happen when he got out of here? His only restraint was the knowledge of what she was up to. Whether that would be enough for him to resist the ultimate temptation, he didn't know.

16

Although the weather began clearing on Wednesday morning and persistent flashes of sun battled to break through the clouds, Suzanne's mood still matched the gloom of yesterday. How ridiculous, she told herself. She and Dave were really strangers, two people thrown together only because of peculiar circumstances. Two people who had not yet progressed to the personal level of sharing private information about themselves or their backgrounds. She only knew he had an ex-wife—and a floozy at that. Suzanne smiled grimly. What on earth would attract a nice man like Dave to such a person? She shook her head. Perhaps she really knew nothing significant about him after all. Yet, when she was with him, she knew he was no stranger. Somehow, in a very short time, she had become connected to Dave Monaco in a personal way.

So—this meant she had feelings for him. That admission brought Suzanne up short. So soon after Walter's death? She smiled as she imagined her mother's reaction to that: "What can you be thinking of?" And her own response: "My husband embezzled money from a lovely old lady." Hardly a basis for continuing loyalty. When she saw it in these terms, she knew a new relationship could be the healing force in her life. Wherever it led. Now they were thrown together by the urgency to solve the mystery of Walter's death. When that was over, what would she and Dave have to keep them together?

Yesterday the picture of Dave lying in the hospital flashed in and out of her mind. Suzanne tried to keep busy answering mail, paying bills, poking here and there with a dust mop, throwing some laundry into the washer. She reached Penny on the phone and listened to her daughter's vivid accounts, negative and positive, of ebullient college life. Life on another planet.

After she nibbled unenthusiastically at a salad for dinner, Suzanne decided to go to the hospital. Immediately she felt cheered and expectant and dressed in a soft pink blouse and swirling rose skirt. She got her coat from the closet and opened the side door from the hall into the garage. Then she stopped short. Common sense took over.

She reviewed her actions so far. After Dave's injury, her initial visits to the hospital were proper, in line, and surely understood in this light by Dave. She was solicitous because he was injured as the result of being involved in her problem. Also, as kind of partners, they had business to discuss. Dave might think that further visits indicated personal interest on her part. That could be very embarrassing for her. If he were involved with another woman, it was time to retreat now. Also, her own growing feelings for him were disturbing. With her heart barely on the mend from Walter's violent action, would it be possible for it to break again and so soon? She was still fragile, still on the edge. She needed to protect herself from any further emotional damage. She closed the side door to the garage and went back through the hall to hang up her coat. Practical Suzanne. Always doing the right thing. Treading the well-worn, familiar paths. No risk-taker, she. Doing the expected thing, the accepted thing.

But when she went upstairs to change her clothes, a picture of Milo and Sophie Romano drifted across her mind. Ample bodies, intertwined. Looking enraptured at one another, seeing past the wrinkled masks of time into the eternally beautiful face of each beloved.

Maybe we try too much to find just the right one in this world, Suzanne thought. Maybe we should let love just happen.

Now, on Wednesday morning, she was glad she had restrained herself the night before. Let Dave make the first move, she thought. About ten o'clock he called to let her know he was being released. The Romanos were picking him up.

"How do you feel?" she asked. A nice, impersonal question.

"A little stiff, but I'm ambulatory. Have to come back in a week and get the stitches out. Then I'll be as good as new."

"That's really good news, Dave."

Silence. Then, "Listen," Dave said, "can we get together later on today? I've got something to tell you." I'll bet you have, thought Suzanne, her heart sinking. "Can't you tell me now?"

"I'd better not. It might be somewhat upsetting for you. I'd like to tell you in person."

"Sure." Her voice was abrupt, flat.

"How about dinner tonight?"

A surprise. "Dinner?"

"Yeah, you know. That meal at the end of the day?"

A giggle escaped. "Well, all right. What time?"

"How about I come around at five-thirty so we can eat early? I have to go to a meeting at eight o'clock." Suzanne hung up and smiled. Took a deep breath. Just hearing his voice made her feel better. He had asked her out to dinner—wasn't that kind of a date? Then she remembered the purpose of this meeting. To tell her something distressful. Probably something about that other woman. Just like a man—thought taking her to dinner would make everything all right.

Once more, she began freezing up on the inside. Then the telephone rang again. It was the law office of John Talbot, Maude Hills' lawyer. A power of attorney had been executed for Suzanne. Would she come in for it? She picked up a piece of notepaper and listed her plans for the day. As it turned out, she had plenty to do before five thirty came.

*   *   *

Charles Rosenthal sat in Walter Wilkins' former leather chair behind Walter Wilkins' former massive oak desk and shuffled the few papers before him. Hollywood couldn't have done a better job at casting the perfect bank president. Carefully groomed sprigs of hair. A plain maroon tie on the crisp white shirt beneath the pinstriped three-piece suit. New horn-rimmed glasses that added to the overall impression of trust and intelligence. All enhanced by the elegant room itself. His buzzer sounded. "Yes, Miss Moore," he said.

"Mrs. Wilkins is here to see you," said his secretary.

"Well!" he said, surprised. "Ask her to come in."

He stood up to greet her, checking his tie, and moving a few feet to the side of the desk. Too late, he wondered if Suzanne would be upset to be back in Walter's old office. A moment later, she stood in the doorway, nervously squeezing her shoulder bag with her right hand. Then she smiled brightly. "Charles," she said smoothly. "How good to see you again." She moved gracefully to his side and brushed a cool cheek against his. A light fragrance followed her to the visitor's arm chair before the desk. Once settled, she glanced quickly about. He thought he saw a flash of panic in her eyes for a moment. It bothers her to be here, he reasoned.

He smiled encouragingly into her lovely eyes. She's bounced back, he thought, somewhat surprised. The last two times he had seen her—at Walter's funeral and at her house when he delivered the box of papers—grief had drawn her drab and listless. Now her cheeks and lips were blushed with crimson, her eyes clear beneath the dark lashes. But what was stranger for a recent widow was a hint of a glow about her, a stirring of something inside. He leaned across his desk for a clearer look through the thick lens of the new glasses.

"What can I do for you?" She arched forward, disturbing him with her direct glance. "I need your help, Charles."

"Of course. I'll do anything I can, you know that."

She exhaled as if in relief and settled back in her chair. "I'm so glad you said that. All the way over here I told myself I could count on you."

"You know you can," he said, a little less confidently than before. What was she getting at?

She told him. "As you know, Walter took care of Maude Hills' business affairs. Well, I'm taking his place. Miss Hills has appointed me her attorney-in-fact and given me an unlimited power of attorney."

Charles was surprised. "That's a big job. She has a sizable estate."

"Yes, I know. But she's confident I can handle it, and I need something like this to occupy me at this time. You understand." Her smile was sweet and wistful.

"And you want me to help in some way?"

"Yes. I have a big problem to take care of. I have part of the solution worked out, but I need your cooperation in dealing with the rest of it." She leaned forward again and widened her eyes at him. He began to forget why she was here. He wondered if he could ask her out to dinner to discuss this further. No, forget that. Dorothy's office was right outside, and, short of opening his mail, she somehow knew everything that was going on in his life.

Suzanne went on in a more conversational tone. "Well, Charles, you won't believe what I ran into. Talk about old people getting forgetful! I was out to see Maude last Sunday—you know—she and I have been good friends for a long time. Anyway, before I left, her companion—the lady she lives with, who takes care of her— cornered me to tell me something astounding." She paused and moved in her chair as if to cross a leg. Charles craned his neck, but unfortunately, the desk obscured most of his vision.

After a moment, he tapped his fingers on the top of the desk. "Yes? What? What is it?"

"It's hard to believe." She seemed to be studying something in her lap.

Charles' patience was ebbing away. "Suzanne, if you don't tell me, I can't help you."

"Well, of course, Charles! I know you want to help me, don't I?" She smiled sweetly. "Well, it turns out that Miss Hills has been hiding money away for YEARS. You know, cash. Like recluses sometimes do. An under-the-mattress kind of thing."

"Really!"

"Yes. Her companion and I feel that we need to get this money deposited into her bank account."

"Well, naturally. That's the best thing. Or else invest it. Is it a great deal of money?"

"Well, we're not sure until we have collected it all. But it could be, I should think."

"So how do you plan to handle this situation?"

"I thought I would hire an armored car service to pick it up and bring it here to the bank. What do you think, Charles? Would that be the right thing to do?"

He nodded his head. "Yes, that's the safest way to transport it certainly."

"Now, because we have no idea how much it will be, we'll have it delivered here to you. You can arrange to have it counted and make out the slip to have it deposited to Miss Hills' account. As bank president you can do that, can't you, Charles?"

"Well—uh, I uh—"

Suzanne opened her purse. "Do you want to see my power of attorney?"

"No," Charles said slowly, "I guess that won't be necessary. I have no reason to doubt your authority in all of this." He kneaded his hands together on top of the desk. "This is certainly an unusual situation. However, I don't see any real problem."

"Oh, Charles, I knew I could count on you. I'm so new to this kind of thing; I didn't know if I could handle it. But now I see that you're going to take care of everything, I know I have nothing to worry about."

Suzanne suddenly stood up and swung her handbag to the shoulder of her blue jacket. Charles rose to his feet and came around the desk to say goodbye. Reaching up, Suzanne gave him a little pat on the face. "Dear Charles," she said. "You've always been such a good friend. Walter often spoke highly of you. Now I know why. People can count on you." She started for the door and then whirled about. "Oh," she said, "I almost forgot. The money will arrive about eleven o'clock tomorrow morning. Just send the deposit slip to me. And thanks, Charles. You make a wonderful bank president."

*   *   *

When Suzanne left the bank, she was shaking. She stood just

outside the entrance for a moment, taking deep breaths to quiet her jumping heart. She had avoided pretending and lying all her life, and it was very upsetting to have to resort to these activities now. Suddenly she despised Walter in a new way. His actions had forced her to corrupt her basic beliefs.

She was relieved that this part of the plan was now arranged. So far, she had pulled it off, but she still had to get the money delivered safely. She wouldn't relax until that was accomplished. As the new attorney-in-fact, a review of Maude's assets was in order. Her report to the old actress would include the new deposit. Maude need never know that, for a time, a goodly portion of her estate had been missing. Suzanne was passing the coffee shop next to the bank when she suddenly decided to go in for a cup of coffee and a corn muffin. Not a bad place, she thought, as she looked around at the floor plants and original art on the walls. I suppose Walter used to come here once in a while. She settled herself at a small table against a far wall and opened a menu. It was one-thirty and only few late lunchers were lingering before settling back into the business routine. Still it seemed as if she were invisible. After ten minutes, no one had appeared to take her order.

Suzanne tapped her well-groomed nails on the simulated oak tabletop and looked around, frowning, trying to catch a waitress' eye. Finally, a waitress tending to tables in the front window looked her way. Suzanne gestured to her and she came over.

"I've been waiting quite a while," Suzanne explained, in her even, cultured voice.

"I'm sorry," said the waitress, an older woman with a thick waistline and ankles to match. "Theda is your waitress. I'll get her for you."

Suzanne watched this woman confront a young girl just outside the kitchen door. In a second, they seemed to be having an argument. Suzanne saw the young woman look at her and then shake her head. Apparently, this made the older woman angry. Suzanne couldn't see her face, but her back stiffened and her arms waved about. She turned slightly to glance over at Suzanne and then put one hand on her hip and shook a finger in the face of the younger waitress.

For heaven's sake, thought Suzanne, what's going on here? It's as if this waitress with the funny name didn't want to wait on her. Suddenly a man appeared and got into the act. Must be the manager, Suzanne thought. He scowled into the young waitress' face and waggled his forefinger menacingly at her. His face was turning pink.

Suzanne had enough stress in her life right now. She decided to leave. Suddenly the waitress named Theda nodded her head and started toward Suzanne's table, pad and pencil in hand. "Is something wrong?" asked Suzanne.

"Wh—ah, what?"

"You didn't want to wait on me. Why not?" Suzanne kept her voice cool, matter-of-fact. She glanced up into an exotic face, whose eyes avoided hers. This Theda was busy looking at her blank order pad.

"Oh, no, uh, it, uh, wasn't that. I just haven't been feeling well today, and our manager had told me I could go home."

"Then why didn't the other woman take my order?"

"I really don't know, but it's okay. I'm feeling better now."

So, Theda eventually brought Suzanne a toasted corn muffin and a cup of coffee, which spilled into the saucer when Theda set in on the table.

"You're trembling," Suzanne told her. "You better go home as soon as you can. Maybe you're coming down with something." Somehow, Suzanne felt sorry for this girl and left a larger tip than necessary.

On the way to Maude Hills' estate, Suzanne decided to stop at her own house to call the Armored Motor Delivery Service. But first, she went into the library to check on the key. She knew there was no possibility that it would not be in its hiding place, but still her heart pounded until she actually felt it lying safely on the shelf behind the book of Shakespeare. Thank goodness by tomorrow it would be unlocking the locker, and then the bag of money would be delivered to the bank.

The armored car people were very reassuring. Yes, they would come to her house to get the key, go to the locker at the train station, and then deliver the duffle bag to Mr. Rosenthal at the main branch of the Monroe Trust Company at eleven o'clock. The delivery service was fully insured and provided two armed guards besides the completely secure vehicle. They were very business-like and handled Suzanne's request as if they received orders like hers every day.

She hung up feeling pleased with herself. Certainly, she had accomplished a great deal today. In fact, she had taken care of the biggest part of obliterating Walter's dishonesty.

The other problem—the why of Walter's actions—still hung over her like an impenetrable black cloud. And his death was the biggest, blackest mystery of all. She got back in her car and put on her dark glasses. The sun was sparkling the wet tips of grass and weaving patterns through the trees. It was turning into a lovely afternoon, and she rolled her car window down halfway as she turned out onto the highway.

She sighed with relief when she spotted two trucks parked in the turnaround by Maude's front door. A crew of five men was digging, weeding, and pruning. Several varieties of bagged and burlaped shrubbery were placed on the lawn near their intended permanent positions.

A large man, with 'The Edgewood Groundskeeper' printed on a gray shirt, put down a shovel and came over to her. "Hi, Ms. Wilkins," he said, flipping up his billed cap, also inscribed. "We're doing what we can. There are several dead bushes, so we figured you'd want us to replace those." He gestured vaguely at new shrubbery.

"Good idea," said Suzanne. "Do whatever you think best. This place has to look beautiful by Sunday." Her eyes pleaded with him. "I mean, it absolutely has to. Whatever it takes."

"Well—" he took off his cap and scratched his head. "We'll see. Can't mow yet, it's still too wet. Maybe tomorrow." He gestured toward the rose garden, full of weeds. "There's a lot to do, and several of the rose bushes are gone. Should have been mulched last fall. We'll get rid of those, do some pruning, weeding, put pine bark around. It should look pretty good." He leaned down closer to Suzanne's car window. "There's still all of the beds in the rear and the rock garden. But there's a nice bed of daffodils near to bloom back by the terrace. That'll help."

"Thanks. I'm so grateful. This is a very special old lady, and it will mean a great deal to her to see her home well taken care of."

"Yes, we know. It's Maude Hills, isn't it? I was a big fan of hers when I was a boy. There'll never be another actress like her. Remember that picture with the red shoes? I must have been ten or eleven when I saw that. I thought that was the sexiest picture I ever saw!" He laughed. "Ha! Now they show everything, don't they?"

"I'm afraid so," Suzanne agreed. "Well, could you give me a call at the end of the week and let me know what you were able to do?"

"Sure."

Suzanne started her car, and then stuck her head out the window. "I'll tell you a secret about Miss Hills," she called. "She's still wearing those red shoes."

Suzanne pulled back the louvered doors of her wide closet and contemplated the blouses, skirts, slacks, dresses, suits, and evening wear that hung in their designated sections. The large shelf above was filled with shoeboxes, the contents noted on red-bordered labels. She pushed hangers slowly to and fro, her concentration as intense as if she were deciding what to wear to meet the Queen.

What kind of a restaurant could they be going to? Not too expensive, she decided. But what did she really know? Maybe he had a little money but was just conservative. No, she thought, it's more like he doesn't care for material things. How wonderful to be so free. She wondered if she could ever have the strength to live without all the luxuries that through the years had somehow turned into necessities. It suddenly struck her that because Dave had shed the trappings of life he was the most real person she had ever known. We go through life like a director in a play, she thought, only we're directing ourselves to play the proper character in each particular setting. We put on masks to be with other people, somehow picking up direction from them, too, and playing the role to please them. After awhile we're out of touch with our real selves. We've lost a little part of the real US to all those other people in our lives.

Through all his difficulties, it seemed Dave Monaco had kept intact his sense of self. She felt some of that when she was with him. His person was open. He was genuine and truthful with himself and compassionate with others.

Suzanne finally selected a designer slate-blue silk sheath with a scarf at the neck that tied over one shoulder. It had its own simple fingertip rough wool jacket. Just right for almost any restaurant, she decided, and its simplicity obscured the price.

It was ridiculous. She felt awkward, uncertain, and uncharacteristically shy. Ready early, she sat in the library and waited, aware that strangely her heart was pounding.

On the way over to Suzanne's, Dave's right side hurt with every breath. The doctors had told him to go home and stay in bed a few days, but the thought of seeing Suzanne made the pain bearable. There was nothing in the world that would keep him from seeing her tonight. All he needed was to look in her eyes again, and the pain would go away.

When she opened the door to him, he realized he was wrong. Another pain sprung up inside him—the agony of desire. He read something in her glance. Was he wrong? Hell, take a chance, Monaco, he told himself. Without taking his eyes from her face, he stepped into her hall. Stood for only an instant and then moved toward her, his arms rising in their eagerness to hold her.

He thought he saw a flutter of alarm in her eyes, and he stepped back uncertainly. She did the same, and a feeling of embarrassment vibrated between them. Suddenly their glances were everywhere except on each other.

"Well," he said, grasping for words to put this moment behind them and then asking the obvious, "are you ready to go?" He risked a look from top to bottom. "You look beautiful," he said, speaking over the catch in his throat. The stitches were aching.

"Excuse me," he said, and went to sit on a carved bench in the hall. "My stitches are pulling a bit," he explained. "Besides, seeing you again makes my knees weak." He grinned at her. Best keep it light.

Suzanne went to stand before him. "We'd better get you something to eat." She was looking at the top of his head with a strange expression. She reached out a hand as if to smooth down his cowlick and then abruptly withdrew it. Dave looked up at her wistfully, and Suzanne stared back with eyes that seemed full of questions.

"Where are we going?" she asked, after they were seated in Dave's borrowed compact car.

"How about La Paloma?" asked Dave as he backed out of the driveway and started up the street. "The Romanos used to own it. As a matter of fact, I think Sophie wishes they still did."

"Sounds wonderful. It has a good reputation."

Oh, Suzanne. Why do we sound like a couple of strangers?

They were shown to a booth in the small, cozy restaurant. Red carnations in a slender milk glass vase decorated the white linen tablecloth. Chair and bench seats were padded in a subdued flowered pattern echoed in the wallpaper above a silvery wainscoting. The carpeting was a soft gray.

"This is very nice," Suzanne observed.

"I think the new owners must have re-modeled," said Dave. "Somehow this doesn't remind me of Sophie." They laughed. The waitress brought Suzanne a glass of white wine and Dave club soda with a twist of lime. "You don't drink?" she asked. "Not any more." He twisted the glass in his hand, and then looked at her. "I have a drinking problem. This meeting I have tonight is AA. I'm a newcomer to the program, and I must go. Much as I want to be with you, I've made a commitment to myself to recover from what seems to be an illness."

She couldn't think of anything to say.

"Look, Suzy. If this makes a difference in how you feel about me, just say so." He didn't realize he had used his private name for her.

She reached across the table and laid her hand on his. "Of course not. If anything, I admire you more. It's a hard thing to handle, I know, but you'll make it."

"I want you there when I get my ninety-day pin." He captured her hand in his. "You're partly responsible, you know."

"I am?"

"Sure. You took your husband's jacket to the second-hand store, and I found the key that led me to you. I could only be sober to deal with all those circumstances."

"You may yet be sorry you met me."

"Never!" he said vehemently.

They sipped their drinks. Then she looked at him. "You called me Suzy," she said. "I kicked the boys in kindergarten for calling me that."

"Do you mind? Somehow, I think of you like that. Suzy with a 'Z.'"

She laughed. "I kinda like it. Informal. Maybe more suited to the future me."

"Or the present you. I think it fits you now."

"Maybe. There certainly have been some changes in my life and I suppose in me."

Over seafood fettuccini, she told him of her visit to the bank, the arrangements to have the money transported, and the progress at Maude's estate.

When she finished, he was grinning broadly. "My God, you're something else. A real operator. I couldn't have done it better myself. That guy at the bank—he must be wondering what hit him!" He threw back his head and laughed. "Suzy the sleuth!"

Suzanne laughed too. "You know, it was kind of fun. Like I was playing a part. Something I've never done before."

"So the money gets deposited in Maude's account. How does this get explained to her?"

"I thought I could just say that I went over Walter's books and discovered he had somehow deposited some of her money in the wrong account." She shook her head. "I don't know. I haven't really thought this part out yet. Once the money is safely back in the bank, I'll think of something. Anyway, I have a strange feeling that Maude will accept anything I say. I don't think she's going to demand a full explanation." They concentrated on their dining for a few minutes. Then Suzanne said, "Tell me about your childhood, your family."

"Well, I was born in Brooklyn. My dad worked in a freight office. He died a few years ago. My mother lives with my sister in Pennsylvania."

"How did you end up out here in the Midwest?"

"I came out to go to Northwestern."

"I didn't know you went to college."

"Only two years. I quit to go to the police academy. Probably a dumb decision, but at the time I was restless sitting in classrooms. I wanted to be part of the action."

"Did it turn out to be a good decision?"

"Yes and no. Looking at my present situation, it could be a definite no."

"But you're going to be cleared, Dave, I know it."

"I hope you're right. In the meantime, I've met you and that's the best."

What a sweet guy! Suzanne felt her eyes mist.

"You and your husband were married a long time," Dave stated.

"Yes, twenty-one years. We met at college. Cornell."

"You're from back East, too?"

"Yes, I'm from Athens, a little town in upstate New York. On the Hudson River."

"That's beautiful country."

"Yes, it is."

Suzanne sensed an awkwardness between them. It seemed they had to get their backgrounds out of the way before dealing further with the growing intimacy.

"I have a lovely daughter, Penny," she volunteered. "She's a sophomore at Wheaton College."

"I never had any children," Dave said. "I guess it's just as well, as things turned out."

Somehow, Suzanne couldn't help asking a stupid question, just like someone in love. "Was there anyone else after your divorce?"

She saw amusement in his eyes and sensed he was seeing right through her. Her cheeks grew warm. "No one, 'til you. But I'm thinking of making a pass at Mrs. Romano. She drives me mad with her cooking."

"I'd be glad to try to drive you mad with mine," she said in what she hoped was a casual tone.

Dave leaned across his plate and gave her a disconcerting probing glance. "You already have a head start."

After that, they both picked at their food for a few moments. An unfamiliar happy feeling fluttered in Suzanne's breast, and she knew she would never forget this dinner with this special man. Over cappuccino, Dave dropped his bombshell. "I think there's another player in our scenario."

Suzanne put down her cup. "What?"

"A girl wandered into my hospital room, pretending she thought it was someone else's room. I didn't buy it. She got very friendly very fast, and had no intention of leaving. So I kinda played along with her."

"Well, of course, that wasn't very hard, seeing she was very beautiful," Suzanne said a bit testily.

Dave's eyes widened. "How did you know?"

"I heard the nurses talking while I was waiting for the elevator."

Dave grinned. "You're jealous. Hey—I'm delighted."

"Maybe a wee bit." She gave him a glance through lowered lids. My God, what am I admitting to, she wondered. I'm being coy and ridiculous.

She sipped at her coffee to dispel her awkward feelings. Suddenly she clattered the cup onto her saucer. "I am so stupid! This girl. She had something to do with Walter, isn't that it?" Dave said nothing. Suzanne's voice rose. "She knows about the money! But how could that be?"

"Can't you guess?" Dave asked gently.

"Oh, no." Tears filled Suzanne's eyes. "Tell me it's not true."

Dave reached for her hand. "The pieces fit, Suzy. This girl—

Theda Krupnick—is a waitress at the coffee shop next to your husband's bank. Apparently, this is how they got acquainted.

She worked at it in her head, putting it together, speaking slowly. "You think this waitress and Walter were having an affair, and he stole the money to go away with her."

"It would seem so."

Suddenly she made another connection. "Wait a minute!" She clutched his hand tightly. "I saw her today. I went to the coffee shop and sat at one of her tables. She didn't want to wait on me, but finally did. Now I know why. She knew who I was." She sat back in her chair, her head bowed. "Oh, my God."

"I'm sorry. I know this is a blow."

"I guess I half expected this. Thing weren't right between Walter and me for sometime. I should have guessed there was another woman. But why didn't he just ask me for a divorce?"

"Maybe he couldn't face putting you through all that agony. Seeing all the hurt it would cause you. Maybe he thought a clean break would be better. Just disappear. Who knows? It was certainly easier for him."

"Now we know for certain Walter didn't commit suicide."

"Well, let's not jump to conclusions. Let's just say that this information helps to confirm our theory that he didn't."

"So now I can complete Walter's suicide note," she said, in a small, tight voice. "Suzanne Dear, None of this is your fault. It is all mine. I'm sorry to run off with the sexy waitress from the coffee shop." She pressed her napkin to her mouth to suppress a sob.

Then her eyes grew big and her voice rose. "She killed him! She must have killed him!"

"Shhh. We don't know that. Why would she kill him if he had the money locked away at the tennis club?"

"Hmmm. I see what you mean."

"Look, Suzy, there's something else. Her name is Theda. I've found out that Cam Castore's ex-wife is named Theda. How many women with this name could there be? She must have some connection with that Cam Castore. Otherwise, how would she know about the money and the fact that I know where it is? I'm convinced that's why she's making up to me. Now, if I just play along with her, I may get enough information to finally solve this case."

"Give me a definition of 'playing along'," suggested Suzanne, a bit tensely.

Dave laughed. "I intend to keep myself as pure and sweet as I am now. I—I—" He closed his mouth suddenly.

"What? What is it?" He had been on the verge of saying something personal, she just knew it.

"Nothing." All at once Dave was interested in his dinner. He swallowed a bite and looked across at her. "I think I'll check out the bank tomorrow morning and make sure the delivery arrives."

On the drive back to her house, she touched on some impersonal subjects—the weather, the homeless, how the president was doing. While they chatted, her heart was silently asking the important question. Would he kiss her? And what should she do if he tried? My goodness, there's no big deal here, her logical mind decided. Don't worry about it. Do as you feel. But if we kiss, then will he think the next step is into my bedroom? That was the natural progression in the movies these days.

As it turned out, he walked her to the front door and then put his hands on her shoulders. Her knees turned to jelly as she turned her face to his.

"Good night, Suzy," he said, smiling. Then he leaned forward, kissed her gently on the cheek, and left.

She stood and watched him walk down the path and get into his car. "Damn," she whispered to herself and went into the house.

17

At 10:45 Thursday morning, Dave lounged against a pillar by the entrance of the Monroe Trust Company. He casually smoked a cigarette and watched the depositors and withdrawers climb up and down the few steps. Just before eleven o'clock, an armored car pulled up in the no-parking area directly in front of the building. Two security officers, armed and in uniform, retrieved a blue duffel bag from the back of the van and carried it into the bank,

Dave expelled the tension from the pit of his stomach in a big whoosh of breath. He smiled broadly. Step one was completed. The money was safe.

For a moment he fantasized that he could drop the rest of the investigation right now. The money was on its way back into Miss Hill's account. Walter's reputation had been saved and that had been the biggest worry to Suzanne. Was the rest really so important? He could probably convince Suzanne that it really didn't matter. Walter was dead—accident, suicide, or murder—and in all likelihood would stay dead. The police were satisfied. In fact, he would guess the police would not welcome reopening a case where their ineptitude could be exposed.

Forget Theda next door and her connection to the money. Forget her weird boyfriend. Forget what really might have happened. Right now he and Suzanne could settle into the real world again, and nurture their blooming relationship. He smiled thoughtfully. He itched to get started on that this very minute. But unfinished business was a persistent companion. You could shove it aside constantly, but you never got rid of it. It could nag and nag.

He sighed and made his way down the steps and into the

coffee shop next door. As soon as he settled himself at a table, Theda was there, hovering over him, looking more alluring than ever.

He gave her with what he hoped passed for a passionate and yearning look and was rewarded by a sizzling one in return. "When do you get a break?" he asked, trying out a throaty, Bogart-type voice, while lowering his bushy eyebrows and peering up at her suggestively. She told him two o'clock in a voice that seemed at least 50% more sultry than usual, and he began to get scared. Luring her into a fantasy escapade with him might be too easy. Hell, he didn't flatter himself that he was very attractive, but what if somehow she really fell for him? After the signals he had dished out, wouldn't she expect him to put out for her as well? He groaned. How could he convince her to agree to go away with him if he didn't get into a little of the physical stuff? Well, maybe a hug or two and a little handholding would do it.

If he held out, maybe she'd pant for him all the more. After a couple of cups of coffee and a danish, he left to go back to Romano's to rest in his room for a while.

Milo said hello at the door and then disappeared into the living room. Sophie came down the hall, wiping her hands on her chef's apron. "You got a registered letter," she said. "I took the liberty of signing for it."

He followed her into the kitchen where an official-looking envelope lay on a flowered place mat on the kitchen table. He picked it up, and the words "Commissioner of Police" in the upper left corner waved before his eyes. A hammering began in his chest, and he pulled out a chair and sat down quickly, still staring at the envelope. A prayer of some sort flicked through his mind. This was it. The final decision of the police investigation. In the first month of his suspension, he had found the adjustment hard. He had felt guilty, disgraced, and dirty. Unfounded accusations somehow managed to do that to him. As time wore on, however, and he protested his innocence more and more to himself, he was finally convinced that there was no way in hell that he could be found guilty.

But now that he held the letter in his hand, he understood in a flash that what he thought had little bearing on the decision his superiors had made. He was broken, defenseless. They had all the power.

He became aware of a movement behind him, and turned his head to see Sophie, leaning against a counter, her eyes squinting and puzzled.

He smiled barely. "Well," he said. "Might as well see what this says." His voice came out in a croak.

Sophie reached into a drawer and brought out a knife to hand him. He turned the envelope over and slit the tape that sealed the edges. He pulled out the letter and opened it. The words jumped off the page to start a dim melody humming inside him. By the time he was finished, Wagnerian cymbals were crashing in a grand finale. Phrases jumped off the page at him: *Investigation completed, no evidence of wrongdoing on your part, exonerated by a witness.* And then the last paragraph: *We deeply regret the necessity of this investigation and the impact it has had on your life.*

The letter ended with: *I would like to meet with you in my office on Monday morning, April 29 to discuss your new assignment. Your back pay will, of course, be restored in full.*

Dave tried to swallow the lump in his throat while eyes grew wet. Without a word, he handed the letter to Sophie. She was more unrestrained. After reading it, she actually yelled something like "yippee!" Then she pulled Dave up out of his chair and tried to dance with him about the kitchen. He winced with pain. She clapped a hand over her face.

"Oh, my goodness. How could I have forgotten you're an invalid?"

"It's okay," he said, smiling. "This news made me forget it myself."

She did a little jig by herself. "I knew it, I knew it!" she said over and over. Dave looked at her in wonder. He hardly knew this woman, and yet she had become his friend and supporter almost from the first moment they met.

Eventually she heated up some chicken soup for Dave. He

could hardly eat it for grinning. Winning is so sweet. Later, he went into the hall to call Suzanne. The minute he heard her voice, his heart seemed to fill his large chest. He loved his name for her. "Suzy," he said softly, tenderly. She whispered back his name to him. After a pause, they both laughed. He couldn't think what to say next. Finally, inanely, "It's good to hear your voice."

"Even though I haven't said anything yet?"

"Well," he searched desperately, "at least I know you're there."

They burst out laughing. "I have something to tell you," he managed. "When I'm more rational."

"Would you like to come for dinner? About six?"

"That would be great. I'll see you then." He stopped. Then, "Suzy." He couldn't help himself. It came out like a caress. She went along. "Dave," she breathed in a whisper, and then hung up.

At two o'clock, Dave parked in the lot behind the coffee shop, and Theda came out from the back door and got in the car. She leaned over as if to kiss him, but he managed to slide his cheek against hers and give her just a hug instead. When they pulled apart, she gave him a puzzled look.

He patted his right side. "I still have to take it easy," he said. "My wound, you know." He smiled, pleased that he had thought of that. She seemed mollified.

He went a step further. "It's tough," drawing his brows together in what he thought would look like anguish. "You're so tempting. I think we have something exciting starting here."

Yuck! That last sounded so stiff. He darted a glance at her and was pleased to see she was looking rather warmly at him.

"This seems to be getting serious," he said. "I think we had better talk."

"What?" Her surprise seemed genuine. "Is there someone else?"

"That's not it," he said evasively. "I want to talk to you about money."

"Money?" She crinkled her eyes as if puzzled. He left her hanging a moment, while he pulled away and lit a cigarette.

"Look, babe, I know what you're after." He turned and looked sternly into her eyes.

"I don't know what you mean," she whispered.

"You've been making a play for me, but I'm not what you're really after, am I?"

"I don't know what you mean," she said again, shrinking back against the seat.

"You want the key."

"What key?" A trembling, high voice.

"Hey, Miss Innocent, do I have to spell it out for you? The key to the locker that holds all the money, of course." Her face was a mask. Silence. "Walter Wilkins' bag of money, remember, doll?" Her face and voice remained frozen.

"Mr. Wilkins was your lover, wasn't he? I gather you were going to leave the area—a neat threesome, you, Walter, and the money."

She finally found her voice. "How do you know all this?"

"Figuring out nasty puzzles is my business. Or at least it used to be."

Now was the time to trade on Theda's distress at being unmasked. He put a finger gently under her chin and looked into her disturbed eyes. "I still think we could have something great together," he said. "It's very obvious we're attracted to each other." He paused. She didn't deny it. "Now, how about a substitute in this threesome?"

"What?"

"C'mon," he spoke gently. "I mean me, of course."

"You?"

"Well, sure. I'm the one who knows how to get the money. If I'm going to help you get it, I expect a cut." Her face jerked toward his, her eyes wide, the rich dark tresses tumbling about her head.

"How do you mean?"

"I mean we should share in the loot. Go away together. I take Walter's place."

Her eyes grew brighter. "Oh. Well. God, how I'd like to get outta here. Where would we go?"

He hazarded a guess. "What about Hollywood? With your looks you've got it made."

"You really think so?" Her hands began waving in excitement.

"Definitely. We can change our names, get new IDs. No one will ever find us. Don't forget, I've dealt first hand with disappearances. I know how it's done."

"Oh, Dave. It sounds wonderful." She leaned forward and gave him a peck on his bearded chin. "So what's our next move?"

"There's only one small problem," he said slowly and took a couple of puffs on his cigarette to prolong the suspense.

"What? What?" She pulled at his sleeve.

"Well, I know where the key is, but I can't get it."

"Why not?"

"I'm under surveillance by the police. They think I took some money during a drug bust, but I didn't. Anyway, I can't do anything suspicious, like breaking into someone's house." He hoped he sounded convincing. After all, it was true until just a little while ago. Then he had a shattering thought. What if the fact of his exoneration was in this evening's newspapers and Theda saw it? Well, this whole operation was built on chancy situations. Theda's eyes were as wide as if she had seen a monster at the car window. "Where is the key?"

"Well, it's at Mrs. Wilkins house, of course. The money belonged to her husband, so I naturally delivered it to her after I got it out of the locker at the train station."

"Oh, shit." She chewed on a long red fingernail. "How in hell do we find it now?"

"I know where she has it hidden."

"What?"

"Yup. I asked her if she had a safe place for it, and she told me she put it behind a book of Shakespeare's plays on her book shelf in the study." He took a drag on his cigarette while his eyes flicked sideways to judge her reaction.

"I suppose I could get it," she said slowly, "if I could be sure Mrs. Wilkins wouldn't be home."

"Even then it might be risky. I think she has a security system."

"Well—I—I know a safe way to get in."

He turned his head and looked at her admiringly. "You do? Well, that's great. Once you have the key you can get the money at the station, and we can hit the road." He bent his head to hers. "Such a wonderful, beautiful girl. We're going to have a terrific life together, aren't we?"

It was time for Theda to go back to work. Dave promised to drop over to her apartment later that night. By then, he hoped to have more information on the right time for Theda to break in for the key. When Mrs. Wilkins was out for the evening.

*   *   *

"But you can't leave him there!" Mrs. Castore was perched on the edge of a section of the circular sofa, peering into her husband's face over the edge of his newspaper. Her face was scrunched as tightly as her hands.

"I sure as hell can," Mr. Castore answered while he flipped to the business section.

"But he's your son!"

"So you remind me, a hundred times a day!" He let go of the right edge of the paper and smashed his fist into the center of it. "And I have told you over and over, I will not have a criminal for a son."

"But he's not, Bill. He really isn't a criminal. If you would just go down to the jail and talk to him, you would know that. He's like a lot of young people these days. They get caught up in bad situations. There are so many more temptations these days than when we were young. He has been trying to go straight. Then this time it seems this Dave Monaco pulled a gun on him and that's why Cam knifed him."

Mr. Castore turned in his seat to regard his wife. "You amaze me. You think this ex-cop pulled a gun on Cam for no reason at all? And what was Cam doing in a dark alley anyway? And with a knife? That's a violation of his parole right there."

Millie Castore brightened. She finally had her husband's attention. "He explained that, too. There were some guys he knew in prison who wanted to hurt him. He had to have a knife for protection."

Now she had his full attention. He leaned his face close to hers and stared into her eyes. "You're dumb, you know that? You believe everything your son tells you."

Her eyes filled with tears. "I have to. I'm his mother."

Their eyes clung for a moment, recognizing the power of this simple truth. Then her glance wavered to a picture on a lamp table. A boy about eight, blond hair tussled, big innocent eyes above a mischievous grin, stood leaning on a baseball bat. "Yes," he said finally, "you are his mother. You gave birth to him. And I suppose we are jointly responsible for his character."

Tears were weaving down her cheeks. "If he's found guilty at his trial, he'll go back to prison, God knows for how long. Until then we can at least give him a little freedom."

Bill Castore gathered up his paper and threw it on the floor. He stood up and futilely pulled his pants further up on his bulky midsection. "Okay. I'm sick of your whining. I'll call my lawyer and see what he can do." He stomped from the room, leaving his wife crumpled on the sofa.

*   *   *

Dave rang the door chimes and unconsciously smoothed down his cowlick. The sun was deep in the western sky, shooting still brilliant streaks across the horizon. May was giving a preview, weaving some balmy little drafts about in the air. In a moment, his miraculous love would open the door. And in his breast pocket, he held the assurance of his future. He glanced about at the foundation shrubbery and saw flat green daffodil leaves pushing through the earth beneath the pink-streaked buds of azalea bushes. It seemed Nature herself wanted to celebrate Dave's reinvolvement with life. He bowed his head and gave silent thanks for the joy that overflowed his heart.

When the door opened, he drowned himself in her eyes for a moment or two, his questing glance hoping to read in them what he himself felt in his heart. A little wariness was still there, he decided, so he simply gave her a light hug while her nearness made him ache down to his toes. When he pulled away and looked at her, her lips were slightly parted in a sweet smile and her head was tilted up to his. He couldn't help what he did next. Filled with the need to celebrate his good fortune, he bent his head and ever so softly and tenderly brushed his lips against hers in a brief kiss. He was unprepared for the delightful sensation that raced through him, and he stared at her in astonishment. She seemed equally as surprised. Then she moved slowly toward him, and her lips were suddenly his again, moving, seeking, burning, yet filled with an indescribable sweetness. Was it something like the first real kiss he had received when he was thirteen? In all his life, had anyone ever shattered him with a kiss like this one?

He ached as he pulled away, looked tenderly at her, and then wrapped her in his arms. "Wow," he breathed inadequately into her sweet-smelling hair. He heard a muffled sound against his chest. They broke apart, and he clasped her trembling hands in his own shaky ones.

"Dearest Suzy," he said. "I think we're moving a bit too fast."

She stiffened and stood still. He went on. "Tell me if I'm wrong, but I think something important is happening between us."

She lowered her eyes. "You're not wrong."

"Then I don't think we should rush it. I want you to be completely sure it's the right thing for you. You've been through a tough time. I wouldn't want you to do something you might regret later on."

She stood still, her head down. He put a finger under her chin and tilted her face to meet his grave look. Then he spread his hands up through her hair and cupped her face between them.

"This is only the beginning," he said. "And it's going to get better and better." He leaned forward and gave her a light kiss. "In the meantime, we have other business we need to get out of the way. Then we can concentrate on us."

She gave him a flirtatious look. "I can't wait."

"Let's go into the library. I've got something to show you."

"How about a drink first? What would you like?"

"I think club soda with a twist is the classic drink for the club I've joined."

She went into the kitchen and came back with two of them. "I think I can get to like this too," she said. She put the drinks down on the coffee table and sat down close to him on the settee. He put his arm around her and groaned. "Oh, Suzy, you have your own brand of torture."

"Would you like me to go sit in the easy chair?" He hugged her to him. "Never. Never an inch of space between us, that's how I like it."

"Have a drink," she suggested, and they raised their glasses to sip and gaze into each other's eyes.

Abruptly he put his glass down on the coffee table. "I have something to show you." He kept his face impassive while he removed the letter from the inside breast pocket of his old tweed jacket.

"I've heard from the police commissioner," he said, trying to keep a grin off his face. She read his eyes and clapped her hands together. "You're vindicated! I knew it! I knew it would happen!" He handed the letter to her and watched the delight grow on her face as she read it. He had been right in deciding to give her the good news in person. It had been a long time since a woman had been openly delighted by his good fortune.

"It's wonderful," she said softly. "You're back where you wanted to be. In the work you love."

"Yes."

"What does the part mean about a new assignment?"

"Just that I'll get reassigned to a new precinct. That's standard procedure."

They were quiet for a moment. Then they each leaned forward to pick up a glass, bumping arms. Laughing, they clinked glasses. "To us!"

"Oh, yes, definitely to us!"

While they discussed how this decision would change Dave's life, his awareness of Suzanne's proximity was scrambling his thoughts. He groaned to himself. It was too early in their relationship for serious lovemaking, but oh how he would like to flip her over on the sofa right now and kiss her into passion. He changed his position and crossed his legs. Suzanne herself might have felt something, for she excused herself in a husky voice and went to the kitchen to bring forth dinner.

They sat across from each other in her house-beautiful dining room and toyed with a chicken casserole, broccoli with almonds, and a tossed salad.

"It's delicious," said Dave, and it was. "But I seem to have lost my appetite. Too much excitement, I guess."

She smiled at him and nodded. "I know. Somehow it's affected me, too."

After coffee, they went back into the library. Dave glanced at his watch. "Ah, huh!" Suzanne said. "You have another date. Cheating on me already."

"Never that," said Dave. "I want to go to another meeting tonight. But first, you and I have to decide how we're going to end this crazy business we're tied into."

"So—I guess I'd better sit over here," said Suzanne, settling herself in the oversized chair facing the settee. She was in pale green slacks with a matching loose sweater, her hair pulled back with a flat green bow nestling on top.

"You look like a little girl," said Dave.

The look she gave him was never learned in childhood. "Well, you look like a little boy with that cowlick."

Dave reached up a hand and tried to hold down the wiry clump of hair. "That's why I grew this beard. So there wouldn't be any mistake."

She gave him that look again. "Believe me, you are very much who you are."

Her gaze flustered him. He got back on solid ground. "I guess we better get on with it." He offered her a cigarette and took one himself. When he leaned forward to light hers, he looked deep into those grey-green eyes and was numb for a moment. Fortunately, a pain from his wound suddenly stabbed him, and he was forced to retreat. He covered up with a couple of puffs on his cigarette and then plunged into the business at hand.

"I've been working things out in my mind. See what you think."
He took a deep drag. "I've been working on Miss Theda Bara. I
met her this noon, and we had a talk in her car." Suzanne sat up
straight. A little gray cloud settled over her features. Dave leaned
forward. "Look, Suzy. I'm going to be completely honest with you.
If we're going to pull this off, expose what really happened to
Walter, I'm going to have to mislead Miss Bara. I don't like it any
better than you do. She may be beautiful, but I'm just an actor in
a role. You'll have to trust me on that."

Suzanne leaned back slightly, "Well—." She didn't sound
entirely convinced.

Nevertheless, Dave continued. "I've led her to believe that you
have the key hidden in this house and that the money is still in the
locker at the train station." She stared at him, waiting for what
came next.

"The idea is to let her know when you will be out of the house
so she can break in to get it."

"What? Why?"

"Because I think when she does that, we'll solve the mystery of
what happened to Walter. I plan to have some invited guests here
to greet her."

She was kneading her hands in her lap. "The police. You're
going to have the police here."

"That's kind of the idea."

"You actually think she'll tell the police what really happened?
Why on earth would she want to do that?"

"Because I think deep down she's pretty scared. So I don't
think it will take much to jar the truth out of her. Whether she's to
blame or not, she's living with the daily fear that someone is going
to discover her relationship with Walter. That means the suicide is
looked at in a different light. In a situation like that, a confrontation
can blow the whole damn thing wide open."

"But taking the chance of coming here—well, I just don't know.
I would think she'd just leave town."

"Not so easy when you think there's a bunch of money lying
around that sorta belongs to you."

"But why would she accept the fact that you're willing to help her?"

Dave stared at her for a moment. Then Suzanne spoke. "Why do I get the idea I'm not going to like what you have to tell me?"

"It's all in the line of duty, Suzy."

"Most pleasant duty, I'll bet."

Dave shrugged and waved an open left palm.

"You're taking Walter's place! You're going away with her!"

"Hey, calm down. You have your tense wrong. It's never going to happen. I only hatched this scheme so I could look like I was on her side and she would trust my information about the key."

The perky young woman in the opposite chair had wilted. He grinned at her. "Hey, I like it that you're bothered."

She gave him a sheepish smile back. "Just make sure you behave yourself, Monaco."

After a moment, they discussed the setup. "We've got to do this right away, before she changes her mind. Like tomorrow night." He paused, thinking. "Who was the detective on the case?"

"A detective named Sohler."

"Oh, yeah. Godfrey Sohler. I know who he is. Well, we'll need him here, as well as a couple of the boys in case we have any trouble."

"Trouble? What kind of trouble? You think—ah—this girl might get violent?"

"Oh, no, nothing like that," Dave said, leaning forward and smiling reassuringly. "I don't think Miss Bara has a violent streak in her. It's just precautionary, Suzy."

"Oh."

"So—I'll tell Theda you're going out to a meeting tomorrow night—you know, garden club, book club, something like that—at eight o'clock. She works until then, so she'll probably show up here around nine." He nodded. "We'll be ready for her."

Suzanne trembled. "I'm scared. What if it doesn't work?"

"It may not. She could change her mind. But anyway, we have a little evidence the detective might be interested in. Might be enough to reopen the investigation."

"You mean the key you found and the fibers from the carpet."

"Yes. And I think it would be good to turn that over to Detective Sohler beforehand. Otherwise, he may not be interested in going along with our plan. Could you make an appointment with him tomorrow morning?"

"Probably. Are you going with me?" She looked worried.

"Of course. Do you think I'd ask you to go through all this by yourself?"

She sighed in relief. Then she stood up suddenly and walked over to Walter's desk and stood beside it, staring at its smooth surface.

Dave left the sofa and went to the other side, bending over and tilting his head to see her face. "What? What's the matter, Suzy?"

She turned questioning, worried eyes to his. "I don't know. I have a terrible feeling about this. Like something awful is going to happen."

"Hey—you're just having a case of the jitters. It happens in stressful situations. People often have kinds of premonitions. It comes from the unknown factors, that's all. Doesn't mean that anything bad is going to happen." She tried to smile, but didn't look convinced. "Do you want to call this off? We can, you know. Very easily."

She stood quietly for a moment, and then managed a small smile. She shook her head. "I'm just being silly. No, I really want to see this through."

Dave crossed in front of the desk and put his arms around Suzanne, hugging her fiercely. "I'd never let anything happen to you," he said. He could have stayed that way forever, her sweetness nestled against his heart. But there was unfinished business. "There's something else we need to do," he said. "Replace the back door key in the dummy rock. Do you have an extra?"

"I think so." Suzanne left for a moment and came back with a key in her hand.

"Good. Wipe it off well and put that in the rock after I leave. Just hold it by the edges." He stood up. "Unfortunately, I better get going now. After the meeting I'm paying Miss Krupnick a visit."

"Don't stay too late," she smiled up at him. "And try not to overact your part."

*   *   *

It was wonderful to be back behind the wheel of the red Firebird. He even had a few bucks in his pocket, thanks to his devoted mother. Cam grinned and turned up the rock music, beating a rat-a-tat-tat on the steering wheel with his index finger. He was minding his P's and Q's. When he had left the jail with his parents, he said nothing, but kept his head down and tried to look as though he might cry at any moment. His shoulders were hunched forward, his steps dragging. He was the image of a beat-down, repentant guy. Going home in the family Caddy, he thanked his parents profusely for their help and their trust, which he would never, ever violate again. His father actually allowed him back in the house, probably figuring that it was just a temporary situation. After the trial Cam's housing could very well be a problem for the state.

He grinned. His father knew nothin'. Theda was working over that dumb big ex-cop. Gorgeous Theda and her ex-husband would be outta here before the shit hit the fan. With a lotta green.

He cruised down the familiar streets to Theda's apartment. It was about ten o'clock, and he spotted her car in front of the building. He drove by on the opposite side and parked. But when he pulled the door handle to get out, he saw the dim outline of a large familiar figure pass under the streetlight and then enter the double doors of the building.

Cam settled back into the driver's seat. This was no time to get mixed up with Dave Monaco again. Not that he wouldn't like to. Love to, in fact. He reached into his jacket pocket and closed his palm around the .38 he had retrieved from its basement hiding place.

He settled back to wait. Theda was only doing what he, Cam,

had told her to do. Pretend to play along with Monaco in order to get the money.

After his release late in the afternoon, he had called Theda at work. As soon as she heard his voice, she froze. Scared, he figured. "Listen," he had said. "I know you can't talk. Just go ahead with the plan we worked out. You know, with Monaco. After you get the money, I'll get in touch with you. We'll still be able to get the hell out of here. There's no fuckin' way I'm going back to jail."

Halfway through the one-sided conversation, he got a dial tone. How much had she heard? "Damn it all to hell," he screamed at the phone. Now after two hours, Monaco's pitiful little Sentra was still parked in the same place, and it looked like he might be spending the night.

Then it hit Cam between the eyes. God damn it! Theda had suckered him! She was really meaning to go away with this piece of fuzz! Leaving him, Cam, out in the cold. He cussed, banged the steering wheel, and snarled animal-like noises, all the time sliding his palm up and down over the gun in his pocket.

*   *   *

Theda sat next to Dave on the worn sofa, smiling wistfully into his eyes while her hands twisted in her lap. How much longer, she asked herself. I can't stand any more of this. My life is swinging this way and that and I feel like all of me is flying apart. Since that frightening call from Cam this afternoon, nervous indecision engulfed her. Maybe she should just go to the police and tell all. If she fingered Cam as the one who actually hatched up this scheme to make off with Walter's money, the police might go easy on her. Only it wasn't really Walter's money, was it? They had really never discussed the source, but deep inside she knew her lover had stolen from some bank account. So, if she went to the authorities with what she knew, then wouldn't they go easy on her if she told them how Walter got killed? There were cases like this in the newspaper all time. What did they call it? Plea bargaining, that was it.

Now Dave was here, and she was afraid that any moment he

would expect to crawl into bed with her. A few hours ago, she wouldn't have minded. Now it was different. Cam was free. He could come slamming through the door any moment. There's no telling what his temper would lead him to do to Dave Monaco. Or to her, for that matter. He would be furious that she had not been to visit him at the city jail. He might also have figured out that she had tipped the police when they picked him up.

Theda rose jerkily from the sofa and went to the window, pulling back the glass curtain to expose a narrow pie-shaped piece of glass. She peered down through a narrow alleyway to a small section of the street in front of her building. Nothing was moving in the dim street light. But she knew he was down there somewhere. Her very bones felt it.

She turned to see Dave observing her intently. He seemed concerned. "Is anything wrong, sweetie?"

His words were kind, but she couldn't help shivering. She wrapped her arms about her upper body, clutching hard.

"No, I'm fine. Just nervous, I guess, about tomorrow night."

Dave got up and went to her. He tilted up her chin with one finger and looked in her eyes. "You'll do just fine," he said. "After you get the key, it will be clear sailing. There will be lots of people at the train station and no one will notice you. It's locker 100—easy to remember. I'll be parked out in front, and when you get back here with the money, we'll take off." She smiled weakly and tried to nod in agreement. Oh, God, could it really be that easy? A lump of black despair seemed to have settled in her stomach.

Should she tell him that Cam was out on bail? If he knew that, the hunted and hunter might get together and blow each other away. It could make for a worse nightmare than she was in now.

"C'm on, honey," Dave said, putting an arm around her. He was looking at her as if he really liked her. A nice man, a good man, she thought. My problem, I've always picked losers. I don't deserve anyone like this. But maybe with him I could get a new start and things would be different.

She forced a smile. "Sure. I'm okay."

"Then I guess I'll be off," he said.

Panic set in again. She couldn't be alone here in her apartment with Cam on the loose outside. At least with Dave here she might get some protection if Cam decided to break in. Somehow, she had to keep him here as long as possible.

She raised her face to kiss him, and he turned his cheek to her. "It's early," she said seductively. "I don't want to be alone."

"Well—" he glanced at his watch and shuffled his feet. "It's a quarter to eleven. I guess I could stay a little longer."

She pulled him back to the sofa and began unbuttoning his shirt. He grabbed her hands and held them. "Look," he said, with a funny little laugh. "I'm getting overheated. I think we'd better cool it until we've blown this town. We need clear heads to pull this off." He reached for the remote control and turned on the TV.

*   *   *

Cam wriggled in his car seat, thumping the steering wheel, and peering at the building entrance every few minutes. Was this guy spending the night? God damn it, there was no way he would let this broad shaft him like this. He'd follow her. Starting tomorrow. But, hell, he couldn't do it in this car. He needed different wheels. He thought of a couple of guys he knew. He ran his hands lovingly around the steering wheel. That shouldn't be a problem. One of them would get a buzz driving a machine like this around for a while.

Eventually he started the car and headed for home. If he ignored his father's rules, he would land right back in jail. Kicking and screaming, maybe, but he never doubted for a moment that his father could arrange it.

*   *   *

"Hullo?" A testy, biting voice.

"Hi, Bobby. It's Elmer. Peep."

"Oh, hi," the voice became warmer. "Do you have something to report?"

"I guess you haven't seen the evening papers. Your ex-husband has been cleared."

"What! I don't believe it! That can't be true!"

"Appears to be. Seems his partner was the guilty one. Gave himself away by living too high on the hog. You should have gone after him. He was the guy with the dough."

"God—" A sound of despair.

"Too bad you didn't believe your husband," the Tail said sadly. "He's a really good guy. I'm glad this rotten job is over."

"Well—thanks for trying and spending so much time. I wish I could pay you."

"What are friends for? Hey—I still remember the fun we had when we dated in high school."

*   *   *

At one a.m. Suzanne lay wide-awake in her king-size bed under a comforter designed in swirls of peach and aqua. Her eyes seemed busy making tears that trickled from their corners. What an idiot she had been! Tricked again by a man.

She thought back to high school and early college days. There was a basketball player who visited a cheerleader after his dates with Suzanne; there was a handsome older man of 26 who gave her a rush before she found out he was married. Then there were several boys who made dates, never to show up. The outstanding example, of course, was Walter.

Now, when she thought her luck was about to change—scratch that—had changed, she had once again given her trust to a man who had trampled on it. A man who at this very moment was probably making love to a sexy waitress.

Suzanne had listened for the phone to ring all evening, while trying to concentrate on a TV movie to make the time go faster. Finally, after arguing with herself, she had dialed the Romano's number and apparently gotten a sleepy Mr. Romano out of bed. After a moment, he reported that Dave was not there. So—what she had suspected was true.

Now her mind darted back to the time she had discovered Dave had the key. Would he have turned the key and the money over to her if she hadn't confronted him? Was he really trustworthy? He had asked Suzanne to trust him. But he was pretending to make out with Theda in order to force out the truth about Walter's death. Was that really necessary? She had seen Theda. No man in his right mind could resist a gorgeous sexual force such as that.

She clutched the top of a peach sheet. Tomorrow would tell. It would soon be over. The hard fact was that she had to trust Dave. She had no one else to turn to. I'm a stupid woman, she thought. And to top it off, I seem to be stupidly falling in love.

18

When Suzanne finally slept, weird dreams tangled in her head and startled her awake several times. She scrunched up her pillow and moved from side to side, searching for that elusive soothing spot in the bed to make her sleepy. Around four in the morning she finally slipped into a numbing, dreamless slumber.

A kind of bell rang far off in the distance. Was it time to go to school? Suzanne struggled to focus her attention. Another chime. She came awake slowly and turned her head to see the clock on the night stand. Nine o'clock! What day was this and where was she in her life? Several chimes formed a tune. It was her doorbell. She found her blue silk robe and hurried down the stairs, trying to tie the belt and smooth down her hair at the same time.

"Just a minute," she called, as she turned the key in the front door and opened it. Immediately Dave Monaco's eyes smiled into her own sleepy ones. "I guess I woke you up."

My God, I must look terrible, she thought, pushing back the bang that had fallen over one eye, and wrapping the blue silk more snugly about her. He didn't seem to think so. He kept smiling at her in a funny way. She snatched at some composure. "Coffee?" she asked. "I was about to make some."

"This is the best way I can think of to start the morning," said Dave. following her into the kitchen. She didn't answer, but went through the motions of grinding the coffee and adding the water. Thought fragments spun around in her head. What exactly had she decided last night while she was in that blue funk? How should she act toward him?

She heard Dave pull out a kitchen chair and sit down. When he spoke, a certain tightness had crept into his voice. "Well, I know a little more about you now. You're not very talkative when you first get up in the morning." She watched the coffee drip down into the carafe and said nothing. She felt his eyes on her back.

When the coffee was done, she poured two cups and brought them to the table. She sat down and immediately Dave captured a hand. "Cold," he said, warming it between two of his. She risked a look into his eyes and knew he wasn't referring to just her hand. When her hand began to tremble, she pulled it away and raised the cup to her lips.

"So what's going on?" she asked inanely, before taking a swallow.

"When did you decide not to trust me?" Dave asked.

"What?" Her coffee cup shook.

"You called last night and spoke to Mr. Romano," he said.

"It was late and my bed was empty. Without even checking with me, you decided that I was spending the night with Miss Krupnick. Am I right?" She put her cup down and stared into it. She could feel his eyes on the top of her head. "So much for trust between two people," he said. "At least between us. I didn't realize we were on such shaky ground that the least little problem could blow us apart."

Neither did I, she thought, neither did I. She didn't know what to say. Finally she brushed back her hair and risked looking at him. Her voice wavered. "Once I was too trusting. I believed everything my husband told me. Then I found out what it was like to be manipulated by a man, how to live with pretense and how to cover up the real truth by continuing to trust." She reached across the table and lay a slender hand on his. "I lived with a man who told me how to keep his house and entertain his friends, how to dress, how to look, how to behave, even how to speak. He made the important decisions for me. Now suddenly my own self, whatever that is, is all I have. I have to make the decisions about what to do and what to feel. And face up to risks." She squeezed his hand. "Don't you see, Dave, it's not a question of not trusting you, it's trusting myself that's the big problem." She looked into his eyes and saw something disturbing. But wonderful. A mixture of compassion and affection. Something she hadn't seen in a man's eyes for a very long time. They lowered their eyes about the same time and became busy examining their coffee cups.

"I'd like to tell you about last night," said Dave. "I felt it was important to gain Theda's complete confidence. She seemed scared and restless, and I didn't feel I could leave. If she doesn't think I'm really committed to going away with her, I don't think she'll go through with our plan." He softened his voice and spoke slowly, emphatically. "I had to put on an act, pretend I was interested in her. I'm not. Not in the least." Dave broke off here and searched Suzanne's eyes. It was important that he convince her that he had no romantic notions about Miss Bara. Apparently satisfied, he went on. "Well, I'm not proud of the fact that I had to mislead her. She's not quite what she seems on the outside. There's an innocence underneath and right now a lot of fear. But often in police work there has to be manipulation and entrapment. You have to make situations happen where the crook will trip himself up." Suzanne gave a little nod. Dave smiled. "We watched television. Would you like me to describe what we saw?" Suzanne held up a hand. her face flushing, embarrassed. "Look, Dave, what you do is your own business. You don't have to report to me."

"But maybe I want to," he said slowly, as if this were a strange idea. "Maybe I just don't want any secrets between us." She didn't know how to answer that, but the look in his brown eyes made her wriggle in her chair.

Suzanne finally brought up the matter of the plot outline for the evening. "I'm scared, Dave. What are we really doing? Maybe Theda didn't have anything to do with Walter's death. Maybe he shot himself accidentally, and she panicked and made it look like suicide. Sometimes this all seems so flimsy I feel we should just stop right here. After all, the money is now safe where it should be. What if bringing Theda here tonight makes it all worse?"

"How? What do you think is going to happen?"

"I don't know. I just have a funny feeling about it." Her face was strained. "I probably should hate her, but somehow I feel sorry for her. Walter got her into a ridiculous mess."

"Look, Suzanne, I think we've got to take this chance. It could bring out the truth, and that's what we're after. And if the police feel our evidence has any value, they'll pick up the ball and run with it. Our part will be over."

"There's another big problem," she said.

"What?"

"I couldn't bear to have Penny find out her father was an embezzler. As well as having an affair."

Dave just looked at her for a moment. "It's always painful to face the truth," he said finally. "But it's better to tackle it right in the beginning. Buried secrets have a way of leaking out, causing resentment and misunderstandings." She knew he was right, but how could she bear giving her daughter such a burden? He seemed to read her mind. "She'll cope," he said emphatically. "She'll grieve for a while, and then move on. Eventually she'll forgive her father."

She was somewhat comforted. But the impending evening and the possible behavior of the actors to be involved still worried her.

"All right," she said finally. "Let's go see Detective Sohler and tell him everything. The chips can fall where they may."

*   *   *

Detective Sohler's eyes widened as he came around his desk to greet his visitors. Suzanne saw the question in his eyes as he swung his glance to Dave and back to her.

"Sergeant Monaco," he said. "I read about you in the papers. Congratulations." He shook Dave's hand.

"Thanks," said Dave, settling Suzanne into a well-worn plastic arm chair and taking another for himself.

"I gather this has something to do with Mr. Wilkins' death?" He's dying to know how Suzanne and I got together, thought Dave. He'll find that out before long.

"Look, Detective," he said. "Let me ask you something first. I know all the evidence pointed to suicide. And that was the final verdict. But were you yourself satisfied with that?"

Detective Sohler didn't answer right away, his glance flickering across the desk from one to the other. Finally, he spoke.

"Most of the evidence pointed to that conclusion. But there were a few things about the case that bothered me."

"Such as?"

"Well, the unfinished note, for instance. Also, the fact that Mr. Wilkins shot himself through the heart." The detective glanced quickly at Suzanne. Dave was proud of her. Her head was up and her eyes were clear. Somehow she's going to handle the unraveling of her husband's tragedy with strength and courage, he thought. The coming hours could be tough. Their visit here was setting events into motion that could be devastating, particularly to the two women who had loved Walter Wilkins.

The detective went on. "But there was no sign of any other presence. No other fingerprints, no access to the house." Dave struggled with what to say next. He needed Detective Sohler's cooperation. He had to present his new evidence in such a way as to not humiliate this official investigator.

He glanced at Suzanne. "Mrs. Wilkins and I have come up with a few ideas. I don't know if they're worth anything or not. But we need your expert opinion."

Detective Sohler seemed receptive. He leaned across his paper-littered desk with questioning eyebrows.

"Let's hear them."

"Well, her husband's desk chair was on casters. We wondered if the blast from the gun wouldn't have tilted him out of the chair and onto the floor."

"It's possible, but he was, after all, found in his chair."

Dave reached into his jacket pocket and came up with a small plastic bag. He laid it on the desk. "There are a few fibers from the carpet behind the chair. I think you'll find blood on them."

Detective Sohler picked up the bag and peered intently at it, although Dave knew the fibers were hardly visible through the plastic film. He looked at Dave with a glint of interest. "You think someone shot him, he fell on the floor, and then this person picked him up and put him back in his chair?"

"We think it's possible, yes. And let me ask you this, Godfrey. Wouldn't such a fall have dislodged the victim's glasses?"

"I would think so, yes." The detective rubbed his chin. "So the killer put his glasses back on, and I suppose had Mr. Wilkins write the suicide note during the death throes so the pieces would all fit?" He leaned back in his chair. "Hah."

"What if that note were not a suicide note?"

"Come again?"

"Remember, it was never finished. What if the victim were saying something like, 'I'm sorry to have to'—ah, 'run away like this.' Or, maybe 'disappear from your life.' You get the idea."

"What? Why would he say that?"

Dave looked at Suzanne. She smiled reassuringly at Dave and then turned to the detective. "Detective Sohler," she said, matter-of-factly. "I have discovered that my husband planned to leave me for another woman. Apparently, he was writing me a farewell note, not a suicide note, when he was interrupted."

He doesn't believe her, thought Dave. Who could ever believe Walter—or any man—would leave someone like Suzanne?

"You have evidence of this?" The detective asked slowly.

"Yes. I definitely have evidence. My husband had embezzled money from an account that he managed, and he planned to use it to leave the country with his mistress."

Dave turned to look at Suzanne with admiration. She looked tremulous, vulnerable. Then she met his gaze and raised her chin defiantly. Damn, he thought, if she hasn't got guts! Detective Sohler leaned an elbow on a stack of paper and cupped his chin. "Where is this money now?"

"We were able to retrieve it from a locker and redeposit it into the correct bank account."

The detective didn't seem to know what to say. Finally he leaned back in his chair. "Sounds like a reinforcement for the suicide theory. Someone found Mr. Wilkins out and threatened to reveal him. A little blackmail."

Dave and Suzanne exchanged glances. "We don't think so," said Dave.

But Detective Sohler was continuing to voice his own thoughts. "In spite of what you have told me so far, we haven't established a motive for anyone to kill him, and there is no real evidence that anyone was there in the room that night. We don't even know if the blood on the floor was the victim's. There could be other explanations."

"But you'll have it tested?" asked Dave.

"Yes, of course. But as I said, even if it checks out to be the victim's, this is not enough to reopen the case."

Dave glanced at Suzanne and she nodded her head. He turned back to the detective and emphasized his words. "We know who was in the room that night, and we can prove it. Access was gained by using this—." He pulled another plastic bag from his pocket and laid it on the desk. "It's a key to the back door. Hidden in one of those fake stones in the ground cover by the patio. I think you'll find some finger prints on it. Mrs. Wilkins had no knowledge of it. So it would seem that her husband supplied it for someone else to use."

"Pretty far-fetched," said the detective, leaning back in his chair. "Still doesn't connect anyone to the killing if we can't prove any one was in the house that night. It could have been used on other occasions."

Suzanne was fumbling in her handbag. "Here," she said, and got up to hand a glasses case to the detective.

"What are these?"

"My husband's glasses. I know they have been handled by some of the police that were there that night, but Dave tells me it is possible a portion of a print might match up with what is on the key."

"Hmm. Pretty improbable." He shrugged. "Impossible if your husband simply stayed in his chair."

Dave saw Suzanne lean slightly across the desk and heard her plead in a charming way. Who could resist? "But you'll have it checked out anyway, won't you?" she asked.

"Yes, I suppose we can do that," said the detective, turning the glasses case over in his hand several times.

"Godfrey," said Dave. "Could you spare a little time this evening?"

The detective grunted a kind of a laugh. "So you can present some more irrefutable evidence?"

"No. So we can present you with the person who was with Mr. Wilkins that night. Who may or may not be the killer. At the very least, a person who may be able to tell us what happened."

"Really! You've issued an invitation to this person and received an acceptance." He smiled and waggled his head.

"Not exactly," said Dave. "We've laid something of a trap. This person thinks the money is still in a locker and that the key is hidden in the library behind a book. We've spread the word that Mrs. Wilkins will be out this evening."

"Hmmm. You've at least succeeded in arousing my curiosity. What time?"

"If I were going to break into a house and I wanted to make sure no one was home, I'd want to see the owners leaving," Dave told Suzanne.

"You think she might show up early?" asked Suzanne.

"I don't know. It's possible."

Therefore, at a quarter to eight, Suzanne, dressed in a grey suit, drove her car out of the garage, stopping at the end of the driveway. She twisted her head to look at the house. Garage door open, coach light and outside lamps were on. All signs that the occupants were out for the evening.

She turned and drove slowly down the street, her heart thumping beneath the white silk blouse. Surreptitiously she checked each side of the road. There were no strange cars parked along the way, and she sighed with relief. But that didn't guarantee that no one was lurking about. It had been a cloudy day with dusk coming early, and a trespasser could be covered by the lengthening shadows.

Theda. Suzanne thought about her for a moment. This was a girl Walter had loved. She swallowed. Yes, that was right. So why should she, Suzanne, be afraid of her? After all, they had a lot in common. Except that now Theda was a desperate woman, wanting to flee with a great deal of money and escape whatever had happened here that dreadful night. For she was the only one who knew what really happened to Walter in his final moments of life. Suzanne was sure of that. Theda was definitely involved.

After leaving her car on the street behind her house, Suzanne lighted her steps with a small flashlight and walked through a neighbor's yard. She was greeted by Dave holding open the back door. They slammed it shut and locked it. "Nervous?" he asked.

"A million butterflies." Her lips trembled.

"C'mon," he grasped her shoulders and smiled into her eyes. "It'll soon be over with. You don't have to do a thing. Just be a bystander. If I'm correct, as soon as she's confronted, Miss Krupnick will tell us her story."

"You really think so?"

"Sure. She's been carrying a lot of guilt around with her since that night, whatever happened. Basically she's a nice person who took some wrong steps and that's got to bother her. She's crying inside for relief."

"I hope you're right. I just have a real uneasy feeling about all of this."

Dave gave her a little shake. "Look, Suzy, I'm here to take care of you. Nothing's going to happen except that the truth will come out."

But after that, what? She wondered. Will you still be around, Dave? Or is this strange drama we're part of the only thing drawing us together? She stared at him, wondering if he could read her thoughts.

"Any sign of her yet?" Detective Sohler came into the hall from the living room where he had been there since seven o'clock.

"No, apparently not." She took a deep breath. "So I guess now all we do is wait."

"Yes," said Dave. "And that can be the toughest part."

"Look," said the detective. "I left a low light on in the library next to the book shelves. I think the rest of the house should be dark. If your theory is correct, she'll be coming through the back door and around the corner into the library. I think we should wait in the living room at the front of the house." He seemed unaware that he had identified the expected visitor as a woman.

"I'll make some coffee," said Suzanne, starting for the kitchen.

"Better not," said Detective Sohler.

"What?"

"Our visitor might smell it."

They exchanged glances, and the men strode into the living room to settle themselves. After a few moments, Suzanne came in with a tray of cokes, little sandwiches, and cookies. "I thought it might be a long night," she offered, as she set the food down on the coffee table. She looked hopefully at Dave, hoping he would refute that. He only smiled wistfully at her. Suzanne settled herself into the squishy sofa and leaned her head against the back cushion. She had pulled back the window drapes about two inches, enough to let in some illumination from the outside lights. Even so, the room was full of gloomy shadows and she felt an oppressing sense of doom. For a moment she forgot why she had to involve herself with solving the mystery of Walter's death. The world had accepted the suicide theory. As it had turned out, his widow should have accepted it too. What Suzanne had subsequently learned about Walter and his affairs had turned out to be far more painful. After the money was restored to the rightful owner, any dispensing of further justice should have been left to destiny.

The minutes dragged. Occasionally they spoke briefly in whispers, or munched on some bites of food. But mostly they sat and listened, straining their ears, thinking their own thoughts.

Suddenly Suzanne heard something. Three pairs of eyes criss-crossed in the semi-darkness. "It's a car," said Dave, softly. "But it could be anyone." He looked at his watch. "It's nine o'clock. Could be her."

Detective Sohler was bending carefully around the drape, peering through the slit. "It's stopping," he said, "on the other side of the street, about two houses down. I can just make it out in the space between the bushes." He pulled back the drape a little in order to see better.

Then he turned back into the room, "It's our pigeon," he said. "I saw a figure get out and start in this direction."

Dave and Suzanne started to rise. He motioned them back down. "No," he said. "A little more patience. This waiting may be the hardest."

Indeed it was. Ten, fifteen minutes passed and nothing happened. Finally, Detective Sohler went to the window. The dark shadow that had been the car was gone.

*   *   *

If that policeman hadn't come into the coffee shop this morning, Theda might not have driven out to Suzanne's house at all. It wasn't the cop's fault. He seemed nice enough. It was just that he seemed overly interested, and he kept looking at her in an inquiring way that made her feel she was about to be questioned about Walter's death. She had seen enough TV mystery shows to know how that works. Coincidence, sometimes. Just some nobody who had seen Walter and her together maybe happens to mention it to someone else who grabs onto the information like a dog with a bone. Little pieces of stuff fitting together and becoming dangerous.

After the cop finally left his table, she pocketed her sizeable tip. She cleaned off his table and picked up the newspaper he had been reading. She caught a glimpse of a headline—something about a cop—folded up the paper and discarded it in the trash.

The only solution was to get far away. And without Dave Monaco. Now that Theda knew how to get the money, she couldn't take the chance that Dave might turn her in someday. Once a cop—well, you couldn't really be sure of a person like that.

Then there was Cam. If he ever got out of jail, he would be after her. By now he had figured out that she had told the police where to pick him up. Plus the fact she hadn't been to visit him, well, that clinched it right there.

Yeah. She would go get the key and the money and run. Hard

and fast. Everything she owned was already stuffed into the trunk of her car.

Her resolve was unwavering. As soon as she left work, she drove to Suzanne's and parked in about the same place where she and Cam had been staked out. She got out and started down the street in her tennis shoes and then stopped. She peered across at the front lights of the house flickering across the yard and shrubbery. Something bothered her. Then she remembered driving past an empty garage under a raised door. Something wasn't quite right here. It was more like an ominous feeling that suddenly crept over her than anything else. Wouldn't a woman living alone be careful to lower the garage door when she left at night? To cover the fact her car was gone?

It's a goddamn trap, she thought. They're waiting for me to walk into it. Shit. Theda got back in her car and drove away. The three of them sat crumpled, their faces blank.

"She's changed her mind. She's not coming," said Detective Sohler finally. He stood up. "I may as well be going." He looked at his watch. "It's almost ten o'clock. If she were simply going to circle a few blocks and then decide to come back, she would be here by now."

Dave had to agree. Nevertheless, he said, "Can't you give us a little longer, Godfrey? I know it looks bad, but maybe she thought of something she had to do first—what the hell, I don't know." His cowlick was sticking straight up in a frenzy of its own. "Just stay a little longer."

"Look, Dave," Godfrey sounded irritable. "I've given up the best part of an evening to go along with this crazy scheme. Looks to me like she's just not going to show."

"So what about our case?" Dave pleaded. Goddamn it, was all he and Suzanne had uncovered and put together for this finale to be thrown aside? He risked a glance at her. She seemed to be in shock. I didn't realize how much we counted on this evening to give the answers that would put Walter to rest, he thought. At the moment, her husband was standing there between them, a looming, never-to-be solved mystery.

"But you'll test the evidence we gave you and reopen the case if it's warranted?"

Dave tried to mask the desperation he was feeling.

"Sure, we'll check it over, but don't count on getting the case reopened." Detective Sohler had a hand on the door, when he turned. "Mrs. Wilkins, I'm sorry it worked out this way." He gave her a weak smile. Suzanne just stood there, staring blankly.

*   *   *

Theda was several miles down the beltway when she slowed down and pulled off on the shoulder. Damn it. If she didn't go through with this tonight, nothing would change. She would still be in the same dumb job, her heart pounding everytime a policeman came into the restaurant for a cup of coffee. Living with uncertainty and guilt all the rest of her life. And Cam. He would surely be after her. She could never get away from him. This last trouble he was in, well, everyone knew the prisons were crowded. Even if convicted, he could be free in no time.

All of her possessions were in the trunk of her car. Ready for some kind of a new life. She had already burned a bridge behind her.

She turned off on an exit ramp to head back the other way. Glancing in her rear view mirror, she noticed the dark shape of a bulky old station wagon as it passed under a highway light and pulled off the road behind her. Hadn't that same car been parked on the shoulder a few yards behind hers? She became aware of it then when she checked the traffic to re-enter the highway.

So what! Another car had decided to make a u-turn. She shook her head. This whole evening was making her buggy. Besides, this was a fairly dark stretch of road. Who could make out anything for sure?

On her way back to the Wilkins' house, she thought of a way to make certain she would not be caught in a trap.

*   *   *

They stood together in the front hall, and Detective Sohler turned the front door knob to leave. Suddenly there was a noise. Really more of a 'plink'. Motionless, they waited. Then another 'plink'. They glanced at one another. Then Dave motioned for them to move back into the living room.

"I think she's testing us," he whispered. "Sounds like pebbles against a window. She wants to make sure no one is here." He felt a bit of admiration for Theda's cleverness.

A few moments passed. Then he heard something else. He held a finger to his lips. "Shhh." The back door gave a slight creak on its hinges as it was opened and then a click when it closed. Muffled sounds that could be soft footsteps came quickly down the hall, fading out when Theda apparently stepped onto the thick carpet of the library. After a moment, the detective whispered, "Now!" and they moved quietly to the library door. In the dim light from the small. table lamp, Theda was busy taking books down from the library shelves and placing them on the library table on the adjacent wall.

Dave motioned Suzanne and Detective Sohler to stay behind him, in the hall. He then reached around the door jamb and turned on the wall switch that controlled a floor lamp by the sofa and the lamp on Walter's desk.

Theda whirled around, a book clutched against her breast. When she saw Dave, she breathed a sigh of relief. "My God, you scared me. What on earth are you doing here? I thought we were going to meet later."

"I got a little anxious," smiled Dave reassuringly. "Couldn't wait to see you." He walked over to her.

"I can't find the damned key," she said, sounding close to tears.

"No, it's not here," he said evenly.

"What do you mean? Where is it? Did you get the money already? Then why in hell did you let me go through with this? That's a rotten thing to do."

"I couldn't agree more. This whole situation is rotten."

He looked at a key lying on the table next to them. "Is this the key you used to get into the house?" He pulled a plastic bag from his pocket and carefully nudged the key into it.

"What are you doing? I have to put that back."

"In the fake stone by the back door?"

"How do you know that?"

"Like you did on the night Walter Wilkins was shot?"

She stared at him wide-eyed. "Hey, what is this? Blackmail?"

He looked at her compassionately and reached out to pat her shoulder. "No, it's an attempt to get at the truth. It's a chance for you to tell me what happened on that night. A chance to clear yourself. To set the record straight and get your life squared away."

She looked at him defiantly and didn't answer for a moment. "Why should I tell you anything, Mr. Know-it-all?" she said finally. Then she gave a weary sigh. "You probably already know what happened. Sure, I was here that night. Walter and I were making plans to go away together. I loved him," she stared at her feet for a moment and cleared her throat. Then she looked over at the desk and a tear rolled down one cheek. "Why would I kill him? It was an accident."

Two other figures moved into the room, and for a moment it seemed to Dave they were stuck in an old movie still. Then Theda screamed. "Oh, my God! You set me up! I trusted you and you set me up!"

She lunged at Dave and beat against his broad chest. Then she screamed again and raked his face with her long red nails. A few drops of blood oozed to the surface.

His strong arms grasped her shoulders and held her away from him. She burst into tears. "Theda, believe me, I didn't want to do this to you. But the truth would have come out someday, with or without me. If it was an accident, you have nothing to fear. Just tell your story truthfully. You'll be cleared and then you'll be free. No more living on the edge, afraid of being revealed."

She continued to sob, and he put his arm around her and

drew her to the sofa in the sitting area. Detective Sohler and Suzanne followed and they all sat down, Dave sat down next to Theda, and Suzanne and the detective took the two facing lounge chairs.

"You know Mrs. Wilkins," said Dave, glancing at a wooden-looking Suzanne, "and this is Detective Sohler." Theda buried her face in her hands and didn't look up.

Dave gestured at the detective, who picked up the ball. "Miss Krupnick," he said, "we need your help to find out the truth of what happened in this room the night Walter Wilkins was killed."

Theda continued to sit, slumped over, her face covered with her hands. They waited.

"Theda?" Dave prodded gently.

Theda sniffed loudly a few times and finally spoke in a muffled voice. "I don't see why you can't leave me alone. You already decided that Walter committed suicide. The case is closed. You don't have anything to connect me to this."

Detective Sohler leaned forward and spoke from his official responsibility. He burned his eyes on the top of her bowed head as if to sear his words into her brain. "The fact that we now know that you were here that fatal night changes everything. You have admitted it, and in the presence of three witnesses, myself included. Ignoring this kind of testimony would put me in jeopardy. You have to tell us what happened here the night Walter Wilkins was shot."

She raised her eyes and turned to look at him, pleading like a little girl. "What if you don't believe me?"

"Just tell the truth. I'll know if you're lying."

"Well—where shall I start?"

"Tell us everything that happened after you drove here that night."

"Well—I parked up the street and walked between the yards to the back door so the neighbors wouldn't see me. Walter let me in—" She glanced sadly at Suzanne who was staring at her. "We talked about the next day. Saturday. That was the day we were going away together. After Walter picked up the money where he had it hidden away."

"Did you know where that was?"

"No, he never told me."

"How much money?"

"He never told me that either. But I guess it was a lot. He said it was enough to live on the island where we were going for a lotta years." Theda stared off into space.

"What happened next?"

"Oh. Well, we went into the library, and Walter sat down at the desk. He had been in the middle of writing a note to his wife when he let me in. I went around the back of his chair to see what it said. Then he took his gun out of the desk drawer. I had a fit, 'cause that thing made my skin crawl. He said we had to take it with us for protection and I should learn how to use it. We kinda argued about it, but he kept insisting on showing me how it worked. He showed me how to cock it before firing and then he kidded around, pointing it at himself like a little kid, and laughing. I got real upset, and I wanted him to put it away. I reached over his shoulder and put my hand over his to make him lay it down." Theda raised her head and looked at the detective, her eyes wide and wild, as if she were back in that moment. "It went off. The damn gun went off. The gun went off, the gun went off, the gun went off, the gun went off—." She only stopped saying it when she began choking on the words.

Dave tried to catch Suzanne's eye, but her head was bent, her her eyes squeezed shut.

Detective Sohler withdrew his gaze and for a moment looked at his hands clasped between his knees. "And what happened then?" he asked in a softer voice.

"I was so startled, I jumped back. I didn't know what had happened for a moment. Then Walter fell out of his chair onto the floor. I saw the blood on his shirt front and then I knew he was dead." She began sobbing quietly.

"Would you like a glass of water?" asked Dave. She nodded. He got up and went to the kitchen. No one spoke while he was gone. When Dave returned, he took Theda's hands from her lap and cradled them around the glass.

Theda sipped slowly like a child. Then she put the glass down on the coffee table and turned to look at Dave. "Help me, Dave, please. I know you set me up, but I guess that's the cop in you. But right now you're the only friend I've got."

It was like looking into the eyes of a frightened child, struggling to wake up from a bad dream. At that moment Dave knew that this evening had already cost more than he had bargained for. A strong feeling of compassion battled against the need to expose the truth. It was nearly impossible to work on the side of justice when you lost your objectivity, when you had become personally involved. But as sad as he felt at the moment, it had all happened, and he couldn't undo any of it.

"I'll help you, Theda. I'll do everything I can." He was making a pledge.

"So Mr. Wilkins was lying dead on the floor," stated Detective Sohler, getting back to dealing with the facts. "Why didn't you call the police?"

"I couldn't, I was so scared." she said. "If Walter had still been alive, I'd have called an ambulance. But I could see he wasn't. Well, I stood there for a few minutes trying to decide what to do. I knew Walter would want me to stay out of it. To protect his family, you know. So I thought I could make it look like suicide. After all the note was there. So I managed to get Walter back in his chair—" she paused and her mouth made a funny grimace. "I have strong arms from carrying trays of food, you know." No one said anything. She went on. "I was about to leave when I noticed he didn't—ah—look right." She caught her breath, apparently seeing the deceased Walter once more at his desk. She leaned forward and took a drink of water. She cleared her throat. "His glasses were missing. I found them on the rug and I—" she seemed unable to go on.

"You put them on Mr. Wilkins," said the detective.

"Yes."

"Then you left by the back door."

"Yes."

"And you locked the bolt on the door with the key that was hidden in the plastic stone?"

"Yes. I was leaving when I remembered it was there." Theda gave Suzanne a pleading look. Her voice lowered to a whisper. "Walter had it made for me to use when Mrs. Wilkins was out of town."

Suzanne got up suddenly and went to stand in front of the fireplace, her head bent, her back to the others in the room.

Dave noticed her shoulders shaking. Let it out, Suzy, he told her silently. Let it all go. Grieve and get rid of it. "Well," said Detecive Sohler, staring at Theda. "this has been very revealing. You understand, Miss Krupnick, you and I need to make a little trip downtown. There you'll be read your rights and then make your official statement."

Theda simply stared off into space, seeing what other demons Dave could only imagine. Jail, perhaps. Then she sucked in a breath, expelled it in an audible sigh, and squared her shoulders under the red jacket she was wearing. She stood up. "What the hell," she said, "let's get it over with." She looked at Dave and then reached up a hand to lightly touch the scratches on his face. "I'm sorry I hurt you." He covered her hand with his and gently squeezed it.

"I'll go get my car," said Detective Sohler and left the room.

Dave, Suzanne, and Theda moved to the front hall. Dave reached out and put an arm around Suzanne. She leaned her head on his shoulder. Theda observed them for a moment and then said almost under her breath, "You're good together."

"You're a smart lady, Theda," said Dave, smiling down at the top of Suzanne's head.

"Sometimes, I guess." Theda's voice was childlike. She stared at Suzanne. "I'm sorry for what happened. I know that doesn't make things right, but I have to say it anyway. I just couldn't help falling in love with Walter. He was the kind of guy I never thought I'd have a chance with. I guess I'm sorta weak. I couldn't resist."

Suzanne couldn't seem to find any words. Finally she responded weakly, "Things happen."

They heard the car drive up. Dave opened the front door, and the three of them stepped outside onto the stoop. The detective got out of his car and walked around to open the door on the passenger side. Dave grasped Theda's right arm and started down the walk.

In spite of a certain sadness for Theda, Dave felt a tremendous relief. But it was more than that. Now he and Suzanne had a real chance at something great together. He couldn't wait to get back in the house with her and hold her close. Whoa there, Monaco, he told himself. After this evening, she'll have some more adjusting to do. He needed to go slowly with her.

When Dave thought back later to this particular moment, he cussed himself for his stupidity. The last few days he had been so caught up in his own plans and feelings he had violated his training as a police officer. Project what might go wrong. Have all the facts in any situation. Know what might trip you up. Be aware at all times of who is out to get you.

He had never even checked to see if Cam Castore had gotten out on bail. Jesus! This ineptness on his part could have gotten them all killed.

So here he was, in a somewhat euphoric state, relaxed and rather self-satisfied that the confrontation was over and that it had gone so well. Walking Theda toward the car that would take her to police headquarters. The case really over at last.

Suddenly Dave's trained eye caught a movement behind a bushy evergreen on the lot line. His brain struggled to comprehend what it might mean. Then he heard a sharp crack, and a split second later a bullet whistled past his head. It's Cam, he knew immediately. He's after Theda for cutting him out. Other bullets would be coming fast after the first bungled shot.

He swiveled, grabbed Theda's shoulders, and turned her away from the direction of the gun. He enveloped her body with his own bulk, his stomach against her back. Then, catching the back of her knees with his, he forced his weight against her until they fell to the ground. Theda screamed, and he himself felt a sharp pain in the area of the recent knife wound. He wondered if any stitches had been ripped open.

Theda had turned her head and was gasping, "What?"

"It's Cam," he hissed. while catching her body to him and rolling over and over together. "Gotta keep moving."

At that moment, there was another shot and a sharp noise scraped along the sidewalk behind them.

Then Dave heard a gun fire several times close by, followed by running footsteps. Detective Sohler was apparently giving chase. Suzanne had run down the path and was hovering over them.

"Oh, my God, I can't believe this. Are you all right? You might have been killed!" She was looking at Dave in a special way that made him feel almost glad that this scary moment had happened. "It's okay now," she said. "The detective's after him."

He and Theda sat up, and Dave reached a hand under his shirt to check his bandage. He seemed to be intact. Suzanne settled herself on the grass beside him and put her arms around him as if forever.

He got a wonderful happy feeling he could live out the rest of his life right here, in this grassy spot in Suzanne's front yard.

"Dave, you might have been killed."

"But I'm okay, and I have you. That's all I care about."

He cupped her face in his hands and kissed her, gently at first and then with the deep commitment of his feelings.

"Hey! What about me?" asked Theda.

They had forgotten her. They looked at each other and laughed.

"Are you all right?" Dave finally asked, swinging his long legs around so he could see her sitting behind him.

"Yes, I'm fine. Really okay. I want to say something, but I hardly know how." She stood up, brushing some dirt and grass clippings from her jacket and slacks. "You saved my life, Dave. Just now. You knew Cam was after me. You could have stepped back, and he would have had a clear shot. Well—maybe that would have been better for everyone. The case really closed, you know what I mean?"

"Yeah, I know what you mean," he said, looking up at her in the half light from the coach lamp. "But now you have a bit of what is known as tribulation to get through. And you know what? You'll come out of this okay. A beautiful, better person." He smiled.

He thought he saw a bit of mischief in her eyes. "Don't forget one important thing," she said.

"What?"

"You saved my life so that means you own me."

There was a rustle of footsteps on the driveway and the flickering light revealed Cam Castore, head bowed, hands behind his back, apparently in handcuffs. Detective Sohler marched along behind, waving a gun in his right hand. Cam raised his head and gave Theda a nasty stare.

She stood with legs apart and hands on her hips. She gave him back his nasty stare. Her words were clipped and bullet-like. "Well— whadya know. It's you—superman. Looks like we're going to take a little trip together after all." She took a few steps toward him. Then her right hand came up, and she hit Cam so hard across the face he might have fallen if Detective Sohler had not been gripping him so hard.

After that, her body relaxed and a strange wide smile swept across her face. "Super!" she said. "I've been wanting to do that for so long. It felt wonderful!"

Then Theda turned around and walked to the car. She opened a rear door and,then called out to Detective Sohler.

"Let's go! I'm ready now."

EPILOGUE

Edgewood was dressed for the Christmas season. The softly falling snow gave it the cloak of angels, sparkling here and there with jewels made by the reflections of the holiday lights.

Police Detective Dave Monaco parked his dark blue precinct Chevy in front of the La Paloma Restaurant and got out. He stood on the driver's side of the car for a moment, gazing across the snowy roof at the building. Dwarf potted pines, dancing with miniature white lights, stretched across the front of the restaurant and along the brief angled entrance walk. A huge wreath festooned with red bows hung on the outside wall next to the door. Celebration, Dave thought. It's good to stop and listen to your heart. Celebrate. Always celebrate.

He walked the few steps to the entrance and went in. He took off his London Fog raincoat and shook the snow from it. "Here, I'll hang it up for you, Dave," said a pretty young brunette, smiling at him.

"How's it going tonight, Penny?" he asked her. He bent down and kissed her cheek.

"Fine. It's not bad being a hostess. But I wish Mom would let me waitress. I could make more money before I go back to college-"

"Hey—tell your mother, not me. This restaurant is her business." Penny turned to greet some other early customers, and Dave headed for the kitchen. Delicious aromas were mingling in the newly remodelled high-tech laboratory of food preparation. And this was one place where two cooks weren't spoiling the broth.

Mrs. Romano was at the stove stirring a big pot of something Italian, and Suzanne was at a long table working with salad greens. Milo stood at a big cutting board, chopping vegetables. They all glanced up when he entered, and sang out in unison, as if rehearsed: "Hi, Dave!"

Dave gave Sophie a squeeze with a kiss on the cheek, slapped Milo on the back, and went to Suzanne, encircling her waist with his arms.

She twisted about and gave him a radiant smile. "Darling," she said, and left her task long enough to kiss him enthusiastically. Then she pulled back, and gave him THAT look. The one that seemed to crumple his knees down into his shoes. He lost himself in another kiss.

"How's my entrepreneur wife doing tonight?" he was finally able to ask. "Making any money for us?"

"Well, we have quite a few reservations tonight. If this keeps up, we'll be okay."

"We're okay anyway," said Dave. Her smile agreed. Then he asked, "What time is she coming?"

"I think about six o'clock. You might check the ramp out in front to make sure it's not icy."

"Sure." Dave got a broom and a bag of rock salt from the utility closet and went back through the restaurant. He stepped outside under the red striped canopy trimmed with greens and twinkling lights and swept a dusting of snow from the handicap ramp. Then he threw down a sprinkling of rock salt.

He put the equipment away and went to sit at a table for four before a glowing fireplace. A miniature city of lighted buildings stretched across the mantle, deep in its own snow.

As Dave sipped a glass of club soda and smoked a cigarette, his mouth carved into contented lines. Finally he heard a flurry of sound at the entrance and Maude Hills came into view, wheeled by Beverly. He stood up to greet her, and moved a chair out of the way so she could be pushed to the table. After Maude was settled, he pulled out a chair for Beverly.

"You're looking wonderful," he said to the old actress, meaning every word. She was wearing a red crepe dress with sequins sparkling on the collar around her crinkled neck. Her thin hair was gathered and held behind each ear by a perky red bow. As she smiled at Dave, her sunken eyes still shone with the eagerness and vitality her movies had captured long ago.

"You look good yourself, Dave," she said in her shaky voice. "New suit?" Dave looked down at his sharply creased pinstriped trousers.

He nodded. Then grinned. "When you have a wife who looks like a model, you have to keep up."

"And congratulations on your promotion," said Maude. "I guess when you solved Walter's death the police knew what you could do."

"Something like that," said Dave. He motioned to a waitress who brought glasses of champagne for each of the women. Maude's eyebrows lifted. "It's a celebration," said Dave, "having you here like this."

"It certainly is!" Suzanne had left the kitchen and was now leaning over the back of Maude's chair, her face pressed against the withered cheek. Then she moved over to stand behind Dave's chair and wind her arms about his neck. A gold wedding band with three small diamonds glistened on Suzanne's left hand.

Then Dave leaned forward, his face serious. "You have on your red shoes and it isn't even Sunday," he said to Maude. They both laughed.

"Well, they matched my dress," She said defensively.

"I remember when you wore them out to visit your estate that Sunday back in April," said Dave. "You wanted to walk around and look at the grounds and peer in the windows. You leaned on me on one side with Beverly on the other and those red shoes got covered with mud."

"I didn't care. I was so happy to see my house again. It all looked so wonderful. Anyway, Beverly got my shoes looking like new again." She smiled at Beverly who looked at her blankly.

Dave glanced around the restaurant at the faces of the diners. The decorations of holly and glowing red candles, the Christmas tree in the corner festooned in white lacy ribbons and twinkling white lights. From the restaurant, speakers came the beautiful sound of a chorus singing "White Christmas," ever so softly.

Dave picked up his glass and stood up. He put his other arm around Suzanne and pulled her close.

He raised his glass in a toast. The others followed. Then they waited. There was a long pause in which Dave had to clear his voice several times. Finally, some words stumbled out. "Best year—ah—friends-ah—my wife—oh, what the heck—let's just drink to the best Christmas season of our lives!"

Low murmuring voices, shuffling sounds of bodies moving, swishing of arms, and the clinking of the rims of glasses. Then the gentle sipping. Faces lifted with the incipient smiles of contentment while eyes turned to share friendly glances that said, "This is a special celebration."

A celebration of life.

FINIS